Day Mover

By
Richard Martin

Day Mover
First Edition
Published by DreamStar Books, March 2003

Lasyard House
Underhill Street
Bridgnorth
Shropshire
WV16 4BB
Tel: 00 1746 761298
e-mail: dreamstar@jakarna.co.uk

Set in 'Times
ISBN: 1-904166-06-7

The events and opinions in this book are fictional and originate from the author.

Printed and bound in Great Britain by Antony Rowe Ltd

Day Mover

Acknowledgements

My gratitude to Clifford Thurlow, who painstakingly helped to produce the finished story. For all his help and encouragement and for his professional editing

To Cor Selen, without whom, this story would not have been told.

Writing a book has been likened to having a terrible illness, or a baby. It is, whichever way one looks at it, extraordinarily difficult to tell a story over a vast number of words and maintain reader interest. In this respect, *Day Mover* is an incredible achievement:

Clifford Thurlow: Author.

www.cliffordthurlow.com

Dedicated to Paddy

Prologue

What we are, we do not know. We have been here since the birth of the planet below. For millions of years, we have observed. 5,000 years ago we had to hide behind the moon. This was due to the dominant species on the planet. The earth then tilted and destroyed one group of that dominant species. They called it 'Atlantis'. We could then re-appear to observe. 400 years ago, we had to hide again. We keep out of the sun and on the dark side of this planet below. We see ourselves as two spheres of light. That is, if we allow the sun to touch us. We hid because the progress of the dominant species has grown again.

We know not, which one of us is male, or female. Over the centuries, we have just merged together and from that coming together has emerged other small spheres. Millions of spheres have left us for the earth below. Normally it has been only in ones and twos. It is only during the last 2,000 years of that earth below us, that multiple spheres have appeared from a merging. They have been far stronger than normal. Each head down to the earth below, seeking a human new born child as it comes from the womb. They move so fast that it is hard to see where they are heading. Each will seek to be there first. If they fail to be first. There will be no choice but to take the next one available.

When this happens the earth below will be out of balance in the future. Far below us, we watch birth, life and death. New creations and wonders, as all the creatures develop. It is the humans below that have moved forwards so fast. We have seen them develop many times in the past. They then destroy each other and it starts again. They can now search the sky with telescopes and have even landed on their moon. We cannot leave until two or more exchange with us. At the moment we are watching one. There is maybe two more with great potential. Others of limited power. Power that the first one has given to them. He can take it from them at will.

Millions of other small spheres are chasing about. Each trying to live again in a new born body. It matters not which body. It can be as a human, or as a small beetle. They each try for a human but it's life again and that's what counts. Some of the day and others of the night. The equation is nearly always equal. It is the warfare of those humans below that changes the equation. This is what happens when they arrive late and have to take another body at birth. We thought that we had one to exchange with us 2,000 years ago.

They caught him and he was destroyed before his power was strong enough. We have watched them all. 'Alexander', 'Ghengis', 'Caesar', 'Hitler', 'Idi' and now those of the present time. The dark and evil win on occasion and then it is the side of the light and the good.

The balance sways backwards and forwards. It is only when two or more appear before us that we will have a balance. It is then and only then that we can leave. At this moment, there is a dominant country. They want to police the world. They will however, destroy what they cannot rule or dominate. This is even though they are on the good and light side of life.

Will it all end again as a dead earth below? So close have they come over the last 60 years? Will it be that the dominant species destroys itself and for us to remain for the next evolution. Be it from the land or from the sea. The choice is not for us to make. Those below must make their own choices. We listen in to everything on the earth below and have interfered only once.

'Apollo 14'. We interfered with and it landed safely back on the earth below. It was just a slight push. You may ask why? Simply really. It was not actually touching the earth. A child of one of those onboard. He became one of our own. We will need the father's guidance in the future.

The one we watch the most. He is writing a book. He has not found us yet, but he suspects. The powers of each country are aware that he is there. They are aware of others like him. All have tried to catch him and the others at some time or other. They have come close at times. Somehow or other, he has got away from them.

Whilst developing he could have joined the dark side. This they were not aware of. How lucky they were. How easy it would be for him to change. He could just take what he wants. Yet he chooses not to do any of these. He observes all about him. Those in close contact with him do not realise what works and walks amongst them. They see him as a simple, yet intelligent man. Even the way he has written his book. It is written in such a way that it hides who he is. He will not publish the book. Someone else will take the credit for it.

When will he find us? Or will, he find us?

'We Are The Sentinels'.

Chapter 1

It's hard to believe that I've lived with it since the age of five years of age. It's when you start to dream that it happens. Or is it a dream because it only happens as the sun rises in the morning. I'm not talking about night dreams or nightmares, but day dreams. Have you never had a dream whereby it seemed that you had actually been there and lived these events? How many of you did not want the dream to end? As if it was better than when you were awake? Yet, while you are dreaming, millions of others are also dreaming at the same time, hoping for something better. Something, maybe a little different.

How many people have disappeared in their dreams and it's never been possible to trace them? Then think of how many people turn insane without any just reason. What's really happened to them?

Most people are afraid of the dark. Why are they afraid? Why are the majority afraid to admit it when they sub-consciously stay up as late as possible?

Who of you people out there have actually seen a ghost? How many people think that they've seen something out of the corner of their eyes and when they turn around it's not there at all? Come on, have you seen a ghost and what was it wearing? Was it a woman, wearing an old gown? A young girl who died at an early age? An old man? What were they actually wearing? Who are you really trying to fool?

Your own mind maybe.

The clothing is in your mind for most people, because it took me years to do it. The ghost? That's another thing altogether. It's another human being that does not want to leave this earth. They appear at times all over this earth and then they slowly fade into the dark. They are spotted trying to come to terms with the fact of making a mistake. Not knowing the rules. A mover forgetting the time or is it a newly born mover who fell asleep at the wrong time of the day. Just when the sun went down.

I'm 58 years old and it's time that I told my story.

I have had to survive by doing things that I've sometimes hated to do. I shall tell how many times that the governments world-wide have tried to entrap me. How my own government asked me to come forwards, saying, that they wished to help me.

Help me.

Use me they meant and then to erase me. If I'd come forwards, they'd have had a name and a family. Then the means to blackmail me into submission. Then the endeavours, by them all, to try to destroy me. All of this when I would not come forwards. Many have they sent out to try.

Always I have hit back. Going for the throat in more ways than one. I'll start at 200. You start counting and keep going. That's how many are dead because they tried to destroy me. Who did I drive into insanity to preserve my own existence? I shall tell how I've had to do terrible things to just to live. Never have I wished it, but I have done it to keep on living.

Governments all have secrets. This secret had been hidden for years. Just the leaders, Kings and Queens, PM's, Presidents and the informed few. All sworn to secrecy on taking office, or sworn to secrecy at an early age. Ingrained in their minds. Do not speak of it.

What is the power that keeps them silent?

Time is one factor and then the power to take away someone's livelihood. Or family. Then another simple fact, who would believe them?

I'm known of throughout the world, in my profession. I have a name and a country. I endeavour to live normally, to look after my family. I am always on the move. Never relaxed, except at sea where I can breathe clean air, keep my strength. Two weeks here and then, two weeks elsewhere. Then I'm off to work, a month at a time. Out of the country of my birth. It's only on land that I can be spotted and then by only a few. At sea I am hidden, unless a mover arrives. Normally, someone lost and having problems finding the way back. The odds of this happening at sea is low due to the distance. It has happened though. Another life lost, maybe lost without good reason. The shock that hits them, when they realise the full truth. That they now belong forever to the dead side of life. Three choices: life, disappearance or insanity. It's hard to choose. Especially when you cannot find your way back.

The first time I remember a day dream was when I was five years old. I fell asleep during a hot afternoon and I awoke in the outhouse. No clothes on and laid in a basket of dirty linen. Screaming.

My mother, she calmed me. The last thing I could remember was falling asleep upstairs on the bed. Sleep walking you may call it. I tried to tell her, but she would not listen. Telling her that I'd been flying, looking from above and diving back down towards the house.

A bad dream I thought at first but it was not a dream. It seemed as if I was glowing, yet the light did not cast any brightness around me. I could see pin-pricks of light far away in the distance. Some were soaring upwards into the sky and then descending down to disappear.

My mother loved me. I was her first born. She soothed me. She used to hold me tight and talk to me quietly telling stories. Do not speak about it. Try not to think about it. Do not repeat it. It's just a bad dream. I believe at the time, she imagined that something was wrong with my mind. Never ever tell anyone. This was repeated to me many times.

'They will take you away,' she whispered.

How would you have reacted in my place? Did everyone have dreams like mine? Dreams you couldn't ever talk about. Part of life and something normal. Not understanding it at all in my young mind I survived it with my mother's help. Too young, to be driven insane. I didn't know how my mother managed. She must have known something was different. I can remember the women's books she used to read. Then the sudden change to books of science.
We call them today "Science Fiction". Most are, but keep reading.

Cast your mind back to fables. Merlin. Wizards of old. Warlocks and Witches. What were they and why were they burnt. Keep going on and on.

What is the real and what is really false in this world of today. Don't forget though, we still live during the night. It is at night that you will dream.

Chapter 2

Bogey man

A stranger started to appear on the streets, criss-crossing the avenues. He came from somewhere foreign, to us young ones. We didn't know? Where south was. Or London. We listened to the grown ups talking about the stranger. He was not known by anyone. For weeks he just appeared in the morning and by evening he was gone. On weekends he started to walk near to us, the children, listening to us while we played our games. Our mothers were getting worried about him. He'd disappear for a few days, but then he came back. Never talking, just looking at us young ones. Staring into our eyes.

We called him the bogey man.

The bogey man of our night dreams.

Remember what was said to us before we slept. Be good or the bogey man will come to take you away. Our mothers started to drag us in, when he was around. Fathers stopped him, but shrunk away. He was a lot taller than any of our fathers and we thought they were big.

It was always after I'd had a dream that he'd appear back on the streets. To me it was definite. I was the one that he was looking for. Even though I was so young, I'd sensed that he was looking for me. For me to say something wrong, for me to tell my mates about my dreams. They would have spread the word to others and somewhere along the line of talk. He would then have a way back to the source.

BM

My father was on the trawlers out at sea. Three weeks on the ship and then four days home. Looking back it seems as if mother was always pregnant, then father went back to sea. I ended up with four brothers and four sisters. I was the eldest.

Playing with my mates all of the summer. Never going to sleep until after dark. We are supposed to be young and innocent. I did not know what was in store for me. Dark nights come early in the winter. No bad dreams.

Spring arriving, days were getting longer. I'm nearly six now and feeling bigger. Learning to read. One day whilst playing with kids in the street. Running, shooting with marbles and hide and seek. Went in for something and went upstairs to find it or hide it. Lay down on the bed. I remember the next moment, looking down at the street. Our house was far below me. A bright light all around me. Pin-prick lights in the distance. Moving across the estate. The sun starting to go down. That early evening I woke up crying on the landing, naked, scared, my mother above me. My younger sister, clinging to her skirt. Why the landing. My mother looked afraid. What the hell was I, she must have thought? Those were my own thoughts. Through tears and pain I tried to tell her.

'No, no it's not true; Do not tell lies,' she'd say.

Bogey man is back searching around. I'm scared and my mother's scared. I try to tell her that he's looking for me. During the day, she tries to stop me having a nap. Even in sickness she kept me awake. I wanted to know what was happening. Occasionally I saw bogey from above and I was back home with fear in my heart. How was it possible for me to do this, I did not know.

Bogey had a woman with him one time, walking round the streets, so I quit sleeping for a time. I noticed that it only happened on bright days. It was only as I grew up, that it was possible to do it during a normal day. I used to come out in the early mornings and keeping low to the ground until I was well away from the house. Never again would anyone have my location. After I'd flown bogeyman would always appear.

I knew that some day he'd find me. What could I do? Did he know about me? Why could he see me whenever I rose into the air? I came out early one morning and did my usual move along the ground before coming up. As I came up I had a really big shock, a thrill even. Another ball of light was about a mile away. Within a few minutes it had moved towards me. I shouted in my mind for it to go away. It stopped and began to leave. Then it went down towards the ground and disappeared. The light had not been that bright. Far dimmer than the light that I could see and feel around me. It was also smaller.

This really worried me and sure enough bogey appeared for a few days. Going out one morning I had another shock. Another light followed me from my house. It was my sister. She too was dim and her light was smaller. It was lucky that I heard her thoughts though. I was angry with her and told her never to do it again. That first light shocked me. I never ever saw it again.

I learnt to fight. I went out of my way to fight kids older than me. Not as a bully, but when they picked on me or my mates or anyone around my age. A right terror I became at scrapping. Mother encouraged me in this for she knew something. Careful, she'd say to me sometimes. I never wondered in those days why I was so strong. Able to fight so easy with kids older than me.

It also became totally taboo in our house for me to sleep during the day. Mother used to shout upstairs all the time. Hope you're not on the bed. Yes, she really kept me on my toes.

I always wanted to be older. My sister told me that she couldn't do it any more. That was something for me to think about. I'd only told her not to do it. Could I just by thinking it stop others from flying up as I did?

That summer, my mates and I started to travel further away from home. To the woods and lakes around an old army range. We netted newts and sticklebacks. Made bows and arrows from the branches of young trees. Catapults etc. We made the lot. Yes and the games we played. Yes we had great fun. Cost me a few jam jars for the elastic. Also sold ginger pop to make money to buy it.

We were playing on the old ranges one day, digging trenches when one of my mates made a find. Yes a golden find.

Shares we used to say on anything, but this he tried to keep. A belt buried in the sand and as we dug it out we found more. A grenade and two very firm ammunition pouches. How close we came to killing ourselves that day. I don't know how we got away with it. Playing at soldiers, hell we had the real McCoy. One pouch had a full magazine of .303 bullets. Bang ,bang ,bang, a machine gun magazine. Luck was with me, because I got 6 bullets and scampered back into the woods. Hide them was my first thought. This was to save carrying our gear home. I mean the cops sometimes took our stone guns off us so we'd hide them. Mine was under an old wren's nest where I'd dug a bottle hole. Narrow at the top and wider at the bottom. Once those bullets were hidden, I got back with my mates.

Grenade.

Well we knew what it was. I mean we all read books and I was around nine years old at this time. We were throwing that grenade into holes all over, playing at soldiers. No, we didn't pull the pin. It was corroded and we didn't know about that. Just that we should leave it in. We never did think about what we were going to do with the grenade afterwards. The damn thing went off. I'm sure we all shit ourselves at the time and we were definitely frightened. What a bang though and how lucky were we to have our heads down, like real soldiers. Yes, even to this day we could have all been dead.

Did we run? Up into the woods and to the top. Along the bushes past the college. A few adults were out. Must have heard the explosion. Police cars had bells at that time not long after the war. They were on the way. We didn't go back to the woods for over 3 weeks. Spoilt our summer that did and it even got a mention in the evening papers. Mysterious Explosion. If only they knew. You want my mate's names, Keith, Brian, and Allan. Mine?

I'm still free.

My dad was at sea when Allan's dad found his bullets. Did he sprat on us. All 4 parents had a meeting. As I said, my dad was at sea. The full story came out and all the bullets were collected but mine. I said I'd lost mine running through the woods after the grenade went off. I remember it was Keith's dad who got rid of them because he was ex army. Anyway it was kept to ourselves, just the four families. My mother though, she knew me better than most parents ever knew their sons. I some times tried to explain it all to her.

She was a cook at a big hotel. I had to look after my brothers and sisters when she was at work. I only went to sleep during the day when bogey man had been gone for a long time. I told her one day everything that she'd been cooking at the hotel. Right down to the puddings that went out. Yes, I counted them.

'You must have been looking through the window,' she said.

'Sure but the lower ones were frosted glass,' I said: 'No way to look through the upper ones without a ladder. No ladder at the hotel.'

That got to her.

Why could no one see me, what was the glow? I could see the same in the distance. Just showing as little pin-pricks. I learnt that I could enlarge it, but it made me weak. If I made it small, then I was strong. It was when I made it larger that I lost control. When it was small, then I could go fast in any direction I chose. I learnt also that I was fairly solid in some respects. The wind I could feel against me. Objects I could not pass through. I could enter some places, but there were limitations. Against any object, I was solid, but not visible. Why was the light not visible to anyone? It took me years to find out.

Bogeyman still came around but I'd learnt to never go straight up. I used to keep level with the ground for at least a mile before I went into the sky. Some of my brothers and sisters had bad dreams. It was me, looking after them that helped them. What I did was to place my light against theirs in my dream and tell them that they were all right. None of them were fully like me. The glow from them was weaker. I still taught them not to go straight up in the sky in the dream. Not to ever speak out of turn. I even took them up one by one just before dark to show them the ghosts heading towards us. Then quickly we were back down again.

Something important happened one day. Keith, was staying with me. We'd been out most of the day when we decided to go up and see some of my "Fag-card" collection. His eyes closed and he nodded off.

I thought maybe, just maybe. I touched him and relaxed myself. Next second we were both above the house and he was laughing. The moment that I let go of him a change took place. It was as if he was lost. Totally lost above the earth. I quickly grabbed him and there we were on the bed as if nothing had happened. He woke up crying to himself, because we were both naked. I told him he'd fallen asleep while waiting for a bath. Once he was calmed down, he explained that he'd dreamed we were up in the sky together and when I had pulled away from him, he'd been afraid of getting back. I started to pull his leg about it and threatened to tell our other mates. That got to him for a bit, because if I told our mates, then they'd think him stupid. In the end I got away with it. He'd keep quiet about it for sure.

I'd discovered something though, a means of being able to do something positive with my gift. From that time on things were steady, except for my shadows. How were they able to trace the area where I lived? I'm suddenly thirteen years of age. Still scrapping when I got the chance. I have a name for it and it doesn't come to me often now. Unless that is, another village lad came to try me out. You see our town was built up of five villages. Ashby, Old Brumby, Crosby and two others. Look them up and you'll find Scunthorpe.

What stops any one? I'll tell you straight. A punch, or a kick in the throat. A brick, a baton, a knife, any thing to put them down. Do you think I'm proud of what I did to others? Even then I wasn't, but they just wouldn't leave me be. The police was always at the house trying to pin something on me. I had my witnesses and never started a fight first.

Best thing I did was take an exam for Navy College. I passed it all right but nearly didn't get in. Never knew if they were aware of my fighting or whether it was because my mum and dad didn't have much money. A letter arrived saying that I was not accepted for college. Two days after another came saying I was in. I figured it out on my own after a couple of years.

Although I was of medium height. I was broad and very fit. I refused my first scrap at navy school. It took another two refusals before I realised something needed sorting out. The masters had seen it all and had done nothing.

All of us lived in lodgings during the week. We'd also found out the short cuts to getting there. I purposely found out which alleyways my tormentors used. Me, a scrapper was going to do it my way and on my ground. Luck was on my side. Two of them lived near each other and used the same alleyways. Now classes never finished together. First one out was it, so one would be in front of the other. Who's crafty? Me.

Told the seamanship master that I had an afternoon dental appointment. That dinner I shot home and got civvies on. Finished at the dentists I waited with one foot against the alley wall. Hello arsehole, this was all I said to the first. He thought it was funny somehow. Sorry but he didn't even make first base. I'll tell you. I even battered him a few time after he was out. Purposely around his eyes. Never again would he fight with out thinking of me. I walked towards the school after leaving him. Trouble was when I saw the next one he was just coming out the gates. Two of his mates were with him.

Hearing them coming down the alley I stepped out.

'It's the coward,' he said: 'what are you hiding here for?'

Couldn't he see that I was in civvies? Was he blind or what? Does a coward walk purposely round a corner and advance? He was a dick head. Fairly sure his mates knew different though. Maybe one of the other lads at the school from my home town had said something. Four lads from my home town had got to college with me. Bigger they are, the harder they fall. Remember the throat. Yes I hit him fully knowing how dangerous it was. I wanted him down. Down, down, down. I kicked him straight on the jaw.

His two mates were astonished at how fast it happened.

'Do you want the same?' so quietly I asked them: 'listen to me. Tomorrow when asked, it was the gang from the top school, do you get me or do you want to be in his position? If I'm expelled through your gobs, then you'd better leave as well. I'll even do it before I leave.'

I was in the shit myself and I knew it. Or was I. Next day I was hauled out of seamanship class to the head captain's office. I asked the master if he'd come along too. He did. I was accused of putting two lads in hospital with severe injuries. Couldn't be me, I was at the dentists. Took my card for it out of my pocket. Even the seamanship master backed me up. I was sent out. Outside his office were the two.

'Remember,' I said passing them.

Even had time to show them my dental appointment. They were the real cowards. Yes, I did get off.

'We are watching you,' said the headmaster.

No one ever tried a thing with me, after that episode. Not singularly that is. Me, two years younger than the bully. I was left well alone, in the matter of fisty-cuffs.

It was only in milling, a form of boxing, that others saw how fast I was, and how dangerous. Never found out who set me up though. Was walking down an alley one night, when wham. Flattened straight out with something. Woke up cold, shivering and bruised all over. My eyes were totally black. I'd been totally hammered. Really hammered. Only rumour at school that I ever heard was that it had been four young fishermen. They used to come down and take tickets. You know, Bosun's and above, tickets to get up to skipper on the trawlers.

It was my dad who gave me the truth of it though. I'd belted one of them a few weeks earlier. Yes me at 13 years of age. I took on anyone out of school. It was win or lose. If I got the throat straight away then it was all over. Had a few close calls but I did it. Anyway my dad came home about two weeks after it had happened and was telling mum about someone at the college been beat up severely. The lad I'd belted was a skipper's son and he'd sent his young fishermen round. They'd got my name from someone. Must have really put the pressure on him, to give them my name and to point me out. I took up Karate after that. The lessons took place at the other end of the city, where no one knew me. It taught me that I was not Invincible. I could be beaten.

It was also during my 3 years at navy college, that I finally figured out why I'd landed up first in a basket and then on the landing the second time. I also got rid of bogey and his girlfriend permanently. Normally it was back in my bed where I normally awoke, but why were those two different occasions.

Clothes, yes that was it. Both times my clothes were involved. First time in the outhouse and then second time, on the landing. Mother used to pile them first on the landing and then take them to the outhouse to be washed. I didn't go home one weekend from school. Stayed in the lodgings to study Navigation.

Fell asleep and there I was looking down on my lodgings and moving around the city, then back above the lodgings. Woke up back on my bed with nothing on. Three days later, I spotted the bogey man and his woman around the estate. It was fifty six mile to home by road and twenty five over the river.

I was scared out of my mind that he'd find me. Took to all the alleys until he went away. We used to hitch hike home from five ways, which was on the outskirts of Hull city. In the mean time, what was giving me away? I was really crapping myself. Would he just appear again every time I soared into the sky. I'm a fighter but he was massive. The woman wasn't much different to him. Why was he seeking me? What was his purpose? It was the same person just older. The same man from when I was four years of age. My mind went haywire during the next twenty four hours. It came to me slowly, not fast like an idea, but slowly.

Bright lights and pin-prick lights in the distance. Not many about, but the odd one or two. It's in bright sunlight when I can do it best but even these lights were brighter than that. They must have been, for me to see them. Just like the sun's rays off a mirror. Was I a spot of light to them in the distance and for bogeyman? He never found me though because I stayed away from him. Using the alleys, always the alleys. I'm sure if he'd seen me, he would have recognised me as one of the kids growing up in the town over the water. I am always on the move.

I went home for a weekend and took some clothes to the woods. Spring bank holiday, so I had a few days. I had to find out how far I could travel though. The sun was out and just a few clouds in the distance. I'd travelled home on my bike. I was tired really, not had much sleep thinking about what I was going to do. I could see myself looking down. How did I move? Simple. I thought it, and I did it. Slowly at first and I was moving, not too fast, but there I was looking down at my clothes in the wood. Think it and it happens. I'm in the woods naked. My clothes were under me. I can move from place to place but my clothes need to be there before me.

Why my clothes?

This was the furthest I'd travelled. A distance of over five miles. I'd learnt how and in what direction I could move. Think it and it happened. Bogeyman, he must have thought he'd made a mistake, or that I'd made one. I'd spotted him getting out of a car about half a mile from my clothes. I watched him start walking in my direction before descending. Me, I was on my bike, hat on and sunglasses. I did a wide detour before heading home.

I knew somehow, that one day I would need my bullets that I'd hidden away all those years ago.

I was good at metal work. Made all sorts. My crowning glory was what I made for bogeyman. I borrowed a Vanier and measured the diameter of the .303 cartridges. I then drilled two holes in a 1" thick plate of steel. It was 6" long x 1-1/2" wide x 1" thick. I added a hinge to another thinner piece of metal drilled it to the centres of the thick section. Tapped two threads and screwed in two screws. These had been ground down to small tips. A flip spring was added to close them together and I adjusted the pin ends to come together even. Nothing left to chance. If one was a dud after all this time then doubling up would cover it I hoped. Two cartridge ends would be hit at the same time. With a good saw that I took from the wood yard and a spade from our shed. A 5lb hammer and some dark twine that I'd dyed brown. Yes I pinch a bloody saw, so what. What I set out to do was going to be far worse.

The pine wood. Possibly belongs still to Briggs the farmer or sold. Yes in the middle is a Crematorium now. Anyway, a saw and nails 6", 4". I was going to do it. I'd made a few drawings, so I had a general idea of what I wanted. I found the ideal spot and commenced to nail my device across a small pathway. I'd also drilled four holes in the thick plate by this time and 2" nails were driven home through the plate into the wooden branches laid across the pathway. I used bark to make it look natural. The dyed cord secured everything in place. Bogeyman was about 6ft 6" so I lined up for 5ft 4". It was the best estimate I could make out. His chest.

I did nearly a dozen tests on the release mechanism of my gadget. It worked perfectly. Over the next few days I had some digging to do. Pits, 2ft wide and approx, 5ft long. Definitely 6ft deep. Carting away the soil was a major problem. Had taken one of our blankets off the bed to use. If you think I'm crazy, then don't walk in the woods if you know I'm around. I cut stakes from another part of the wood. Even got some bamboo from a small garden shop. All were sharpened and embedded in the ground at the bottom of the pits. It is in the books, how to set an animal trap. This was a man trap.

Summer 1958.

I did it. Took my bike and some clothes to Fairy Dell. (For some it will ring a bell.) I had a day to wait because dark clouds were over the sun. I wanted nothing to go wrong. I actually did it the next day. Mum knew something was going on because I wouldn't leave the house. Up the stairs and onto my bed, to force myself to sleep. I'd kept awake all night readying myself for this day. It was going to be a turning point. I just knew it. Just to get the bogeyman off my back. No one knew how much he terrified me. I'm just fourteen years old. Over the woods and down, I somehow felt that it was hard to awaken that day and only wondered about it later. Naked I awoke in the woods once again and got dressed. I set both 303 cartridges in position. Checked that all was set correctly and then I was away on my bike. I'd worn gloves and mittens. Wiped everything clean of fingerprints. Dumped every thing in Silica Lodge at the opposite end of town. A large, man-made lake developed from old quarries. What the bogey man never knew was that I'd found out something important. The way he walked through the woods, off the main tracks. Travelling only on the really small ones. You see I'd been reading a book on wood craft.

Scout-style.

Little pieces of twigs set on the little tracks gave me his route. It had taken me hours to set them and hours to find his route. It was all on my maps. Written on paper and tree bark cut with minute nicks to show me the way. You want to know something. I made Head Lines. Man shot dead. Woman seriously with injured from animal trap. It was in for three nights running. It gave all the details of how it had been done.

No one had seen me making my weapon. Kids can go any where with out suspicion. They could in those days. I sodded off, back to college across the water that Sunday. If they came for me, I'd fly.

What my mother's feelings were I didn't ask. She just knew that I was involved and all she did for two days was silently cry. I saw the tears in her eyes but she said nothing. Yes, I'd killed a man. He'd been a shadow for nine and a half years. Finally he was gone. What happened to the women, I don't know because I never saw her again. I was free of him.

Yes free.

Chapter 3

BM

Fourteen and free. Forget it. You are never free. There's always someone looking for you. It was my mother who spotted the message in the classified section of the evening paper. Quite simple. Scunthorpe Mover. Will you please call this number? We know you are young. We can help you. Then the telephone number. It had been in every night for over a month. She'd cut the lot out for me to see.

My mother and I didn't get much chance to really talk. I was either studying or out chasing girls. That part of growing up came naturally. Mother was always busy. Working at the hotel when she wasn't pregnant, washing, cleaning, knitting or sewing. It was late at night and I'd just got in from a church dance.

We really talked for the first time that night. Not as boy and mother, but more like man and women. She truly surprised me for the first time that night. She was able to do what I did but not fully. All she did was find herself above the house and then she woke up. It had happened to her the first time just after marrying my father. She couldn't do it automatically. It just happened. If she'd told it to anyone, they'd have carted her off. You now know the reason why my father never found out. She'd hidden it totally. Her words to me to be very careful had paid off. What had shocked her was what had happened to bogey man. We reached an understanding from that moment. Never to do it from the house or the immediate area. Never again would any one be able to trace me back.

What a lie.

How can you stop something when you don't know how to control it. I learnt how to get home totally unseen. My base for operations would be at my lodgings across the water. Devonshire Road, Gypsy Ville, Hull. Remember all the alleyways between Hessle Road and Anlaby Road.

Care and planning came first. I'm coming up to another year of my life and I intend to keep it. I also have the yearning to find out what I can do, my limits, why I can do it. Most of all who are the bright lights on the horizon. Some times they are on and some times off. Who also wants me to telephone them and why. What's in it for them and most of all, what in it for me. I know a little about value. What is my true value. Could be someone wants to put me down, just like a dog. You see, bogeyman never once put an advert in the local paper, asking me to come forwards.

Why?

You know for a young one, it's hard not having money. Mum always had to give me some for the week when I first started college. Not as much as some but enough. Got a job in a bike shop. Going out with the daughter that's how. From 5 to 7 Monday to Saturday, repairing the bloody things. Night off, on a Wednesday, destination unknown. Punctures, spokes alignment, brake changes, cables, you name it, I could soon do the lot. It lasted right up to nearly Xmas. Fancy though, you think I got in the daughters pants. No way, she was a right prude. Got trouble from another direction altogether. Edith and Val, two others, who fell pregnant. I'd had it off with both of them, so had half a dozen others by all accounts. I'm out. Yes straight out. It was conduct not becoming a future officer that they got me on in the end. I was bitter about it to begin with but in the end it came down to one thing.

Caught out.

It was only on a Sunday though, through those last six months at college that I found out more of my ability to soar, move and arrive at another place. I kept a good look out for any prowlers. How I could do it was simple. Every one has it. Even though at that time the world did not have a name for it. It made it possible for me to do it. My clothes were the clue. What was on them. Me, or any little micro particle of me. My skin was the secret. Just one little particle made it possible for me to move to different places.

How far could I do it? How fast can I move?

I broke a promise to my mother in the end but it was worth it. Never told her. Under my bed was a heap of all sorts, books, magazines, shoes and boots. I ended up putting some of my skin in a little pile in a cleared area under the bed. It couldn't be seen by any of my brothers and sisters. They never had a reason to go under the bed. I'd commence from my lodging and come home through the air. I'd do it on a Friday night. I had to check that all was as it should be.

I added a little more skin from the side of my thumb. Mum always thought that I bit my nails but I didn't. Saturday, I went back to my lodgings. This was it, a test beyond any thing I'd ever tried before. You know, I think that I can now sleep with complete ease. I'm up and thinking, turn to the river, cross it and move pass the sluice. Head for the smoke from the works. Hell, I'm already close. Skirt around the smoke, follow the Kingsway, turn left half way over the houses and I'm there looking down. Wake up. I'm home and under the bed. It was so quick. Got dressed, out the window, came in the back door. 'Hello mum,' I said: 'just came home for an hour or two. Where're the kids?'

'Out, playing at the park,' she replied. She gave me a funny look though, I'm sure of that.

Do you know any thing, about trigonometry? If any of you do, then

Use it.

I did. It was part of college, learning about navigation.

'Some Officers Have Curly Auburn Hair Till Old Age.'

Take the first letter from each word and what does it give you.

$$\text{Sine} = \frac{o}{h} \qquad \text{Cosine} = \frac{a}{h} \qquad \text{Tan} = \frac{o}{a}$$

It tells you all you need to know about how to measure distance on land to within a few feet. At college I had plenty of sea charts and a few large scale, land charts. These were for places like Goole at the end of the Humber. I took the land mass charts. I needed them. Not really worried about the advert in the paper for now. I'll talk about that, maybe later.

What were the pin prick lights in the distance. To me, they were something more important. They had to be part of me and what could I possibly do to find out? First though, I took stock of high buildings, chimneys and such. All were placed on my chart. The cement works at South Ferriby had a high chimney. Just off the fish docks was another. Two really good points. High in the air and easy to line up to. I had to be far enough back to be able to move slightly left or right to see or not to see a light in the distance? Could they also see my light. I'm sure they could. Ten to Fifteen minutes was my allowance at that time. Looking down I could see people walking. Kids playing out in the streets. In fact I could see almost everything. Could they see me. No. Definitely not. I'd already determined that because I'd flown right down in front of them. Started with small children first and then some adults. No one could see me at all.

One problem I found, unless a window was open or there was a gap under a door. I couldn't get in. I struggled with anything less than a 1/16". That was my estimate, with a lollypop stick on one door. I needed to know why I hadn't passed straight under this door. It was a bank door. The main thing was never to be trapped.

As the sun disappeared over the horizon I found it very hard to wake up in my body. I wondered why so I stuck solely to daytime. Knowing that it would take me about fifteen minutes to line up one of the lights. I did it just after school. My landlady had already sussed me out as a mysterious person. She and the old man were pensioners making up on their pensions. Didn't blame them. This time I shot up telling her I was going to have a bath. Laid down and closed my eyes, just relaxing now and I was away. Straight over to Ferriby. Took a good line up, from one of the houses half way up the hill. Straight back over the water and another line up from near the centre of town and back towards my lodgings. Something was wrong though. One of the lights was becoming brighter. It was getting nearer very fast. I woke up sweating and very worried. Damn, what had I done?

Nothing happened though, that's the part that I couldn't work out for a time. Anyway, I had my triangulation. Trouble was, the house in Ferriby was not on the map. Had to take the Ferry across the Humber to New Holland. Hitched to Ferriby. Found the house and lined myself up from the ground. West of the Trent river and slightly east of Doncaster. Nothing. Yes, nothing showing on the bloody map that I had. I'd it a dead-end and was very pissed off.
You see, I'd got Admiralty Charts. Not Aerial Charts.

I had to rectify that quickly. Trouble was I'd no cash to spare. I found some at the library but in those days you could not copy them. Borrow yes, but I was too young to take anything from the adult section. At the back of the library I found an area that suited me fine. Bit the skin off the side of my thumb and fingers and placed it just at the end of a shelf. Trouble was. It was only mid week, and I had to go back every day for three days. Luck was with me on the Friday. Heard one of the women taking about the stock-taking for Saturday afternoon. I'd planned to be there that afternoon when it shut. Sunday it was. I walk down early to check that all was clear. Even stuck a lolly stick under the flaming door. There was a huge gap. No wonder the place was cold, even with the doors closed. I settled down at the lodgings. I knew it wouldn't take long and in no time, I was there totally naked in the library. I actually started laughing. I took two maps into the kids' section and stuffed them into an ABC learning book. Lets have a look round I though while I'm here. Head Librarians Office. That'll do. No sooner had I pushed the door open when a bell started ringing. I'd set an alarm off. Should have known, but I'd not really done this before. How the heck was I to know about alarms? It was only supposed to be banks that had them. I needed the maps damn it.

I was in a rush. Lay down relax. I couldn't at that point, the thought of the police coming was overpowering. Relax, relax but it was so hard with no clothes on. That was the worse point and a turning point at the same time. I did relax and within about ten minutes. The police were there because as I left in a flash of light they were parked outside. They were waiting for the keys. Fancy that, they are delayed on entering I thought. I wore my navy uniform on the Monday morning. Collected the map, cheeky as hell, and walked out with it in my pocket. Trouble was that by the end of the week I was out of college for good. Never to wear my uniform again.

Dunscroft. Yorks. It was the approximate light area. It was the light that came for me and missed.

Hey. I'm only fifteen years of age. I've done things that most will never do. I am a Wizard. Free to roam at will. Why only during day though. I was fifteen and having to share a bed with two other brothers. Top to tail we did it. Two one way and two in the middle from the other end. Single bed with another brother and kid sister at the bottom. In the box room three other sisters with bunk beds. Two in the one on bottom and the oldest on the top.

She's was fourteen.

Family's large and my dad's finished on the trawlers. Packed in like fish, my dad says.

My dad has no job and no money. He gets one in the end. The filthiest job I've ever seen in my life. He comes home black and coughing his guts up most nights.

We got a four bedroom house just after. On a new estate. I'd done no day sleeping for over six months. I had to learn more before I went a searching for the first light.

Remember that advert. I hadn't. I'd rang a few times.

'Hello, Edith here,' a voice used to say: 'can I help you?'

'It's me,' I used to say: 'I'll call you again sometime.'

Never used the same phone twice and never in the town of my parents. I suppose they had an idea about them tracing the calls so I stopped them. Kept the number though. Might come in use one day.

I found a job as a motor winders assistant. Monday to Friday. 7.30am to 4.30pm. Hour for lunch. Learning about electricity. I needed to know all about it. An alarm had nearly trapped me. I picked that man's brain for over two years. Study, you don't know the half of it. Every single book on electric's, Magnets and Magnetism. I read them all.

I was just fifteen when I had my first contact. I went soaring into the sky, the light around me was larger. The light that missed me had been far smaller than mine. I got the idea that person was younger than me. I allowed it only to get so close, before I sped away from it. I then dipped down to hide and woke myself up, before it made contact. I think it was because of the short distance, that it headed my way. It was the same one, from my measured angles taken a few months earlier. The distance on the map made it around twenty three miles. I only had my bike. I went on Friday night. I carried some of my clothes and a pair of soft canvas shoes with me in a packet. Bits of skin that I'd scraped off the side of my arms and legs. A piece of wick from next to my nails. I was making sure this time. I'd also cut my toe nails and carried all of these bits and pieces. Three hours later I was there in the general area. I stayed in the woods until dawn.

I lay down just as the sun came up and closed my eyes. Trying to relax, relax and relax. I flashed above and commenced to spin around slowly. Keeping to a steady height, I waited. Slowly spinning, spinning. It happened so fast that I barely caught it in time to think, 300 yards away. I had time to note the rise point and thought myself awake. I dressed and waited, looking up to show my face.

I knew that it couldn't hurt me in that form because I'd tried it with kids back home. Put my hat on, got on my bike and rode away. Yes it was smaller than my light, someone young. I travelled into Doncaster for the first ever time. I'd found the house. What was I to do. I had some thinking to do. It only took me a few minutes and I rode back slowly and waited.

It was other kids on the street that gave it away. They were playing marbles on the side of the road just like I'd done when I was younger. A little girl of about ten had come to the gate. I could hear them shouting and teasing her as I walked up. Crazy, crazy, my mum says you're crazy. She was just standing there crying. The tears were rolling down her cheeks. What had she done wrong? Nothing. She'd been born like me. Did she ask for it?

No.

I growled at the kids for teasing her and they ran off. I stopped and looked at her. What a little thing she was.

'Do you like flying,' I asked her.

She just sniffed, and looked at me with big brown eyes. I turned to walk away. Hadn't got but a step when she said it.

'Where's your hat,' she said.

Bloody hell, I'd left it on my bike handle bars. She knew me. She must have come right into the woods where I'd hidden to go to sleep that morning. Hell, I'd been chuffing naked. I'd not thought about that part of it. The embarrassment of it. A few times growing up and flying, I'd seen people in the nude but I soon got fed up with it. Didn't turn me on. Privacy goes a long way. 'You know me,' I said to her and she nodded her head.

Quickly I asked her if she ever went out. The park when the kids are at school she says.

'What's your name?' I asked her.

'Rachel,' she replied.

'Monday, if it's not raining,' I said.

Only problem with that was that I was working. Had to evaluate there and then what was more important. She was, I realised because I could see what a state she was in. Was I going soft? No not really because I just have a soft spot for those in trouble. I could ring in sick. One day wouldn't hurt. Wouldn't need my bike on the retur run because I went back to the woods. Checked out that everything was hidden up a tree and my means to get there was in place. I placed bits and pieces a few yards from each other and then had a slow ride home.

Went to a dance that night. Had no money, but had plans to get some. Mainly stood and watched for the first hour. 'Rock and Roll.' I did have friends, even though I was classed as a hard case. I even had a few rows with them but never once did I threaten any of them. They knew me well in that respect. They could shout their heads off at me, as long as they wanted, so long as hands were never raised. Even had a nip of whiskey that night for the first time. Someone had sneaked half a bottle in, so we drank it in the toilets. Had a few dances with the girl from next door. Year younger than me, but she looked even younger with her pigtails and flower patterned dress. Tried reading a book on electrics on Sunday, but some how I couldn't get into it. I needed to stay up ready for the morning.

I felt sure that some thing would go wrong some how. Was I going to get collared. Had she said something to her parents? I was going to fine out soon enough. I planned it for around nine. No one was in, kids at school. Lets do it. Next thing, I'm up and away. I'm actually finding it easier to do. It's just as if I can will myself to sleep. Think, forwards, and go. Takes just a minute. How fast can I move. Over the woods, a quick check to see if it's clear and another look for any bright lights that may be moving towards me. Just one pin prick, far away. Woke up with my back side in a thorn bush. Got my gear down and got dressed quickly. I did a casual walk around, up and around the streets. I was looking for the police. No one about but a couple of young mums playing with their kids in the park.

That was where I met her. It was nearly dinner time when she appeared.

She worked a right crafty one to get me near her with the mums about. I was sat on a bench near the swings wondering how we could speak. She waited till they were pushing their young ones in the baby swings.

'Hey, mister, give me a push,' she shouted.

'OK,' I said and as walked over. I asked the mums if it was all right. They looked me up and down. Must have passed approval because they said it was all right. I just pushed her up and down for about ten minutes.

'Where are you from,' she asked me.

General told her that was waiting for a mate to finish work and that he lived just down the road. That was for the benefit of the mums close by, because I said it loud enough. She just laughed and I think she was enjoying herself, for the first time for ages. I then walked back to the bench and sat down. One of the mums walked over and said quietly.

'Humour her, she a bit touched in the head,' she said quietly to me.

Hell, what could I say to that? I do say "hell" quite a bit, but it's far better than being foul mouthed like some I know. I quickly asked the girl how often she appeared to be flying. Her reply wasn't what I wanted to hear.

'Only when they don't watch me,' she said.

No. I couldn't believe it. She was been watched.

'When do they watch you?' I asked.

'Not much now,' she said: 'but about a year ago a real big man used to come and ask me questions and watch me when I was sleeping. He stopped coming one day.'

What she had said sat me back I'll tell you. I knew him all right. He'd just come back to haunt me. It could have been no other.

'OK, listen, you're not crazy and you do fly,' I said to her quickly: It's real, do you understand me. Don't say anything but listen carefully: Bite a little bit of skin from the side of your thumb. Bite your nails, quickly,' I went on: 'Give the bits to me. Listen. In that direction are some quarries, dug into the ground.'

I pointed the direction out.

'No one can see you, if you're down there at the bottom,' I carried on saying: 'your light is blocked out from those in the distance.'

I'd discovered that if you went low down, you couldn't see any of the pin prick lights in the distance. Neither could anyone see you in reverse. A quarry was perfect for what I had in mind.

'I'll be back next Saturday, if the weather is clear and if not then it'll be Sunday. If that's not clear then, it'll be the following Saturday. Don't worry I'm going to come back.'

Okay,' she replied.

'What time does your mum and dad get up?' I then asked her.

All of this I put to her quickly.

'Around eight to half past on week ends,' she told me.

'If you see me on either of those days, just think to yourself, awake when you are close to me,' I then said to her: 'I've got to go now before some one catches us.'

Another thought and I asked her what sizes shoes she wore. Got sisters at home remember.

'Make it sun rise.'

I got out of there quick. Back to the woods and I stripped off. Stashed my gear. And lay down well clear of the thorn bush.

Back home, I had to hover awhile just off the ground. Popping up and down looking through the window, until one of my brothers left the bedroom. I thought that as I was travelling home I'd seen a dim light. Not been sure, I forgot about it for a long while. Was getting better and better at it, but I always watched out for other lights and went really low miles before arriving home. Zigzagging along the roads around cars and people walking or riding. I covered my base. No one was going to find me, not if they had a value on life.

Weather was really bleak on the Saturday. A bit of rain and low cloud, so I decided not to risk it. I thought I was going to get the sack the previous Tuesday though. I forgot to ring in sick. What got me out of it was that it was one of the few times that I took a day off. I always needed money, so my time keeping was normally good. Especially to help mum with grub and such. I fixed that though.

Sunday, It was clear. I got out just after dawn. In a few minutes I was there. Woke up in the tree though, not on the ground. Nearly fell off. I'll after figure this out later, because I'd left plenty of skin around. Got to the quarry and sat down. Took a paper bag out of my pocket and sprinkled it on the ground a couple of yards away. I was just staring at it when she appeared. It startled me to see it actually happen. Nothing one second and there before you, in less time that you can blink an eye.

To see is to believe.

All she did was burst into tears as soon as she appeared and then tried to cover herself up. I reached back and gave her a parcel. In it was a vest, pair of pants, dress, jumper and some plimsolls.

'Put these on,' I said and turned my back. I'd a sister, same age and size. Plimsolls stretch a bit. I'd had a five hour bike ride to get those clothes to the woods.

'Mister, I'm dressed,' I heard her say.

I turned towards her with a smile.

'Just relax for a minute,' I said quietly to her: 'take in the sun. You know by now, that you can do something that others can't.'

She just nodded.

'Listen to me,' and I carried on: 'don't tell anyone what you can do. You only do it when you want to. You think it and it quickly happens. Only when the suns bright, can you do it quickly. When it's cloudy, it's dangerous. It slows you down when the suns not shining. I'm still figuring it all out.'

I paused then and added.

'The tall man will never ever be back, I can promise you that.'

She then began to open up to me. A lot of it was garbled and mixed up. What I did get most of all, was the fact that her mum and dad used to hit her hard. Various doctors and been to see her through out her life, from the age of six years of age. Her mum and dad used to hit her for wasting people's time. She told me that whenever they watched her sleeping, that see could sense them there and had never soared while been watched. Every one thought that she was crazy.

'I'll sort that out for you,' I promised: 'but it may hurt your mum and dad. Will you trust me totally?'

'Please, please do it for me,' she said then: 'they hurt me all the time.'

That did it. I pulled a finger nail off and for good measure, I gave her another one.

'Put this at the side of your bed and grab a pair or your dad's trousers and a belt. Put them under your bed. I'll come next weekend, if I can. Listen, I also want some rope and a knife. I promise you this, I will not harm your mum and dad much. But definitely they will never strike you again.

'Promise,' she gasped.

'I promise. They are only hitting you because they are frightened just as much as you.'

I really hoped that these words were true.

I spent the next few days on my plans and hoping that I was doing the right thing. I arrived , just as I had told her. Touched her awake. Her eyes just shot open and as she gasped, I thought at that moment she was going to scream. It was recognition that stopped her. I grabbed the trousers and I was in them immediately. Belt on and tightly fastened.

'Shush,' I whispered. 'Where's the rope.'

She pointed to her wardrobe.

'In there.' She whispered back.

The knife was there but it was a flipping table knife. Blunt as hell.' 'Shush,' I whispered:. 'I'll come back soon.'

You know how hard it is to get down stairs. There's always a creaky step. Keep to the sides. Down I went and found the kitchen. I crept back up. Into her bedroom and cut the clothes line to the length's that I needed. I made my way to the parents' bed room. Door was ajar. If anything went wrong I'd run. This is it I thought and there her father was, just like my dad, his arms slightly out at the side of the bed. Good at knots. Seamanship at nautical college had done me proud. Two half hitches crossed between and two others to lock it. Both ends to the bed end. The girl's mother had only one hand showing. A nice little double hitch and a slow half to secure it.

Both ends to the bed end again. It was a detached house, so no one could hear next door. Round the bed. Thumped him in the chest and it took a fast hard jab to the jaw to stun him. Back to the mother. She was sat bolt upright, her mouth opening when I grabbed her throat. She couldn't squeak.

'What wide eyes you have,' I said to her and glared into her eyes from real close up…

She was terrified.

'Listen to me, lady,' I finally said. 'I'll not harm you or him if you'll listen.'

'Do you hear me,' I shouted.

She nodded as best she could. I then lowered my voice and called Rachel in.

'Listen misses. I am here to help your daughter. Do you understand,' I said in the same quiet voice.

I think she calmed down when her daughter walked in. I could feel it and sense it.

'Will you scream,' I asked her.

She gave me a slow shake of her head. No.

'Please don't,' I said again: 'I am not here the hurt you, but to show you some thing. If you do anything I'll have to change my mind.'

I'd have got out of there first, but she wasn't to know that. Dad was now coming out of it.

'Listen I will not hurt him any more either,' I then said: 'I just need him a little more secure though. Look, I'm giving the knife to your daughter. Take it to the kitchen Rachel and then come back. Wash it all over first.'

I knew about finger prints. I just slipped a rope around his foot and secured it tight. It took just a couple of seconds. Rachel's mother was just staring at me all the time.

'How did you get in,' she whispered.

I then began to talk to her, giving her bits and pieces of my life. I told them that I could soar and fly, free as a bird whenever I wanted to. Totally unseen. I didn't tell them about the pin-pricks of lights in the distance. I never told them how I could appear in different places.

'I don't hit friends' mothers,' I told her.

She'd got the message.

Rachel's father was listening even through his pain. I told him that he'd got off extremely lightly I told him how I'd hammered people down for most of my life. He believed me, I could see it in his eyes. Rachel was sat there quietly listening. I saw a few little tears. She herself was hurting.

No matter what, it was her mum and dad. I explained first of all that from now on they would have to protect Rachel until she was older. To always assist her whenever possible.

'I'll show you now, the proof first,' I said to them both: 'but be aware, I will always be in this area. I hope I never have to return. Lay between your mum and dad, Rachel. You can think it safe to do it, relax and do it. You are safe to do it now for the first time.'

She looked at them both, as if to ask them if it was all right. Her mother even gave a little nod.

'Relax,' I told her again.

She did and was gone, a glimmer of pure light.

'God Almighty,' burst from Rachel's dad.

What remained between them was just a night dress. Mother had her hand to her mouth.

'Rachel,' I called: 'get dressed and come back in.'

In she came within seconds, and her mother burst out crying holding her free hand out to her daughter. I stood up and removed the rope from her wrist. Both mother and daughter crying and holding each other tight. I looked at her dad. He was just laid there totally bewildered, speechless and unsure what his mind had seen.

'Got any beer,' I said.

That brought him back. Yes, it was early morning and I wanted a beer. I took the ropes off him. He wasn't going to do anything now. I opened his wardrobe and put one of his shirts on.

'See you down stairs,' I said.

He came down real quickly right behind me.

'Where's my beer,' I said.

I could just see the smile, not big but it was there. His hands though were really shaky. I noticed it, when he handed me a small bottle of brown ale. Still not believing what had happened he sat down.

'You do realise that I'm going to do the same as your daughter, don't you,' I said.

He just looked at me and then bent forwards with his hands over his eyes.

'I'll never come back,' I told him: 'as long as I can see her light.'

Well, we just sat there just the two of us for about twenty minutes and then we heard them both coming down the stairs. In they came with their little smiles. It's going to be all right now. The fear was over for all three of them.

'What's your name?' Rachel asked me.

'Day Mover,' I replied.

I'm sure at that time they just expected me to stand up and leave. No I lay down, relaxed, and flashed out and away.

Chapter 4

BM

Remember the Thorns, well something had been niggling me for some time. There was no sign of me being pricked by the thorns when I had arrived home on that particular day. Not a mark. The other thing, why was I up the tree and not on the ground? Why was I so strong? Why was I big in the chest and arms? Most of my friends were far smaller. It worked out that no foreign bodies travelled with me when I moved from place to place. Was it automatic for me to have such a clear skin? I'd not a single spot on me. Any bruises from scrapping disappeared after a single move. My legs were thin but I had incredibly strong muscles. I'd not a bit of fat on me. It was as if I had subconsciously proportioned my body to my best advantage. I knew about mass and that it is still equal in weight or area even in different forms. I tried it slowly and it was true. Just a little on the stomach I thought whilst moving onto my bed one day. Sure enough it happened. I'd suddenly got fat around my waist. I'd lost it from my shoulders and arms. Had to go back out moving, to get rid of it. The conclusion, I reached about landing in a tree was simple. Insects had taken my skin. Something to watch out for. If it was buried or eaten, then I cannot land and wake up. Never try to go underground where the sun does not shine. Keep to the light.

I spotted Rachel a few times over the next few months and flew over. She was limiting her ability, for her parent's sake. We'd discovered that we could converse by thinking, even while hovering. I could also block out her thoughts at will. Her parents had changed for the better she told me. Even to protecting her. She told me that occasionally someone from London would arrive to ask about her. Her parent used to tell them that their daughter was normal and had stopped having dreams of flying. I asked her not to mention my visits. She soon began to have normal friends. I'd explained to her how she must follow certain rules to protect herself. To always watch the pin-prick lights.

'Always keep yourself safe,' I told her.

Slow but sure, I let Rachel build her own life with what she had. She was growing up the same as me and getting wiser every day. Always have an escape route planned. I taught her that.

What is a Burglar? To me, it's a person who enters into other people's homes to steal. He doesn't care where. Houses, shops and company warehouses. I decided that I would never break into a person's home to steal.

Shops and offices were my meat. I used to walk into the entrances and drop some skin. If any one spotted me, I'd ask for a job. Under a gap in a door was one way in, or through a cracked window. I'd size a place up on a Saturday, just by hovering in front of the windows. I could sometimes spot cash being put in drawers, or being hidden away. I'd cruise round on my bike at night dropping my clothes and shoes in a safe spot. Sundays, I did the deed. In I went. First thing was paper, to cover my hands whilst opening drawers. Check the windows for an alarm. Open it if safe and drop the cash outside. If the window was alarmed, then I used side doors to slide the cash under the gaps. Half in and half out. Never a front door, always a side door. Elastic bands were a boon to me. My radius was around thirty miles so I had endless scope. I carried this out so neatly it was unbelievable. My mother used to find extra money in her purse. We were happy for a time. Always be careful she used to say.

She should have said it to dad. You know, between life and death it doesn't take long. It was in the last three months of his life that my dad was diagnosed. He'd got Cancer of the Lungs. Six weeks and he was as dead.

I'd not really known my father but I'm sure that he loved us in his own way. The sea had been his life and to put him on the works, in all that Basic slag dust was the end. Did my mum get compensation, or course she didn't. All she got was a widow's pension to keep us on. We would have starved. I gave her most of my wages. Saved enough for a couple of beers. I always dropped some extra in her handbag when I'd done a job. I did a few rush jobs to pay for my dad's funeral.

Insurance you say. She'd got me insured for death and not my father. He was only insured for accidents and disability.

I'm just over seventeen now and courting the girl from next door. I kept disappearing and would never tell her why. Known her all most of my life. They moved house and then we moved house.

We lived right next door to each other.

Used to walk out most nights or go to church hall to Rock and Roll. Yes man, I can do it. Both of us were really good. Long and the short of it, mum took in a lodger. Didn't take them long.

Thought I didn't know. Collared him up the pub one afternoon. I'm sure he though I was going to have a go with him. He knew of my reputation. Didn't though but I told him straight, get on with it but don't mess her about. Did you think that I'd stopped scrapping. I hadn't. Never started any though. I did have certain principles. My words were simply this to anyone. You want to try. Nothings stopping you. I'd never mention Karate, to any one back home. None of their business. Bang, bang ,bang. Sometimes that's all it normally took.

'At least he tried,' I used to say.

The police were involved a few times but let's face it. Word was out to them. Never did I start anything. Never ever threw the first punch. The only time was the two at college. I put four of them away one day. One started it and the others jumped in. Too late for them but it certainly made my life easier from then on. It was down town on a Saturday and the town was growing. I'd been away for three years and most people didn't know me in town. Packed with shoppers it was. Him and his mates were supposed to be the hard nuts of that part of town. Well known for making trouble. Everyone kept away from them. I fancied a quick pint at the pub near the market. Blue Bell they called it. I was walking to the door with my lass when out they came. Couldn't have timed it worse.

Fancy a screw darling. That' all it took.

'Watch your mouth,' she's with me.

'What ya gunner do,' came this sharp reply from one of the four.

We'd got in the door at that point and I thought know more about it.

‘Foul mouthed idiots,’ was all my girl said forgot about it.

We didn’t know what was happening out side. The four were waiting and mouthing off about a coming scrap. A crowd was gathering outside to watch the gang. A lot of young lads and lasses from fourteen upwards and a fair few shoppers. I spotted this when glancing through the window.

‘Don’t tell me,’ says my lass: ‘They’re waiting for you.’

I went out all right, but with something in mind. The second I got outside, I shouted so all could hear me. These guys insulted my girlfriend. They asked her for a screw and now I’m telling them to sod off. Yes I had my witnesses all right. Spinning to the first one I told him to get the shit away from me. Not him. Up came a fist and forwards it came. Too slow sonny, because I grabbed that fist in both hands. Quickly transferred one to his wrist. Spun round against the back of his elbow and I broke it there and then. Did he scream? I grabbed his mate’s hair as he came in, down to a knee coming up. Fingers to another’s jacket cuff and a straight back flip over on my feet.

That really shocked them to see me do it. Just that little support against him gave me the leverage to do it. Straight jab to the throat and elbowed back number four. He tried to come back. He’d probably never heard of a drop kick. He felt one though. Drop kicked him hard in the face. Did I stop? Did I fuck?

Not often you’ll hear me swear but I did then. I did the rounds on them. A stamp in one face, straight hard down with your foot. A kick to the jaw. Number three was out of it. Hard to breathe I’d say. Now back to number one. Straddled him while he was still screaming. I didn’t have a once of regret for what I’d already done.

His good arm pulled out straight and then twisted. Again I hammered against the back of his elbow. Twice I hammered against it. I broke his other arm in front of every one there. Dropped him and walked back to my lass.

'Jesus,' I heard: 'It's BM. He's back.'

Yes I could hear them telling everyone who I was. Held my lasses hand and walked through the crowd. Coppers were coming through at that time. Big Jock was one of them. I'm sure he saw me but he didn't stop. We got the bus back home. The police found out who I was and where I lived. Down they came. Four of them together but in two cars. I told them there and then. Why four of you, when it only takes one. They got the message and three of them left. Now that's one thing about me. I respect the fact that the Police have a job to do. No way would I start a battle with them. You're on a loser straight away if you did and I had a lot to hide. I invited him in. He was new as a DC and about four years older than me. We had a good chat. From what schools and college I'd been to. All sorts, until he got round to asking me if I'd been in town at such a time and did you have a fight?

'Have you got any witnesses that will identify me?' I asked him.

He said that he had. Four of them. The four I'd belted. Not one from the crowd though. I was home free.

'Put it this way,' I said to him: 'I never start anything. Can you prove otherwise. I will if necessary produce twenty witnesses. They will all state that I only protected myself. If you want me to go down to the station, that's fine. Keep this in mind, you'll never get me to say one word or to sign anything.'

Sure enough, I went down with him. They kept me inside for two days. Every hour or so they brought me out to make a statement. I was totally silent for the full two days. Open your lips once and they have you. Never even took up the offer of a solicitor. With one of them present, they expect you to say something to him with them listening. No thanks, I didn't need one. I'd already told my girl friend what to do if I got lifted by the police. The word was out that if I got prosecuted, then the hard boys would really be in trouble. Out on remand I would have done it, without any witnesses present. Word was that the guy whose arms I broke, was told first. One of my mates had walked up to him. All he said was that 'he could have been BM' and to think about it. He must have asked about all right because I was let out with a caution.

Met big Jock on my way out. Had a word with him. He laughed and told me that he'd told DS that I'd never speak. I'm sure that bets had been made on the outcome. He was the copper on our estate whilst I was growing up. He knew that I never ever started one fight in all the time he'd known me, but that I'd always somehow come out on top. When I'd scrapped years ago, he never said a word to me. He knew that it was me because I'd done a standing back flip. The last time he'd seen anyone in town do that, was three years earlier. Me, showing off. That day in town he must have heard someone mention about the flip. Smart to put it together. A straight back flip and landing on my feet. Try it some time.

No sooner was I out the cells when I had something new to face: My girlfriend was in the club. It was totally my fault because I never liked the rubber goods. Done nothing but row with her. Told her mother that I'd marry her.

'Over my dead body,' she said.

It could have been arranged, I thought at the time. I even approached her father. He didn't say anything and just carried on cleaning his motor bike. If he'd thumped me, I'd have taken it better but he didn't. I think that I'd have let him do it at the time. Carried on rowing with my girlfriend and she said that was it for the last time. It was over.

I'll show them.

Quit my job and headed south on my bike. I'd bought a Norman B4 250 cc sports bike with some of my illicit gains. I ended up in Dorking Surrey. Riding in, I went over the new overpass that was being built. Slept in the woods that night. Went in the foreman's office the next day, cheeky as hell, and asked for a job. He gave me one. Must have liked the size of me or my cheek. I remember that it was a Thursday and I had to start on the Monday. Had a few bob so I was all right. My cash was safely hidden in my pannier on my bike. I had well over £500. Had that phone number with me also. I'd kept it all these years. I wonder I thought. Rode out to a little country pub just out side town. Red phone box, handy at the side.

'Hello, Edith here,' she said: 'Can I help you.' Funny isn't it. Same name and the same words from long ago.

'I can't speak for long. I used to live up north. Where can we meet,' I said all of this to her quickly.

'You can come here,' she said.

'No way,' I told her: 'you'll have to meet me. Neutral grounds. I'll call you back.'

It only took a few minutes but I was away on my bike, just in case. My job though.

Started work on a Monday in my new job and finished on a Monday. Wasn't making tea for nobody, not me. Left something in the corner before I left though. The petty cash would be there. Waiting for me.

London was so large for a small town boy like me. Where could I meet her? How safe would I be? Not safe at all. Was she going to come on her own. I didn't think so. I had to think it all out, step by step. First thing, they must have known bogey man. They must have known of my involvement because of the advert. Only another of my kind could get close to me. How many others were there like me here in London? I knew that whilst in mover mode that I was fairly safe. It was only whilst awake during the day, or sleeping at night that I could be caught.

Timing, that was how I did it, and got away with it. I found the perfect place. Leaving it in the straightest line possible. I started to memorise all the high buildings. Heading south and then west. Always keeping, in the same direction. I'd bought a map.

Just south of the big airport. On to a small place called Leatherhead. I'd found some digs. Told the lady that I was looking for work and that I'd always pay in advance. A beauty of a room. At back was an alleyway. I was looking out on it. A safe way in for me. A safe way out if I needed to leave fast. Parking for my bike. Called Edith and got the same words again. Once she knew it was me, her tone changed.

'Where are you,' she asked.

'That's my business,' I said and carried on talking: 'exactly 100 yards in, from the South Gate. Regents Park. There's a brown bench. Eight o'clock tomorrow morning. I then put the phone down before she could say anything.

I told the landlady that I was going to have a lay in the next morning. I was then clear for a home run if all went well.

Laid reading for most of the night. It was light before I decided to go. I'm ready, relaxed and I close my eyes. Lets go do it. Let's discover the future. I can now feel my body go, as I become a ball of cold but bright energy. I stopped and looked back at where I'd been laying. It was one of the few times that I'd done this. Just to look back and not see my body on the bed.

I kept low that morning for the first few minutes. I stopped and rose up slowly, to look around. No other pin prick lights. Good, down close to the ground. Moving fast along. Up and down over obstructions and heading into London. Three times I stopped in as many minutes to rise up and check. Still there were no lights.

Regents Park. He was there, as I'd planned it the night before. A tramp was fast asleep on the bench. It was seeing him the previous day that had given me the perfect way to do it. I was waiting close by, unseen. I watched him stirring in his sleep. I had to go by the position of the sun whilst hovering.

Sure enough it wasn't long before it happened. The previous day I'd seen the Park Keeper move the tramp on before the visitors arrived. He got up, ambled a few feet away and waited. I'd spotted something not quite normal though. Two other tramps had only moved to sit up. I moved in close to both of them. Mid twenties was a good guess. I was sure they belonged to Edith. Tramps have long hair. These two didn't.

I carried on waiting and a few minutes later, a woman of about forty appeared at the gate. She was smartly dressed. She walked towards the bench. I could see her eyes moving from side to side as she sat down.

Looking at the sky I could see the sun. Yes, I though 8 o'clock. Edith, I know your face at long last. I then watched the tramp amble over to her. My envelope was in his hand. I told you I was smart. Did they take me for some country bumpkin?

I watch both the other tramps stand up as if to come towards Edith. I even watched her shake her head. She took the envelope and opened it. A piece of paper and a fiver folded inside. It had cost me ten pounds for the tramp to stay where he was and with a promise of another five if he hung on just to hand over that envelope. It had worked out. I'm sure if he'd known that the other five had been in the envelope it wouldn't have worked. He would have been well away. I kept my eye on him as he left.

Sure enough two men stopped him as he left the park. I looked back at Edith. Just a quick check I thought. Went up really slow turning and checking for any lights. Nothing, it was clear for the moment. Moving quickly in I positioned myself right in front of Edith. She'd read the letter and sat there thinking. She then composed herself and began to speak. If any one had walked by during the next few minutes, they'd have thought her insane. Talking to herself of all things. That's how I'd planned it. The only way to get information, from Edith. They had no way to trap me. I was free.

Chapter 5

Edith

My name is Edith Reynolds. I am a doctor. I have worked for a Government department in Harley St for fifteen years.

No.

No.

We want to study you.

Yes.

No.

Yes.

Yes.

That would have to be decided.

Poor doctor, she was talking to herself. Three times she said the same thing. I think embarrassment came into it, because the two supposed tramps had approached her by the third time that it was repeated.

'Where the heck is he,' asked one of them quietly.

'If only you knew,' Edith said quietly back to him: 'If only you knew.'

I could see them looking around.

'There's no point in trying to find him,' she said: 'He's here but not in sight.'

I moved away at that point. Slowly, low down. Stopping once in a while just to make sure that there were no more lights. Then I moved behind buildings to hide my light. I'd mark out different places where I could have hidden myself from view. A garage here and then another one. Machine shops. A barn out in the country. Every entrance faced south west, away from London. I'd worked this out from the quarries when with Rachel and from my own methods back home. Keep low down, buildings will hide your light from another mover.

Do not go underground.

A dimly lit building was just OK if you kept out of the dark corners. Dark corners were where the night ghosts were waiting to pounce. They appeared as transparent shimmering shapes. Not visible to humans but just visible to me. All of them were hiding there waiting for the sun to go down and for me to make the one mistake. All of them were facing outwards, towards me.

The hunger was plain to see.

..... Harley St. That's where all the posh doctors were.

No. She wasn't married.

No. There were no children. They want to study me.

Yes. She knew of others just like me. Other movers.

No. I could not speak to them.

Yes. They were in London.

Yes. Will I be safe and allowed to leave, at any time?

I'd a few answers, but there was no way that I was going to trust anyone, just like that. That advert was put in just after bogeyman. Had they forgotten that episode so quickly? It was the last question where she gave me the wrong answer. They'd never forget bogey. One thing I am sure of though. In a dark room, I'm fucked. That's all it would take. There was also something else wrong. Where were the other movers now? I'd not seen anyone up and about. Were they as strong as me? Could they move like me? Or were the majority just like my family, not fully developed and not able to do it at will. The other question was who was faster and stronger than me. Or was I the strongest of them all. All of this was passing though my mind.

I needed answers to many questions. Let's give them a little rope. Maybe, just maybe, a mistake would be made. I waited for four days before I rang Edith again. Never gave her a chance to question me. Just told her straight that I'd been there, and had listened to all she had said to me. I telephoned from the other side of London, just in case.

Got £237 that Sunday. Let them think on. No sign of entry and nothing at all broken. The gap under the door was large enough. I also did a little touring round on my bike. Checking out a few places ready for the future. Then went back at night hidden from view. Plenty of them, all thinking, that they were safe to hide money. Some of the places were so unbelievable. False floor boards, false wall panels, false books, hidden under papers. A bank is the only safe place. Even that's not always safe.

Do you think you're safe, to play with things when you're locked away in your office or home. London must have the largest amount of illegal weapons in the world, or so I thought at the time. Well I was going to have some, to stash away. It was only by chance that I'd found the first one. After that it came easy to find them. Anyway, this day I was just laid there and I'd not even thought about going aloft. One second it takes and them I'm up. Quick check because I'd not prepared myself. Just went East for a few miles when I spotted this man acting a little strange.

He was just stood there looking out from a car showroom. He was checking all over the area. Ran to his car, jumped in and locked the doors straight away. I'd never seen anyone do that so fast. Decided to follow him and I got right down beside him, looking in. Blimey, there was a gun at the side, on the passenger seat.

That was also the closest I came in years to hitting something. Have I not told you? I have to avoid hard and solid items. I'd misjudged once a few years previously. Hit the side of a building. I bounced back spinning, little sparks were flashing all around me. It took me nearly a minute to stabilise myself. I'd never taken that chance again, that is until this time. Never knew out if the sparks could be seen.

I broke one of my own rules that night. I had to have that gun. The bag he carried was safe for the moment, even though I knew it contained money. That was in his house. The gun was in the glove compartment. It's easy with the windows of a jag. A little jimmy, and I'd got a gun. It was wrapped up and buried. Right next door to my lodgings. It could still be there as far as I know, even after all these years.

I was always in my digs before 9.30 pm. Only ever had a couple of beers at any one time. I wanted to be the model lodger. No women in my life. Didn't want to know them for the time being. I didn't want anyone at all knowing what I did. Sneaked out soaring twice a day looking north east towards London but always I checked my rear. I'd done a sighting on a map of London. I found Harley

Street. Sight lined it up from eight different angles. If anything appeared from London, it would be from that area. I now knew within a couple of hundred yards how far it was. As the Crow flies, that is.

It took eleven days for something to happen. I'd come out for my daily spying session. Two pin prick lights were showing brightly in the distance. I went dramatically low in a few seconds. I could just see them from where I'd hidden, behind a high rise. Spun around every so often to check my rear. Right I thought here goes. I moved north, very fast and very low. No way could they see me at ground level. It was a really quick ten mile run by my estimate. Up I shot for them to see me. Stayed hovering until I could see the change. Definitely moving towards me. Down I went for my quick run south again and headed a little East as well. Did not want to be near my base. Stopped behind another high rise and waited. The angle of approach hid me very well.

Only one came into sight, so I had to go right and look around the right side of the block. Could not understand it at all. The second one was heading back. Barely moving. Came back slowly to the left side again. Just sneaking quick looks. Well one thing was certain at that point. I couldn't be seen at all. The light was smaller than mine. Not quite as bright, as Rachel.

I remained because I had an added advantage. I could make it all the way home up North in one run. I could estimate an arrival time. Just before dark, that's when we had to reform as a human body. Even if it meant heading at a tangent, to my final location. I knew to the minute how long it would take once I came upon my home stamping grounds.

He or she would have to turn back some where along that route.

After just a few seconds of rising. The light started coming my way. This was the second time I would meet someone like me. I felt tense, exhilarated. Ready to move instantly, if need be. Definitely it was smaller than myself. It was slightly larger than Rachel but not as bright. I waited.

The ball of light came forwards slowly, stopped for about a minute just a couple of hundred yards away. Then inched again towards me until it was but a few feet from my own outer rim of light.

'Who are you?' a voice projected into my mind: 'Where are you from?'

It was a boy's voice not yet broken. I waited for a few seconds, just to hear more. He was hovering quietly. I could literally hear his brain thinking.

'Why do you wish to know?' I asked.

'It's not me but the doctor who wants to know,' came his thoughts: 'She sent me and a friend out to find you. He cannot stay long, so I carried on alone.'

That's one down and out of it, I thought.

'Just a minute,' I thought back to him. Then I shut him out completely. I could feel him try to speak to me, so I opened up and asked him to wait. Then I shut him off again. We were just there hovering, unseen to the world of man. Two balls of white light cold and bright, yet totally invisible.

'How often do you leave your body?' I asked him.

'Not very often,' he projected into my mind: 'because we have to take tablets to keep us alive. The doctors have told us, we need them every day.'

Something wrong here. My body heals itself, every time. The vague thought was coming into my mind by then. I was the one they wanted. They should have concentrated in trying to catch me when I was younger. Now I was able to avoid them. Sending out this young one proved they had nothing much at all.

'How long have you been at the doctors?' I asked him.

'Since I was six years old,' came back his response and he carried on. 'My friend since he was seven years old.'

'How old are you now, and how old is your friend?' I asked him.

'I'm thirteen and he's twelve,' he told me.

'Have you seen any others?' I next asked him deviously.

He thought for a moment then continued, 'There were two others but they died. A boy slightly larger than me. The other, she was a girl and she was younger. The doctors told us they died because they stopped taking the tablets.'

'Can you remember what time of day it was?' I asked.

No, we never saw them that day,' came back his immediate answer.

'What's your name by the way?' I'd forgotten to ask him.

'Michael,' he replied: 'My friend's name is Geoffrey.'

I thought for a moment. 'So what you're telling me is that you have been there for seven years,'

'Yes, ' he mumbled.

'Do you ever go out to play?' I then projected to him.

'No, the doctors told us that other kids would not like us. We have a garden to walk around in. A slide and a swing. We have to ask, to play out. Then the doctor's come out and watch us.'

'Is it open to the sky?' I butted in to ask him.

'Yes,' was his reply.

'What else do they do to you,' was my next thoughts to him.

'We have to lay down for the wires to be put in place.'

'Where?' I asked.

'On my head and body,' he replied.

'Do they take anything from your body.'

'Blood,' he replied.

'Anything else?'

'No.'

'Tell me have you ever bruised yourself in any way or cut yourself?'

'I was bruised for days when I fell off the slide,' he answered.

'Can you remember flying whilst you had the bruises?'

'No, but what has bruises to do with it?'

Think hard will you, did you still have the bruises after flying?'

'No,' were his thoughts back.

'Bingo.'

'How long does it take you to come up in the sky?' was my next question?

'I can only do it when I dream of doing it. They always talk to me about dreams. They say it makes it easier for me to do it,' he replied.

‘Slow down a little Mike,’ were my thoughts to him.

My own private thoughts were on overtime by now. They had nothing to compare with what I could do. They had nothing at all really.

There was only one of us in any danger and that was Rachel. Poor sod little thing. They had no idea that skin had anything to do with it. No idea, at all.

What had they been doing all this time.

‘Listen,’ I said to him: ‘It’s one thing for you to find me, another for you to follow me. DON’T. It would be dangerous for you.

‘I’ll see you in four days,’ I told him.

I’d something to do. I had to give a message, to Rachel. I slid away very fast but something was wrong. Something crazy. One second I was going smoothly along and the next I was spinning and twisting out of control. What a relief when I smoothed out just above the ground. It was my own stupid fault. I’d forgotten about the Heathrow airport west of London. I’d nearly got hammered by a passenger jet. I may have crashed the damn thing if it had hit me.

Chapter 6

BM

I'd been so concerned about hiding my base. I'd clean forgotten it was in that direction. That decided me. I was going north on my bike. Sod it for a couple of days. Play safe. Having a bike gave me freedom, not speed. It was only a 250cc and I'd yet to pass my test. I got home during the night and had to knock mum up. What a smile she gave me. Maybe it was relief, I don't know. I was happy enough to see her smile.

I'd got another three days before I needed to be in London again. I was up and out early and had no choice but to use the bike. I headed for Rachel's house. I needed to know how she was fairing. I checked all around the roads to the school and couldn't see anything amiss. Drove back to her house and hung about at the corner, waiting for her to go to school. She spotted me straight away. Or had she been out above that morning having a look around as I'd taught her to do? Mornings were always the best time to check out the lay of the land. I risked it just taking her to school. Mind you another helmet would have to be thought about if I did this more often.

On the way I asked her to meet me at lunch time. A couple of her mates eyed me up when I dropped her. She'd already an answer though and beat me to it.

'It's my cousin,' she said to them.

Some how she'd got her act together. No longer was she a frightened little girl, afraid of what people thought. What they said behind her back would never effect her ever again.

I went to a little penny arcade to pass the time and got back just as they were coming out for the lunch break.

First thing I asked her was had any one been snooping about.

'Not really,' she said:

A couple of times she'd seen strangers but they'd also called on other houses on the estate. There was only one change that she'd noticed and that was that a new man and woman had moved into an empty house a few weeks previous. They didn't mix with anyone.

'I have seen them walking passed my house at weekends and sometimes when I get home from school. Real strange they are,' she said: 'I've tried to spy on them but their curtains are always closed.'

'Rachel, have they ever taken any blood from you?' I asked her: 'Or anything else?'

'Just blood,' she said: 'That's all they ever wanted.' 'That's what used to scare me a lot because I don't like needles.'

'OK,' I said: 'Now I'm living in London. If you ever really did need to get away, quickly like. Just come south.

She seemed puzzled for a moment and then I added.

'Ask your dad to buy you a road map of England. You must only come in the mornings and never late in the afternoon. Do you understand this?

She nodded.

'Practice, reading the map and work out the way south. Look at the sun before you leave. It rises in the east and sinks in the west.

She nodded once more.

'At twelve O'clock it is approximately south. It'll take you less than two hours. If you cannot find me. Follow the same road back.

'Okay,' she said.

'Remember the suns direction always. Look also for church spires. They normally have a clock on them. This will also help you to get your direction correct.

'What's that long road called?' she asked and I was pleased that she was taking it all in.

'The A1,' I told her: 'It goes straight to London.'

She smiled.

'One more thing,' I said: 'You'll see some planes on your right, when you get closer. Do not ever get near them. Go well underneath them if you have to, but stay clear otherwise. Do you understand that bit?'

'Yes, of course,' she said.

'Look on the map for Leatherhead,' I continued: There's only one small set of Terraced houses down there and it's easy to spot them.

I paused at that point before continuing.

'Now give me a piece of skin and a nail. Just think yourself awake when you're there and you'll be drawn to where I'm staying.'

'I'll keep this safe so you can do it. Is your bolt-hole still OK in the quarry?'

'Yes, no one can find it,' she said.

'Listen,' I then said to her.: 'You should have another hiding place.'

I then commenced to tell her about my place. Time was up and it was back in school for her.

I had debated whether to see her mother at one point. May have to in the future but not just yet. Father I didn't trust still. It's maternal with mothers. Had a nice steady ride to see mum. Still got a couple of days. It never worked out how we planned it though. The other bogeymen, they got to her first.

Once my brothers and sisters were in bed, we started to talk. I told her that for the first time I was really going to show her what I could do.

'It's got to be tomorrow morning though, after they've all gone to school or work,' I said.

Then I started to tell her about Rachel. As much as I dared say.

I even explained a little about what had happened to bogey. A little about those down south. It was getting late by then so it was off to bed.

In the morning I was woken by the family getting ready. My brothers and sisters knew I was a strange one. They were used to it and never said anything. Mind you my brothers and sisters are strange as well. I just put some shorts and a tee-shirt on and went for some toast and a cup of tea. The lodger worked night and was in bed by this time. He'd got home just after 6.30 am. I sat there patiently waiting. By a quarter to nine the house was silent except for the TV.

'Are you ready mum?' I asked.

All she did was nod her head.

I'd prepared her for this. I some how knew she'd be all right. I just relaxed and it was done just like that. Right in front of her. One second she was watching me. The next all she could see was my clothes, a tee-shirt and shorts. She actually cried out. I heard her as I arrived in bed.

'It's OK,' I called down to her: 'I'm just getting dressed. I'll be down in a minute.'

I came down and she was still sat there in the chair. She was shocked. It was in her eyes. I put my arms around her.

'It's OK, I'm all right,' I said soothingly.

Just sitting there put a lot of heart break from the past few years totally right. She kept looking at me. I asked her if she was all right.

She said that she would be, but it was just the fact that she'd seen it happen, something so special so amazing. The one thing on my side was that she'd thought that it had happened to her once when she was younger. Just the once, she said.

I know now, that it could not have been true. We started to smile after that.

'Here,' I said: fifty pounds.' I told her more about Rachel and she promised that if she ever appeared, she'd hide her until I got in touch.

I'm going south mum, I said: 'I'll send you a letter as and when. Hell, I could beat the post.'

She now knew exactly how and that made her laugh.

You know, it's tiring being a human. I'd done a fair bit of travelling and the bikes not running too good. My muscles were tired. I was tired. I spent the next twenty four hours either sleeping or just relaxing. Prepared myself for the next day. Planning and thinking now went into everything I did. Was going to be daring in some ways. Did they want to stay or not? Would these two boys believe me when I told them about the lies told to them over the years? I was ready for it now and went back to London.

I was there waiting for them, as they rose upwards into the sky. Shook them rigid. All I'd said to them was, I would be there waiting. I'd not said where though, so they did not expect me to be above them. Here we are not fifty feet above, three cold bright lights.

Two were looking towards one, and one looking towards two. Only in your minds can you visualise it.

'Hello, we did not expect you to be here,' was the response from the gleam of light on my left.

'You must be Michael,' was my thoughts to him.

'Yes, and this is Geoffrey.'

'Geoffrey, think yourself smaller and you'll be able to stay longer.' I'd noticed how large he'd put himself, to match his friends glow.

'Some of us are stronger,' I channelled to him: 'the smaller the better, until you get older.'

He slowly became smaller.

'That's much better,' I added.

We hovered for a moment in silence enjoying this sense of being with our own kind.

'What are you supposed to find out about me,' I then asked.

'We have been instructed to find out where you staying. We're to ask you to come and see the doctors.

'Hey,' I thought. That's plural now. Before it was just one doctor. Edith.

'Are you happy where you are, or do you miss your parents? Can you leave when you want?

Michael already had the answer.

'I've asked them since I've been here and they always say no,' he channelled across to me: 'We need the injections.'

'That's bullshit,' I responded: 'What if you could leave and never go back. I can teach you how to look after yourselves.'

'Can we think about it, for a moment,' came back from Michael: 'We've to meet a new girl tomorrow. She's supposed to be really strong. They say she can teach us a lot of new things. They have been watching her for a long time. Word is that they are after someone else and have been for a few years. Is it you? Do you come from the north?

My heart dropped. Who have they just got? What do they mean up north I thought?

'Listen, never try to follow me,' I said and channelled it loudly to them:

'Go back and awaken and do it now. Just keep away from me until I find out what's happening.'

I watched their lights move away and fade to mere specks.

I went fast. I don't think I'd ever travelled so fast. Arriving above my house, I checked fully around. Just mum's washing. All was fine at home. I then journeyed west and came to the woods above Rachel's home. My secret stock of clothes was still there wrapped in a bag. Got dressed and hid till dark. I had to sneak up to Rachel's house that evening. A knock and the door was instantly answered. It took just one glance at her mother's face to see that my worse fears had been realised. Rachel had been taken. It could only have been in the night, when she was defenceless. I told Rachel's mother that her daughter would be home again soon. I went straight to that odd couple up the street. I already knew what they looked like. I'd spied on them when Rachel had first told me of them. I'd only been gone from that door for a few seconds when police cars appeared at each end of the street. They were on to me. They'd definitely spotted me. I was over the back yard fences fast. Dogs were barking at me as I passed them. OK, I was leaving a trail but it wasn't long before I hit open ground and I was over that in a flash. Someone was going to pay and pay dearly. I spent the worse night of my life, that night. What had gone wrong? How had they found out again? I had to damn well hitch hike home. It was dark and I was utterly powerless. At least I was lucky with a lift though because I'd just got in the car when two more police cars shot by at speed. Got home after midnight.

I slept badly haunted by nightmares. Relax, I told myself. They cannot see me when I'm out of my body. Let's go back unseen.

This I did. Straight to Rachel house to hover there listening. Sure enough the reason came out. The odd couple were sat down talking. Dad had been drinking one night. Had a little too much and opened his mouth to the spies from up the road. I went in through the kitchen window. They had binoculars, cameras on stands. Headphones and other equipment I'd never seen before. They were talking about how long it would be before they were re-called to London.

Too late I thought. You're mine. I'd learnt that with a touch, I could take anyone up with me. It had happened by accident with my mate first and then my youngest brother. I'd been touching his shoulder one morning when I went up for a look around. Hell, he was up there with me, just coming awake. I never moved so fast in my life. We were down and awake that fast that all I got from him was a strange look.

I travelled back to the woods again. Had to dig up a tent that I'd hidden. It was raining so I spent a really miserable day. Damp for most of it and wishing for darkness. I crawled on my belly to the front door. A slow push and I dropped my nail through the letterbox. Now I was ready. Early morning could not come soon enough.

The sky was just light as I let myself leave my body. Could see a couple of night ghosts slowly fading away. Slowly moving to the house. Fancy that, the window was still open a crack. I passed through to the front door and materialised on the floor. Creeping upstairs was easy. Feet to the sides, slowly, slowly placing my feet. Putting my weight down softly. It took me fifteen minutes to cautiously reach that bedroom. They'd left the door slightly open to help me. I touched the man lightly, relaxed and took him up. I can now relax and sleep in an instant. I let go of him and went straight down for the woman. How easy it was becoming to take them with me through the smallest of openings or gaps under doors. I let go of her and hovered there watching them both. The man kept streaming his thoughts at me. He was desperate to get back down to earth. They would both quit their jobs if I would only do it. The woman was going insane. It was too late for her. Then he started to threaten what he would do to Rachel.

'You're dead just for thinking that thought about Rachel,' I projected to him. 'You will be a shadow. A ghost of nothing.'

I left him up in the sky. The woman, I took down to her bed. Not one intelligent thought at all. She would never be able to speak again. She would live, if you could call it living. I hadn't even a thought for the one above. I then split back down south as fast as possible.

Here's what happens to those I leave in a spirit form. For those to whom I do not pass on the power to get back down to earth. As the night darkness comes in, ghosts of the night are waiting for the unlucky ones. To rip from them the day-time essence. They are then split apart by the ghosts of the night. This is when a person of earth will tell you a tale. I saw a ghost last night would be the word from one. In another part of town, it would be others. I saw an apparition or something. Sure enough the papers will give the stories out. Yes, I knew it was true because they'd nearly had me before. I had learnt quickly, what they were. The light from a day mover can be split from a day mover. It is this way that you can see them, as a grey form. I am a day mover. I intend to stay that way.

I arrived back at my digs in the afternoon. Got a bad look from the landlady coming down the stairs? Something was up for sure because I wasn't supposed to be there. Straight back up, grabbed some things and out the back, I was away. I was really lucky that day. Bike started straight away. It had started to give me problems. What I'd done to the couple would be found out. My full intention was to put fear into them all and that I'd achieved.

The days that followed, I hid out in the Surrey woodlands and moved in the early hours through every little gap and space seeking information.. They had managed to get Rachel into the Harley Street clinic but I was determined to get her out again.

The kids were being kept sedated during the day. Listless, drugged and not able to do anything at all to help themselves. I watched someone inject Rachel with a drug. Then the questions commenced. Backwards and forwards they went with the questions. They had my approximate location within the first day. Then they got from her the hiding places and what she'd hidden at the quarry. She did not have my name. That was always the one thing that I'd kept secret. Now was the time to get back at them.

I was back to my hide away and dressed in a moment. Straight to a phone box and I made a call.

'Edith here.'

It was the voice that I wanted to hear on the line.

'Listen carefully to me Edith,' I said: I have been watching you. I suggest you stop. You wouldn't get another chance.'

At that I slammed the phone down.

The Orderly at the clinic had been touching Rachel while she was drugged. I'd seen him do it. He spent his spare time in Soho watching porn movies. Thought he was safe being a big man. No one's safe. I had my plan: three properties to burgle. I bought some glass, cut to the correct size and a little pot of white gloss. With a carpet blade, I trimmed out the wood from around a pane of glass. Two small screwdrivers prying it out and that was it. I was then into the place. The glass was just in case I broke a pane. I left a little of me in the orderlies bedroom and then made sure by drilling a hole through the wooden frame using an hand drill. I did this high up and out of sight behind a curtain. Cleaned up the mess and then it was back outside. The glass was then replaced. Putty made up onto the holding area to look normal and painted to look the same colour. Even dropped a few bits of muck into it to normalise the effect. I checked it out from various angles and it looked all right. Then it was around to the next house. Key from under the mat and I was in and up the stairs very fast. A bit of skin just in case and then another window at the back of the house was drilled into, just the same as the first one.

Why not just enter as a sphere you may be thinking. It's like this: I will never take anything for granted. Hidden in the gardens of the first two were some clothes and shoes. I was covering myself just in case. Number three was just as easy. All three pieces were placed well under the beds, where no one cleans. At all three premises there were people sleeping. Not one of them heard a sound. That's how quiet I am. Just like a ghost.

Back to the woods to wait for the right time. I will put the scare of god into two of them, the third, well. All three of them worked with movers. At Harley Street, they thought they were safe. At their homes they had felt insecure and had sealed up the easy ways in for me. Now you know why I had to get inside by other means.

If Rachel's said too much then at least what I do will make her safe for a time. Here goes, I thought time to do it. The sun was coming up brightly over the horizon. I arrived first at Edith's house. I entered through the drilled hole and quivered my way upstairs. I touched her lightly on the arm. Just a light touch and I have caught her dream. The next second she is pulled high up into the sky where the sun shines bright.

'What's happening?' I heard the projected words from Edith.

I just let her go and projected my own words to her.

'I'll be back soon'.

With that I was moving back downwards but then I stopped. I could read her troubled mind and I returned.

'Calm down.'

I then held her mind, calming her.

'I will return you to earth later.'

The next, I thought. I needed to move urgently for this to work. Another doctor. This one was a little older and he was the one with all the questions. The one who gave the drugs out.

'Come on,' I thought: 'Lets go aloft in your dreams.'

No sooner said and we were up there. Edith, I could see in the distance. I took him closer to her. Dropped him straight off and down again. It only takes but a few seconds, to do this.

Number three. This one should not have touched Rachel. He's dreaming of girls and I can feel it as I touch his hand. What a surprise for his dream to be broken so quickly. What a shock for him to feel it dissolve and to find himself hovering hopelessly above London. I didn't let go but pulled him north. Well, well north. Faster and faster did I travel with him in tow, listening to his screams? Right up to the Scottish Mountains.

Loosened my grip and fled west to the sea. Dipped down and changed direction south and away I sped. Dragging him up there had taken twice as long as my normal speed. I was in a rush now. Blackpool was now below me. I recognised the area and where they strung the lights. Passed it in just a few moments. And then sped south east back to London. It was around 4.00pm and I spotted them at around ten miles from the start point of the morning. They'd been slowly drifting.

They were getting totally fucked up in their minds. Edith was not as bad. She'd heard my promise to take her back down.

'Hold it,' I thought across to both of them: 'Edith I want you to come with me now.'

I commenced to talk to Edith. I knew of the healing powers of my form. It took some time but her mind was adjusting. I wish I'd known earlier what else I could do with my healing power.

'What about me,' screamed the other doctor into my mind. I shut him off totally.

I grasped Edith to me. Just two spheres gently touching. Pulling her back to her home section, I thought us both down towards her bed.

'Beware,' I said: 'I could leave you above at any time. One other little thing I have to tell you though. The orderly, he will never be seen again. Night ghosts will pull him apart.'

'Why,' she managed to project back in the few seconds left.

'He touched a little girl,' I replied: 'He was sexually abusing her while helpless on the drugs you gave her.'

I left her to awaken and then went back up. Clasped the other and took him towards his home. Now it was real timing for the next stage. I had to judge between light and dark.

'Look around you,' I said to him. Spinning him gently around. He could see them all right.

'They are the ghosts of the night.'

They were just becoming visible and coming in fast.

'They are coming to rip you apart.'

'Help me,' he whispered into my thought stream.

Then he started to scream more and more.

I took him down and left him also awakening. No healing for him. I wanted him to suffer and for others to see him suffering. I had just a few seconds left to myself. Never have I felt so close to failing. Only willpower awoke me in that man's garden on a pile of clothes. The sun was down. A few wisps of shadow were around me. Slowly fading away. I was safe. I got dressed and headed away.

Chapter 7

I telephoned Edith next day.

'Enjoy your dream?' I said to her.

With that she went quiet.

'One of you will never come back,' I said quietly: 'Believe me it was not a dream. You were there with me. You heard me tell you why, he will not be back.

'What did you do to the other,' she asked: 'All we can get out of him is something about ghosts coming for him.'

'All true,' I said: 'I gave him a glimpse, into his future.'

'Oh my god,' she gasped.

'Keep your hands off my friends,' I continued: 'No more drugs. I'll be watching you all. Who is your immediate superior?'

I could feel the fear in her as she gave me the name straight away. Yes, I'd read papers and his name and stories about his exciting medical discoveries. A brain expert. It took me a further two days to track him down. I must have followed over a dozen cars that arrived and then left the residence in Harley Street. One of them ended up in Downing Street and that was the one.

I also arrived at one other point. A guilt feeling came to me for the other doctor. I took him back up that morning and healed his mind. I warned him that this would be his only chance. It took some doing. I wanted the real boss. Mr Brian Smyth the consultant. He disappeared the following morning. It was another lesson for me that consultants were Mister, not doctor.

Rachel, Michael and Geoffrey had also been up in the sky over the last few days. Some thing had scared the people down there. That something was me. They'd watched me working and had seen it all. I told them what I was doing it. I rang Edith.

'Yes,' she answered.

I let her say another five words.

'Thank you for my friend.'

I cut her short at that point.

'Your boss said good-bye this morning. Safe guard my friends, or you will be next. Bye.'

The phone was down and I was off.

The next morning it was only Rachel that came up to see me.

'You have them scared out of their minds,' was her first few words: 'They told us last night that the boys would be awoken before dawn and that I was to come up to see you alone.'

'First off,' I said: 'You will give them my conditions.' 'If they are not met straight away, then I start tomorrow at the top and will work downwards. You will tell them that I will not accept any conditions whatsoever. If the top people try to hide. It will be the next in line. If you come up tomorrow to ask for time to consider, then that means they have not accepted.

'OK,' she projected: I have all that.

'Freedom to be given immediately, that's for all three of you and not just one,' I continued to project more into her mind: 'You are to be allowed to grow up as normal as possible. All of you back to your parents. Nothing less. No more drugs.'

She was not to know my future plans and I could not tell her them because of the drugs she's been force to take. I could have taken Rachel away from them at that moment but wanted freedom for the two boys. Down she went very fast. I'm sure that there would have been tears in her eyes if it had been possible. I didn't tell her that I would be following her down to listen. Checking first that I could get back out.

It was a good job that I did go down to listen. A minister, mentioned the word, destroy. Well he was going to be next. He had not got the message. What a fool. I followed him around London all morning. He went for a drink to his club. Even settled down for a nap. He was mine there and then. Told you I'd been busy. I'd spied on the rich and famous. I'd even listened to the Prime Minister one day in this very cosy snug. The minister was alone and not to be disturbed. I'd listened to him say it to the waiter. What a shock. He could do nothing about it.

The window was open and I was clear to take him up. Just took a little touch and he was mine to take up.

'Do you want to be destroyed,' I said.

All he could do was scream. That was it. Totally insane in a moment. I took him back down. Watched him screaming and foaming at the mouth. Totally naked as the day he was born. Bang went the doors as everyone in the place came running in. He was totally fucked.

I then left. Back up I went. Out of the city. Down to my clothes and on to the bike and away to another phone.

'Edith,' I said, 'the word, destroy, should never have come into the equation.

‘What?’ she said loudly.

‘You will hear shortly about the minister and he mentioned that word at a meeting,’ I said.

‘I had a feeling somehow, that you were listening to us,’ she said.

Down went the phone.

The morning papers said it all. No mention of the real reason. Just the fact that a prominent minister had a stroke. No mention at all about him being found naked. No mention that he’d gone totally insane.

Rachel

Much of what I can remember up to the age of 10 was a real nightmare to me. I could do some thing totally abnormal to what other kids could do. I could leave my body and soar up into the sky. The trouble was that I always ended up naked when I came back down. My mother and father were always beating me. Right back to my earliest memory. Doctors came to see me all the time. Never once did I let them see me do it. They even put cameras in my bedroom. I just knew that they wanted to see me do it. In my mind, I knew that I would lose my mother and father if I showed them how I did it. I hated the needle part of it. Always they wanted a blood sample. They even put wires on my head. This was to monitor my brain waves. I’d been taken away at one point. When they got fed up. I got sent home. They would not believe my parents. Maybe it was because I never did it for other people, that they beat me.

All the other kids called me crazy. I know that I was well behind in my learning. I also knew that it did not take long to catch up with any of my school work. All my teachers found this very unusual. I was very bright and that was it. Even though I was younger than many of the other children. I could run and jump far better. It was the name calling and teasing that hurt me most of all. Nothing else, but that. I wanted to have friends but none of them would become one for me. Possibly they would be tarred with the same brush and be called crazy, just as they called me that.

Many thought that I was way behind the others of my age. It was the exact opposite. For a long time now I have seen this other light in the sky. It was there for as long as I could remember. Sometimes they're brightly and sometimes not. It was the closest to me. Always I wanted to move towards it. It used to disappear very quickly. That light meant to me that out there, was another like me. It seemed to have freedom to move about.

My main area was within what I could see and recognise. I never did lose sight of where my house was when I was really young. At around eight years of age, the other light it started to be seen from a slightly different direction. You see, we had a tall chimney down the road. Before, it was always on the right hand side. Then it changed to mostly on the left side. I was over ten when I got the closest to it. Then I nearly lost my way back. That really frightened me. I have seen little road maps that my dad had for his old car. I used to try to memorise it and to try to see if I could follow the roads when I went up in the early morning. That is when I felt safe to do it. The closest that I got to it, was at a river called the Trent. It's a good job that I could see the river the day I tried to move close to the light. I only just found my way back. From my child hood knowledge I estimated a place called Scunthorpe. And then a city. Hull.

It was a shock to see it in my area one morning and then to see the much older boy. It was a bigger shock to see him at my front gate. He just sodded off the kids that were calling me names. I even remembered asking him where his hat was. He was the boy in the woods getting dressed. I remember also crying when I got back home. Something new had happened. Some one who was the same as me, was close He'd come to find me, of that I was sure. Who was he? Why had he come?

I met him on a Monday at the park. He was really funny with me. I was a little scared at first but slowly I could feel myself relaxing. No harm was going to come to me from him I was sure of this. What he did to my parents was so unbelievable. Things really changed for me from that point. I was really happy for the first time. Dad took a real interest for the first time. It lasted for just over two years. That was until they knocked on the door one night. A legal paper was given to dad, it said that I was to be taken into care.

They'd kept records from before, photographs showing me with bruises. Mum and Dad had not smacked me for two years. It was all from before. All of it, just to take me away. Yes. The two people from up the street were there. Sure enough, spying on us all the time. Why now, why the questions? I did not know where they took me. It was along way. That I did know. They made me sleep at night and injected me with drugs during the day. Always it was just before day light. One of the helpers made me feel dirty all the time. It was how he touched me, whenever we were alone.

I knew if I said anything, no one would believe it. I hated that man right from the beginning. I only had to take it for a few days. The boy appeared down here in London. How he knew of how to find me I don't know but find me he did. The woman Edith, she was nice. Always she tried to protect us from the others. She'd warned them that there was one out there that could take them all. I watched her answer the phone one day and I could tell something important had happened back home. I had heard the word Dunscroft. Injections stopped immediately for me. For the boys, I didn't know. They started to treat me very different and then they sent me up to speak to him. They sent me up with allsorts of questions to ask him. He refused to speak about anything they wanted. He just out and out told me what to tell them. They had the day to prepare for him. He was definitely coming for them all. He would not back down. When I told them where he was going to start. That was when they began to panic.

Over the next few days, I watched how he did it. How he got them all scared. How he put the fear of god into them. They sealed up everything to keep him out. All the windows and doors were sealed up tight. The fire fronts were bricked up.

'He'd get to you still,' I thought to myself.

I could hear them talking about him. I heard that one man up North had disappeared and a woman was insane and could not speak a single word. I caught again the name of my village. Dunscroft. Yes, he'd got the spy's. Edith and the old doctor disappeared with the dirty man for a day. That's what I thought of that one. She came in the next day without the other two, withdrawn and very quiet. Then someone important was found naked in a club. Yes, I could hear every thing. When possible I would go up and observe for the rest. It seemed to go on for hours.

It was Edith the woman doctor who gave us the news. We were all going home. We had to promise to be good. We were requested to keep secret, what we could do. I was going to be all right, but both the boys had been away from their parent's for a long time. Help would be given them. I asked for Edith to take me. I wanted to talk to her for some reason. My friend, he had not harmed her. Why had he also taken up the other doctor twice. She took me home by train. I asked her how long they had been looking for me. How had they found me. Who was the first bogey man mentioned by my friend. Word of mouth from doctors had first put them on my trail. It had been hard to convince anyone at first, about me. I was in line with another one she said. We used to send someone up for years, but he could never seem to catch him. A women used to go with him at times. He died in a shooting accident and the women fell into a hole with stakes at the bottom.

'Him?' I asked.

Yes, I think it was your friend whilst he was growing up.'

'How did it all start?' I then asked Edith.

An old man had started it all off. A few years previous, he'd been a Naval Officer. They had sent teams out towards the lights when ever this old man saw them in the distance. He proved to them that he was doing it by disappearing before their eyes. There was one time though that he'd come back terrified. One of the lights had shown so much power that he refused to go near it. That light had told him to go away and the old man had to do it. He started to warn us all about this one. We felt that if we could combined others together, then we could control the strong one. It's the opposite though because this one can give or take at will. That is my opinion. The old man, he went out late one day and never came back.

Late, I thought to myself. My friend had warned me never to go out late, up into the sky. They'd only managed to get the two boys before the old man had disappeared. We know of the general area of another weak seven of you. We talked more of other things. Then she was quiet for a while.

'Rachel?' she asked me: 'If and I mean if. Will you take me up with you in the future, if it is possible?'

I looked at her for a few seconds.

'Maybe,' I said: 'Maybe, if I get permission.'

I had to think on this one. There was a motive for wanting to go up again. What had my friend done to her, that she wanted to do it again. Had he changed her in some small way. Edith, even though I am only a young girl. I understand only one thing. My friend, the boy. He wish's for only one thing and that's for you all, to leave us alone. It will be for him to decide for now. When I'm older, then I can decide on my own what's best for me. I know one thing out of all this. He will only attack those that want to hurt us. He will not threaten you the next time. He will just carry out what he has told you. You will have no warning at all and it will just happen.'

We were met by my dad, at the railway station. Edith gave him her telephone number. Told him to call at any time. Dad gave me a hug and a kiss once we were in the car. Things will be changing I thought. I am not yet free of danger. It was too easy. Some one had given in easy. Yes too easy. Yes, I am getting to be like him. A Day Mover, but I have a name. They know where I am. Planning my friend used to say. Keep planning and never give in to anyone. I'm nearly a teenager. Soon I thought. I wanted to grow up fast at that point. Where was he, will he come to me. I had what I thought was a wet dream that night. It wasn't though. It was the other thing. Yes, I am growing up. Far faster than I should be, for my age. If I'd known at that time about the next few years I would have cried. My friend just disappeared.

BM

I'd got a visitor's passport from the Post Office, one week whilst I'd been home.

France. What a place. They drive on the wrong side. I was on the run. No way could I trust anyone to really leave my friends alone now. Not for long anyway. I had to be out of the country, just in case they came back for us quickly and without any warning. Maybe they would have my name, the next time.

Chapter 8

BM

Here I am in France for the first time in my life. First time for me in any foreign country for that matter. Well here's me, heading south towards Paris. Bike not too good. I'm having to stop and clean the plugs every few miles. It's evening and I need to rest. I have decided to hide the bike permanently and I've been crossing a few rivers when an idea hits me. Under water will do it. That's what I did on the outskirts of the French capital. I then hitched to get south. How far, I don't know. One thing that I do know is that no one's going to know me here.

I spent the night on some hot air vents from the metro. At least I was warm. For some reason, I wasn't bothered by anyone throughout the night. Maybe it was because early on in the evening I'd laid a guy out. He'd been waving his hands about and sticking his face in mine. Hadn't a clue what he was going on about. He'd left just afterwards and that was it. Just walking around all the next day. Spied a few things, seen some legionnaires. They were on guard at the entrance to a fort of some sort. Just a big old brick monstrosity to me. I'm heading south towards the sun. What ever happens, will happen.

It took me four days to get to Marseilles in the south of France. It was nothing but a hot place and full of foreigners. Every nationality under the sun. I had enough money. But I'm going to need more soon. Anyway it's in and out all the cafés I can find.

Listening to every one and to everything. Most of which I couldn't understand. Then I hit upon a couple of English girls, both looked no more than eighteen. Good looking and with what I thought were London accents. They were just sat there having a coke when I walked over to them.

'Hey, I'm new down here; can you give me some idea of digs and what not to do?' I asked them.

I'm not what you call clean at this point and they were giving me a right looking over. I'd not had a shave or a wash for a couple of days so I must have looked a sight. One of them told me outright to sod off.

'Look would it make a difference if I went away and got cleaned up?' I said.

'No, not at all, sod off,' said the girl and she wasn't even really looking at me.

Here's me, just wanting some advice and she acts like this. It wasn't as if I was going to try it on with her. At that I lost it completely. This one was going on a little journey. She wouldn't like it at all. Not one little bit, because she would now give me the information willingly, from tomorrow. In fact she would do everything I wanted. Everything. I walked away, then turned back and said to her.

'Same place tomorrow afternoon, you'll be here. Your friend can stay away.'

'Fuck off,' she said.

It took me all day to find where she was staying. Into different shops, both looking at clothes and jewellery throughout the morning. Then they stopped for lunch. That gave me the opportunity to book into this little hotel. Up and showered double time. Clean clothes on and I still made it back in good time. They were eyeing men up as they passed. I could imagine the remarks they were making about every guy passing. Both laughing. Then more damn shopping. It was hot stood out there. They then headed down to the yachting marina.

Now this is a sight to see. Massive private boats motor and sail. Money land is what I could see. I will have a piece of that and more, but first a lesson. I watched carefully which boat they went on. I even made sure that they both stayed, waiting to well after midnight. Back to the hotel.

First light, awake and relaxed. I change, to hovering above the bed, then out through the widow up a little to check the surroundings. Nothing's there and I'm clear to move down to the marina. Along the quayside checking for the right boat. A couple of port holes are open on the starboard side and I move down towards the first one. Looking in I see a man and woman. I moved on. A quick look in and there she was. Her friend was in a bunk across from her. In and hovering just above the girl who though she was too good to help a stranger. Nice figure, nice to look at until she was awake. Here goes. I touch her and bring her out. Her body just disappearing in an instance.

At that precise moment, I let her go and shot out of there. She is now stuck in limbo. It came within about ten seconds, a scream so loudly projected that the dead would have woken. Trouble is, I'm the only one who can hear it. She's lost to everyone. I'm just hovering above the deck listening to her screaming. I decide to have a look around. She is not going anywhere.

Time is going to pass quickly this morning for me. I keep looking in and out other boats, checking out the best of them. Cash will be coming my way soon. You've got to see what's on these boats to believe it. Gold chains, jewellery laid strewn about and the money. It's unbelievable. People are now up and about. On the boat where the girl is, I spotted three people and a small mellow looking sphere. It was slowly rising up and being blown gently with the light wind. The man and woman I'd seen were talking to the quiet girl from yesterday. The small sphere was trying to gain their attention. Not a chance. At that I went slowly over, she could see me coming.

'What's wrong with me,' she was screaming: 'Why can't they see me.'

She was definitely having a right fit this one. There is no way for her to see me as the boy she'd insulted. I only have to think my words and she will receive them. I just touched her sphere with my own bright light and transfer enough thoughts to calm her down in order to read her mind Basically, a good kid. Been with a couple of men. Spoilt rotten by her father and mother. At that I had enough to go on and let go of her.

'Can you remember yesterday?' I projected: 'What did you do all day?'

This I'd put into her mind for her to answer. She commenced to outline her day. I wasn't even in it. She'd no recollection of even speaking to me. Well I was going to change her thinking. I touched her to pull her gently back to the boat.

'Do you see down there?' I said across to her and continued: 'There are three people down there looking for you. You are lost to them forever. You're a ghost. You have died.'

I was really sticking the boot in on this one. Just at that moment I could see some French policemen coming down the quay and I continued again in her mind.

'Do you see the police? Because they are here to view your body. They'll have it in the morgue pretty soon. Trouble was, I was lying to her. There was no body for the police to see and she wasn't aware of this. She wasn't very happy either I can tell you, not happy at all. Did she start to wail. I just touched her again to stop the racket she was making and pulled her towards the café where I'd first seen her.

'Remember someone asking you for assistance yesterday. That was a really good friend of mine.' I stressed: 'Can you think back to what he asked for.'

At that she started to communicate through her mind to me

'How was I to know, he just looked scruffy.'

'That's not the point is it,' I said: 'He offered to go clean himself up.'

I then pulled her back to the boat, hovering just above and watching. She was hovering at my side. We waited for the police to go. I could see that I was giving grief to the others left on board.

'Listen,' I said to her: 'What would you do if it were possible to return you onboard. Alive and in your body.

'I'd do anything,'

'If you tell anyone what's happened no one will believe you. I then paused for a moment: 'There's a boy waiting for you at a certain café and he'll be there at one minute past twelve.'

'I'll be there, I promise,' she transmitted to me.

'Now listen carefully,' I said: 'When you get back, you'll be in your bed. Tell them you've been out since early morning and swam back. You'll have to be quick and as soon as you arrive, do all of the following. Swimsuit on quickly, and then go out through the forward hatch. Get into the water so that you can then swim to the stern to get out.'

I'd read her mind, on that one, she could swim. I pulled her in and allowed her to appear back as normal. Naked of course and then I couldn't resist it watching while she put the swimsuit on.

I got back to my room easy enough. It occurred to me that all I had was in that room. Had to remember to buy some plastic bags and rubber bands. Tomorrow was going to be a bank day or should I say, a collection day.

She was there before me, subdued and quiet. I was looking at my watch whilst crossing the road to join her at the same little café. I sat down opposite and smiled.

'See how I clean up,' I said: 'Where would you like to go or would you prefer to stay here.'

Glancing at the table I realised that I'd forgotten my own manners and asked if she'd like a drink.

A quiet 'yes,' was her answer.

'Coke, or would you prefer a strong coffee.'

She then asked if what had happened to her was a dream or real.

'Read it how you like,' I said: 'What's your name by the way?'

'Susan,' she replied.

She never asked mine for some reason, maybe fear or something.

'How is it possible and how can it be real?' she asked.

'Let me ask you something,' I said. 'What if it were to happen in the next hour to you. You couldn't even run away from it. The minute you stop to rest for sleep. That would be the time you're taken. It would be a one way, trip and no return ticket issued.'

She thought for a moment.

'You mean it was not a dream, that I was taken and I could do nothing to stop it?' she said.

'OK, you got that one in a nut shell,' I said: 'Now what if you could be returned, or that you were able to return to your body at will. What would you say to that?'

'You're twisting it now,' she said.

'Yes, I'm twisting it all right,' I said.

'But what is it?' she asked.

My reply was meant to shock her to the core so I told her.

'It's very simple really. It's a ghost of the daytime and he's got you in his sights.'

She cowered back in her chair.

'Come on, lets go for a walk,' I said and stood up.

Although I could feel the fear in her mind. I'd done enough to ensure her silence. She was now an entirely different person. Gone was the fuck you attitude and in place I had someone who I could do something with. Maybe I've been a bastard, but she started it.

We carried on towards the beach and headed for a secluded area. Up onto some rocks and hidden from view. I sat on a rock and she was facing me on another one.

'What would be your feelings, if it were possible to do it when you wanted to?' I asked: 'Look. Forget about the ghost, waiting for you. What if it was possible to just disappear at will.'

I was wanting someone to fly with, some one to trust. She also showed me that she could be a bitch but maybe it's how she'd been taught. Money does that to some people. If she's willing, then I can change her forever. Then I can move onto another person, be like a shining knight or something. There is a need to have more like me. No way would she ever dare mention what she could do. Same as in England, they are unforgiving to my kind. Anyway, on with finding out whether or not she'd do it.

'If you were able to move from place to place at will,' I said:

'What would you do to achieve it? What would you give to be able to change your body? I don't mean deformity, but to be really healthy and fit.'

She was as I knew taking it all in. Fear is in the unknown and that was in her mind.

'How is it possible?' she asked: 'Will I be safe? Can I come back at anytime?'

It's one thing to talk about something, but having already had a taste of it and returned. Well it's a different matter. It's like if you can do it once, then you can do it again.

'By the way,' I said casually: 'Who's your friend?'

'It's my younger sister,' she told me.

'Right, how old is she?' I asked.

'Seventeen,' she said and then there was a little smile on her lips: 'I'm over eighteen.'

'Are you ready to go back now?' I asked and she jumped up.

We rambled back towards the cafe on the front. I was kicking sand about, dodging in and out of the water. Anything to relax her I thought. The closer we got going back the more she seemed to be perking up. Just before we hit the steps up from the beach she stopped and sat down. Her head went down into her hands and she began to sob quietly. I sat on the steps waiting for the tension to leave her and for her to gain control of her emotions. After a while she began to wipe her eyes and a few words started to come from her.

'I was so frightened, so frightened of you,' she said: 'I had to follow you and I was so scared of you. Scared of what your friend would do to me. It was so awful. I nearly ran away just before you came to meet me.'

'Don't worry,' I reassured her: 'You'll be all right. No harms coming to you. I'll see you around.'

I got up and left her on the beach. My answer would come from her if she needed it. I'd done my part. I walked happily back to my hotel for a shower. I had some tea and then changed for the evening. Put my washing out for cleaning. It was time to be out. There were six little cafes along that row. In between was a dance place. It was neat the way it was all set up.

It was around nine when I spotted Susan again. She was walking along talking with her sister and another woman. I was at our café. She was searching for me. I knew it. Along they came towards me and sure enough she saw me. Said something to the other woman, her mother, I guessed; they looked alike. Then she came in with her sister. She headed straight towards me.

'Can I sit with you for a while?' she asked and sat down next to me.

Her sister was clearly surprised.

'This is my sister Sam. Can we have something to drink?' she then asked me.

Her fear had gone completely. Maybe Sam was surprised at the way her sister was now talking to me, but she never let on and we all started to have a really nice time of it. The boats were on the sea outside and the music was mellow. No mention of her experience whatsoever came into the conversation. It was when Susan went to the toilet that I talked to Sam.

'Do you know something,' she said: 'It's the first ever time that my sister has not tried to pull a man down. She's normally so uppity with them. What have you got, because yesterday, you were nothing to her.'

'Maybe it's my persuasive personality,' I said.

'You know she disappeared yesterday morning,' Sam said.

'Really,' I replied.

'Did you by chance have anything to do with it?' she asked.

This just came rattling out from her. I just smiled and left it at that. I could see Susan on her way back.

'What have you two been on about?' she inquired as she sat down.

'You of course,' I said and she gave me that same little half smile.

I could see her parents coming back down the road.

'Your chaperons are coming,' I said.

Sam got up to go but Susan just sat there.

'Sam, tell them I'll be there in ten minutes,' Susan said to her sister.

She then settled back looking serious.

'I want to try it again,' she said.

She had just asked to be a Day Mover. She had been reeled in, hook, line and sinker. Bitten by the bug.

'Yes but not from the boat,' I said: 'Once from there is enough. See you on the beach around nine and bring you swimming gear.'

Up she got and down the road she went into the dark.

I took my swimming gear with me early next morning and planted them safely in the rocks out of view. Left my watch wrapped in the towel. Got back to the steps just before nine. Sat down to wait. You never know if women will be on time. It was well past nine by my reckoning when up she came. It was a real good smile on her face but I could see she was tired. I soon found out why, she and her sister had been talking half the night about me. We got to the rocks and settled down.

'Listen to me, you have to listen and follow all what I tell you to the letter,' I said: 'If you do not want to do it then it's OK? You have the choice. There is no way that you are going anywhere unless you understand what it is and how it will change you.'

She was listening to me. She had no fear I could tell. I then commenced to tell her what happened, how she would come back naked. The methods of how to move from one place to another. Think yourself moving and you will move. Think small and you will go smaller. Avoid objects at all times. Always have two ways back. Always remember the dark and what it hides.

'Where is he at this moment?' she suddenly asked me.

That put me off my stride for a few seconds.

'OK, you have asked me where he is,' I said: 'Before I tell you where he is, you have a choice to make. You can get up and leave now. You can go back to what you were, or you can be like me.'

She was looking at me while I was talking to her and I could see understanding come to her.

'There is no friend is there, it's you isn't it?' she whispered.

I looked up and then lay back for a moment.

'Yes, it's me. I'm a Day Mover,' I said:

She to look at me. I smiled back. Then we both burst out laughing.

'Tell me that this isn't a dream,' she said.

'Do you really want to go?' I asked.

'When we can,' she replied.

'Go to sleep then; I know you're tired from last night. Once you sleep it will happen.'

It took her a long time but she slowly dropped off to sleep.

At that instant, I looked about us to check it was clear. I relaxed myself, transformed and then touched her to take her aloft into the clear sky. Her thoughts were mingled to begin with and then they came clearer and clearer.

'It's wonderful and so beautiful,' she beamed her thoughts to me: Please take me back now to prove to me that what you said is true.

'Just a few more minutes and you'll be able to do it on your own,' I projected across to her.

The power was entering her. Not to heal, for I'd learnt already how much to give.

'Ok, your ready now. Think of yourself moving downwards.'

She began to descend.

'Think of a direction to go towards,' I projected to her.

Sure enough she went in that direction.

'Now think small.'

She got smaller.

'When small, you're able to move fast. Remember this. Time for you is always best in the morning. Never in the afternoons. Darkness will kill you. I'm going to let you follow me in.'

At that I shot down and transformed to human form. Grabbed my trunks and put them on quickly. She arrived a second later and went bright red as she scrabbled into her costume.

'You bastard,' she said laughing at me.

I'd warned her about it, but got a good look. Nice. We then got talking again, her on about what she could do now. How she had to keep the secret.

'I've a problem already,' she said: 'My sister.'

I said joking to her.

'She can be changed can't she?'

Got a look from her, for that one

'How old are you and why have you not mentioned your name?' Susan suddenly said.

'My name is not important and never will be. My age, well I'm nearly eighteen years old.'

Then she said: 'How did you get so broad, because most boys of your age are skinny?'

'Put it this way,' was my reply. 'If you really saw me move it would be in fighting. I've had many enemies, including the people at home. Why do you think I'm down here? I've had to fight all my life to survive, because of what I can do. You still have a choice, even now. I can take the power back. You have only to ask. Me, I cannot lose it at all, but will have to live with it always.'

'Can I now do it just as you say, this very minute?' she asked.

'Try it for just half an hour.'

'If your not back I'll come for you,' I said to her.

With that she settled back down next to me. Even got closer, to feel me next to her. It didn't take her long and I felt her leave. I put my watch on to check the time. Half an hour and I'd be there for her if required. It's time that's the problem up there. So easy to forget the time. I read it by the sun. That's something she has got to learn. She was back in ten minutes. Not even a blush from her as she put her costume on. I then got a big smacker on the lips, totally unexpected.

'I watched you put your watch on and check the time for me.'

'Learn to tell the time by the position of the sun,' I told her.

I got up, grabbed my towel and said: 'Coke time and you're paying.'

We then scrambled down from the rocks and set out walking along the sea shore, towards our café. She'd put her arm in mine. Coming towards us was sister Sam, wanting a little piece of the action or was it knowledge she was after? She could see her sister had changed. She had suddenly grown up. Her sister somehow looked healthy, gone were the pimples from her face. I imagine for the first time Sam saw how her sister would appear to men and felt a little jealous. We carried on to the café. We were becoming regulars. Twice in a café and they know you. Our drinks were there as we sat down. It was Sam who went to the toilet this time and it gave me a chance to talk to Susan quickly.

'Listen, if ever you need help,' I said: 'Put it in the *Daily Mirror*, on a Friday and if I see it I will come running.'

'Vise-versa for you', she said.

'Put it as such,' I then said: 'Mover Needed One other thing, your children will have the power. Look after them safely. Tell me if you want to convert your sister.'

'Let me think on that,' she said.

'Even if you tell her, no one will believe her.'

That was the last of our small talk as Sam got back and I could tell by the way she looked at me. She knew we had been talking about her.

'Fancy going out dancing tonight?' I asked both of them.

'Only if you can Rock & Roll,' Sam said.

At that I burst out laughing. The only dance, I can really do is Rock & Roll.

That a great time I had that night. Two of them, both could dance and do it well. We certainly showed a few people. I can tell you. Non stop we were at it. One dance after the other. Brilliant it was and I enjoyed every moment. All I had was a couple of beers all night. Hard as it was to say it, Sam was the better dancer. At this point that I knew she would be converted soon. She enjoyed my company as much as her sister. We were laughing and joking all the way back to the boat. I said my goodnight to them both and off I went into the night.

Up at the crack of dawn and hovering over the boat. I waited for the demonstration I knew she would give to her sister. I caught it through the porthole and then her entrance back into her body after a few moments. Had it been a demonstration for Sam or a test, of her own power? I'd arranged to meet Susan at ten o'clock, just as the café opened. It was great to see them both coming together. They were like one, neither had secrets from the other. Susan was all laughter and smiling, whilst Sam was feeling unsure about it all.

'Let's not rush,' I said: 'we've time to talk it through.'

It was a relief to Sam at this point I could see. I gave her a smile and said:

'Cheer up, you're in safe hands. I don't bite.'

'Tell you what Susan,' I said: 'To be fair to your sister, why not get off and practice. We'll mosey down soon. Why not come back and spy on us.'

She jumped up straight away and virtually ran to the beach. That left me and Sam alone together for the first time.

'Did she show you?' I asked. I got a quick nod from her.

'You don't have to do anything you know.'

She smiled back at that.

'Come on; let's have a beer for a change.'

'We lay awake talking about you last night,' she told me: 'I couldn't believe anything, not one word until she did it this morning in front of me. Who would ever think that it was possible?'

I let her talk about it for a few minutes. In the end she stopped as my smile got through to her. I just sat there looking into her eyes, her into mine. Sam smiled; her eyes were full of life.

I looked up and whispered quietly; 'Are you there Susan?'

'It's entirely up to you Sam and what you want. No strings are attached and definitely no threats. If your sister asked me to reverse it, I would do so immediately.'

At that I got the smile and a quick hug and a kiss. She just got up and did it there and then.

'I wanted to do that last night, to kiss you, even before she told me all about you,' she said.

Boy did I feel good at that. Then she went on.

'I told Susan last night in bed that I'd wanted the night to go on and on, so that I could stay dancing just to be near you,' she said:

'She's not jealous of me that way, she has what she's always wanted. She now has the power, to be able to stand on her own. You see our father has a big company. Neither of us were strong enough to keep it secure, if anything happened to father. Now it's all changed. Susan is going to ask for a seat on the board later today and he'd better not say no. She's now got the drive to do it and it's all due to you.'

'Listen to me Sam,' I said: 'I'd love to be in your company any time, but sooner or later people are going to come after me. They will be playing for keeps. Do you understand that and what it would mean if you were caught in between?'.

I got a nod from her in return. We carried on talking. We just wanted to be with each other for a time.

‘I’ve made my mind up though, I want the power as well,’ she said suddenly.

We had by this time forgotten about Susan and she interrupted us. She’d done it and returned.

‘How are the love birds then?’ were her first words.

We had lost track of time.

‘Susan, tell me what he whispered to you,’ said Sam.

‘He asked if I was there,’ said Susan looking into her sister’s eyes. Sam had the confirmation she’d wanted. Susan in turn had listened in to us both.

‘By the way,’ Susan said next: ‘We are being spied on. Possibly one of daddy’s people, you know what he’s like with us.’

They then went on to tell me a little of the last few years. Of how people had been warned to keep away from them.

‘By the way Susan,’ I said: ‘Where’s the spy now and what does he look like?

‘He’s sat a couple of tables away from us,’ she whispered across to me.

‘Do you want him to stop spying on us?’ I simply said to both of them.

‘How?’ both girls asked me.

‘I’ll show you,’ I said and got up.

I just walked straight over to the guy. Sat down and looked across the table at him.

‘Yes, can I help you,’ he said across the table at me.

‘You certainly can,’ I said: ‘Fucking well stop spying on us.’

I just got up and left him sat there. A couple of minutes later he got up and left. Maybe trouble was coming my way, at least I was now aware of the possibility and would be on my guard. Susan got up a few minutes later and told us she was ready for her father. It was time to have it out with him once and for all. All or nothing

'What are you two going to do?' she then remarked.

'Me,' I said: 'I'm going to take your sister to bed and make mad passionate love to her.'

'OK,' Susan said without blinking her eyes: 'She's on the pill, enjoy yourselves.'

Away she went for a war of words. Sam was looking at me strangely somehow and then said.

'You and who's army.'

'Come on let go for a walk,' I said and both of us got up to walk down the street.

As we walked along I told how we'd fox anyone following us.

'You see the shop in front,' I said: 'It has a back way out. As we come level, turn in and point to something in the window. We'll go in together and just carry on straight through to the back. Then we run like hell along the next street for 100 yards. Turn right at the end.'

We did exactly that, but turning right when we got to the end was my surprise. Straight up the steps into my hotel. I'd managed to get her where I'd wanted her in the first place. Into the lift we went and straight to my room.

'Didn't need that army,' I remarked to her.

She just turned towards me and was in my arms. It was straight to bed. I'm sure we both enjoyed it because I know I did and she wanted second helpings. Lying back later half asleep, she quietly asked me.

'When?'

I had to check the time first. It was OK, so I said to her to try and sleep and it would be then. We lay there cuddling up to each other.

Slowly, but surely her breathing got lighter and once I was positive that she'd dropped off. I transformed and took her up for the first time. I held on to at all times, transferring to her the power.

'You have now just twenty minutes to do a quick tour around,' I projected to her: 'Off you go but watch my light. If you see me high up, come back quickly.'

I went high after fifteen minutes. She came hurrying towards me shortly afterwards.

'How long was that?' she asked.

'Too long,' I replied.

At that I descended down to the bed and under the covers to wait for her. It was love time again. The second she reappeared, she was all over me. Then, we showered together. We were both going dancing again. Sam left me at the café to rush to the boat to get changed.

I'd totally forgotten the guy from earlier on but was rudely reminded when he sat down beside me with two other men.

'Now, we will have a little chat with you. You will leave before morning, or trouble will find you. Our employer wants you to leave his girls alone. Have you got that? he said just sticking his head forwards into my face.

I gave him his reply to his face.

‘Just run back to him and tell him, he’s too late,’ I said: ‘You three are not enough for me to break sweat on.’

He couldn’t believe what he was hearing. He stood up and backed away. The two friends were coming forwards though. For me to break a persons arm is to simply grab his or hers wrist tight and to then jerk it down hard. This was the first out of it immediately. The second hadn’t realised it yet, that he was now on his own. His fist hit me on the side of my chest. I grabbed his other fist in my hand, just as it was coming forwards. I curled my fingers around his fist and squeezed hard. The fingers broke and he screamed. Letting go, I managed to grab the mouth of the party by the hair as he turned to run. I dragged him back towards my table, pulled him down further to put my foot on his head.

‘Stay, don’t move unless you want a cracked head,’ I said.

Here was I just sitting back down foot on someone’s head and casually drinking a coke. The waiters and a few people around had seen the action. I was the one that had been attacked and they’d seen the result.

It was good to see Sam on her way back. Just seeing the guy under my foot said it all to her. The other two were stood a few yards back wondering how I’d done it to them so fast. Just as she got to me I released his head, got up and walked towards her.

‘Your daddy’s been busy,’ I said.

‘I know,’ she said: ‘We’re also leaving in the morning. Susan has really got him going. He can’t believe his ears. She has him totally surprised with what she’s now demanding. One good thing about it though, our mother’s now on our side.’

‘Just one second,’ I said.

I then turned to the three men.

'You have had a final warning. Any more and you will be screaming for your mothers, but they'll never hear you voices calling. The one I'd grabbed by the hair was actually getting a little colour to his face and I could see a malicious glint in is eyes. That one would try again, of that I was sure. I approached him and put my head close to his.

'Let me make it permanent for you, just give me the pleasure of doing it,' I whispered in his ear.

He went totally, grey in the face. The colour just left it. He could see his own death approaching from my eyes. I turned and left with Sam on my arm, heading for another place to dance the night away. Our last night together and did we make the most of it, in more ways than one. Sam left me around eight thirty the next morning. She would be soon heading back to England.

We'd gone hovering and twirling through the sky for over an hour before she left. Susan had joined us and gave us both the latest update. She'd got her way, on the condition that she studied first to be an Accountant. It was a start for her and that's what she wanted. Sam never let on to either of us what she wanted to do. We had time just for a quickie, before she left me though.

Me, well I had some people to face down on the ground. They had mis-read my message for some reason. I didn't let on to either of the two girls that I was now being watched. Let them come for me. I would be ready to accommodate them all to the sky so bright and blue.

Chapter 9

BM

I went shopping for some plastic bags and elastic bands. It was just a quick trip across the street to a shop. Then straight back to the hotel. Banking time had to start at some time or other. I then had to get other info. Onto the bed and transform to hover. Out through my window and down level to approach my watchers.

Remember this well, Siesta Time was normal in this country. Not wrong either. They were on shifts all right. At around 11.30, the first one signalled his intention to the others. A hand up with one finger told me, one hour and at that he started to walk away with me close behind. He walked into a bar and straight into a private booth. He had a sandwich and a beer. Then he put his feet on the bench and relaxed for his forty winks. It was his last, for I only warn once. He'd just not believed it when I'd told him what I'd do.

I took him, just as his mind went blank in sleep. He could do nothing at all to stop me. His clothes were there for others to find. Up and up I pulled him. He screamed all right, he screamed and I left him for the night.

Back down quickly, dressed and headed for the steps of the hotel. I now needed to be seen. To be seen in full view of the remaining watchers. I headed down to the quayside and joined the crowd. I had the intention of heading to a quiet area. Only two left to deal with. I went over some rocks onto a second beach and knowing I was out of sight, I cut round and then back behind them.

They were just starting to climb over the rocks when one of them happened to see me. A quick word passed from him to his friend and they turned and headed back to me. They were both older, probably mid-twenties. I was too young looking to them to be a danger. It's always the one mistake that people make.

'My advice to you both is to quit now and head off somewhere else,' I told them.

A knife was now in the hand of the guy on my left. I went for him and under the knife I went with both feet hitting his knee solid and hard. The knife just got through. I'd a cut to my left leg, high up. He went down though with a smashed knee. Scrambling up, I met the other coming in hard and swinging. I took maybe three or four blows from him before my hands met around his body and then I started to squeeze. My head was buried into his shoulder where he couldn't get to it. With muscles straining, I just carried on applying pressure until I felt the first of his ribs go. Dropped him away to the ground and then I hammered my foot fully into his face. Turned to the first one again and did the same to him. Both out cold. Pulled them both close together.

Down beside them to relax and away I took them into the sky. The other one was up there still screaming and there were two more to make it a chorus. I shut all three out from my mind whilst my leg wound healed and then I descended to my room. Night was coming. I expect that a few apparitions will be seen tonight. Me, well I am swimming during the night. Slowly but surely, around the boats in the harbour, leaving plastic bags and elastic bands tied up within reach from aboard. Little bits of skin, placed on the deck, or through an open port hole, all ready for an early start in the morning.

It was just after day break when I reached the first one. I slowly appeared within the boat. Reached out side for my bags and rubber bands. Commenced to place rings, jewellery and cash within. Sealed it tight and dropped it overboard. There was enough air in it to float slowly away. On to the next one, exactly the same method, just like a ghost. Two was enough and I flew quickly back to the hotel.

Dressed in swim gear, I was back quickly. I could see both bags now around fifty yards away. Blowing towards the harbour entrance, slowly but surely. I dived in and soon had both together. Squeezed the air out of them and then dived down to the bottom. That harbour sea bottom is full of all sorts of rubbish. I spotted what I required. An old tyre. Inside I placed both bags. With the air out of them. they now had weight for them to remain. There were always people about and there was no way I was I bringing the jewellery ashore until I was ready. I swam back, towelled off and walked to my hotel. A good morning's work. Estimate for the cash alone was over two thousand pounds. All done and dusted in less than an hour.

I showered and then dressed in shorts and a shirt. I wanted to be at my regular café by nine, for the appearance in sake. I also wanted to see a French girl I had my eye on. Every place I'd been with Susan and Sam, this girl had turned up. She used to watch us dancing. Seeing her looking not just once at us, but fairly often. Once, I'd heard her talking to another girl whilst I'd been at the bar. I did feel sorry for her because for some reason she limped awkwardly. She was really nice to look at, until she moved.

Just sitting there and watching down towards the harbour is a great view. You can see everyone coming and everyone that leaves. I miss nothing at all that morning. Not a damn thing. The police appeared on a couple of boats and after half an hour left. It was a beautiful day. I'd still plenty of ready cash. More in my bank down below. What more could you wish for? I took a little stroll around ten. I was stiff, and knew I'd better start back into training.

I headed down to the beach and stripped off to my trunks and started to limber up. Into a series of knee bends and then on my back, for stomach training. Press ups, to finish that section and then into balance. On one leg I commenced to position the other first forwards high, and then slowly down towards the rear. Twisting slowly around to face the opposite direction. Changed legs, after ten tries and did the same again. I then walked slowly forwards to some hard sand. Stood still for a second and did a full back flip, feet off to feet down, then a series of hand stands and full somersaults to finish. This I would have to do regularly again, because I'd just felt that little stiffness this morning. I needed, above all things, to maintain a high level of muscle and strength at all times. I didn't care at the time for the audience watching me do it. To them I looked fit already. But I knew that I'd lost a little edge. After that I hit the water for ten minutes. Heading back in, I still had an audience, but it was only one.

The girl was standing there, with her hands placed on the rail beside the path. Staring down at me. I was certain she was yearning to be able to dance. To be able to spin and turn gracefully. She saw me turn to stare hard at her and she flinched away. If she could have ran, she would have done so at that moment. Not giving her a second chance to think of running. I walked up towards her and stood my ground just looking up into blue eyes.

'Parley Anglais?' I asked.

'Yes, a little,' she replied. She spoke it better than I did English. It sounded really posh.

Being in a good frame of mind. I became a bit of a devil in what I said next. I didn't know how she'd take it either.

'How about a meal for two and afterwards, I'll grant you your dearest wish.'

At that I then jumped onto the path beside her. I grabbed her gently and gave her a kiss on the nose. She was astonished; I'd seen that first little expression of pain come into her face at my first words but I'd not given her a chance to let it come out. The kiss had put her mind askew, it was so unexpected. I stood waiting for her to make her mind up. Just looking and not a smile or frown on my face. Not a damn word from her.

'At least do you want some thing to drink at the café?' I said.

She nodded.

'Are you French?' I asked.

'No, Swiss,' she replied

'What are you doing here then?' I asked her as we sat at the table.

'I'm here because my leg cannot take the cold weather and I have to visit two to three time a year, just to feel the warmth,' was her reply.

I ordered a beer for me and she had a coke. She then asked me about the two girls. I told her that they'd gone back to England.

‘I enjoyed your dancing with them both,’ she said: ‘Where did you learn it?

I told her, I’d grown up with it back home. I could hear in her voice that she wanted to be able to dance herself.

‘Got a boyfriend at home?’ I asked her.

She shook her head.

‘You are playing with me aren’t you? She added and I could see a hard look in her face.

‘No I promise you,’ I said.

I asked her name and she told me it was Helga.

‘Let’s have a walk, I need to get changed,’ I said.

We took it slow and easy walking and I steered us both in the direction I wanted to go. I headed for a shower on my own. I dried myself and asked for her to pass some clothes to me. She passed them through the partially open door. I dressed and then went back into the room. She was laid on the bed watching the TV.

‘What’s on?’ I asked her.

‘Some men have disappeared,’ she said: ‘and there’s some people supposed to have seen ghosts all over town last night. Two sets of clothes were also found on the beach yesterday and a set in a café. There a big investigation going on.

‘Amazing,’ I said without irony.

‘A robbery occurred on two boats down at the harbour. The owners say that everything was locked up and there’s no sign of any forced entry. It’s going to be in the papers from tomorrow they say.’

‘What a funny old world,’ I said and lay down at her side. She tensed up at first, but slowly relaxed. Every so often we both moved a little and in the end we had our body’s facing towards each other, even though we were both still watching the box. I honestly don't know when we started to look at each other. I pushed the hair out of her eyes. Got a smile back in return. Then she reached over and flicked some fluff off my shoulder. I leaned closer and kissed her once and laid back again. Her hand was on my arm a few minutes later and I gazed at her. She was looking back into my face. Both of us moved close together, hungrily. My hands explored her body. She stopped me only for a moment, then relaxed to let me explore her body slowly. She and I slowly stripped off her clothes. Both of us kissing each other's body and lips. I'm on top in a moment and then I entered her gently. She gave a little start and as I sank into her she gripped me harder. Slowly we began to entwine ourselves together. I felt her shiver below me as she started to come and when she started she kept going. Rocking back and forth until I was exhausted. It had been her first time and for me the best time.

Now I was going to give her some thing back in return. Something that she had no knowledge of. I let her go to sleep, contentment on her face. I relaxed myself beside her and took her up slowly from the bed. Holding her tightly to keep her calm.

'Where am I, what's happening to me?' she asked in French and had to repeat in English.

'It's OK, you're all right and you are safe,' I put into her mind: 'Your wish was to be able to dance. Your leg is healed and in a few moments this will only be a dream. Before we descend, listen carefully to me. The boy you are with is your friend. He made you a promise and has kept it.'

I took her down slowly, calmly, putting both our spheres on the bed. As her body transformed, mine did the same.

She shot up in an instant.

'I had a bad dream,' she said.

'What do you mean? I promised to grant you a wish,' I added and smiled.

She hopped straight out the bed naked and a split second later sat down sobbing. She was fully recovered for there was no twist in her leg. She gently flopped down on the bed crying and I stroked her hair. After a while her sobs lessened and her questions began.

'Who are you? She asked.

'Just a boy,' I said.

'What's your name?' she asked next.

'I have no name to give you,' was my reply.

'How old are you?'

'Around your age.'

'How can you do it?

'How do you do it?'

'Just a gift.'

This went on and on. Questions from her and me then replying. I then commenced to tell her what she could now do. You too have the means to leave your body. I went through it all with her. Then the most important factor of all. I then explained what she must do to protect herself.

'The television,' she said: 'It's you who caused all the strange things to happen.'

'Yes, they were caused because certain people would not leave myself or the girls alone,' I told her.

She had moved closer to me in the bed. Just to let her feel secure in my arms.

'How am I going to explain about my leg?' Helga suddenly asked me.

'Take some papers home with you. Some funny things have been happening in the last few days. A miracle will be just another thing to read about,' I answered: 'Always be on your guard. Let's shower and go out. Have a walk and a drink and then let's she if I can teach you to dance tonight.'

Helga smiled at that, she was so happy but we never did get to dance together. She'd gone to get changed for the night and all I received was a little note delivered to the café. She was flying home to see a medical specialist. I wonder why. It didn't matter in the long run to me because I had her address and a telephone number: All taken, directly from her mind. I also had a little book for names and numbers. One day, I may need one of them.

I felt that my time here was coming to a close. People could be looking for me. Remember one thing, three men had disappeared and their employer could point a finger my way.

Instead of the dance lesson, I went for a swim as dusk came. Found the tyre and recovered my bank. I returned on the beach in darkness, dressed and hit the road, back to the hotel. Packed my gear, checked out and I was away heading east toward the French Riviera and Monaco. There was no rush. I buried the jewellery, except for one ring under a railway bridge where I spent the night.

My estimate for the cash had been low, so I was in good spirits. Get to the place I wanted first. Get some more bank money and then consider the next move. I was well hidden before I started my plan.

Chapter 10

BM

Its day break and I am eager to move. Into hover and away I went at full speed, just flying past main flow of traffic east. It's absolutely marvellous to see these two places for the first time. My first place to visit had to be the boats. I went through twelve of them in a matter of minutes. Not much in the way of cash but the jewels were a different matter. Had these people no regard, for what they had? A beautiful Rolex just laid there on a small table. Diamond rings. Gold bracelets and necklaces. I was going to have a field day.

It's now back to the road and heading west. In just a matter of minutes and I'm back and transformed to human form again. I needed to be at least five to ten miles out for my plan to work. Walking distance, easily.

I found a little B &B that suited me fine. Enough people staying there for my purpose. My swimming trunks were on under my trousers and I was wearing a new shirt. Plastic bags and elastic bands in my pockets and a reel of black cotton. I also had a spare shirt and shorts, a pair of slip on shoes and enough money for a cab in a little rucksack. I took a cab and ten minutes later I was dropped off in sight of the harbour.

I did not under any circumstances want to be seen anywhere near the boats. I did a full detour down to the side of them. It was just over 300 yards away by water and worked out the best way in. From that moment I left the area until night had fallen, then moved in slowly towards a little beach. To the left was a small shaded area where I could leave my clothes. I stripped off and swam slowly across the harbour. As I got to the area where the lights were brighter, I took a check on my bearings to the first boat on my list. Breathing slowly and deeply I took in oxygen for a long swim under the water.

Down I went and with a long smooth breaststroke headed in. I came upon the bow before I knew it, just a dark silhouette above me. Surfaced slowly where I couldn't be seen. I'd already prepared small pieces from my nails and had placed them in the pocket of my trunks. Two little pieces for each boat. A piece flipped on the forward deck and the other through the open port holes. An elastic band to hold two folded bags just above the port hole on the lower upright of the hand rail around the boat. Too small for it to be seen in the dark. A length of cotton, double the distance from boat deck to water.

These are big boats belonging to the rich and famous. Most would be out for most of the night and would also be dead to the world in sleep well into the day. They were night people and had to be seen out on the town. Over two hours silently moving from one boat to the next.

It was an easy swim back to the beach and no problem to get dressed in the warm air. I even removed my trunks to stop my trousers from getting wet. I placed my trunks under a stone in the water to hold them in place, ready for the following morning. I was set except for burying my rucksack in the sand. A couple of pieces of nail onto the sand and I was ready to leave. A quick walk away from the area and then circle back to check my cache of clothes. In the dark, you never know who could be watching. I stayed silently waiting for over an hour to ensure that it was secure and in place and it would all be there waiting for me in the morning.

I left the B & B at first light and was hovering at the first port hole within minutes. It was easy to move inside and I could see it was all clear. The couple in the bed were well out of it. It was a very simple matter to pull in the bags and cotton. I took a couple of bands out of the bag and filled it. Three necklaces. A bracelet. Four watches and all the cash off the bedside table. I even took some notes out of his trouser pockets. Securing the bags with elastic. Fastening the cotton to it double and I lowered the two bags out the port hole. They were then secured with a slipknot. Remember my college days. This knot would be released from the outside and no trace would remain.

I was always extremely careful, not to touch any thing not going into the bag. Not even a fingerprint on the port hole. First one done in less than three minutes and I'm out and in the next.

Same procedure again and out. I'd done seven boats when I spotted a few early risers taking the air. Enough was enough. Out and onto the deck of the last one where I transform to human form. Slipped into the water and slowly moved back to each boat. First pulling on the slipknot carefully to release the bags. Squeezing the air out and then diving out to the mooring buoys. At each buoy, I secured a bag of jewellery. The other ones held bank notes. There was no way that I'd leave the cash underwater, just in case. As I was finishing the last boat I could hear people starting to move inside.

Were they getting up or what? Just the toilet I hope. All the jewel bags are tied secure. Cash bags are going with me.

Well I'm away rapidly now and though I'm moving slower with the bags in each hand. I'm covering distance underwater until my lungs were really bursting and I had to surface. What a distance I'd done. A distance well beyond what I'd imagined possible. A few fast breathes and a bearing, and I'm under again for another silent swim. Then up for surface breast stroke for the last short distance. My trunks were there for me to put on. A quick jog across the sand to my buried rucksack. A quick sweep down into the loose sand and it's out. I'm getting dressed in double time. Bags go into the rucksack and I'm up and out of there.

OK, I may have been seen but it was from a distance. Into a run down the road to a taxi rank. I pointed east away from the boats and asked the driver to drop me off after five miles. I walked for a minute until the taxi had gone, then I was sharply into the hedgerow. Across a grass field into some woodland. I was home and free. All together I estimated that I'd done the lot in just over an hour and half. I found an area covered with bramble. I secured the bags together and tossed them into the centre. They were totally hidden from view. I walked for another couple of miles east. Stripped and put my clothes in the rucksack and threw that into another bramble bush.

Laying down, I relaxed and within seconds I took the correct direction west and I was back on the bed in no time. Up and showered to remove the smell of salt water and down stairs for breakfast. Here's where I joined the rest of the guests. Around ten I ordered a taxi to take me to town. It would be my first appearance in any of the cafes near the marina one of which gave a perfect view of the whole area. The marina was going mad for some reason. Police cars were arriving. People shouting and ranting and then more police arriving. People were being questioned. It was a joy to see. My waiter arrived with a coke for me and I asked him what the heck was happening. He told me that there had been a series of robberies in the night. On the posh boats. Some film stars were on one of the big ones and he pointed it out to me. It had been number two on my list and I'd not known and neither did I care.

I was waiting for some thing else to happen. I had another coke, then wondered down to the harbour to listening on the questioning because the portholes were too small to get in the thought of water did not enter into the equation with anyone. Who would ever imagine what was hidden underneath them and just twenty feet out from each boat?

More confounding was that some people had only arrived back just before dawn. Yes, I can understand what's been said. When you can read minds a language is no problem to learn. I left the immediate area and wondered back to the café for dinner. It was excellent to eat and enjoyable to watch the drama for the rest of the afternoon. No one entered the water at all.

I was walking about later on when I passed a motor bike shop. What did I spot but a Triumph T 100. It had two good panniers on the sides. It was just what I wanted but it would have to be the following morning before I could buy it. I had ample spare money, insurance to ride any bike and a licence. These I'd kept with me after I dumped the first one.

I paid cash for it next morning. First I'd left my passport with the man selling it and I had a good trial run on it before the money changed hands. I bought a leather jacket and helmet.

I was mobile again. What a feeling it is to have something of your own again. I'd missed being on a bike.

I spent the next two weeks riding around the countryside. I recovered the jewellery from under the bridge in broad daylight after stopping there and pretending to tinker with the bike. Recovered it and buried it closer to home. I had also bought some new clothes and had started to frequent a couple of night-spots. In the mornings after a quick hover to check around the area, I continued with my training.

When I first began training I'd had a few startled looks from people living in the area, but they soon got used to it. Even a couple of young lads had watched me one morning and asked if I could teach them how to do it. Balance is harder to learn than you think. Rhythm comes with practice. To harden your hands takes forever.

The night has arrived for me to recover the banks. I've not sold a thing yet and I already know the value of what I have. The papers had given out the sum and I had cut it in half to be sure. Well in excess of over fifty thousand pounds worth of jewellery. The night-spots were a place to get information. To find out who was who. Maybe they wondered who I was, being so young and the fact that I always had money. Not too much on me though at any one time, but just enough for any night.

At one club I watched the younger ones. At around seven thirty most evenings they used to come in all aged eighteen to around twenty five years of age. Girls clearly with their boyfriends, I left well alone. Maybe an occasional smile, but that was it. I'd bigger fish to fry. Then about an hour later the older ones with classy women. Later, a man came in with two or three companions. This was a man of around five foot ten, in his early forties and with a big barrel chest. I would say a very strong man, a very hard man. What I'd noticed about this group was the fact that it was only the young ones who paid for drinks. Whenever this big guy came in, there was always a waiter in attendance at all times. His glass was never empty.

Go in any bar and sooner or later, you will see someone showing off. One of the main attractions is arm wrestling and a means to show the girls what you are made of. It was also a betting game, with money on the table. Normally the best of three. I'd edged close one night and casually put a note down at the side of the guy taking the bets.

'Which one?' was all I was asked.

I pointed and that was it. I lost my money. It was hit and miss for a couple of nights, losing more than I won. Third night I was invited to have a go. The rules are simple. Right hand to right hand, across the table and elbow bent. One trick I'd learnt is to squeeze your opponent's fingers as you gripped his hand. With me it made no difference. I allowed them to nearly press my arm down and then without any emotion, turned the tables on then. One after the other I did exactly the same. At no point did I waver. A few drinks of coke and I continued to take them on. I was hoping that the big guy would take the bait and one day he just sat down opposite me. I never knew what time he'd arrived. Nor the fact that I'd been observed by him, just that he was there. Now, this is what I'd planned for the last few nights. He took his coat off and rolled his sleeves up.

His elbow came to the middle across the table and his palm opened to meet my own. Both of us gripped hard. Applying brute force into the grip. Not once did I break my concentration or give him any indication of my reaction to the pressure he was applying. It was the opposite for him entirely and I could plainly see the surprise in his face. He eased down the pressure and I followed him down pound per pound. Next came the applied pressure sideways. I held him there without budging. Then I slowly cut down on the force to let my hand slowly, slowly bend back onto the table.

The place erupted with shouts from all sides. I stood, went to the bar and sat on a stool. I was on my second beer, by the time I realised that I had company. On my left side he sat looking at me. Then the question from him came,

'Why did you let me win?' he said.

I looked at him and told him the truth: 'No one beats the boss in is own territory.'

I got a startled look from his eyes and then the little nod of his head. Understanding of what I'd actually done for him was plain to see. I had taken on his group, young and old and yet not beaten him. Hell, he was damn strong in his own right. An indication of his hand got me another beer. At that he left me alone to drink it. I had all the time in the world. He had two choices, one to let it pass, or two, to approach me again.

It took another six days for this to happen. During that period, I carried on training, hardening my body. Always, I was up early in the mornings. I'd be up soaring around the area. Checking and re-checking that all was normal. Then I spotted the car parked down the road. Came close and two of my wrestling friends watching the B & B. They'd followed me back.

It was then back to the bed. Training gear on as normal and in full view, I commenced a full routine. Not once did I glance in their direction. Back flips and somersaults. Hand balancing and then karate practice. I finished off with more balance training. First off one leg and then the other. Back in and showered and then out on the bike, heading into town. I had a complete list of places where money was stored overnight.

It was on the fifth night though that I met another girl. She came in the club one night while I was watching the arm wrestling. I was now banned from joining in after that first time display. The girl just happened to sit down at my side and as I turned to pick my drink up I soon realised I had company. I continued to watch the wrestlers. They were having a good match. It was one down each.

'Who do you think will win?' she said.

'The one on the far side,' I replied without looking at her.

He did win. I then just turn back to the bar.

'Your from England aren't you?' she asked me.

'Sure,' I said taking a drink at the same time.

Here's me, now replying to a girl in French without any bother at all.

We then commenced to talk about music, singers and customs. I asked her what she was doing there alone at the club?

'Just waiting for my father,' she said: 'He'll be in soon.'

Me, I just fancied going for a ride on my bike for an hour, just to get my head cleared. I told her that I was leaving and that was it. Now it wasn't that she didn't take my fancy, but I couldn't put a foot wrong for the moment. An involvement again so soon could put me back to square one. Keeping things in the right prospective meant that I had to be just free to go when I needed to and not be tied down. We'd already spent an hour talking so no harm was done by just leaving her at the bar.

I left and headed up the coast on the bike. Instead of heading back to the same night-spot, I decided to try another for a change.

I was in there maybe half an hour when who should come in but George Delacourt the big man, at his side the girl I'd been talking to. The minders were there of course. Just for him to enter caused a rumpus. A couple of young ones were cleared from a table and offers of drinks given to shut them up. Definitely, this man was important and very well known.

Me, I'd only dumped his daughter. I sat there watching them settle in. This club was not normally as packed as the other one. Slowly but surely, I spotted faces arriving who were known to me. This was going to be interesting for sure. Here I am just sat out of the limelight, having what I thought was a quiet night.
Monsieur, Mr George would like to speak to you.' The waiter whispered this into my ear.

'OK,' was all I said.

I walked over and sat down on the chair placed there for me.

'Evening,' I said as I sat down.

'My father would like a return match, a true one this time,' said the girl: 'He will accept nothing but a true test from you.'

'That will be fine,' I told her as I stood up to take my jacket off.

He in turn did the same but he also limbered up. I smiled and sat down waiting. By now there was silence in the club. The music stopped and the crowd began to place bets, huge sums of money heading on the tables. One particular pile caught my eyes. It was big and thick, just as if it had just come from a bank.

'What's the odds?' I asked across the table.

'Two to one that he takes you two out of three. Evens that he takes you for three.'

'For me?' I demanded.

'Three to one on the first and five to one on the second.'

Should I do it to them I thought, damn it I will.

'OK, who will give me odds that I take all three?' I said: 'Each in less than six seconds.'

A hush descended. Some had seen the last match and were nervous. It was the girl herself that broke the silence.

'What have you to put forwards?' she said.

I reached into my pocket and brought out a really beautiful necklace, and a solid gold ring with a big clear diamond. That did silence the people present. They could see plainly that what I'd put down before them wasn't paste. One man began to put his hand forward.

'No,' said George sharply.

'Eight to one,' came from the girl quietly.

I picked them up and handed them to her with the words: 'Hold these for me for a moment.'

Elbow onto the table and then my hand open to receive his. I expected it and held it, as he had no sooner touched his hand to mine that he tried for a quick one. I looked across into his eyes and then just applied force without stopping until his hand touched the table. Five seconds gone and that was the first one. While flexing his arm and hand he just stared at me.

'Ready,' he finally said.

At that our hands clasped again. One two three four and down his hand went again. What a silence in that room. People were standing on chairs to view, others on the bar. From the information I'd gleaned from others, this man had not been beaten in fifteen years. Here was I, just one month off my eighteenth birthday, taking on this man. If only he had known what I could do if I really tried.

Like breaking all his fingers just by tightening my hand.

Round three and he's ready again. I could see the determination in his movements. Elbows out and hands together hard. Me, I just started counting to myself again. One two three four five and down, I put his hand hard onto the table.

'The necklace will look fine on you, I believe I was a fraction out,' I said to the girl.

I then left the table for the bar and got a beer. What an uproar I'd created. Arguments were starting about my timing. George came to the bar and sat beside me. In his hand, he had the ring. He placed it in front of me.

'Dinner tomorrow, all right,' he said.

'Sure, you know where to find me,' I replied and his eyebrows lifted slightly at that remark.

I'd set him up and he knew it. I think I could have been the first to dare to in a long time. He was now definitely well curious about me and would want to know more.

At dinner next day, I asked him if he knew my name?

'Your passport reads BM,' he replied.

He then asked about England and why I'd pitched up in the south of France?

'Nearly eighteen,' he said: 'What will you be like at twenty.'

'If I'm allowed to live that long,' I replied and that did put him back a bit.

'Jewels, now that's what I'd like to talk about,' George added: 'The necklace came off a boat in Marseilles harbour, did it not.'

'Yes,' I said.

His mind was ticking over and then he began to chuckle to himself. I'd never seen this man even smile before.

'You, he managed to say at last. You did it.' His laughter continued for a few more minutes.

'Why Me?' were his next words.

'Simple really, when I see the young ones, they don't actually work for a living. Then the older one's to overseer the young ones. Then there has to be a boss. That's you,' I said.

How he laughed at me telling him this. He then became serious. Very serious.

'Do you want to know something, people wanted you beaten and dumped out of town. I wanted to do the same. Thank your stars that my daughter asked me not to. You've been getting in the hair of my people for over a week now, you don't know how lucky you are.'

I smiled at him then, a cheeky smile maybe. But I then had my say.

'You think I'm lucky, but listen and I'm serious in what I'm saying. I have all the jewels from this marina. I had to find some way to dispose of them. I chose you.'

That really shut him up then. He became quiet for a few minutes then. At last he spoke; 'What you are telling me is that you robbed seven boats in the space of one night on your own.'

'Correct,' I said finally without any hesitation.

He whistled at that. It was through to him, that it was not a joke.

'How do you know, that you can trust me?' he said.

'Put it this way, one hundred men with guns could not stop me getting to you,' I told him. He was looking at me astounded at these words.

'Where are the jewels hidden?' he asked.

'Where they have been all the time, at the boats,' I said simply.

'When can I have them?'

'Some time tonight, if I can borrow your daughter for a couple of hours.'

'My daughter?'

'----- to watch my bike----.'

'By the way,' I then said to him: 'Once your daughter gives you the jewels, I will show you in the morning why I trust you.'

Her name was Frieda and I picked her up on the bike around eight and we rode back to the marina. Took a towel out of the panniers and then stripped off to my trunks.

'Come on, you can watch me swimming,' I said: 'It shouldn't take long.'

I crossed the beach and then into the water swimming. She looked nervous when I left her. It took a few minutes there and quietly I moved from one buoy to the next. Collecting the bags. I then swam back to the beach and dried off. Her eyes were now brighter with the relief that I'd done it. No sign of any trouble.

Bags into the pannier and away I rode, slowly, not wanting to be stopped for any reason by the police. I kept away from the B & B that night.

I stayed in a motel twenty miles away. My eyes snapped open as dawn broke and then I relaxed. Let myself change quickly and I was outside in an instant.

Up I soared, speeding fast I came upon the house. I had a look around and counted seven people on watch. Another three were asleep in the lounge. I moved around until I saw an open bedroom window. In I went. He was fast asleep, curled next to a woman. An older version of his daughter. His wife no doubt.

I touched him slowly and he disappeared as normal into a ball of dim light. Pulling him out was so easy and taking him high into the dawn sky, I let him go.

'Be quiet and be calm,' I passed the words to him as he realised that something was totally wrong with his senses: 'Your perfectly safe, I'll be just a moment.'

I sped back down. Only a minute later I had them both before me. Father and daughter. Both of them together up in the sky and wishing that they could wake up.

'It is not a dream, but you are both perfectly safe,' I projected to both minds: 'I'm not going to hurt you at all. In fact you both now have the power to do this at will. Only I can remove it from you.'

I then went on to explain the rules to survival. I gave them telepathically an address in Switzerland. An emergency number.

'One good thing,' I explained: 'both of you will be in good health. Frieda, go down and then come back up to show your father that you can do it.'

At that she descended and disappeared for a few minutes. It must have taken her a little while for her to get back to sleep. This I was explaining to George when suddenly she appeared back in the sky, shooting upwards to join us.

'Papa, I can really do it,' she was shouting into our minds.

'Trust, George.' I then said and left them both.

'Trust you shall have,' was his mind shout behind me.

I went back to the motel, checked out and headed back into town. An hour and I drove up the drive way to dismount at the front door. No one was in sight. Frieda looked and she greeted me differently. It was a warm welcome smile and a kiss on both cheeks. Her father asked me in, and appeared to be a little quieter than the daughter.

'Are you both fine?' I asked.

'Yes, came a double chorus.'

'Let's go out the back and join my wife,' George said.

It was a pleasure to meet his wife, Anna. A lovely pleasant woman. She was from Germany which accounted for the name of her daughter. Anna was aware of what her husband did and who he was. We all sat down at the table and it was Anna who broke the ice.

'These two have been telling me of something that happened just over an hour ago. I think they are both crazy,' she said: 'What is odd, is the fact that he told everyone to leave about fifteen minutes ago and that we would have a guest arriving for dinner.'

Tell you what Anna, if I can call you that,' I said: 'Ask your husband if he'll trust me again?'

'George,' she said to him.

Now George he was looking at me now. All three with the power would be better for this family.

'Let me think about it,' he said.

I would need his help in the future, but he didn't know that yet.

'I have a question for you,' George said to me: 'You could see this morning that I had taken you up on your challenge. There were thirteen men here waiting to beat you senseless.'

'Not enough, George,' I said: 'A hundred maybe.'

I was smiling at him while saying it. I think we all saw the funny side of it in a way. I needed to talk to George now for a while and I asked the women if they would let me talk in private. They both stood up and walked away without a word. I needed him to wipe out all records of my ever being in the area. I needed a new passport and a new licence. All had to be untraceable. They had to come from a real person. I would be using them for only one year. It was a small price. A bank account was needed. One of the younger members of his gang looked enough like me for me to take his place. He would be paid of course. Not his life but in money.

George approved of all I asked of him. I was going to get it all. By the time it had all been sorted out it was dinnertime and we all ate together. Anna went for a nap. The other two were both sat there staring at me.

'What's your answer George?' I said.

I was looking at Frieda at the same time.

'Do it when you're ready,' he simply said to me. A nod came from Freda.

At that, I disappeared before them. Astonishment was plain to see on their faces, just to seeing how it happened. Especially how quickly it happened. They were stood there looking at my pile of clothes. I caught Anna just as she was nodding of to sleep. Took her gently up and then around the side of the house to look down at her husband and daughter. 'Now do you believe them?' was passed to her mind.

I kept a really good hold on her and let no fear enter her. I brightened her light to give her enough to be able to help the poor in small ways. In her mind was a feeling for charity, to do good. Not a lot but something. Then we both reappeared. Anna in the bedroom and me naked in front of them. I dressed quickly and a few moment later Anna rushed out to her husband and daughter.

'All true,' she said: 'All true.'

In the next two weeks a bank account was opened in my new name. A sum eventually appeared and I whistled at the amount. £78,000. This I would be transferring slowly over a year to my own account in the UK. The other bank was named Delacourt.

It was now time for me to leave. First thing was to have a new licence and documents for the bike. Insurance was a must. I'd covered most every thing possible including a little compartment behind the panniers on the bike. This held my real identity and spare cash. The last thing was a strong chain and two big padlocks. That bike was not going to be stolen.

I had a last night out with everyone. I had been given the green light, by the boss. For me at the end of the night, it was time to move on.

Chapter 11

I'd important phone numbers in a book and I destroyed it after I'd memorised them all.

'Salema', I think that's how it's spelt. The first town in Italy, beyond France. That was my first real stop. Customs had been no bother at all. Just a quick look at me and a stamp on the passport. I was in. Coffee shop first, then to change money. French francs into Italian lira. And I was set again for the road.

'Rome, here I come.'

It's winter time and not really suitable for a bike. I stayed just a day, touring around and not really liking it. My idea then, was to head down into Southern Italy where the weather was warmer. Three stops overnight and four days later I was at a ferry terminal looking out across to Sicily.

It was a warm day and so I lazed about making up my mind on what to do. In the end, I thought why not and bought a ticket one way. First I had to make sure the way back would be possible. I stuffed four plastic bags with bits of my clothing. Added some nail clippings to each. Then I rode out of the port to a nice quiet area. Two hours later, my real passport and cash along with some clothes had been buried in a new rucksack I'd bought. Four sites had been picked to hang the bags hidden from view. The denser the undergrowth, the better. I was set up and pleased with my work. A route back and double covered with back ups. You never know.

Stayed the night at a little hotel and I had double chained the bike. Up early, to catch the first ferry out. Can't speak above two words of the language, but I'll learn it fast.

Now let's face one fact. Every one knows about the Mafia and where it evolved. It was never my intention to have anything to do with it. Me, I'd just parked myself in a little fishing area. Booked into a hotel. Cleaned up and went for a walk. Just sat there, a total stranger to everyone, watching the fishermen mending nets. A couple of old men were doing this work and were damn fast at it. I sat there having a drink and watching them working.

Always something will happen to spoil the day. A young guy came along and started to bellow and shout at the old fishermen. Even pushed one. Me, I wasn't standing for that and walked over. Grabbed his arm and literally heaved him over a low wall into the sea. It was only waist deep so I thought no harm done. He climbed out and started towards me. As he swung a fist at me I caught it and squeezed hard. That brought him straight to his knees. With my other hand I gave him the international sign. One Finger stuck up in front of his face. Telling him to fuck off. A little extra squeeze before I let him go.

Now the old men were getting hysterical by this time and from what I could gather, they were telling me to get the hell out of there. Trouble was coming. With a capital T. No bother to me and I sat back down to finish my drink. The two old guys disappeared and not long after, I heard a car drawing up behind me and I span round for a look. I stood up to face them as they left the car. My young friend had brought some muscle, to assist him.

I stood up and wagged my finger at him as if to say naughty boy. That did piss him off and he ran towards me. He met a solid fist that put him straight out. The next met a straight chop to his Adam's apple and fell gasping for breath. I'd held back just a fraction on that or he'd have been dead. With the other three I was bundled over the wall into the sea and they then came at me. I grabbed one and jabbed a finger into his eyes before he knew it. The other two had scuttled away from me by this time. I grabbed the one out of the water and heaved him back onto the land. Jumped out after him and calmly sat down. The one I'd hit in the throat was catching his breath by this time. The one who'd started it was still out cold. I'd a little audience watching and some were shaking their heads. It was over and the two remaining men knew it. They picked their friends up and left.

I waited for the car to disappear and ran back to my hotel. Up to the room and into hover. Outside and smaller, I'm on my way to catch the car. It was climbing slowly up an incline into the hills. I needed to know who I faced. I followed slowly behind them until the car turned into a drive and approached a large farmhouse. Just looking at it and you could see where it had been extended over the years. Out they all got and dragged the last one out with them. He was just waking up by that time. It was around the back and on to the veranda facing the sun. Some old men sat there. One in particular was older than the others. He was in a wheel chair, facing the five. I was just hovering above them and listening to what went on. In this form, reading minds, understanding the language was natural, although it was visually pretty obvious when the old man in the wheelchair raised his stick and suddenly whacked the boy that had started it all. He just stood there and took it, I'll give him that. Next it was a scene to see. Piling the old guy into that car and his chair stuffed in the boot. Two others, in the back and another to drive. I knew where they were heading and was back before them. Into the hotel quick, dressed and outside in double time. A stroll and I'm back to the wall where I sat down to wait. The old guys were back working by this time, looked at me but they didn't say a word.

That damn car came that close to me when it arrived that I if I'd not lifted my legs up onto the wall, the driver would have taken them off. Round one to the old men at his method of arrival. Out they got, next the wheel chair and then they helped the older one into it. His stick was waving everywhere. Over they came towards me. Stopping just over afoot from me, that stick rose up.

'I wouldn't, if I were you,' I said looking at him.

'English?' He said to me in an American accent.

Now that damn stick was still up there, in the air ready to come down on me.

'Why don't you ask, why?' were my next words: 'Ask these two gentlemen behind me why?'

His face, although still purpled up with rage, flickered to the two men in question. A few words from him and I even felt a little afraid.

This was due to how the fishermen acted. I couldn't believe what I was seeing. These guys were actually bowing and cringing. Who the hell was he. My eyes never left that stick though and as I listened to words passing back and forth, it slowly came down.

'You have till morning to leave this country, or I will feed you to my dogs,' he snarled.

I just laughed in his face and said to him in plain English; 'Before that order could be given in the morning by you, death will have claimed you.'

That put him out all right, but I didn't care one hoot at the time. 'Tomorrow morning I will give the order at nine, be gone,' he said.

'OK, here's what I will do in the morning,' and I literally stuck my head forwards whilst saying it: 'I am coming for all four of you.'

The gauntlet had been cast, a direct challenge given by both sides. I didn't care who he was. I knew I could be away at any time. I got on the bike and rode out the opposite way to where they had come from. I hid my bike down an old gully. Then I walked back to the hotel for a cold beer. In the morning, I would take all four of them for a flying lesson. No one spoke to me all night, not even an acknowledgement. It was as if I wasn't there.

I went to bed early and slept until dawn when I set out for the farmhouse. Shutters were closed but windows cracked open. No problem at all and I squeezed through them to hover above a bed. Wrong room, but there was a stunner to look at. I'm coming back for you, I thought. Into the next room and I had the first one, out and up above the house in no time. Down to search for another one and then up with him as well. Next one was the old man. No problem, he was collected and taken out. Last one and they were all in the bag. I held all four together, just to give them rational thought, but not to take from them the fear of the unknown. Then I released them and headed into the house again, to collect a bonus.

This one I brought outside and took her high in the sky with me. I let them know who it was in passing. This one would not believe what was happening. I held her to me, passing over information. Instructing her on what she must do and why. Her light was starting to glow as I gave her the means to do so. I withheld the healing power The girl would pave the way for me to descend amongst them and for me to stay the winter in peace. At the same time, she would be unable to tell others what she could now do. She was no longer one of them, but a free Day Mover.

She did not believe this until I pointed down to the old men hovering below us. You're free to go down and try what you want. I let her descend on her own. It was now back to the old men, and their thoughts. Fear was in them all right. They had taken my words lightly yesterday. Had looked at my youth and thought I was nothing at all.

'My profession is assassin.' I projected into their minds: 'How would you like to see my dogs, to feel them tear you apart?'

I then went on to tell them of what the night ghosts did to those they caught in the dark. Piece by piece you will cease to exist. That did put the frighteners on them.

'Now watch what happens next,' I put across to all four.

Below us I could see the family, all coming outside together. The girl had followed my instructions. Already they knew that the four men had disappeared. Young and old were now gathered.

'You,' I said to the nearest: 'When you arrive back down there on your bed, you will drive into the village. Then bring back some clothes of mine from the hotel. Be quick.'

At that I took him down to his bed. Just a few seconds later, he was outside screaming for the car, double quick time. A gang jumped in with him and off they went.

I took the other three with me and we followed the car. Waited for them to get my clothes. All this time, my company were silent and watching the events below us. Then we followed the car back to the house where I took another one down to his bed.

'It is but a fraction of what I can do,' I mind spoke to the remaining two: 'Be very careful of me. Think, before you do anything. Think, before you speak. Think, before you breathe.'

I was looking down at some very frightened people by this time. They all knew what had occurred yesterday, but it was totally reversed and they didn't know how or why, except that some of their older men folk were acting very strange and frightened.

I then dropped the last two down but appeared beside the old man. Dressed beside him while he looked at me.

'Would you like to set your dogs on me?' I asked him.

He just sat there looking at me in silence.

I walked down the stairs and out of the house. Looked at them, pointed at the car and the old man who mysteriously now had the power of his legs.

I could see the women crossing themselves. I was a devil to them at that point and I would be left well alone watching the two fishermen mending nets. It still took some time for them to even accept the fact that I was still there and that nothing was happening to me. When the girl came down and sat with me, they knew something had happened, a miracle. I already knew that her English was enough for us to get by on so we began to talk. We walked together to fetch my bike back. I going on to explain more about what she could now do. I got the bike out and away we went. She held on tight at every corner as I cranked it over. This was probably her first time on a motorbike.

The word was spreading fast around this community. It was small and most of the people knew each other. I was to be left alone. The manager at the hotel could not do enough for me. I continued to watch the men mending nets. I noticed various strangers appear in the back ground, but they never came close. A policeman appeared one morning. He'd stopped his car about twenty yards away. Young, not much older than me, and he was very nervous, I could see it in his face. They wanted answers about me. Some one was speaking out of turn. That is not normal for Sicily. My passport said I was French, but they knew I spoke English all the time, but I spoke to him in French and not English. The passport he looked at page by page. Nothing was wrong with it. My other documents were in order. They all gave the same name. That must have really stumped them all.

He handed back my papers and I turned away and walked down to the nets. He'd not even written a thing down. I surprised them all then by commencing to mend a net. Taught at a school, in seamanship. I could have done it the first day, but was rusty and had wanted to check if my knowledge was still there.

All day I worked alongside those two old men. People watching me and not believing it. Even the policeman had stayed for an hour. Talk was certainly buzzing around.

Over the next few days, I started to follow the two men to a small bar for lunch. The first time I entered with them, the place emptied, but slowly they remained in place to watch. I was always watched and every little thing was noted. It was when I started up my daily training that they had the biggest surprise. To see me, turning and twisting and stretching my muscles. Karate kicks and thrusts and most of all to see how I did a back flip. Lifting weights that I'd hung off a metal bar. Little kids tried to imitate me until mothers caught them at it. I just laughed when I saw it. The girl used to come down to see me every few days. I'd seen her practising in the sky. Not a word had she said to anyone. Only the four men had seen me take her and had no knowledge of what I'd given to her.

Chapter 12

Sicilian Girl

Something happened to me early one morning. I was laying there thinking of a certain policeman, when I found myself in the sky

Alongside me were four dim lights and next to me a really bright one. I could feel myself glowing and I could hear words being given to me. For me not to be afraid in any way or form and that soon I would be back down in my bed. Awake in my body and perfectly safe in all respects. I could feel the fear in my mind been erased even as I thought it. And then the explanation of what had happened came to me. Why it had happened me, also what I could now do. I was to follow the instructions given to me to the letter.

I had become some thing called a Day Mover. It must forever remain a secret. I thought of my bed and I was down on top of it totally naked. I screamed very loudly as I'd been told to. That woke the rest of the house

'Grandfather has disappeared,' I was screaming out.

It worked and everyone began to rush about. Quickly it was discovered that his two brothers and an old friend were also missing. It was only a few minutes later that one of his brothers came out of the house shouting for the car. They were back within fifteen minutes.

Another brother had reappeared by now. His face was pale and grey. It was as if he'd seen a ghost. I had been asked to take the clothes given to me to my grandfather's bedroom and to leave them there. In just a few more minutes, my grandfather appeared. He was walking for the first time since long ago, when I was a small girl and he'd been shot with a shotgun. All of us were seeing a miracle but it was the sight of who followed him outside who took my breath away.

He was my own age and from abroad with light skin. Not, what you can call tall. But very broad in the shoulders and he walked as if he'd not a care in the world. My mother and aunts were crossing themselves. To them somehow, he was unnatural. An unknown young man and he'd just appeared from the house.

All he did was point at the car. It was grandfather who drove him back to the village. I was questioned later on by my grandfather and the other three, in secret. I got away from them later and headed for the village. I had to see him and I was not afraid to see him. He'd given me something without me asking for it and it was wonderful. He was on a wall trying to converse with two lovely old men. I'd known them all of my life. I'd been out fishing with them once. They'd retired now and just mended the nets.

I walked across to him feeling a little afraid and felt much better when I saw him smiling at me.

'How are you,' he said to me.

It was beautiful to hear his voice for the very first time. He got up and asked me to follow him. My fear returned in an instant and then he told me that never should I ever be afraid of him.

'I'm just a boy who wants a little peace,' he said: 'I'm fetching my bike".

Sure enough it was true. I sat on the back as we rode through the countryside and into town. It was really great.

Over the next few weeks my life was a whirl, finding out all that he'd given me. I wanted to give myself to this person and one day he told me why this was not to be. A promise made to my mother. Even though I was grown up, I'd never been with a man. This one I would have slept with if he'd only asked. I learnt that he only struck people when they came for him. He was never the first one to attack. He always warned people first to leave him alone and to let him live quietly. To see the interest that he had for two old men was unbelievable.

The policeman in my dreams arrived one day to talk to him and to check his papers. I'd always wanted him to notice me. He never had. That is until he saw me with the stranger. It was from that moment on that he started to speak to me, whenever he found me alone. Mother and father tried to stop me seeing him but it was grandfather who told them that I was the safest person in Sicily at that moment.

In the end, my grandfather was the wisest of men. I hadn't known anything at all about the promise he made to my mother until he told me himself. How he stood it, I don't know. Every day someone would be there at the village. Some were important people but the remainder were the Mafia. I recognised a few from photographs in the papers.

BM

There were still strangers. Arriving in big cars. Silently they used to watch me. Finally, I could take it no longer. I became a Day Mover and followed the man who'd been observing me out to a large mansion. That seemed out of place in Sicily.

I hovered unobserved and followed him in. I was fairly safe, having seen a couple of open windows. I listened to the report given to a man I'd never seen before. The way he dressed though gave me enough to know he was important in that area. He was mine tomorrow.

I took him the next day in the early morning. Flew him back to my little hide away and explained in Italian to leave me alone. He knew after two hours with me of my power. I even stressed this time that a gun would not stop me coming for him.

When I took him back there was a panic below. People were milling around and trying to find him. I didn't even ask his name. Just dropped him down onto his bed and headed back for a quiet day. I got my peace from then on.

I then started to explore a little. Even against the wishes of her parents, the girl carried on coming to see me. In the end I just rode up and told them straight that I had no wish to harm the girl but her mother still crossed herself when I left.

We took to travelling around the island. On the first run we went through a road block where everyone coming into the village was stopped. I asked the girl what it was about. She laughed and told me it was to keep people away from the village. All the people on the island had got wind of strange happenings.

All were talking about it and were wondering why the village had been sealed off to strangers. Rumours were rife everywhere she told me. Only village people were allowed in and out. It was totally cut off. This was not the place that it normally is.

This is where the Mafia originated. Around 1878. My being there was not breaking the code of Omerta. The code of silence.

Now Sicily is not as small as people think. It was on one of our outings for dinner that brought it to me how things had changed for me. My bike must have been known, because while we were having dinner it went silent about us for a start. Then the whispers started. When I came to pay the bill, there was no charge. I could hear them talking and heard the village name mentioned a few times. I was out of their confinement. What's the point of sealing a village off if I can ride out at will. I was the mystery, out in full view.

'Can you ride my bike back?' I asked her quietly across the table.

She had already learned. The girl was a quick learner and off she went.

I needed some new clothes and thought why not. Up I got and left the café. Just a slow walk down the street looking for something to wear. Spotted a shoe shop and entered to buy some. The assistant was all smiles and helped me pick a pair of leather ones. It was while fitting them that she became aware of people looking in the shop. Looking at me and all wanting to know who I was. I told her not to worry about them. Got a little smile back in return.

That bike of mine would have to go soon. That, I was sure of. It had become a trade mark. I paid the girl the money for the shoes. Then went shopping for clothes. A Shirt and trousers at the next shop. Paid for them and up the road I went. A new jacket was next. I paid for it and asked them to deliver my goods to the village. I paid cash for the delivery and a little more besides.

Next step was a toilet. Here, I just disappeared leaving a pair of old jeans, shirt and old shoes. Let anyone work that out. I was waiting for the girl outside the hotel when she rode up on the bike. Her face was flushed with the wind and her eyes sparkled. Word would be breaking soon of my trip and of my mysterious departure. I gave it another week and I would have to go. A week, I calculated, before anyone took a chance. Just a few more runs in and out of the village and that would be it. I would be set to leave.

That's what I thought.

The old man appeared early next morning. I'd heard the car door slamming just after dawn and looked out to see him enter the hotel. My telephone rang shortly after that. Now this is at 06.30. They must have really been keeping an eye on me to know that I would be up and awake. Would I come down to speak to him. Sure enough I went down. His first words were a formal introduction.

He was he said; 'Mario Broley.'

He next asked if I'd mind having a chat. Well away from the hotel, and somewhere quiet. The beach is a good place. It's fine for walking along. His legs were healed and strong. Anyway off we went. His English was perfect, even with the American twang. The brother of a very important person was held in the Ucciardione prison. He had been locked away for over eleven years. He had not long to live. Eighty one years of age. They wanted him out.

'Straight out,' Mario said: 'Could I do it?'

Money would be no object. Except for the fact that his legs were healed, he still had great difficulty in believing what I'd done for him. Even his brothers were now beginning to disbelieve. It had been the disappearance in the town that had brought the truth back to him, in a sense.

In total, I knew of only six people that knew the full truth of it.

'How were you approached?' I asked him.

'I wasn't,' he said: 'I went to see this person. It is known by all, that he wants his brother out for his last years. I will make money for my family and this is the truth. I have told this important man that you can get his brother out.

My secret is now out to another. This was my thoughts for a few moments. Definitely I am going leave soon.

'Give me his name?' I said: 'How much does he believe of what you have told him.'

'He believes me all right because he was there when I was shot many years ago,' said Mario: 'He saw the state of my legs. There was no other way for me to make him believe in what I told him.'

'One million dollars cash,' I said to him.

That I thought would put him off but I was the one to get the shock.

'Done,' Mario said to me.

'First though, I wish to show him a demonstration,' I said next: 'Also I need to know where he lives.'

'That I have all really anticipated,' Mario told me.

He produced a couple of photographs; 'This first one is the man in prison. The second is the man who wants you to do it. He also wants a demonstration of what you can do and I have to stay there overnight for a week.'

‘A week?’ I said.

Mario went on; ‘In that time he wants you to take me again, from his house this time. His house is guarded by at least twenty men every night. All of them armed with automatics and the best of alarms have been installed. I have told him that nothing could stop you taking me from there.’

‘OK,’ I said to him and then smiled. I think that he caught on to what I had in mind. Because Mario smiled himself.

Why had he shown me two photographs? Back to his car and away we went. Mount Etna was a beautiful sight in the distance that morning. Only took us just over thirty minutes and Mario pulled up overlooking a lake.

‘That’s his house,’ he said and he pointed across the lake to a beautiful mansion.

‘See you soon,’ I said and I relaxed and I disappeared in front of his eyes.

The shock at me doing it there and then was on his face and the shiver through his body was plain to see. I was over there and through the house all within fifteen minutes. The master bedroom was easy to find. I was back and following Mario without his knowledge and he was definitely smart enough because he had my clothes with him and was heading back to my hotel.

I was sitting on the steps waiting for him as he drew up.

‘Please don’t do that to me,’ were his first words: ‘It scared the living shits out of me when you did it.’

‘I know it did and that’s why I did it,’ I said: ‘It was another demonstration to make you aware of what I can do.’

He then walked into the hotel and made a phone call. He was out side again within ten minutes.

'OK, it's in your hands now,' he said: 'See you whenever.'

I spent that evening treating the two old fishermen to a meal.

I was up and away at first light and in a matter of a few minutes, I'd arrived on location. Straight down and I took the old man up into the sky just high enough for him to see what I was going to do.

'Observe all of it,' I projected into his mind and at that I was down and out with the man in the first photograph. I kept him calm and let him feel safe enough before I descended and brought back all the sleeping guards two at a time. I kept them all safe in mind by explaining that this was just a demonstration and they would soon be back down again.

Then leaving them in a huddle of light I approached Mario and the man I knew now as Franco Vittorio.

'Is this a good enough demonstration for you,' I put across to Franco. Franco wanted back down. He was cussing me telepathically and that takes some doing. He would have killed me if he had the chance.

'Stop right there,' I bellowed across to him: 'One more word and I'll leave you here permanently.'

That shut him up.

'Come on Mario I put across: 'I'm taking you home.'

At that I touched him and headed for his home.

Mario put a few words across to me on the journey. One was that he'd hoped I'd do what I had done. For years he'd waited for someone to get the upper hand with Franco and it had finally happened. Also to tell me that the money would be made available once Franco had calmed down. He so desperately wanted his brother out. One thing though he put across to me.

'I will always be safe from him,' he said: 'but within a period of time Franco would maybe try something against you, so be warned.'

Now those words coming from Mario made me realise how much he thought of me, for giving him back the use of his legs. He then went on to tell me why he'd put me at risk. He was running out of money and he needed it for his family. I dropped him of onto his bed and a few minutes later I was back at the start.

A total silence met me. I could read the thoughts though. All were scared stiff and I mean scared. I put across to them that I was now returning them to the earth. I left Franco until last.

'One warning I give to all,' I put across to him. 'Never try to make me mad at you.'

It was now up to him, so I took him down. As I let him appear on his bed, all hell was breaking out in the house and the grounds. I listened the commotion for just a few minutes. Franco was threatening everyone but the ones I'd taken up with him knew what had passed between them up in the sky. All of them had been totally helpless.

They made it known to some of the others that I was unstoppable. I had heard enough, so up I went and was back on my own bed within a few minutes. I had a quick shower and was down and out for 8 o'clock sharp.

My girl was there waiting for me. We had planned another day out and nothing was going to stop us.

'What were you up to this morning?' she asked quietly.

'Business,' was my reply: 'Is your grandfather fine this morning?

'I think he spotted me,' she said: 'He came over this morning to ask me questions but he got nothing from me.'

'That's good,' I said: 'Keep your secret well hidden".

We were by then heading away from the village, to a place she knew in another small village down the coast. No one would bother us because she'd been there a few times in the past with her grandfather and he was well known.

It had a very small beautiful beach and during the day that as we lay down on the sand we had another really good talk. The subject of sex did come up very early on in the conversation.

'Why?' she asked me: 'Why have you not tried to take advantage of the situation?'

She said that every day, she'd been expecting me to do something.

I gave her the answer.

'I told your mother that I wouldn't.'

That was it. Promises do work both ways. In the end she gave up on the matter and I commenced to train her for the future. Going into detail about what she could do and how to do it. When to do it and when not to do it. I repeated it all to her and then I taught her the sun clock. To take note always of the position of shadows cast by the sun in the morning and then the afternoon position. To be able to know the direction of travel at all times. Always remember what is waiting there in the dark of night. I could not stress this enough. I did give her a kiss on the cheek at one point, when she got the directions correct.

It was in the afternoon that I caught the flash of light from the sand dunes. They were a good quarter mile away. We'd been found. At least it had taken them a while and had given me time to teach her.

'Let's go,' I said: 'People are coming.'

We hurried up the beach to my bike.

It was on the third day that Mario appeared in town. He arrived in his car and simply cruised up slowly. I was chatting to my two old friends, the net menders.

'Franco called this morning,' was all he said to me.

At that I stood and walked around to the passenger side and got in the car. I let Mario drive just outside the village before I asked him where we were heading. He told me that it was to see Franco.

'Change of plans then,' I told him: 'Franco will have to come to me and he will have to come with you on his own.'

I then told Mario that I would be covering the route my way. I told him what I needed from Franco's brother: A lock of hair, some nail cuttings or old clothes. Also I needed to know the exact whereabouts in the prison to save time looking. I also needed Mario to take a journey with his brothers to an address in France. I wanted the money in small suitcases and it would be collected at that address, by an unknown girl.

No questions to be asked at any time, but to simply give her the money and for her to be allowed to take it away.

'That will be the only way that I will do it,' I said: 'What you do with your money is not my concern.'

I then left the car and walked back into the village. It was Franco's call.

I made a phone call to France. George Delacourt was pleased to hear from me. When I told him a little of the happenings in Sicily, he quietened down to listen. The mention of how much was heading his way really must have set him back. He had an address to give me and his daughter would be at that address at the appropriate time. He would cover her from a distance to ensure all went accordingly to plan. I told him to ease back on the cover and that the old man could be trusted. I gave him two other words to give to his daughter and I explained why.

It only took an hour for Mario to get back with Franco. A much subdued Franco. Me, I didn't let on that I'd not covered the route. Perhaps they thought I had and I let them think it.

'Let walk down to the sea away from here,' I said.

Franco was giving me a good looking over. Maybe it was my age or maybe it was the way I was built. I slowly walked down to the sea wall to sit down. They followed. All my requirements were easy to obtain. He was in the hospital wing at the prison. I also had another two conditions. One, his brother was not to be told. Two, I would deliver him to the mainland of Italy. That way he would be safer. To my surprise, that was where Franco had planned to take him. It made it easier for him and had reduced one of his worries. He opened up from that point on. I'd solved something for him and cut down the risk of getting his brother into Italy. Another factor would be that Franco would be seen leaving Sicily by the authorities. This would be prior to the escape and therefore he would be clear of any involvement.

‘What type of car will you be driving?’ I asked him.

I was given that and then continued; ‘Leave a window open and have all the things I requested in the car. Your brother will also need some clothes to put on.

Money, that was my next step. I then told him what I wanted Mario to do. This quietened him but he agreed. I gave Mario the address in France and explained that he was not under any circumstances to speak to the girl in question. That he understood and told me so.

‘Leave tomorrow,’ I said: ‘Call me when it’s delivered.’

I then arranged the dates with Franco and where I needed him in Italy. Also what time to expect his brother. He’d have a good few hours start. That I assured him and I then told him why. He could not have wished for more. He got inquisitive then about myself and I told him to forget it. My plans were my own.

I was also thinking of what Mario had passed on to me about not trusting Franco and had decided to create something in my favour.

‘Franco, I want a private word with you,’ I said.

At that Mario moved away from us.

‘How is the health of your brother at this moment?’ I asked and hoped for the truth.

‘Not so good, maybe six months to a year if we are lucky,’ he told me quietly.

‘OK, what if your brother is fit and healthy when I deliver him,’ I said: ‘I can do this and I will because I never want you to come looking for me and I also don’t want you to give out any information about me. The money I need, but I also need a clear get away from here.'

Now I had his full attention.

'My brother's health can be restored to him?' he asked me.

'Yes, fully given back to him,' was my reply.

'My oath on it if you do it, you will have time to leave freely.' He said: 'Also I will give something in return if you do give my brother his health back, then I will protect you. My family will be in debt to you. I then told him of an address in the north east of Italy where his brother would be hidden away. He'd told no one at all and I knew this. It takes only a few minutes up in the sky to get what I want from anyone. How did you get that address?'

It was my secret. Maybe he'll work it out.

My strength and power was growing daily. It was time for us go our ways.

'Mario, don't forget to call me from France,' I said: 'Call me between 7.30 pm and 8.00 pm.'

At that I headed back to the hotel. It was up to them to move the money. Three days I waited. I helped mend nets. It helps to harden your skin on your fingers. Business was done between us, in secret. The fishermen, even the folk in the village knew that I was different, but they were beginning to trust me. Even the little ones were now allowed to mimic me whenever I exercised. I laughed whenever they fell over. They sensed that I would not do them any harm.

I had just gotten ready to go out on the third night when my phone rang promptly on 7.30 pm.

'It's Mario here, I have been told to give you two words, he said: 'Day Mover.'

He'd delivered the money. That was the words Frieda had been told to say to him.

'Have a safe journey back and enjoy yourself after,' I said. 'I will be gone Mario.'

I then put the phone down. Tomorrow would be my last day here. Tonight was going to be a party and the village people didn't know about it. I walked across to the bar. All the regulars were there and I gave the landlord an envelope.

'This is a free night for everyone,' I said.

When he looked in the envelope he understood why. Over a thousand dollars. The place just erupted from that point. I came close that night, close enough to being totally pissed out of my mind. Only knowing that I had work to do in the morning stopped me.

I rose with the alarm clock just before dawn. All my clothes were packed and I moved them to where I'd planned. Slotted another envelope into my key box for the hotel manager. Then back up and I relaxed. Up and away very fast indeed.

Down to the prison, into the medical block to arrive above the bed of a very frail man. Looking at him you would have thought nothing about the life that he'd led prior to his incarceration. He had been a power indeed in more ways than one. Looking down I could see that he did not have long to live. I touched him and took him up and out of there. Keeping him very calm and at the same time, forcing the disease out of his body. I was thinking about my father. How I wish I'd known then that I could heal a person with the power I had. He would still have been alive. It took just over fifteen minutes to cross from Sicily to the mainland. The car was there. An impatient Franco stood at the side smoking. His brother was inside the car before he knew it and a startled Franco was peering inside as if he couldn't believe his eyes. He jumped in and the car sped away.

That was it. It was over and done with. I turned in the sky to observe a light hovering in the far distance and then moving backwards and forwards.

My girl in Sicily was up and about early. I headed straight for her. To tell her I was leaving today. I asked her to meet me at the hotel as soon as possible.

Watch your children well I told the girl on the last day. I gave her the bike and signed it over officially. She and the two old men were the only three who knew which way I was heading.

I paid well over the odds for a twenty five foot motor/sailing boat. It had belonged to the two men. I also gave them a letter to deliver to the old man with the stick. Do not question them or ask them were the words on the envelope. They needed someone to look after the money that I'd given to them for the boat. He would understand all right because I put him back on his feet instead of putting him six feet under the soil.

I called George Delacourt, to ask him to set up a money transfer to Malta. He then told me excitedly that Anna was pregnant. It was something that they'd always wanted, more children. He even offered to fly over to Malta with the family for a holiday. Now that was a change in the man. I declined, for one reason and that was to be certain that no one followed me across the water from Sicily.

Chapter 13

BM

I had a really good break in the weather and that evening when all was quiet and still, I made the breakout. Heading south. The total of foreign movers was growing fast. Except for those back home. I had two more English, one Swiss, three French and twenty six Italian (Sicilian) and I would make that number grow. In Sicily, I was a marked man, but only with the French name. No one but the two old fishermen were aware of my new identity that George had sent to me by post and it was staying that way. I'd practised signing the name by torchlight and saying it over in my mind. Name, address and birth date. Thirty miles or so and I could see lights appearing in the distance. Gradually they were getting closer. I anchored about 200 yards out and waited for dawn.

A quick shift into hover and I was away to find the best place to moor the boat. It was two islands really. Large one is Malta and the smaller one is Gozo. I picked the smaller because of the fishing village alongside the daily ferry run. It was far more suitable for me. Back to the boat and pulled the anchor up.

Two hours later I was tied up and asking in English for customs. I wanted to clear immigration at the same time. I had the boat checked out and my passport was duly stamped. A couple of beauties are walking up and down. In fact the more I looked around the more beautiful girls I could see. Paradise on legs. I'm definitely going to enjoy this.

Next step the bank and followed up with a phone call to arrange a transfer. I've still the equivalent of £500 pounds in my pocket, so I left all the details with the manager at the bank and told him to expect a transfer in my name. Preparation was far better than just going in blind, asking about money or to see if it was there. Leave it for a week.

I kept £50 in my pocket and stashed the rest on board. Locked the cabin and headed for the ferry terminal. No sooner on the ferry and then your off it. An old London Bus was waiting so I jumped on to see where it went.

Valletta, capital of Malta was interesting to see. Many, many churches. They say for everyday, there's a church on Malta. Try counting them. Always building somewhere. Every last little bit of land has its use. For the first time in along while, I started to hide bits of clothing and nail cuttings. I walked everywhere, stopping to see the views and dropping in cafes for a cold drink. Then back to Gozo where it's far more open. I hid plastic bags all over because I had a feeling that something was coming my way.

Just a feeling about something. It was warm at this time of year. The full force of tourists would be starting in a month's time. Apache Ville (Paceville), that's the night area for the young and the old, wanting to be young. Just sitting in a bar and having a quiet time, just is not possible. Me, I'm eyeing up the girls and they know it, because they are there for the boys.

Some are holiday reps getting ready for the season. I've already talked to half a dozen. Questions asked and answered. Boat in Gozo, alone and free. Two out of three would not believe I had a boat. Normal for them not to believe, due to it being a likely chat up line.

Who cares, the invitation is to come and see. I've money that they do know. Paula, she takes up the challenge. A day off for her tomorrow, so she's on the prowl. I'm her choice, and she's curious to find out the truth. No strings attached to anything. I'm intoxicated. So is she.

Just to take her back to her place would have been enough for the first night, but I was going to prove a point. The boat. Sure enough we arrived back on Gozo and I walked her to the boat. The surprise for her was to see me jump on board and unlock the cabin.

'No strings,' she said and then jumped all over me.

I had a damn good night. The next night was totally different because I'd proved my words about the boat and Paula the nymph had spread the word. I could now take it easy with whom I wanted, a Maltese girl or two would be fine if the opportunity arose. I had more than just a couple of drinking friends throughout the weekdays until Friday night. That was when the locals came in. Some really good looking girls. I had a little circle of friends by then. You're not the average tourist when you have a boat and money. These people had to work for a living and for the reps it would be a hard season. For the girls I was a bit soft with regards to drinks but the boys found out that I was no easy touch. They got one drink and sometimes two if they were lucky. It's sorted out easy though, when you go for drinks and don't bring back a third. The message to them, don't push your luck.

Another thing that helped me was the punch ball machine. Money in the slot, then pull the ball down. Hit it hard to get a score. Under my shirt they could see that I was well formed. With my sleeves rolled up they could see the muscle. I was watching some guys trying to hit that ball. All laughing at each other, each trying to beat the records set up. It was a male rep who suggested that we have a go. Now he did have a little muscle on him, so I joined him in front of the machine. Sure enough that rep got his name on the scoreboard. Before I had my turn I asked one question.

'What if I break it?'

They all just stood there and laughed.

'Seriously,' I said: 'What happens if I break it?'

One of the guys called an attendant over and put that question to him. It's not possible to do, but you can always try your luck and he laughed.

'OK,' I said: 'You asked for it.'

In went the coin and down with the chain. Ball steady and still. Laughter was still in my ears as I hit the ball. The glass at the back smashed and the lights went out. There was no spinning arrow to register the score. I returned to my seat. You could have heard a pin drop. The attendant was over at the bar talking to the barman. He came over a few seconds later and loudly demanded that I pay for the damage.

'Go play with yourself,' I said to him.

He just stood there unsure of himself for a few seconds and then stormed off back to the bar. The barman or owner whoever he was came over and started to rant and rave, threatening to call the police.

It was a voice over my shoulder that shut him up. I didn't turn at the sound of it but I could hear perfectly what she said to him. He stood there for a second or two and about turned and walked away. Remember, I'd asked first about breaking it and this person behind me had heard the response from the attendant. A really soft hand was on my shoulder as if to protect me. I glanced over my shoulder. This one was not your average, no way at all. She was dark haired, brown eyed and just the one I needed. She had come looking for something, as we all go looking at a young age. I asked her to sit, but she just walked away and sat with some other girls.

Throughout that evening, I was only half listening to the conversation. My mind was on the girl. Occasionally, I'd look across at her and I could see the merriment in her eyes and face. She knew what she was doing, teasing me. Making me be the one to go to her. How the hell was I going to keep my pride with this one?

She wanted to dominate the situation her way. She was well aware of her womanhood. OK, let's play the game, I thought.

'Any of you fancy a sail tomorrow?' I said to the group around me: 'The weather forecast is really good.'

Three bit the hook. Two of the boys and a British girl.

'How do we get over to Gozo?' one said: 'We're skint, until pay day.'

'I'll be across at eight sharp, next to the ferry jetty,' I said: 'I took twenty pounds out of my pocket and placed it on the table. That's your drinks for the night.'

At that I was up and out of there before anyone realised it. Straight out but not to head away from the place. It was around the back of the building, into the shadow outside. I could just see them sat there and I was just able to listen into what was being said. I could hear them discussing me.

A boat mentioned more than once, twenty five foot and well built. My age, they estimated it at around eighteen and the comments on how well I was built. A couple of girls said I was too big for comfort and too strong, as was demonstrated with the ball. Yes, but did you also see how fast he did it. He knew he'd break it before he did it. He's one strong person that I wouldn't like to cross.

Money, he certainly seems to have plenty, money to burn if he wanted to. English, but speaks French and Italian too. Speaks all three as if he were a native. Name, now that was the queer part of it all, to all of them. I'd never given out my name. Even Paula didn't know my name.

By this time the girl and her friends had joined in with the conversation. Why did he leave so quickly, and this came from the girl I wanted. One of the lads gave her a good answer to that.

'You frightened him off,' he said.

That voice would be in free beer for a week. The one with a few muscles, Dave was his name. He was on the trip tomorrow.

'Not my type,' she said to them. All of them could hear the uncertainty in her words.

'Oh yes, not your type is he, well why were you looking at him half the night then. We could all see it,' said Dave: 'Come on Maria, we all know what you're like with the boys.'

At that I shot back around the front and came straight back in.

'Dave, I forgot something, see if you can round up some food and such, beer included,' I said and I dropped another fifty pounds in his lap. Turned and walked out. That sum of money meant nothing to me, but to them it was a fortune. Money can buy most anything, but true love.

It turned out to be a really good day for sailing. They'd managed to get food from a late night store. Cans of beer stuck in a couple of carrier bags and enough for a couple of days really. I'd been there waiting for them at eight sharp. Off we went for a sail around the island. Dave had done it before and we took turns on the tiller. Dave had tried to give me the change from last night shortly after we left.

"Keep it,' I said to him loud enough for the others to hear. My plan I hoped was working. I wanted Maria. We pulled in at one little beach. Just to laze about and relax. The sun was just starting to give out the start of summer heat. The day had to end though and by six I'd dropped them off. One beer is all I drank all day.

'Can't sail and drink,' I said. I was setting an example of how I normally ran my life in the daytime and not as they'd got to know me by night.

'Take the beer with you Dave. I don't need it on the boat.' I told him: 'See you all tonight.'

Eight o'clock was normal gathering time. For me it would be around ten, even though it was Saturday. Time would be given them to discuss the day. Now Dave would just have to dip in to buy some drinks to night before I arrived. He'd have no choice because I'd given him the means. Also nearly two weeks worth of beer was in his flat.

At ten I walked in to see a couple of hands wave me over to the group. All there, including Maria. She'd taken the bait. I squeezed in opposite her. She was looking at me all right and something was different in that look. Drinks appeared and for once I'd not paid directly, but indirectly through Dave. He was all right really.

He was proving to be one generally good person to be with. Known to everyone for his carefree way of life at night but a hard worker for one of the holiday companies. Anyway it was general chat about the day's sailing and then around to work. Who was doing what and how. Then a few questions came my way. By the way, what's your name Dave asked?

'Je suis, Richard Martin,' I replied. This in a perfect accent and out came my French passport to hand over to Maria. She was looking at me as I gave her it.

'Why do you speak perfect English with a northern accent though?' This came back from a British girl.

'Parents, English and French", was my instant reply.

'Italian then,' came from another girl.

'Just left there,' I said.

That had certainly settled another mystery.

'What do I do for a living?' one asked.

'Nothing I replied.

'Where do you get your money?' another asked.

It was typical for the British to be so nosy.

'It's none of your business but I just collect it from the bank when ever I require some.'

That silenced them. They must have thought my parents millionaires or something. Maria smiled across and just said to them all.

‘He’s right, if he collects it from a bank,’

She was quick and caught me fast.

‘Which one,’ she said.

‘Tomorrow on Gozo, if you’d like to come,’ I said.

The challenge was out and she couldn’t refuse. A dance had started on a small area set aside for it.

‘Can you dance?” I asked her.

Dave heard me and butted in quickly. ‘She a real mover, any dance but especially at rock & roll,’ he said: ‘None of us can keep up with her.’

That got him a really bad look. Maria was still trying to keep the upper hand. I just sat back to watch others dancing. Two can play at this, I thought.

Wait until you do start and then you’ll have a shock in return. I went off to the toilet about two minutes later and coming back, she was up there dancing with another girl. I stopped by the bar. Ordered some drinks and stood watching for a moment. Done on purpose, while my back was turned. A definite way to show me that she was in control. She was I think showing off a little, as if to say to me that if I could follow her moves then maybe she’d allow me a little closer. She was fast and definitely in tune with the rhythm.

I went and sat down to finish my drink with the gang. All of them were watching her but me. I’d seen what she could do and she wasn’t going to be a problem. Little did she ever dream that she was doing was perfect, just like a female bird challenging the males to show their bright colours. Who would take her up on it? Me. But not yet because I would delay it for just a little while longer.

Another drink in my hand by now, I'd bought another round at the bar. At the finish of the next dance she came back and sat down. Bright eyed and flushed, a smile at me, as if to say, can you beat that.

'You missed a beat half way through,' I said to her.

I'd spotted the hesitation from her friend. Her smile dropped and a thought came to her.

'Show me,' she said.

At that I stood and walked onto the floor, not even stopping to see if she'd followed me.

'Jitter Bug, Bee Bop or just plain old Jive,' I said turning to her.

At that a funny expression was on her face as if somehow, the tables had turned.

'Jive,' was her reply.

At that we commenced to dance. I caught her rhythm immediately. As she went over and round to the right I spun under and left to meet her face to face on the turn forwards. On the side turn I reversed away and calmly waved to our friends. Then I spun back forward to take both hands in mine to do a double hand over. I taught her new things even on that first dance. Clapping and shouting began around us. We were now fully alive, aware of our mating ritual. Could Maria move, going on and on. One dance stopped and the next started, off again, and again. I glanced up to check the height of that room. High enough for me and as she spun on a single turn around I did a back flip to land on my feet just catching her hand in time to spin her back again. Let me tell you something.

With rock and roll generally, it's the woman who will normally stop first, because she is doing the hardest part of the dance. Most men just stand and swirl the woman around and back without moving a foot either way. Well Maria danced six times before she had to stop for a breather and by that time we'd both brought the house down with cheers and clapping. She just fell into my arms and buried her head on my shoulder. Trembling with the effort of dancing so much and so fast. Her muscles were vibrating through me, as I held her tight. I let her relax and then, only then did I take her back to sit down and it was beside me, not opposite and her hand for a moment in mine.

Maria's head was now on my shoulder, relaxed and calm. She was telling her girlfriends without a word spoken to them, that she was claiming me.

Chapter 14

Dave

Although this young man appeared in our circle, none of us thought for a minute that he really own a boat. We all thought that he was an early tourist out to score. We thought that we were taking him for a ride. Paula, our resident nymph, could not resist taking him on for a night. The next day though, we found out that the boat was there and he owned it. Money, he had, that much we couldn't believe it. I tried it on a few times but his message came through clear enough. He just didn't bring a drink back. Not a word at all from him. With the girls, you could see the difference. Just to sit next to him was as if something was not quiet right. It felt like electric, yet I couldn't place it.

The night of the punch ball was a turning point for all of us. I classed myself as a strong person, bigger than average, but sat beside him I looked puny. His arm muscles just rippled. He walked light for all of his size. He just stood there and asked us all.

'What if I break it?'

When he said it I knew even then that he would. Every one laughed at him, even me, but in my mind I could see it happening. What he'd actual asked for, was permission to break it. They gave him that permission so he did it. What I saw, I couldn't believe. He'd actually hit it with the tips of his fingers. If I'd mentioned it to anyone they'd have laughed at me. No way would I get in this one's way. Tip toe around him for sure, that's me from now on. Somehow or other a sailing trip was arranged. He dropped the money on the table on purpose. I can still see it now, how he was up and away quickly. He let us all have our chat about him. We all voiced our opinions and suddenly he was back in our midst with some more. He knew that the first amount was enough and he just put the boot in with the rest. It took me the rest of the evening to figure it out. How the heck can you tell people that he'd been listening to us through an open window. What proof did I have to give anyone.

That next day sailing showed he knew perfectly how to sail. Navigation he talked about it as if it were natural for him. Latitude, Longitude, D'Lat, D'long and Distance. He explained that latitude is the angular distance north or south of the equator measured from the centre of the earth. I had to look it up in a book. He could just quote them all and I'm sure he could put them all into good use correctly.

Maria, was prick teasing as usual. Not one man I know had got anywhere with her. She only allowed a kiss and that was it. We teased her about staring at him and he at her. Side long glances at each other, casual like but something was happening for sure. I felt the change in her attitude. We watched him go to the toilet and then Maria get on that floor to dance. It hit me about then because normally, Maria only showed up occasionally. This was twice in two nights.

I watched him come back. He paused for a fraction before going to the bar. It had been hard to catch that pause and even now I think it was his eyes that paused and not his body. I was only half watching Maria dance. My eyes were on him but I didn't want him to know. He came back and sat down. All he'd seen for a few seconds was Maria dancing. Once he sat down he never even bothered to look any more. He even asked me if I was all right. I can still see it now, the way Maria came back and sat down opposite him. She did it on purpose. I heard him tell her about the missed beat. I thought she'd give him a mouthful, but she challenged him instead. Something wasn't right. It hit me again for the second time. They'd somehow both been taking each other on and we'd missed it. This was going to be another challenge between them. Who would win this one?

Others in that room had caught on, I'm sure of it. He'd taken us in hook, line and sinker. I just knew that I was going to see something fantastic happen. Never to this day have I seen a person rock & roll like he did that night.

On that first dance he took control and then he started to teach Maria how to really go with that music. To see him turn and spin with her was unbelievable. To actually see him do that back somersault was beyond me and he still caught her on the spin. Never have I ever seen this place so quiet and it lasted for a few dances. How people cheered them in the end. He'd won the challenge and it showed in Maria's actions.

BM

Closing time and we had to leave, Maria knew that there was not a chance of me getting back to Gozo.

'Where are you going to stay the night?' she asked me.

It was two thirty in the morning and not that warm.

'I'll have a quick kip on a bench,' I told her.

I was walking her home. At her door, we stood kissing for the first time. Not long though and certainly not long enough for me.

'What are you doing tomorrow?' I asked her.

'Don't you mean today,' she said smiling up at me.

'Alright today,' I said: 'I've to go to the bank on Gozo, will you be there.'

'Yes, I'll see you in Gozo,' she said and the door closed.

'Yes, yes, yes,' I said to myself.

I had made it. It was not warm that morning on a bench, waiting for the first ferry. I should have brought the boat over. I booked into a hotel at eight that morning. I explained that I had a boat tied up and that I wanted the room for two weeks minimum.

I collected some clothes from the boat and returned to the hotel. I would have to get all my clothes cleaned at the laundry and buy some new things in the morning. Damn, damn it, I suddenly thought. It's Sunday and the banks are shut. Wait a minute, who really was the crafty one now? The tables had been turned around again. She damn well knew it. Who had reeled in whom? The dancing had been in my favour, but she'd known all along that the bank would be closed on a Sunday.

Would she come, I had to wait a couple of hours to find out. I wandered down to wait for the ferry. It came in, my heart started to race as if I'd been exercising. Next second it leaped as I spotted her on the gangway.

We met. I held her hand. A little peck of a kiss and we headed for my boat. As soon as she saw it I knew it was just right for her. Ideal for two. I'd planned to take us out for a sail but the weather was bad. The boat was clean, well maintained and that she told me. I wasn't to know at that time but she'd been brought up with boats all her life. Her father had a bigger boat than this. He'd always had them ever since she could remember.

'What shall we do for the day, seeing as the banks are closed and the seas too rough?' I asked.

She smiled; 'I have my costume. Maybe we can find somewhere to sit out of the wind and talk.'

That was more than I could wish for and right next to a wall on the beach we found an area out of sight. Out of the wind, but still in the sun. Chatting about this and that it came out that she had known all along the bank would be closed. Winding me up, but then dancing with me, had changed her mind again. Never had she enjoyed dancing so much before. I told her it was only half of what I could show her with rock & roll. How there are different ways to turn and twist to break the speed down, instead of just turning all the while. She was looking closely at me at one point and then asked me to tell her why I had come to Malta, and who was I really.

'You wouldn't believe me if I told you the truth,' I simply said to her.

'Try me anyway,' she said quietly.

So I laid back and told her that I could fly through the sky.

'No the truth,' she said.

'It is the truth,' and I looked straight at her as I said it.

Now she was really looking at me, as if to say, just keep going on with this and I will be leaving. I told her what I thought she was thinking and she just nodded her head.

'If you want the truth, go to sleep and I will take you up in to the sky and show you wonders.'

‘I wish,’ she said.

‘Remember the last two days, how I believe we have been challenging each other. Now it’s my direct challenge to you, go to sleep and find out who I am.’

At that, she simply stood up and said goodbye. I walked slowly behind her to the terminal and watched her get on the ferry.

She was looking directly at me as the ferry left and saw me turn and run up towards the hotel. Upstairs quickly because she’d left her towel. That I slung on the bed.

I relaxed and felt myself transform and away I went up and across to a little stash of my cloths, under the quay on Malta. I was waiting for the ferry just as it arrived. I waited until she had her foot on dry land before I called her.

‘Maria.’

Up and around went her head towards me and in the next second she’d ran to me. Into my arms and holding tight.

Then she looked up. ‘How?’

‘You asked for the truth and I told the truth,’ I said to her.

‘No, it’s not possible, it’s not possible.’

‘All you have to do is sleep,’ I said.

She again broke away from me and ran for the bus, not looking back and I heard her sobbing. I crossed back over to Gozo. Back to the hotel and up to the room.

Went into hover again and shot up in to the sky. Here I could holler and shout to vent all of my frustration without a soul hearing me. A light was showing across the waters, in Sicily. I’d missed it at first. I checked the time and zoomed off. Faster and faster, so fast that I nearly overshot her. How are you, I put across to my Sicilian girl, and then she told me that for a week she'd been trying to get my attention. Her grandfather had heard rumours that a search was on for me. They knew about the boat but not the name of it. No, he didn't know what she could do and she'd never tell anyone either. At that I gave her my thanks and had to rush because time was running out.

'Get down it'll be dark soon,' I projected just before I left. Off I went fast. I made it with a few minutes to spare. The darkness came.

Maria.

I'd heard from friends that there was a strange guy at the bar. Paying for drinks all week and that he was supposed to have a boat in Gozo. Another typical tourist, wanting to spend all his yearly earnings on a couple of weeks holiday. They say he's not what you call tall, but his shoulders were massive.

I went for a look. You couldn't miss him. They were hitting the punch ball again and showing off as usual. Trying to beat each other for that magic first place. I watched Dave hit it. Sure he always had his name on the score board. It was only when he walked forwards that I saw the guy for the first time. I couldn't believe it when he asked them what would happen if he broke it. I stood there with the rest of them and laughed. He just took it all. Here was the tourist making a fool of himself. OK, he looked above average in size. Another week and he'll be gone like all of them. No one could believe it when he did break the machine. I heard perfectly what he told Manuel to do. The manager, George, should have known better than to threaten him with the police. Especially knowing that I was there. Only George knew that it was my father who owned the place.

I tried all night to keep from looking at him after that. Nice looking, that was definite. Big across the shoulders. That was an absolute fact. Around eighteen. Maybe a teasing session in it for me. I could hear them planning and listened to it all. Let them have fun with him. He's nice though, yes a teasing time would suit me again. I'll come in tomorrow for another look. Maybe a dance. I'll get the gossip about the day's sailing. Fancy though, leaving them with that amount of money.

I came in to tease him all right but the more I looked at him the more I thought about something not being quite right. Dave was bragging about how good he was at sailing. The day's outing had gone well for them. They were all asking him where he came from. He's not the average person when he can speak three languages, that's for sure. The way he told them about his money. It did shut them up. An account at the bank in Gozo. Not for a tourist there isn't. He caught me on the hop when he asked me to go to the bank with him. No harm in it, maybe have a nice day with him.

Sure I liked to dance and I did purposely get up when he went to the toilet. He was correct when he said I'd missed a beat. My biggest shock though, was to dance with him. Never had I felt so alive and natural dancing with anyone else. He controlled me all the time. I could feel the power of his strength, yet it was so gentle. I lost myself to him at that moment and for me it was the first time that I had ever lost control. I want this man. I want him so badly it hurt me. Even if half of what he'd told us was true, I'd still have him.

I met him as arranged. The boat was well maintained. I'll give him that. Up until the time when I began to ask him where he came from, I'd enjoyed his company. Just go to sleep and I'll show you how to fly and who I really am. I told him to tell the truth. I just left him to his lies. The last view I had of him was from the ferry when he was running to his hotel. He called to me as I stepped off the ferry on the Malta side. The shock hit me to see him waiting there. I had fallen in love with him, but I still could not believe what he was trying to tell me. I ran to him crying and yet he still said the same thing again.

BM

I was slowly getting intoxicated, just like a normal young tourist. They were used to it and left me alone in my sorrows. I remember vaguely going to bed. I awoke late with a hang over. My first ever. My head was really pounding. The only way I could think of curing it was to start my exercises. This I did next to the boat. Stripped down to some shorts, bare foot and I started up. I started up and as I built up the routine my head became clearer. I did a slow hand stand and then transferred to just one hand. Perfect balance, mind in tune with my body, and I held myself in that position. I let a full minute pass and then lowered myself gently down. Numerous inquisitive people were staring. Maria stood there with them just looking at me, no smile and no wave from her hand. I stood up to show them a perfect back somersault. Then jumped lightly down onto the boat and into the cabin.

At that moment it was her choice, not mine. I'd told her the truth. If she went away from me again, I would not chase her, I would leave and that would be it. I felt the boat rock as she came aboard. There, silhouetted in the hatchway and then in, to sit opposite me. Not a word passed between us for a few minutes. It was as if we'd had a lover's quarrel.

'The bank is open,' she whispered.

I grabbed my wallet and passport. I took her hand and pulled her with me. Up onto the quay and we headed to the bank. She listened to the conversation at the bank; £5,000 had been transferred and I withdrew £500 of it. I headed for my room with her in tow. Inside, I turned and pulled her close. Just a long kiss, our first long one, and we both fell back on the bed. I held her there, not trying to make advances. Just a kiss given to her now and then.

'What I saw you doing earlier was so unbelievable,' she whispered to me: 'So wonderful to watch. I am beginning to believe it.'

'Believe me, you will fly soon,' I whispered.

I could feel her relaxing, neither of us had slept much the night before. It would come soon. So peaceful, that we could hear the birds in the background, people walking by the window on the path below. So nice to feel her against me, to feel her slow breathing, steady but firm.

I could finally feel her asleep in my arms and I relaxed and disappeared from the bed. My light was gleaming bright and a gentle touch brought her with me into the room. I held her light, dim for the moment, and then I allowed it to grow brighter.

Maria

I could not eat my evening meal or sleep that night. I just tossed and turned thinking of what had passed between us over the last few days. The ball, his dancing, the money, the boat and the way he made me feel when I touched him. I could feel what I thought was an electric current coming from him and yet there was no shock. I'm going back. I need to know.

BM

If only humans could see us, I thought. In what spectrum is this light was also in my mind. I sensed when Maria looked around. She knew that everything I had told her was the truth. We could really fly. Maria was obtaining knowledge from me. I let her read so much from my mind. Who I was and where I was from. A little bit of my childhood. My money and where it had come from. She discovered about the others, that I'd changed, and why I'd changed them. I gave her everything, except the power to heal.

We both went outside to soar and twirl. Up and down, all around the island. The light of a girl across the water could be seen. I explained who she was. Maria descended to the bed. I followed and appeared beside her. Not a word was spoken. We were as one together, sweaty, hot, sticky and loving each other within just a few seconds. She was there with me for a while afterwards and then disappeared on her own. I let her go; she had to learn.

An hour later she appeared, a little quiet for some reason, and then she explained where she'd been. She'd made a journey to get information. She had been jealous of the girl across the water and had gone to see her. Now, she knew she had no reason to be jealous. She dragged me back to bed and we made love like two perfect animals.

We spent a really glorious week travelling backwards and forwards. I moved the boat over to the mainland, Valletta harbour to make things easier for us. I found out why Maria never gave men a chance to get to know her. Her parents were wealthy and she'd never let on to her friends. She'd been looking for someone who did not need her parents help for the future. At last, I hoped to have someone forever, to share what I'd had on my own,, for years. It was early morning when it all changed.

Maria

I caught the early ferry with some tourists going over for a visit. Just as we were landing I looked towards where the boat was tied up. A knot of people were standing about watching something. It took me another five minute before I found out what it was. He was doing exercises, balance, poise and a karate style movement of which I'd never seen before. I know because I'd had lesson in self defence. Then to see him balancing just on one hand and then to change over from one hand to the other.

He just stood up after that and seemed to flip over backwards with no effort at all, just as he'd done while we danced. He'd seen me but never even acknowledged me. I had the message. It was my choice and I took the first step. We ended up on the bed and yet he never attempted to fondle me at all. Just lying there and holding onto me, talking quietly to me.

I let my mind relax and it was the lack of sleep that finally overcame my body and mind. I awoke in the air. At first I felt just that little bit of fear and then it passed. I could hear his voice in my mind and looking around I could see a bright sphere of light. I could also feel a light brightening around myself. Telling me what I could do. How to do it. Twirling up and down and through the sky. Then we descended again. We made love and it was everything I had ever hoped for.

Dave

I went to have a talk with him. I was thinking about Maria. For some reason I missed her on the ferry. I could see something happening and I watched the last part of his routine and then I watched Maria follow him onto the boat. I gave them ten minutes before I stepped on board. There was no one there which was astonishing. I sat at a café wondering what to do about it. I was frightened. I even had a couple of beers. I just couldn't believe it. I had sat there for over two hours when they just appeared again, getting off the boat hand in hand. To see her kiss him was unbelievable. Somehow they had still been onboard but where? This guy was something else.

BM

It was only pure luck that made me hide my passport and other bits on the boat or was it intuition?

I'd rented a flat and we'd moved in against her parents wishes. That had quietened Maria down for a few days. She went to see them both daily and told me that they were coming around to accepting the situation. That brightened her up and it made it easier for me.

It was on a Tuesday morning, early and I was opening the balcony shutters ready for our morning sky dance. Just as I turned round to speak to her I felt a tremendous and was flung back into the room. I was almost unconscious. I could hear Maria screaming dimly in the background. There was blood everywhere. We must go, I was trying to tell her, we must go up into the sky.

My message was getting through to her and in spite of the pain. I was trying to relax my mind. I'd been shot high in the chest on the left hand side. Later I realised that turning to speak to her, had probably saved my life.

It took me a long time to relax and I quivered out really slowly. Maria was beside me by this time. There seemed to be sparks flying from me in all directions. Every time they hit something it burst into flames.

We moved out slowly upwards. Glancing down we could see people running for cover from the sparks. Never had this happened before. People having heard a loud bang had come outside to find themselves defenceless against flames shooting into the sky. Wc were slowly moving upwards. The flat below was ablaze. We were going to be homeless. Slowly I commenced to settle. Maria was assisting me with her own powers. Keeping me calm. Not allowing me to drift earthwards. For over an hour we just held each other until I was totally healed.

'Maria, appear at home quietly and then meet me at the boat,' I told her.

Off she went as fast as she could. I had to find a cache of clothes under the quay again before I managed it back to the boat. Maria appeared breathless and then we just held each other tight. Her parents hadn't known that she was in the house and when she appeared from the bedroom they'd had a shock.

I had to find out who had shot me and why? I need to get to the airport fast, to check the flights. I grabbed hold of the engine cowling on the outboard and lifted it out of the water. On a tag was a spare key to the boat hatch. I then took a screwdriver and removed a small cover. Inside was my original passport with the other identities and some spare cash.

'Now listen to me carefully Maria,' I said: 'It was me that they wanted. This is the phone number of the booth over there.'

I pointed at the phone booth.

'Get to the airport and check all the flight times to Sicily. Ring me, I'll be waiting for your call.'

A taxi arrived within five minutes and she left. I was pacing up and down outside the box thinking. Ten minutes to the airport. Five minutes to check. The phone suddenly rang and I saw the plane in the sky as she told me that one had just left.

'Listen, go to the flat and act surprised. 'We were on the boat all night,' if you're asked and I returned to the boat. The gun wound had gone, not a damn mark on me.

I'm away quickly and as small as I can make myself. Up I go very fast and heading towards that plane. I'm fast overtaking it and I slow down. It's only a quick hop by plane from Malta to Sicily.

There I am waiting just above the bottom steps. Checking out each face descending. Oh yes, I found him. The one who liked to push about old men. But who had sent him? Surely not the old man with the stick. I watched him enter the terminal and shot up and over to the other side to see if someone was meeting him. At that precise moment I had a visitor at my side.

Chapter 15

BM

The girl was there.

'It's my cousin,' she projected to me spotting him coming out of the building: 'He's nasty and likes to hurt people. He even hit me once.'

'You can have the pleasure later,' I said back across to her. I told her what had taken place that morning. Sure enough a car was waiting for him. He got in and away the car sped. Not towards the village but away and up to another big house. I'd warned this one and now he'd find out that my vengeance was long. To be up there defenceless only feeling them as they pulled you apart. Freeing the ghosts of the past, to roam for a night amongst the people below. I'd make this island suffer and tremble before the week was out.

'Are you ready to take your revenge?' I asked her: 'It will be permanent for all of them.'

This would be the second government hunting for me and they would keep looking for years. Or maybe it was the Mafia. It made no difference to me. They had been warned not to mess with me ever.

We both descended. We needed to study the faces of all the men below. To mark them well in our minds, so to recognise them all tomorrow morning. I followed one car from that place. Then back to catch another leaving. They were laughing and congratulating the marksman. It was afternoon by the time I was satisfied. She would be waiting for me in the early hours of tomorrow.

I travelled back towards Malta. In the distance I saw a light coming up to meet me. And as we met, the message was that she couldn't wait any longer and had to come and met me. The fire had already been blamed on an electrical fault due to the people speaking about the sparks. We were considered lucky to be alive. She'd told the police that I'd be in with her to sign the report later and that I was at the other end of the island with a friend fishing off the rocks. We circled slowly around the boat before descending. Down we went and then made love. We were growing closer; the problems do that. I finally told her what I had to do. Why, if I left it, they would be back for more. Next time it could be her in the line of fire. I only warn people once. She cried herself to sleep that night, laid in my arms.

I was away before Maria woke up. I looked back as I arrived on Sicily. She was up there in the sky. I could feel her looking over towards me. Another light was coming in from the side. Behind her was a really dim one hung suspended.

'First one down,' she said.

At that we both split up and gradually there were fourteen dim lights hung up in the sky. Each one hovering above the house from where they had been taken. Slowly they started to drift about. Franco had not been at the house yesterday. The next one would be the last and down we both went together. Both of us touched him at the same time. We let the shock come to him.

'Beaten any old men or young girls lately?' I asked him.

He screamed and we just left him there. Just above a young girl of no more than fifteen. She could not hear him screaming and as we left him and flew away, his voice dimming as the distance grew greater. I said good bye and back I went to Maria.

The reports in the papers over the next two to three days were quite some reading. Fifteen men had disappeared and ghosts had run havoc through the night. Frightening people, so badly that many refused to leave their homes even in the daytime. An old man's picture was in the paper. It was reported that he'd warned people to behave and not to mess with a certain person. An unknown visitor, one who had just stopped for the winter. All he'd wanted from people was to be left alone in peace. No he could not give a name to the person. Yes, he had met him. So had many others, but no one knew his name. With him at his side on the photograph in the paper, was a young good looking girl.

Franco had kept his word. It was not a rumour but a telephone call from an unknown source. He had spoken to the grandfather and he in turn had spoken to the girl. There was also a photograph of her in the paper. Me, I'd ignored her warning. Never again would I do that again.

'Is that her, in the paper?' was the question asked over my shoulder by Maria.

I just smiled back over my own shoulder at her.

'Is it over now?' she then asked me.

'I really don't think so,' I replied: 'I don't think it will ever be over.'

She hugged me tightly and kissed me on the head. Why, you may ask. Why did I destroy so many men at the same time and all together. I'll tell you why. My two old friends were tortured, that's why I did it. They are both dead and yet they knew nothing. The cousin had arranged it all. The full betrayal of two men who were very close to me in a short period of time. They all paid a high price. More will follow them somewhere and in the future. Beware of me for I will end up close to you.

I'll give you now the name of this young girl. 'El--------a. That's all I can give out. She married a certain young policeman. He has moved quickly up the ranks. They have five children and the eldest now have children of their own. He is possibly the only one who could have given out a name. El--------a got to him first and took him for a flying lesson. Then, she married him soon after. He never had my real name though.

Day Movers are in Sicily at this very moment. The family is growing stronger. I have been back twice in recent years. No abuse of what they can do. No abuse whatsoever.

I'm eighteen. What is the future going to be? I have so much money now that it's not worth me counting it. The boat was sold within four days. It was the boat that had given me away. My new name though was not known. Only my friends had that and yet they did not place me as the person in the papers. To them I was in Malta and not in Sicily. I was just a rich kid to them. Maria and I talked for long hours about what I could do and what she now had the power to do. We were in love. I became accepted by her parents but the word marriage kept cropping up. We talked this subject through. If and I mean if, one of us got caught in any way, then the other would be caught in the same trap. What we decided though was to give ourselves a date. A date in the future to split up, for good. Yes, even though we loved each other.

Both of us knew that it would not last. We planned it together. Not letting on to anyone at all. To every one else it seemed as if we were made for each other. Over the next three months we had also to choose some more Day Movers. That was in our plans. Now Dave was courting another Maltese girl. He had by this time become a good friend of mine. If and when they announced an engagement both would be chosen. This came about quicker than we expected. A shotgun wedding. Maria told me about it because Dave's girlfriend had come sobbing to her one morning. She wanted to know what she could do about it. Termination, abortion and all that crap.

Dave was in a bit of a state about it all. Money was the biggest problem for him. He knew not to ask for anything. In the end I had a talk to Maria about the situation. It took me just an hour to sort it out once and for all. Two more hard working days to complete it. We both then got ready for a night out knowing that all of our friends would be there. I had in my pocket two envelopes. I was going to seal a friendship In we both walked, right into the evening's entertainment. Crowds of tourists were about and all of them wanting beer and fun. Dave and his girl were sat down talking. Maria and I spotted them as soon as we arrived and across we went. I let Maria take the lead while I stopped at the bar for drinks.

A few more of our gang were in the area and it made it perfect.

'Toni,' I said to the manager: 'Drinks are free for my party over there tonight. When that's gone, tell me.'

He passed over a beer for me and then I headed across to Dave. 'Drinks are on the way, it's a party,' I said: 'A party to celebrate an engagement. Here you are Dave.'

I gave him the first envelope.

'Open it,' I said.

He took it from me slowly and I could see him looking at me closely at that instant. Then a quick glance across towards Maria. She just nodded to him, as if to give approval for him to take it. By this time friends had gathered around us. Knowing that something important was happening at the table. Dave just looked at it for a few seconds and then opened it. I could see the disbelief in his eyes. It was a check for £5,000. Did he stand up and shout?

No. He just flopped back in the chair and stared up at Maria and me.

'Why?' he then asked me.

'First it's for friendship and the rest I'll tell you later,' I said. 'By the way, I've also bought you a wedding present.'

I then gave him the second envelope.

'That one is between you and your girl and for no one else. Open it later on,' I said: 'It will only need my signature to make it legal. What I will need is a full day of your time and your future wife must be included.'

Drinks were by then appearing on the table. It was party time for all and rock & roll music was on. It was time to dance. By the end of that night there was only two other people sober besides Maria and myself. That was Dave and his girl. He had opened the second envelope sometime during the evening. He'd read it and then read it again before passing it on to his girlfriend. He stopped drinking for the evening after reading it and so did she. Both of them had got up and walked to the door. Something across the road was taking up their thoughts.

Maria and I knew what it was and said nothing about it. We just left them alone to think about the future together.

Dawn was coming by the time the party ended. It was time to leave and we said our goodbyes. Straight across the road and we were there.

A fifteen bed-roomed tourist hotel with one speciality. A flat, up on the top section of the roof. Totally self contained and with a private entry. Dave and his girlfriend had followed us across. We entered this first time though the front door. Waiting for us in the lobby was the owner. It had been my request for him to wait for us. Or should I say now, the ex-owner of the hotel. We all shook hands and keys were given to me. At that he wished us luck and left.

I gave them to Dave. The facts were by now hitting both of them. I had told them that it would only take a signature. Would they take in what I was offering them once I told them the truth? That was something we would be finding out very soon. I thought that they would and Maria had no doubts whatsoever. She'd known the girl from childhood.

'Dave,' I at last said to him: 'Let's all sit down. What you are going to hear will astound you and its better heard sitting. Have you not ever wondered about me and where I come from? You have here the deed for this hotel. It will only take my signature and it will belong to both of you the day you get married. You have seen the conditions. It cannot be sold without my consent or Maria's. Either one of us can give that consent. It only takes one to sign. The stipulation about the flat on the roof must be kept at all times. That flat must be available at all times for strangers. They will appear at any time in the future. You will know them as my friends because they will be like me. That part of it neither of you understand yet. The question is this. Over the last few weeks, I have learnt to trust you. Do you trust me? Take your time on answering.'

Maria broke into the conversation at this point; 'Believe me, both of you. I trust him fully.'

Dave broke in; 'You know, I've always thought there was something strange about you. Good in a crowd, mixing well and yet I've felt something not quiet right. There's something been puzzling me for weeks. You move about so lightly and I've never seen anyone as fit as you are. I've watched you dancing and I still can't believe what I see. I came down to your boat one day and stood back to watch you exercise. Never have I seen anyone do what you do. I watched Maria go on the boat. The biggest puzzle was that I came down afterwards and you'd both disappeared. There was no way that you could have done it and yet you were not there. There's definitely something about you that I don't understand, yet you want to give me all this. I want to say that I trust you but it's hard to say after what I've seen you do.

'OK,' I said: 'Let go about this another way. If I can just give you this hotel now and without any more talking and you will accept what is written down. I will then have nothing further to say about myself. Only if you approach me in total trust will I tell you. Maria, you can tell him how long I will be remaining here on Malta.'

At that I signed the deed.

'I'll see you all later on,' and I left them sitting there to have a talk between themselves. Dawn was breaking and another surprise would be with them soon. I had in some ways expected this to happen and I was quite happy about it. Soon he'd be back for the some more. Especially when Maria had finished talking to them both. What happened next is what was related back to me by Maria herself. It had been Maria who had planned the surprise.

'Is he mad at us in any way?' Dave asked Maria.

'No not in any way at all and in fact he told me what you would possibly say,' Maria replied: 'Listen to me, both of you. I love him very much. What would you say, if I told you that I will never be married to him. He will also leave us in the next few months.'

Both Dave and his girlfriend would not believe it at all.

'You mean that he's just going to get up and leave us with this hotel?' said Dave quickly: 'It's uncanny and can't be true, all this and he'll just go.'

'Yes perfectly true, all of it,' Maria said.

What I can tell you is that there are many people searching for him. He has in his bank account over a million dollars and he earned every penny of it. Certain friends of his got hurt though and this was after he'd warned people not to mess with him. He hit back at them really hard. They will always be looking for him. The people he trusts, he would give his life for them.

'You're telling us that he's got over a million dollars and he's earned it,' Dave burst out and said: 'He's younger than me, damn it. What the heck does he do for a living? For the last few weeks he's been here playing with us all.'

At that moment a door opened to admit another young girl. Her name was El-------a, and she introduced herself to Dave and his girlfriend.

'I was asked to give you this,' she said and she handed over a newspaper: 'That's me in the photograph, stood next to my grandfather. It's up to you now to either trust him or not to trust him. I do and so does my grandfather.'

At that 'El——----a' just said goodbye and went back through the door she'd come from.

'That's one of his friends,' said Maria to both of them.

'Where does that door go to?' said Dave's girlfriend.

'Straight up to the flat,' replied Maria.

Dave's girl was up and through that door fast. Not ten seconds behind El-------a. She was back down within two minutes. She just walked back into the room and said; 'She's not there, she just disappeared.'

Dave was studying the newspaper. He was reading once again about what had happened in Sicily. He then gave it to his girl to read. For a time he just sat there thinking and then he sat up a little in the chair.

'What this is leading to is that he is the one responsible for what happened, over in Sicily. That's the girl in the photograph. Yet, he's been here all the time on Malta. I don't know how but I do need to know,' said Dave to Maria.

'I only met her once before today,' Maria told him next.

At that remark Dave's girl butted in really quickly; 'You've never been to Sicily before.'

'I have though, just to meet her,' Maria said: 'I went to find out about her relationship with Richard. Do you want to know something. That girl would give her body and soul for him. He never touched her at all. He'd promised her mother that he would never touch her and he kept that promise. I'll tell you both only once more. I trust him and if I could marry him tomorrow, I would do so.'

El-------a.

I know that he did something for them one day and the next he was away. He made money out of it but why did they go after him?

He cried on my shoulder when he heard about what had happened to his two friends. They shot him and if it had just been my spiteful cousin involved then others would have lived. He took all that revenge because of what they did to his friends. The pain that they both had to endured, long before dying. I'd read it from my cousin's mind before we left him in the sky. I'd read other dreadful things that he'd done to others. He fully deserved his punishment. I can do many things now. I had a visit from a girl in Malta. I flew there just for ten minutes to give a truthful message. I am courting my policeman. He will be as me if he carries on.

BM

I had just walked back in at that moment and I heard the last few words spoken by Maria. I paused for just an instance.

'Hello, I'm back,' I called to them.

This was to help me forget what she'd just said. I walked in and sat down smiling across at each of them in turn.

'All OK?' I said.

Dave now started to ask me about the paper and what was in it.

'It's all true before you go much further,' I just said to him.

It was Dave's girl who at last told him to shut up. Then she just up and walked across to me. Leaned over and gave me a quick kiss on the lips.

‘I trust you, even if that Dave of mine doesn’t,’ she said: ‘You’ve already given us a means to have a good life together.’

I knew at that moment that I would have some more Day movers. Dave just stood up then and with a small smile on his face, he held his hand out.

‘Tell us the rest,’ he said.

‘How would you like to be able to fly?’ I said to him smiling back.

That little smile on Dave’s face just dropped away.

‘Just get comfortable,’ I said: ‘Think of all your future work in this hotel. Tomorrow morning Maria and I will tell you the rest but not now. I’ve just seen one of your kitchen staff coming in to start the breakfasts for your guests.’

Dave was going to be very busy from now on. He’d told me of his dream a few weeks before and had pointed out this hotel to me. His wish had come true sooner than expected. Plus tomorrow morning he’d have something else. He also had to make a phone call. So had his girlfriend. Both rang in to quit their jobs.

What did Maria and I do all that day? We lay on the beach sunbathing. Sleeping sometimes and then up for a swim. Then we went for dinner. Just the two of us together. That is until about 3.30 in the afternoon when we were accosted by a couple of friends from the previous night. It was spreading around. What I had done for Dave and his girl. Soon it would be all over the island. Maria was looking anxiously at me.

She knew that my time was up. I would have to go very soon. That night we made love passionately. More so than ever before.

Dawn broke and up we went. Not far at all. From my new flat, which was just a few feet above where Dave and his girl slept. They were laid there in each other's arms when we appeared above them. I touched Dave and at the same time Maria touched the girl. Both were instantly aware what was happening. I began by telling Dave a little about myself. What he could now do. Telling him about what he now had to learn. Explaining about the night-time and what would happen when the shadows fell. Always to protect and to never tell a soul about who we were. No fear did I allow to enter his mind. Maria was doing the same with the girl. I took Dave back down and let him appear on his bed using his own new power. I then went to wait for Maria.

Five minutes later, she was beside me. She pulled me towards her. Afterwards it was into the shower and then we dressed. I had a case packed and that was it. I'd also left some new clothes in a wardrobe. Maria also had a sealed envelope. In it I had placed my true passport, licence and an address in the UK. I'd also done one other thing for her. She now had a five zero account in the bank. It was half of what I had in the world. If for some reason I was caught, then at least someone would have my money and not the banks.

George had done me well on this one thing. The remainder, he was looking after. Time to leave. We went down together, to meet two people. They walked over and spotted my case.

'Can you not stay for just a little while longer?' Dave said: 'I need a best man. The flat will always be ready for any visitors.'

What I was worried about was the fact that people can put two and two together. That knowledge would be in Sicily before long. If they were going to come for me again, then maybe I could throw them off. What if I wasn't here, but in Italy? I'd had a thought about this for the last couple of days. I could use Franco to throw people in the wrong direction. Since the last attempt on my life I had been careful to take out all of those who knew where I was. Taking a private plane out would be too obvious so a daily flight it had to be. I rang the airport and booked a first class ticket to Rome. I withdrew what was left in the bank and that was it. Maria watched me go, knowing that I would try to get back to her. Even if it was just for Dave's wedding.

It was 2.30 pm. That's the time that I cleared the airport in Italy. I took a four hour taxi ride. Booked into a posh hotel, room 503. The key was on a fancy transparent tag. Good job that I wasn't drunk. Looking at it from the opposite side it looked like room 203. I was not to know it at that moment but that key tag saved my life.

I'd made a phone call at a service station half way through the journey by taxi and was expected at a given address. An old voice had answered the phone and all I'd said to him was two words. Day Mover.

'Your safe to come,' had been the immediate reply.

Showered, shaved and in clean clothes it was only a matter of a few minutes to a secluded bungalow. Two men were at the gate waiting for me. One was clean shaven and big built. The other one I should have taken more notice of. He was younger, in his mid twenties and had a heavy black moustache. He looked vaguely familiar, yet I couldn't place him. Inside I was met by an old man. He was really pleased to see me. The last time I'd seen him was when he had been in a car with his brother Franco.

Giovanni Vittorio. He was still free and looking in good health. We sat down for small talk. He'd let his brother know that I was here in Italy. That had been my intention from the beginning and I told him this. I asked him if word would be passed about discreetly, that I was on the mainland. He understood. I also let him know that I would be travelling north within a couple of days. Now that I'd set out my plans.

After that I would be clear away and hidden again. The damn key tag was a bulge in my trouser pocket so I took it out and laid it on the table. It was just at that moment that drinks were served by the younger of the two men from the door. I still could not place him. I stayed for half an hour and then left to conclude my plans for the journey north. I was back at the hotel in time to see a group of British reps checking in for a convention. It made me a little homesick, just to hear them talking in English.

You know it's good to be in a nice posh hotel. Room service is always excellent. But not that next morning for one guest. I was just laid there at around 7.00 am when there was the loudest explosion that I've ever heard. It was right underneath me. The building shuddered from the blast. My ears were ringing and yet I could still hear the sound of falling glass. I was relaxed and in hover inside of a second. Straight out and downwards to find out what had transpired. Three floors down directly below my own room. The room was totally demolished. I could see a crowd gathering below me. I headed down to check it out.

I was looking for a face, a face that I'd managed to put to a place. The country where I'd last seen that face. The village and what that face meant to me now. I knew who he was, only the moustache was new. I found him. He was in a phone booth making a call. It was his mistake to make another call whilst I was behind him. I memorised the number. I was back in my room in seconds. Packed and out in five minutes. It was straight out the back and to another hotel up the road. Booked in and went straight to my room. I called Giovanni on the phone and asked him if his young minder was in.

'That's funny about you asking that,' he said: 'He disappeared last night and hasn't come back.'

'Get out of that place now, leave now and don't wait to pack,' I shouted: 'I'll call your brother. Come to this hotel.'

I gave him the hotels name and then I called another number. The code was Sicily.

'Peppino here, who's calling?'

I heard then, a few cuss words before it was slammed down again. Was I relieved that it had not been Franco. I now had the name of the person who gave permission for a bomb to kill and maim innocent people. There had been six people killed in the explosion and twenty-seven injured. It was on the television. A few of them had lost limbs. Now a few more were going to follow the dead. Those responsible would face a worse terror. I would tell them of the night ghosts and how they ripped you apart. Sicily will tremble once again. I will be there in the morning but first I have something to sort out here. I was now looking for a person called Pietro. I'd poked this one in the eyes a few months back. This was another cousin of El-----------a. A dead cousin, when I've finished with him.

It should have been me. It was my key tag and it had been viewed from the wrong side and upside down. They had bombed the wrong room. I heard it just then, a dull sounding boom of another explosion and wondered if he'd got out in time. I headed down to the lobby deep in thought. Old men, that's all any of them can really hurt. A telephone call and some one else to do the dirty work for a few thousand pounds.

Looking up, I saw him walking into the lobby. He was sweating and behind him came another man with a worried look written all over his face. They had both just cleared the house when it went up. That called had saved them both. It was the first time in my life for me to be hugged by two men. It felt strange but I could feel the emotion. It was a thank you for saving them.

'Where's the phone, I need to call Franco?' Giovanni asked me.

I pointed him in the right direction. He warned Franco.

'Let's go to my room out of the way,' I said: 'I need to do something but I need you both out of the way first.'

As soon as we got up to my room, I called down for a taxi. I then emptied all my pockets except for a few lira.. I put some of my other clothes on the bed. I knew exactly what time the first plane left for Sicily and I had time.

'Stay here,' I said: 'I'll be back soon.'

Fifteen minutes later I walked into the airport reading a paper. This was to hide my face until I'd chance to get to the side section. I then searched as far forwards as possible. Every little group of people, waiting to check in. I slowly moved forwards. Just enough to be able to look right or left into shops and bars before coming level with them. He was there all right, tucked into a corner. What a foolish man to sit in a position where by he couldn't see the full area. He was talking to another man and a woman. I didn't care about anything at that moment. I just walked in and hit him hard. He was out cold. People around had all jumped up by then. I just stood there glaring at them, waiting.

A couple of young, strong men came in and they got a taste of my anger. Both out in seconds. I still waited. I could see them coming. Guards, all with weapons drawn charging towards me. I disappeared before everyone's eyes, touched Pietro and he did the same. All that was left on the ground were two sets of clothes. You should have been there to see those women and men screaming and the mad scrabble to get away from that area. Even the guards withdrew before moving slowly forwards again. I left Pietro at ceiling level screaming. No one could hear him. Away fast and I stunned two more people in the next few minutes by just appearing on my bed back at the hotel.

'Pietro,' I said: 'He is waiting for the night.'

Giovanni, understood immediately; his brother had told him. The second man, the minder, saw me appear out of thin air, yet he'd hardly blinked. It was a first to me. I asked Giovanni's minder where he came from whilst I was dressing. Luck was running with us again. Just thirty miles away was his home. He was married and had two children. One a boy of ten years and the other, a girl of seven years. He'd been a bit wild in his youth. Had a reputation for fighting. Never knew who he was minding at any time and even if he did. He was in it for the money.

'Listen to me, would we be safer in your area?' I asked him.

He gave me the answer with a nod and a yes, both together and then his address. I called once again for a taxi. Took all the money off the table top and gave it to Giovanni. I also gave him both sets of my ID's and passports. Spun round and hit the minder hard. I had to hit him one more time to make sure.

'Why?' asked Giovanni stunned.

'He's seen me and knows what I can do,' I told him: 'Soon he will be another Day Mover. Here's my clothes.'

I just stuffed them in a case and gave him them. 'Get down and go to this address we'll be there waiting for you.'

A few minutes later, I had him with me, moving towards his house. On the way I kept him calm. Mind you it had not taken much. This one was hard. I read his mind: He was also honest and loved his wife and children. It was up to him now and I explained everything.

'Use it if you want to, if not don't,' I said: 'It is your choice. You cannot tell anyone in any case. You would just disappear if you did.'

That he understood. I then told him what would be happening to Pietro when night came. He was silent for a few moments then said that he'd have liked to have done it himself. Not to have left Pietro for the ghosts, but to have actually ripped him apart himself.

'My wife was nearly a widow and my children nearly lost their father,' he said: 'Thanks for my life and this.'

We arrived and I explained that I would be travelling away soon. Down he went and within a few seconds he was dressed and outside watching. I caught the casual look upwards, as the old man arrived. I left. The minder had a call to make to the newspapers. To tell them that the person who'd bombed the hotel had been dealt with. His passport or ID would be found in one set of clothes at the airport. Those who had given the order to bomb the hotel would be dealt with in the same way. The morning news confirmed the death of Pietro. He had been ripped apart. The news was on the television from 6.00 am. All the Italian paper put it in headlines. That bomb had been connected to the airport activities. Apparitions had appeared in the airport just after dark. Everything came to a standstill within a circle of five kilometres of that airport. Nothing and nobody dare enter the circle. All roads leading up to it were closed off and guarded.

I had a wedding to attend. By 3.00 pm, I was on the bed in my flat on Malta. What a surprise they all had to see me appear through that door. The news had been on the television about the explosions. Somehow they had connected it with me and had been worried. Maria grabbed hold of me. I had to explain it all to them. Every last single fact of what had taken place over the last few days. Also of my suspicions and the possible action that I would have to take. I had four days at least, maybe six at the most. Tracing me would be very hard. This would be the last place to look but they would look regardless. The next message would more than likely be to the Maltese authorities. OK, they could take me in and lock me up but unless they had the full knowledge of how to contain me, I could be out and gone in seconds. It was only in the UK that this was known. That I'm sure of because even they would never divulge anything about what was happening to certain children.

I had a great time. Best man at a wedding that was held on the second day of my return. It all went smoothly. Most of our friends and the holiday reps were there. For once I never paid a penny. For Maria, it was if I'd never gone away. I really did want to stay with her. Even though we were lovers, Maria told me what she was going to do after I went the next time. For me it would be no more sex with her. The love for me would always remain. She'd actually started to court with a young Maltese boy. This was before I arrived on the scene. She had dropped him for me. I was really chuffed to hear that part. He'd stayed in the background ever since my arrival, hoping that we'd break up in the future. He'd seen me leaving the other day and had approached Maria. She'd had dinner with him and during it she had given him hope. The fact that she had told him I would be leaving and she would not be marrying me. It must have made his day. Maria also liked him very much.

She wanted him to be the next Day Mover. Although she readily admitted she loved me she also knew that I could not give her a future with children. That she wanted more than anything in the world to have children. Be careful of your children I reminded her. She just laughed at that.

I agreed with her entirely. It was time for me to leave again. We went to bed late that night and just lay cuddling each other. We could have had sex at any time during that night but it never happened. We had our love. That would never change. She now belonged to another man.

I was away by twelve, speeding fast and high towards Sicily and I passed 'El—--------a' far down below me. I did not stop until I saw that she had another dim light at the side of her. I wondered who, and circled around towards her. Poor man I thought, she's got you good and proper now. It was his first time up and it was just hitting him at that moment. He'd had his way with her in the fields and as he lay sleeping afterwards she'd taken her revenge in a way. Her first man and this is how she repaid him.

‘Policemen, you have to watch out for them,’ I projected to her.

Little did I know that in the future, those few words would come true for myself. I did meet a very clever policeman indeed in the future. El——-a was still holding her own policeman tight and transferring knowledge to him. A clear strong mind was beginning to emerge. His light was getting stronger by the second. Enough for now.

‘El——-a,’ I need to talk to you: ‘It was Peitro who caused the explosions that killed all them people.’

She hovered silently in the sky not saying a word. Then the cry of ‘Bastard’ burst forth from her loudly.

‘I’ll get him when he returns,’ she said.

She’d been too busy with her boy friend to hear the news of what had happened at the airport.

‘Peppino, he ordered it,’ I then told her.

I was surprised by what happened next. A policeman came up to me then but not in his human form. He came as a sphere of bright light.

‘Leave that one for me,’ was what he put to me through the air: ‘He’s mine at last.’

I understood that outburst from him and as soon as it passed across.

I just said goodbye and left them to serve out what they wanted to Peppino.

I was in Malta in 1988. I stayed for two years on and off. I used to fly in on BA club class from the UK. Stay the night to see old friends and then travel across to Tunisia. I’m still on the move, even today. There are a total of sixteen Day Movers on Malta, so be careful.

I was heading for my clothes and my ID's. Around 5.00 pm I arrived and slowly moved inwards towards the house. What a relief for me, to see the old man upstairs asleep. His minder was around the back playing with his children. My suitcase was in the spare room. All my clothes were laid out neatly on the bed. All cleaned and ironed. I appeared on the bed and dressed. I opened the window just a little more to watch the minder playing. For a hard man, he was very soft and loving. He just happened to glance upwards and saw me leaning there watching. Only his eyes showed surprise.

'Do you want a beer?' he called.

I nodded.

He told the kids to fetch two beers from the kitchen. This gave me chance to jump down from the window without frightening the children. A shake of hands and an Italian hug of welcome.

'Welcome to my home,' he said: 'The old man is fine. He actually loves to be around the children and will miss them when they go back to school. To me that was really good to hear.

'Franco is coming here in a few days time,' he then told me: 'He also sends his thanks to you for what you did. He has requested that you wait to see him.'

All of this information I had within just a few minutes of arriving. 'I'll see you in the sky when he arrives,' I said. I explained that I was going to Venice. Just for a look around. I did the opposite and went to Rimini, down the east coast. Booked into a hotel brimming with Brit tourists and settled in. I then called George in France to arrange a transfer of funds. Gave him the ID I was using.

I'd gotten the equivalent of £150 pounds back from Giovanni. He'd offered to get me far more but I had enough until the transfer came through. George thought I was crazy giving all that money away in Malta. He'd sat down with his family and they'd all had a general discussion about it. Wife and daughter won the argument hands down. They thought it wonderful that I'd done what I did. Their point was the fact that it was so easy for me to obtain more.

George now found it easier to control his area. The word was out in some respects that anyone could disappear. All was under control.

Me, I'm sat on a sofa watching tourists. There's a show tonight, so the place is full. It doesn't matter where you go in the world. Someone on their own is always noticed.

First to sit near me is a couple with very young children. Two small boys of around six years of age and a little girl. The little girl was around nine years of age and is right by my side. She looked pale and very thin. I didn't look like your average tourist because by now I was deeply tanned. They didn't even know that I was British until the girl spilt her coke on me. Mother started to scold the little girl until I spoke up and said it was all right.

'Your English,' were her first words.

'Afraid so", I said: 'Clothes will wash. I don't mind at all and it was an accident.'

They'd not seen the little girls foot slip off the wooden cross bar under the table. I had seen it and explained it to them. From that point I was accepted in their company for the night. Just chatting away through the evening it came about that their flight in had been diverted at the last minute. Me, I knew the reason for it but made no comments. I also found out the little girl a hole in the heart. Around ten and half way through the show. I had a little girl fast a sleep against me. I couldn't move without disturbing her so her dad bought me a beer. Here's me, a total stranger in this position. I was really happy and content that night for the first time in a long while. It also got me out of being dragged on stage as part of the act. The night ended around eleven thirty and the family departed.

I headed out towards a night-club. A couple of bouncers were on the door as usual. Paid the entrance fee and I was in. The place was packed solid. Standing room only. A fair few lads worse for drink. That's when the trouble started. Two gorillas had collared one of the drunken lads. Not content with just putting him outside, I watch one of them hit him in the kidneys really hard. It was totally not called for. That lad was hurt bad. He was on the ground and in real pain. Should I or shouldn't I get involved? I didn't for a full thirty seconds. That's all it took for a girl to first find the boy on the ground and then for her to go for the bouncer with her handbag flailing. That bouncer just punched her straight in the face.

I stepped forwards. My hand curled around his windpipe and I held him rigid against the wall with one hand. His surprised mate started forwards and he felt my fist. Released the first, grabbed his wrist and then full force with my other hand. I broke his arm. Second one coming in felt my foot on his shinbone, breaking his leg. I walked away from it then, heading back to my hotel. I headed for the bar for a last drink. Ten minutes later a group of about twelve lads and lasses appeared. Two were well blooded. It was one of the lads who spotted me and he came straight over.

'It was you who put the bouncers out,' he said.

He then called to the group and told them who I was. I had been recognised. So much for me having a quiet and peaceful few days. It was handshakes all round from the lads and a couple of pecks on the cheek from two of the girls. I didn't feel good about it because it shouldn't have happened in the first place. It was time for me to head up to bed, so I said good night to them.

Up early, I went for a swim in the pool and then to a sun bed. A couple with two children were sat near me during the morning. It was about eleven when I heard someone getting settled on the bed next to me. I never even looked to see who. I felt thirsty so I just got up and headed in for a drink. I not gone five paces before a voice behind me spoke.

'Fetch a coke for me Richard.'

I just blinked out in a split second and hover above the voice. I could hear the little girl telling her mother.

'Mammy, mammy he disappeared,' she was saying: 'Mammy, he disappeared.'

'Who dear,' came from her mother.

'That mister from last night,' she said.

Her mother just looked up, and then laid her head back down. I was hovering around to see the person who had spoken. It was Frieda. I was in my room fast. Slipped some shorts on and was back down on the double. Two can play at this game I thought. So I headed for a quiet spot in the lounge. It took another ten minutes before she stepped into the area.

My towel and trunks were over her arm with her own towel. She looked beautiful and I wondered why I'd never noticed before.

Up she came to me and bending over she gave me a full bloodied kiss on the lips.

'Daddy knows I am here to see you,' she said:

'Does he now?'

'My mother's due in a couple of weeks time. I just wanted to see you,' she said.

She sat down beside me she then explained the rest. That she'd been rowing with her father but in the end he'd been made to realise that his daughter was now grown up. Instead of a bank transfer, she brought the money. Her father was handing over most of the business to his brothers. He had decided that he wanted to give far more time to his wife and the baby when it was born. He knew that he would have to be there for the first flight of the child. And wanted to teach it everything.

Somehow, the authorities had got together with the British, French and Italians. They knew that someone was loose. What they didn't know was the power I had to given to others.

The apparitions appearing at the airport in Italy had put the shits up them. The biggest surprise for me was another passport, fully stamped and up to date. I'd really struck it lucky with George. Now his daughter was here with me. Would I lose his trust?

'Frieda,' I put to her quietly: Your father, he trusts me. I don't want to lose it. You being here means that if we become lovers and then split up, what's he going to think?'

'We're not lovers though are we,' she broke in and said without a smile: 'On the other hand though.'

A smile then appeared; 'We could be and it would be none of his business. It's mine. You'll never lose his trust through me.'

She reached over and I received just a little peck that time.

'Where's the drink you were fetching me?' she asked.

I just laughed and told her that she had the money and to fetch them herself. The men in that lounge bar watched her and I was thinking of the night to come.

Chapter 16

BM

We had lunch just after noon at a restaurant a few doors down from the hotel. A bottle of red wine went down beautifully. Then back to the sun beds where we carried on talking. A swim in the pool and then a game of water polo with a few others. The atmosphere between us became electric and it wasn't all me making it happen.

Evening mealtime was approaching and neither of us wanted to make the first move upstairs to get changed for the night. Sorry, but it was me who made the first move by picking up my towel. It was arm in arm to the lift and up we went. I was on floor seven and Frieda was on six. It took me about four minutes to sort out clothes for the evening. Shower had just been turned on when there was a knock on my door. I found her there with a suitcase.

'Can I move in,' she asked.

That door was nearly taken off the hinges, the way it slammed shut behind her and she began stripping my clothes off.

It was a dance night. I'd never danced with her at any time and didn't know whether or not she could. We were sitting there talking when a cheeky sod came up and asked her for a dance. I was surprised but she at least looked across to me and I just nodded my head. I thought to myself just for a moment: I'm jealous, but it soon passed while watching her on the floor. She knew how to keep them from getting too familiar.

What did I get during that dance? I got a sleepy looking little girl next to me.

'Mister, where did you go today?' she asked: 'You were there and then not there.'

If only she knew, but I'm certainly glad that she'd not been older. I got up and fetched the little girl a coke. Her mum and dad had noticed me and waved.

'Where did she come from?' he said: 'You're a dark horse.'

'Shut up Allen,' his wife said.

'It's my girlfriend,' I replied and sat down with them.

'By the way, I'm Sue,' she said.

That dance ended and Frieda headed my way. Introductions were made but it was by then getting late for the children.

'Did you see the little girl, Frieda,' I said as they took the children off to bed.

'Yes, she's pale isn't she,' was her reply.

I then explained what I could do to help her.

'Let's go to bed and talk about it,' she whispered to me.

First light I was up hovering and seconds later Frieda was there beside me. Up we went very high. Checking all about us and ensuring that all was clear. Then we went twirling and turning for a few minutes before zooming downwards.

It was Frieda that found the room. Window was open and we both entered. The girl was peaceful and sound asleep. I brought her upwards slowly. Speaking softly to her and ensuring that she was safe. A small dark area was visible near the centre of her sphere of light. I commenced to heal her body, slowly. All the time talking to her, making her believe that it was a dream and then returning her safely to her bed.

The little girl would always think of it as a dream. Doctors however would not. Frieda was watching me carefully and listening to my thoughts.

Then it was back to our room for sex. This time it was slow, loving, tender and caring. It was around ten that morning when we had settled down on the sun beds. Not five minutes had passed before the little girl walked up. First she gave Frieda a hug and then she turned to me. A smile was on her face and then she kissed me quickly, held her arms around me and whispered; 'I like you.'

Then away she went to play. Frieda smiled broadly. I'd spotted colour on the child's cheeks. We watched the amazement dawning on Sue's facc, then Allen's. They were watching their daughter play. Using energy that she'd never had before.

During the afternoon I gave Frieda an account of everything that had happened and what I was expecting in the next day or two. The signal for Franco's arrival would be the time to leave. Frieda and I made some plans of our own. Sure enough the minder was up there as a signal for me on the fourth day. We then parted just to show him not one, but two lights. Then we went back down to pack for travelling.

Frieda hired a car for both of us but it was going to be separate hotels on arrival. On the journey there we stopped on a bridge to tear up all of my previous ID's. All I kept was my true passport and the new one. She'd brought me a small holdall. It was sewn at the sides with coloured cord. A needle with a big eye was the next little item. Just by taking a knot out, one side opened up just by pulling the chain stitch. It revealed two pieces of thin cardboard, to form the base. It was a perfect good hiding place for my British passport and licence. It only took me another ten minutes to sew it back up. The needle then clipped into a small hollow to form a safety pin. This went onto the carrying band with two others.

I was expected sometime that day. I could see four men in pairs strategically placed within easy reach of the property. This I'd observed from the taxi I'd taken from my hotel. My friend the minder was there to welcome me. Everyone then relaxed. I had with me a small valise. It was placed on a chair carefully. Franco smiled, but now he smiled as if I were his long lost brother. He grabbed me in a bear hug. Then he turned around and pointed at a briefcase that he'd brought and said: 'That's for you.'

He then began to rattle on about the future and most of it was about me. I stopped him dead in his tracks at that point. No one was ever going to control me in any way. I would never take anyone's orders. He took it in but then smiled. He'd tried and that was the end of it. He opened the briefcase. On top was a sealed envelope but below were layers of dollar bills. It was time for me to show them another surprise. I went upstairs and three minutes later I was back down. With me was Frieda. Now that did surprise the hell out of them except for one. The minder. He had just proven that he was committed to what I'd given him and had not mentioned the second light seen in the sky.

I opened the valise and took out four stacks of bills and passed them over to him.

'Family,' I said and he understood what I meant:

‘This man looked after your brother.’ I was looking at Franco as I said it.

Franco by this time knew that there was another like me and this shook him to the core.

‘How many of you are there?’ he asked.

‘Many,’ I told him.

I was not alone, as he’d been led to believed. My plan had worked far better than I’d hoped. He did eventually get around to asking me how many were in Sicily.

‘More than one,’ was my reply and it was left at that.

Dinner was a great success and even the minders wife came with the children. That had been Giovanni’s suggestion and with them there it allowed us all to relax more. The ultimate news was that Giovanni was going home to a secret house. Franco then surprised me. He gave the minder the same sum of money that I had given him. Where that money came from that evening I don’t know but all it had taken was a phone call from Franco for it to be delivered.

It was at the end of the evening that I took Franco to one side. ‘There’s just the one left in Sicily, he will be dealt with, by a Sicilian. It may have already happened.’

I told him that I did not intend to come back in the near future unless I was called for. I had just one other thing left to do. That briefcase was to be delivered to the British Consul in Rome.

Typed instructions were inside with the money. Orphans of those killed would receive most of it. The remaining amount to go to the injured. I sent it all. Frieda would be taking a plane home and I was heading north. She’d come just for a crazy week, to be with me.

She just kept one little secret from me. Just one. She wanted a child. Not a child with just her powers but a child with mine. All my powers transferred and combined with hers. That wish she got. It took me a long time to find it out and then she had twins.

Franco had also surpassed himself in another way. Another ID and a passport to match. That passport was unbelievable. How the heck he got it, I don't know. This was a passport for an emergency. With it was a letter on which were various names. Frieda and I had a crazy week in Rome. She flew home on the seventh day. I took the train out of Italy. It gave me time to relax and gather my thoughts. I arrived at my destination. Lucerne, in Switzerland. I was hoping to meet Helga, up flying in the morning.

It's turning towards winter and this year she would have no need to travel. I booked into the first hotel I could find. Upstairs to my room, to take a quick shower. Then down and outside, to find some shops. I needed some new clothes and shoes. I went for a full rig out of good clothes. I wanted not just to feel smartly dressed, but to be smart. I bought the best of everything and I sent it all back to the hotel by courier. I even bought some winter clothes for skiing.

My days will start later as the nights draw closer. Just a few minutes a day up to check for another light. I had her address but was very uneasy about approaching the house. I was avoiding having my photograph taken and didn't want to get caught by a hidden camera. Three months up front at the hotel had the manager purring at my feet. I'd the penthouse room. It took me a few days to make other plans. I'd spotted her walking to college and at the same time I noticed the very discrete tail behind her.

Helga

What do people want to hear from me? That what happened within one week could not be true. That I'd never been a cripple with a twisted leg. My parent knew the truth, so did many doctors. I'd seen them all while growing up. In one week it all changed. I was sent to the south of France every year for the warmth. I loved watching people dancing. I arrived early that night to watch and what I saw was beautiful. The evening started quietly until in came a young man escorting two girls. They sat down a few metres away from me. Both girls were beautiful. They were laughing and joking between them and I heard him ask for that first dance.

He started slowly dancing with one of them and I could see what he was doing. Learning the rhythm of his partner before using his own moves. Throughout the night I watched him dancing with both of them in turn. I could not take my eyes off them. Never will I be able to do that I thought. Not with my leg. Over the next few days I sought them out. There was something different about them. Something not quiet right and very unusual, especially in boy. I watched him deal with some men and he made it so casual. As if he was afraid of nothing at all.

That day. I watched him on the beach exercising. Afterwards when he came up to me and spoke. Then that little kiss he gave and what he'd said. I was in shock in just seconds. Sure I was ready to spit back and curse him. I'll never know why I didn't. I even followed him for a drink. I was being drawn towards him and felt that I couldn't resist him. I had no boyfriend. The way he asked me if I wanted one. Why me? I'm crippled. We ended up in his room at the hotel. His excuse was to take a shower. Mine. It was in my mind. I wanted to be with him. What happened between us was the first time for me. Afterwards, I lay back thinking about what I'd done and what it meant. He was there besides me, just holding me and the last thing I remembered was falling asleep.

I dreamed that I'd flown into the sky. I was soaring above the house tops just like a bird. A white, bright light surrounding me. I woke on the bed with him beside me.

'Try your leg,' he said.

I can remember jumping up and then collapsing back crying. I was cured. My leg was perfectly formed. Then all of the questions I asked and the answers given back from him. The teachings, I received from him, of what to do and what not to do. What happened during the rest of that day happened very fast.

The people with whom I was staying took one look at me and phoned my parents. Then they wanted to know where I had been. Who I had been with. I just stayed quiet about it. I was full of joy though because I could walk normally. In less than an hour it had all been arranged for me to fly back home.

I just scribbled a quick letter and gave it to the gardener to deliver. One day I hope to see him again. I spent the winter at home. The doctors were stumped. I refused even to go and see them. It was glorious to be able to walk, run and to be able to learn to ski, just like all my friends. The fuss gradually died down and from then on I practiced in great secret. That is until my parents started to have the house redecorated. They insisted that my room should be the first room to be decorated. That caused a row because it had only been done six mouths before. I liked it how it was.

Bringing in the decorating manager was a mistake and I didn't miss it. There was no way he knew anything about painting. I gave in though to allay their suspicions. I moved into the spare room. My doubts were confirmed shortly after. The painters van used the left side entrance road up towards the house. It had been snowing a little during the night and you could see the tyre tracks clearly.

Now I went out to see a friend not five minutes after. Mother had been informed that I would be half an hour. On arriving back I asked her if anyone had been? Her answer was no. I went upstairs to look out of the window. There in the snow were tyre tracks coming right up to the front door. The right side entrance road had been used. My mother had lied to me. Why? There was also one more thing on my mind. Why was the room next to mine having fitted cupboards?

It had not been mentioned at all. I just knew that something was amiss. None of the people doing the work lived locally. That's when I recalled what the boy had said. Look for something that is not an everyday occurrence. I'd found it alright. Something not right and I walked down the stairs to confront my mother.

'Tell me the real reason for the men upstairs,' I said to her. The look and the colour coming on her cheeks confirmed it to me.

She told me not to be so silly at first.

'To put it bluntly mother,' I said: 'I will not be moving back into that room. In fact, now that I am over eighteen. I can use some of my legacy, left by grandma.'

That really put my mother in a flap because she called father. He was home in ten minutes to confront me. Everyone could hear his voice. He shut up after I got my word in.

'Do you think for one minute that I don't know what's going on,' I said: 'The spies may as well pack in now.'

I'd got it clear, right from the start because not only did he shut up but he sat down and just stared up at me.

'I'll be back in one minute,' I told him and left the room to run upstairs. From under my bed I pulled out the papers I had. I ran back down and thrust them onto his lap.

'Is this what you are worried about?' I said: 'If so you're all fools. The mysterious events that had happened in France, were in the papers on his lap.

'Now father, you have just one choice to make,' I said: 'Either the people upstairs leave now, or I do.'

At that I stormed outside. The people upstairs had heard me all right. It took just five minutes for them to pack up and leave. Government was written all over them. I'd gotten away with it for now but how long would it last?

I never flew all of that winter, nor in the spring time, just to be sure. I spotted some of them watching me on the odd occasion. Never once did I try to hide or to evade them. I did not want to go into banking like the rest of the family. I wanted to own my own hotel. My studies in this area took me to college every morning and two evening. The rest was taken up with learning how to dance. It was only on a Saturday evening that I stayed out late. Maybe twice a month I stayed really late. Winter came and I learnt to ski. Then an early spring came.

I'm sure that it was around that time that my watchers were reduced. I knew the faces of them by now and had even nodded my head to them on occasions. Summer was beautiful around the lake and on warm days after college, I used to sit by the water's edge. I'd had a couple of advances from boys but I kept then away. Sitting there day dreaming besides the lake I came up with a means of being able to do what I'd wished for so long. Father's little boat. It was perfect with a covered cabin and a small Envinrude 25 outboard.

I never even bothered to ask him. I just arranged with the boat yard to put it in the water, ready for the following Saturday. I arrived around ten the following Saturday. Into the boat, checked the fuel and straight away the engine fired. Quickly released the mooring line and I was away across the lake. It took only ten minutes to reach my destination. Threw the anchor over the side and entered the cabin. Just to relax and to feel myself become that sphere of light, after so long. It was wonderful to lift up and soar through the sky like a bird. Down and moving fast, back to the starting point.

Sure enough a face was there, known to me from winter and spring. He was trying to hire a boat. Laughing to myself I headed back to the cabin. I'd refreshed and cleaned my body on just that one flight. I waited until I could hear the engine of another boat coming close before I appeared. I pulled up the anchor. Started the engine and headed back to the quayside. In total I'd taken just over thirty five minutes and it had been worth it.

Summer passed too quickly for me. I had by now some good friends at college. I talked with girlfriends about boys and music. Dancing and new films. The bets on who would get pregnant next. It was the sixties and we enjoyed it while we could.

One story came into the conversation about a boy of about nineteen. He was at a hotel in town. A daddy's boy they said and rich. Dressed in all the latest clothes. Big wide shoulders and could he dance. Every girl he danced with wanted to dance with him again and again. He did a back summersault one night while dancing on the floor. Everyone's waiting to see him do it again. A couple of lads jealous of his dancing had tried to pick on him one night. He didn't even bat an eye they say. All he did was pick up an empty glass and crushed it into pieces with one hand. The boys backed off. It was the talking point of the night because even the doormen kept away from him. It's said that he even paid for the broken glass and for it to be cleaned up. He laughs and jokes with everyone. Who would be the first girl? Bets were on.

My heart bumped. I caught my breath and asked again for it to be repeated slowly. I knew of only one person who could really dance and I'd met him last year. He'd come all this way to see me. He'd arrived at a time of danger but was not aware of it. I had to warn him but was unable to break my routine because I was still being watched. I would have to wait until weekend.

He was normally to be found just 200 metres from my own regular dancing places. Somehow I had to get at least two of the girls to ring my home. The phone I rarely used. Whenever I did use it, there was always a small little click shortly after I picked up. I asked one of the girls to ring me and told her I would refuse first off and explained that it was just for my parents benefit. If another rang up then it would be a threesome going out. Suspicion would be averted by any possible listeners. At least that was my plan.

We were all three out by nine and down town. Heading for new pastures for a change. Heading out to see this one man. I'm sure that many more girls were doing the same. He was at present, the towns' new peacock strutting his body before us. Waiting for one of us to claim him as a mate. The difference was that none of them knew what he was really doing. He was purposely trying to draw me out if I was there. Without giving away, who he really was.

For some reason he'd not tried a direct approach and I realised that he must have known I was being watched. At the entrance there was a crowd waiting for the doors to open at nine thirty. Friends from college were in front and we waved to them. I could hear about six different languages around me. We entered fast to claim a good seating area and two of us claimed a table just off the dance floor while the other went for drinks.

I'm feeling apprehensive but trying not to show it. Couples were up to dance as soon as they came in. Had two offers but turned them down. Both of my friends were up dancing and I'm sat watching. I was just starting to have a drink when I saw him across the room. Just standing there. Then he looked around the room slowly. His eyes were registering every face. As his eyes swept towards me he must have missed me due to the dancers. I could see him between them, his head moving around. I watched that face and it turned back and looked straight at me. He'd realised that he'd missed me and had swept his eyes back to look again. I caught the change in his expression, the smile beginning to form and then he turned away from me. I'd been found at last and he would approach in his own good time.

How he had grown in the last year. Even in that glimpse, I could see how he'd changed. He looked stronger. I next spotted him dancing with a lovely blonde girl from college. Everyone watched. That dance ended and he disappeared. I then saw one of my watchers. He'd a cut lip and was being escorted outside. Word was around quickly that he'd insulted one of the girls. She'd complained to one of the doorman, hence the cut lip. It was the chair scraping back that announced him sitting next to me. Then a very light touch turned me towards him and he kissed me gently on the lips. Both of us felt the hush descend upon the room. He sat back and laughed. I started to laugh with him and it became just a night club atmosphere again. We were left in peace.

All bets were now off. Even my two girlfriends took the hint and left us too it. It's like this. I, too, am beautiful and I know it. He told me about the face. It had cost him £200 pounds to arrange that cut lip. Just for a kiss he told me.

'What now though because they have been watching me since last year,' I said. '

'Taking a holiday south will be the best thing to do,' he said: 'I've already a plan worked out but I need your passport number. I will be flying into Paris tomorrow. Two days later you will take the same flight. I will be waiting with a package holiday flight to Tunisia. It will be off one flight onto another. They will have no chance to get on that flight. We will delay our check in until the last minute. Your ticket will be at the information desk waiting for you. I'll be just behind you. What I do need you to do is linger in the lounge until I give you a signal. Then collect your ticket then.'

This was all related to me in minutes. My mind was whirling with the speed of what was happening. He kissed me and left so fast that I couldn't say another word to him. Did he leave? Did he hell. What he did do was dance with all the girls. I took up the offers given and danced with a few of the boys.

The next morning I set in motion the plan. Booked my flight to Paris with an open return. Rang the college and informed them. Then I told my mother. She wasn't very happy about it and neither was father. For once I told them straight. Also about the watchers that I'd had over the last few months. That shut them up in a sense. I'm positive that they knew all about it and somehow I knew that I'd been linked with what had happened in France, Italy and Sicily. I was a link to him and the governments of those countries had combined forces to find him.

BM

My flight out was straightforward. I'd a valid French passport which I used. A full case of clothes and my holdall. First thing I did was book a package holiday for two. Next step was the airport to check it out thoroughly. First day, walking around on the ground and the next day in hover form. I'd hired a car for this purpose. I was going to change my tactics. It was going to be something entirely new, something that I'd been practising hard at.

It'll shock a few people but it will allow us to get clear. Here's me, I've followed people as they've opened doors. Allowing me access inside the airport. I had the gate arrival of the aircraft. I was just hovering patiently at the exit way from the aircraft. Two men were before me along with other airline personnel. The difference was that one of them had a photograph of Helga. Sure enough she came past them and they set out to follow her at a distance. She went through passport control and then down to baggage reclaim. All the time they watched her. When she cleared customs and moved outside the terminal, I put my plan into force.

I cannot pass through solid objects but down I came to commence circling the two men. I'm invisible but I can put up a barrier that cannot be seen. Every direction they took, I blocked them off. Startled people cleared away from the scene. Two men trapped in what appeared to be a cocoon of air. Shouting and bellowing in surprise, I kept them there. In whatever direction they tried to move, I blocked them. More and more people were moving away. Gendarmes were approaching cautiously. After ten minutes I soared up through an open window. The two men had collapsed on the floor. Explanations would delay them further. I sped straight into my hire car and back into human form. Dressed quickly, grabbed my case and then delivered the key back to the hire company on the way into the terminal. I nearly got knocked over by a group of very excited men. I arrived in the hall and gave Helga the nod to proceed as planned.

When they did get around to check, we would be long gone. I had other plans made and this was on top of my first plan. George had made the arrangements for me. His daughter was pregnant and yes, he knew who the father was and the reason why, and he wasn't mad with me. He even wanted his daughter to marry me and it was she who'd said no. We cleared the airport and it was then that I spoke to the holiday rep. A double change of plans. We would not be going to the hotel until around the last two days of the holiday. We had made other arrangements at the last minute to go to Porte El Kan Tewi. A boat was tied up there and it's a beauty. All I have to do is show my passport and the keys are given to me. Try to find us now, I was thinking. My ID was a secret.

All they had for Helga was a photograph. The timing of our arrival had been planned also with two ladies arriving at the vessel. Hairdressers especially requested to change Helga's hairstyle and colour. I wanted freedom for us both for at least twelve days. Sunshine and pleasure, we had both. Around the Madena, we bartered for trinkets. Meals were taken at the quay side restaurants. We must have tried every one. We had two little boys following us from day one. Both of them, wanting our loose change. We used to toss it to them once a day. On the boat was the only time we were free. No one was allowed to come onboard once the gangway was hoisted up. We were free to soar up into the sky at will. The future was always in our thoughts. The boys now, I was going to leave them with a far greater present. Both could speak French and that had decided me. I explained my reasoning for more Day Movers to Helga. The more we are, then the odd of survival are greater. I had noticed that the boys only left when the gangway was up. They had our timing off because they used to be there waiting, just before we left the boat for the evening meal. I went straight into hover on the seventh day to follow behind them. Just over the road from the entrance to the harbour was another hotel. They went around the back and into a small dwelling. An old man and woman was there with a meal for them. Cash was always handed over at that point. Just at the side, some old mattresses. Here the boys rested. A hard life for beggars and for these two I was going to change it.

I took two screaming children up into the sky, very early the next morning. Two hours later, before the boat, were two smiling boys with a secret. I gave them both an envelope. It was a little start in life. They were African Day Movers. The first and they would be choosing the next ones on that continent. They had the means to change and move from place to place and the latest details fully installed in their minds. Abuse would destroy the means to fly. It was a kind of mental block really.

The last twelve days, has been heaven for both of us. We've mingled with everyone and made many new friends. It was time to join the real world again.

First though, I had a parcel to post to Switzerland. It was registered and I paid for it giving a big tip to the collector. A taxi took us to our original destination for the last two days. Both our passports were taken as normal, when checking in. This I'd expected. Up to the room and back down immediately to check. Sure enough, I could hear the conversation announcing our arrival. It was then back up to inform Helga of the development. I knew that I had to go. The one place left for me was the boat. I kissed Helga.

'See you back home,' I said.

I was out of there and at reception in two minutes flat. I walked straight around the counter to confront the startled manager. Picked my passport off the desk and turned to move away. He'd just placed his hand on me, when I spun around and gripped his wrist and squeezed hard, bringing him to his knees. I felt like breaking it. If Helga hadn't been there in that hotel, I would have.

I left by the front door and hailed a taxi. I paid him even as we left the place. Then I commenced to tear that passport into pieces. Along a four mile length of highway I threw it out the window. The photograph was in smaller pieces and that followed.

I left the window down and followed the photo. I hovered just above the road for a few seconds and then headed back to the hotel. Straight up to our room and through the window to find Helga packing. At the open door was the manager and two other members of his staff. All three were shouting at her. She was smiling broadly at them. It was as if she knew what was going to happen in a few seconds.

It did happen and it was my sphere hitting them like a ball from the bowling alleys. Just like skittles, they went over fast into a heap. I could not follow her into the lift so I went in again to reception through an open door at ground level. Pulled up fast to see the gentlemen from Paris approach her. I listened to them and I realised I had to let them take her. She would be far safer out of Tunisia. She would be flying straight home immediately. Not one single act of deceit had she committed. They wanted her back where they could control her.

I stayed the night on the boat and early morning, I was up and hovering silently. Two other small spheres came up to join me. I said my farewells and I'm up within seconds speeding due north. I'm back in my room in Lucerne by dinnertime and it was a surprise to the manager to see me. It would be Helga's father who would be the first to see her. Of that I'm sure.

All it took was four days of waiting before he changed his morning routine. He drove that morning to some army barracks. Parked his car just outside. Two officers were waiting for him at the gate. Four days for me in hover from early morning and I never once let up my vigilance. It paid off because I got really close up to look through a window.

There she was in a room on her own, silently reading a book on hotel management. Her father entered and they held each other for a few seconds. Behind was a group of men and women. Typical isn't it. In would come the doctors next. All governed by someone from above. I was now going to put the shits up them. I withdrew away from that window and then hit it hard. It shattered completely and the glass splayed inwards over them. I was right behind it and then I commenced to hit them. Not a damn thing could they see.

To them it was as if the air was boxing with them. Not too hard but enough to make them retreat out of the room. The only two left were Helga and her father. I left then for her to talk with him. I did not go far away but waited patiently.

Helga.

It was now up to me. We knew this would happen. His actions at Paris airport had proved that he could stop people from moving. If he did the same to a window, it would shatter. I had to lie from that moment on. I had to convince them that he would attack the next time anyone stopped me leaving. I had to convince them that I had no power to do what he did. The first to give me drugs would suffer. Gradually people were entering back into the room. Most were to warn me except for one who'd just arrived. Pinstriped suit and a regimental tie. There's always one and it doesn't matter which country you're in. That one will always appear.

I saw this man lifted so fast and hitting the wall unconscious that even I could not believe it at first. Then he just disappeared in front of everyone. His clothes crumpled onto the ground. They scattered and my father grabbed hold of me in shock. Not two minutes later that man reappeared naked on the floor. Screaming. Screaming like a wounded animal. Frothing at the mouth. Then he disappeared again right in front of those re-entering. There was now a deadly silence throughout the building. I'm sure that they were wondering: Who next?

Four long minutes and then he reappeared again. Calmly this time, not speaking for a few seconds as he looked around him. He quietly got dressed.

Then he spoke to them all. 'I would suggest that you set this young woman free now. I would also suggest you never bother her or her family again. Anyone caught following her for any reason will just cease to exist.'

At that he left the room.

I stood up: 'Come on father, it's over and finished with. We are going home.'

I walked right by them with my father to his car. I told him he had a right as my father to know the truth. All that I want is to be allowed freedom of movement. To be able to study for the future and to marry someone. To have a couple of children. Much would have been denied me if he'd not cured my deformed leg. Ok, I'm prepared to talk now with anyone who will treat me with respect. But never will I be caged up like the children in England.

I have his promise that he will start at the top and work downwards if I disappear for no justifiable reason. He will keep that promise. His demonstration was done just to prove how easy he could do it. It was one of our ministers whom he terrified. That I didn't know about until I met him again. He came to see me at home. It was to ensure that I was well and would I accept his apology for his attitude.

That unknown boy, I first met in France. He lived within sight of me for the next two years. No, except for the time in Tunisia, we were not lovers. He moved into a small flat and became a bit of a recluse. He had enough money to last him and in secret we used to meet up in the sky to talk. He was my hidden guardian. He stayed to protect me and give me a chance to find happiness.

I found it all right. An invitation to a party out of town and I went to it. I had a lovely meal and then dancing started. I took up an invitation to dance. I danced with that man for the rest of the night. A minister's son. You know who I'm talking about. His father had told him all about me. He'd told him of my beauty and who protected me. He'd told him of the ghost that protected me. Even told him what the ghost had done with him. The son had come to see me, hoping to see a ghost. He saw a woman he wanted and he got me. What he didn't know was that his hope to see a ghost was right in front of him the night we met. He is now my husband and a Day Mover. His father was the second to become A Day Mover. It is worth it to have some one in his position.

My friend told me that it was time to find out about his family back in England. He left one day very early.

Chapter 17

BM

Just before I took the ferry across to England, I hid some of my old clothes in the woods. I used four different places to be sure that at least one set would not be found. They may have been waiting for me. If I'd have spotted anything unusual, it would as only taken a few seconds for me to disappear back to Belgium. Then I'd have moved east as quickly as possible.

I handed over my passport and in Italian I asked him to ring a number. Three minutes later it was handed back to me.

'Thank you sir. Enjoy your stay,' the official said. I had often wondered how anyone had got close enough to me to take the photograph inside the cover of this passport. This passport gave me more freedom than I'd realised. I just wondered how much it had cost. I travelled by train to my old home town. More than three years had gone by. Mum opened the door, screamed with joy and grabbed me. All the news came out that night. Mum had married the lodger and they had a little girl. My ex-girlfriend's baby had been a boy. He'd been adopted. In a couple of year's time I would find that boy. He'd show me the way towards him. Of that I had no doubt. When I at last ended up with just mother, that's when other questions commenced. Could I still fly?

'Yes, but with great care,' I said.

It was then that she took from a drawer some newspaper clippings.

It detailed of strange happening in London and then on the continent. France, Italy and Sicily. She sat there staring at me until I finally just nodded my head. She had the answer and that was enough for her for now. I screwed them up and threw them on the fire.

I'd enough money to get another bike. My intention was to become a good citizen. You know something. I had to then sign on the dole. What a farce it is. Will not be doing that for long. I purposely went into every office that I could find down town. Any jobs going I used to ask at the desk. Leaving a bit of skin here and there. I was going to get some more cash fast. Even went back towards Doncaster, then back to Hull. Bits and pieces were left everywhere. A took a few pence, at some places and up to over three grand at another. I created my own crime wave entering 188 properties in less than six weeks. Did I go back to sign on the dole? Did I hell. I never kept more than what I needed. All was hidden in little tins. Sealed up tight and buried in the surrounding woods. It was in the papers quite regular. No sign of any forced entry. Some remarked that it must have been an inside job or that keys were available.

I never stopped looking for pin prick lights in the distance. Sure some were shining on odd occasions and from different directions. None near enough to bother me though. I also never rose up in the sky until I was at least two miles away from my home base. I bought the motor-bike on hire purchase. The one thing that I did avoid was a certain bank. That bank had a massive amount of money in my name. I kept well away from the place. The moment I went to withdraw any money, there would have been a trail back to me. George just kept putting small amounts into it and he always put on the transfer an address in France.

I wanted to see Rachel. The house was empty. After making a few enquiries from lads at the park. I had a few answers. It had been emptied overnight. That to me was wrong for a start. Rachel's dad was buying it, not renting it. For over three years, I'd kept a phone number in my mind. I rang the number but it was no longer available.

Edith, now where the hell was she? Empty house, Edith gone. 'Bastards,' I thought.

If I found out that what I was thinking at that moment was true. Hell would be unleashed in London and the surrounding countryside. I started to visualise where most of them used to live. Not all could have moved. Somehow I would find her. I travelled home that day making plans. I needed more money than I had ever had before. Where could I get it from? Not the bank for sure. Then I cast my mind back to the car salesman with the gun. Would he still be doing the same thing on a Saturday night. Taking a bag of money home with him? Would he still have a gun. Let's find out.

Told mum that I was going travelling for a few days. No trouble, just going away. Less said the better. I needed another home base near London. Just south of Hatfield where I found my digs. Room to let. I spotted that sign at the house of a couple of old pensioners, man and wife. They needed some extra money. I gave him £100 there and then.

'Let me know when you need some more,' I said.

What a smile he gave me. It took some explaining to him that I would be in and out at odd hours due to my work. Next thing was to get some old clothes. I went all around the second hand shops, the markets. Every thing I bought cheap. Three tents were on the list. I then had to put everything on. I needed my body odour and flakes of skin on everything. Odd thing though. On occasions I landed away from my clothes. I t gave me something else to think about but not for the moment. Four days scouting around and hiding things here and there. That bike of mine gave me mobility. There had to be always two or more routes out from every hiding place. Never put yourself in a trap. I was lucky in one respect. I'd done a little bit of scouting early on in the mornings. This was before I stashed the clothes. I'd gone up to Harley Street and hovered about. I used to wait there just above the door. I could still recognise a couple of faces, even though they were older now.

That evening, I followed one home and into the backyard to see if I could stash some more of the old clothes I'd bought. I found a place at the bottom. Old grass cuttings in a pile. I pushed the parcel of clothes in. One edge was left open to the air. Just the one for now, I thought. I didn't want any alarm bells ringing just yet. At first light I relaxed and left my body. Keeping low to the ground I headed for his address. In I went and travelled slowly through the room. It had been the child's room where I'd entered. I could see a girl of ten and she was tossing and turning. I could see straight out that she was sick. I'd come for another reason, something more important, so it was into the master bedroom. A touch and he's mine. I purposely let him come fully awake in this hovering form. I let him feel the horror and pulled him slowly back through to his daughter's room. I paused just to let him see his daughter sleeping. Then I pulled him outside. I released my hold once we were well outside.

Remember this well all of you. No one can go back without my assistance.

This man was just in total shock. Just hovering around fifteen feet above the ground. He could not understand it, what had happened to him. 'Am I dreaming this?' his mind said quietly.

'No, you are not dreaming this at all,' was my reply.

'What happens now?' his thoughts came to me: 'Have I died or what?'

He was calm, this one. One of the calmest that I've ever taken up into the sky beside the minder back in Italy. Never again would I find another like him. Totally resigned to what had happened. As if it was normal.

'No, you have not died,' was my thoughts: 'I need information, otherwise you will be dead. The next one will be your daughter.'

He didn't know that I'd never have done that, but the threat was there.

'Where's Edith?' I asked him.

'Oh,' he said: 'They left about a year and a half ago. I work for the company upstairs.'

It was at that moment I realised that there had been two different groups of doctors. What I had was an innocent man.. I'd made a mistake. I just hovered in front of him. I could feel the fear welling up in him now. Fear yes, but he was still calm in his mind.

'OK,' I said: 'First of all I need information. Where are the doctors and the group from down below you. The ones who moved out. He explained the events. 'They'd heard only snippets of information. Winchester was heard quite often. That and the difficulty, of getting houses in certain price brackets. I have seen one of them quiet often though. He comes in on the tube twice a week. He's Dr Randolph Brunswick. Yes, that's his name.'

I remembered him very well. Now he's one of Edith's friends. I remembered that name because he just missed been taken by me. I'd left him out because he rarely stayed in his own bed. He was a bit of a ladies man.

'Can I ask you a question?' he asked me shortly.

'Yes, if it appropriate?'

'All of us have only heard rumours, about you and what you can do. I know the truth now and that has put me in jeopardy. We also heard another rumour about a doctor. He was taken twice. The first time he was taken and returned sick. I'm talking about very sick and yet on the second time, he came back cured. Am I to be returned to the earth? You see, my daughter is very sick. I need to be there for her.

'One question for you,' I said: 'How sick is she?'

'Terminally. She has another six to ten months.'

'Do you want to make a deal on your daughters life?' I asked. 'What do you mean?' came his thoughts back.

'Simply this. I will cure your daughter if I have your promise to never repeat what has happened this morning. Break that promise and I'll be back for you both. No warning will be given you.'

I could feel the answering thought before he even knew it himself.

'I promise,' was the reply: 'But how do you do it.'

I began to tell him how I could do it.

'Look at yourself now. You are a sphere of light. The light cannot be seen from below. A dark section would be a bad section. Remove that section away from the light. It's then done. Your daughter is going to disappear for one hour. She will then return. What's your name by the way?' I asked him.

'Simon.'

'Let's go down.'

Just a touch of my light drew him down and back to just above his bed.

'What's her name?' I asked him.

'June,' was the reply.

I then let go of him and I took his daughter above. Her light was dim. Very dim. Below me I could see that Simon had the windows open. Frantically looking around the sky. We were well hidden, just three feet above his head. The girl was awake and looking around. I was watching her mother. She stood there crying on Simon's shoulder. I could hear him telling her. I started to work.

'June my light is going to touch yours,' I communicated across to her: 'Think of nothing, but your mother and father. He has asked me to help you. I need a promise from you. Never repeat anything about today. You know what a bogey man is, don't you. You repeat anything and he'll come and take you away. Is that clear?'

'Yes,' was the quiet reply.

'Just relax now,' I told her.

I touched my light to hers. Healing thoughts were being transferred to her now. A clean up of her light was happening. It was getting brighter by the minute. The darkness was leaving her. Within a few minutes I'd completed the task. I had the best part of an hour to use up and spent the time taking her on a mad dash over London. June was happy, I could feel it. We headed back. It's time I said. I took her through the window. Her parents were sat apart, but staring at the bed.

'Bye June.' I let her come awake and appear in front of them both. I watched them stumble forwards to grab hold of her. Both were now sobbing. Simon, he looked around and I could plainly hear him saying it.

'Thank you. Thank you.'

I read in the papers a few days later, about a little girl being cured from Leukaemia. It was confounding the specialists. Her father, a doctor himself, never said a word. He had been warned.

Give a life and take a life. Randolph, I'm coming for you. I will wait forever if need be.

Five days of waiting paid off. I thought that I'd spotted him on the first day. Wrong man. He was older than what I could remember. It was five days of walking, sitting, drinking and generally getting pissed off. I was propositioned on the second day, followed him down an alley and kicked the shit out of him. Each, to their own. I was left alone after that. I watched every train coming in and every one going out. The fifth day, I saw him step on board and jumped on behind him with my parcel of old clothes.

I remained in the carriage behind him. There was a little clump of trees and bushes about fifty yards from where he left the train. He got into a car. I'd never thought about that happening. I'd got the number and the colour. It was a mad dash up the road and into the bushes. A really quick look to see if I was hidden and I relaxed and up I went into hover.

I caught him about thirty seconds later and settled down to tail him. Out into the country, along some winding roads. Had to keep popping up to check which way the station was. It was an area I'd never been to before. Up ahead there was an old mansion with high brick walls all around the place. I could see only one way in.

He stopped, left the car and pressed a button set in the wall. I listened to him talking into a box. A camera was visible at the side facing towards him. The gate opened slowly and after he'd driven in it closed automatically. That camera made me feel unsure for a few minutes. How many more were there? I found eleven hidden all over trees and pointing towards the walls. Others were pointing across. All high tech.

It'll not stop me. I don't need to get in for the moment. Remember the old saying. Cut off the head and the body dies. Believe me it's true. The windows were all sealed tight. The doors were sealed with rubber.

Let's have a look. He'd driven straight into a garage and never came out. On roof, the tiles were loose in places. There's one way I thought. New digs was my next thought. Sod it. I'll be back.

Took it slow returning, kept low and made sure I was safe to get dressed. I decided to take another look at the lay of the land. I was just rising up steadily when I spotted it climbing. I descended once more and dressed quickly before heading to the station. Hell did I start scratching. I'd left my cloths on a ants nest and they were all over me. Success and hell, both at the same time. I'd seen someone coming up to hover. But who? I tried to remember, or rather picture how bright the other light had been but I'd gone down fast to avoid it. I'll be back soon enough, I thought.

I'd time to make some plans now. I'd found them. Of that, I was sure. First of all, I needed to ensure that money was not going to be to be a problem. The gunman made it easy over the next few days. I watched him selling cars. I knew where the money was coming from. Deposits made on HP. He was still doing it the same old way.

Home every night with the cash bag. Same routine as before. I'm very surprised that someone has not tried it before. It had to be his office. The money was in his office when he was on the sales floor. Be cheeky, let's have a look at some cars. Anyway, I needed one myself by this time. I waited for him to go to his office that afternoon. Went in, poked my head around the door and asked to look at his motors. I dropped some skin, just by opening my fingers. The money was locked in the bottom drawer.

'Feel free,' he said.

He'd normally let you have five minutes to look and then he'd be out with his chat line. I'd spare shorts and a tee shirt inside my coat. I would need them to get back to my bike. These I placed in the toilet. It's only fifteen minutes before he shuts up.

As he came out of the office, I was already walking towards the street door.

'Maybe I'll be back tomorrow,' I says over my shoulder.

I was on my bike and parked two hundred yards away. I was hidden well enough. I pulled my helmet off, placed my head forwards on the front of the handlebars and I was away. Up and forwards and inside, right beside him, just as he was locking the main doors. Hovering behind him as he went to the office, not a hand's width between us. Out of hover and I moved forwards behind him.

He sensed me, but too late. I grabbed his hair and the back of his jacket. Ran him into the opposite wall. It took two quick bangs of his head and down he went. I went through his pockets for the keys and opened the drawer. Bag was already closed and waiting. Out, toilet, shorts and shirt on and I'm away in thirty seconds on the bike to my retreat, where I counted the cash and found I had enough for a fair few weeks.

Chapter 18

BM

I've now got enough money to last me for a few weeks. It will allow me to concentrate fully. I am going into battle with people who have only to request and they are supplied. I am one. They are many.

Rachel is sixteen years old by my reckoning. I've never really asked her right age or birthday.

I have now to find places that would be safe for me to hide. I need to store equipment. I also posted some money home for the family. I needed total commitment and didn't want anything else on my mind.

I then bought another motorbike and began to dig. It took me two days of digging. Two damn solid days, of carting away dirt. I'd bought a couple of light block and tackle units. These were stored safely away. Small hooks were fastened in the trees above where the bike was hidden. I knew I could lift it out within ten minutes. I had to make a narrow design otherwise I could have used my own strength to lift it out.

This was a fast ground based escape route made in case I could not get back to my first bike for any reason. I can remember that bullet in Malta and what it had done to me. Two tents were hidden and spare clothing. All of the clothes I'd worn. My nails had been cut carefully. Small bits of skin were taken from the sides of my fingers and hard skin off my feet. In an area of ten miles, I had twelve hideaways. I kept enough for immediate use in a small pouch I carried at all times. Getting a licence from a pub in London was also a must for me. It forms an identity for many people. Cost £50. When you know where the down and outs hang out, just giving them a little and you can get anything that you require.

It was now time to start. I moved to within a quarter of a mile of the place. I needed to log everyone in and out of the mansion. I was hidden under a roof of bushes that had carefully been pulled together with green twine. I'd fastened a piece of cardboard over the top of my binoculars to eliminate any sun reflection. I'd moved in under cover of darkness, taking with me an army poncho, sandwiches and a bottle of water. Car numbers were taken and make and colour of the car. Men or women. It became a routine for the first three days. Watching and noting down the main route in, checking also for any car that looked important. I noted how long each vehicle stayed. Who drove into the garage and who didn't. The garage was an extension on the side and it could hold up to fifteen cars. Most were coming from the town area. My next step was to check the railway station.

I hung about waiting. Sure enough some of the cars were parked there. Two of them were use by different people. Pool cars. Now to start following. Over the next three weeks, I'd the home addresses of twenty three people. I knew that rail line like no one's business. Each of them had different habits. Four went 1st class. Some smoked. Others dozed.

All had travel cards.

I then moved back to London. Each address was memorised and visited when I knew they were at the mansion. I kept myself solidly on the ground for this part of the operation. Night time was for hiding things. Bits of skin through open windows. Other bits pushed through letterboxes. Just rubbing a small piece of material could give me access. Sitting next to someone on the train and secretly touching a jacket, bag or briefcase would do it. I can get in anywhere, given the slightest opportunity. They were mine.

'Edith,' you should have listened to my warning.

Rachel

Life was great when I got home from London. I was allowed some freedom now. Mum and dad asked me to be careful in everything I did. I was starting to enjoy school. Had a couple of friends. Laughter and fun came into my life.

At first though, I had a few problems from the older kids. This was stopped by the headmaster. It was at the morning assembly. He caned the culprits, right in front of the school. They were warned to leave me alone.

You see, dad had a phone number to ring. This was just in case I had any problems. I never left my body for weeks on end. Whenever I did though, I learnt to twist around as I rose upwards. Just like my friend had taught me. I often wondered where he'd gone. No word came from him. I didn't no whether he was alive or dead. I was very frightened at first not knowing but as the next two years went by, I thought less and less of him. I'm growing up fast now. The best runner and athlete in the school. I can even beat the boys. I know that it's because of what I can do. It makes me far stronger. When I return, I'm healthy again, in mind as well as body. I can occasionally see other lights in the far distance. It's not that they are bright. It's because they are just there and I can see them. That's when I'm afraid. Mum and dad know this, because I told them one day. They know when I'm frightened. They just ask me to be really careful. What does upset me though is that sometimes the telephone will ring. They think I'm asleep, but I'm not.

I know that it's them calling. You see, we never have a telephone bill. The telephone came just after I got back. I've heard them talking about bills, but never the phone bill. I'm getting smarter by the day.

They came again for me. Mum and dad must have been expecting them because they never caused a fuss. It had been arranged this time. Two years of happiness and it was taken away in one day. It's always about money. I heard it: Your money will be paid.

We arrived at this big dark place. I was in total isolation for the first few days. Only one visitor allowed at a time and always watched by the attendants. I was never allowed to sleep during the day light hours. Then the dreaded drugs and wires started again. Miss Edith was in charge. Or I thought so in the beginning.

She never allowed anyone to hurt me. She was always kind. Gradually, I lost my fear of the others. My room was nice and always clean. I had a double bed, a wardrobe and a dresser. A big mirror was set into the wall. I was even allowed to put pictures up.

It was only by chance that I learnt that Edith was not in charge. No names were ever mentioned. It was very strange. I'd heard raised voices from the room behind the mirror. I'd put my ear to the wall to listen and I could only recognise the voice of Edith. The other voices belonged to men and they were telling her what to do and how to do it. She was trying to protect me because I heard her refuse at times. Then I heard someone ask where I was. I realised that they could see me through the mirror and I was now hidden against the wall. They had been spying on me all this time. I cried then and I prayed for my friend to come back. Edith came in quietly, not saying a word to me. I just pointed to the mirror and said two words.

'You bastards.'

From that point on I refused to do anything for them. They removed all my clothes as a punishment and said that they'd burnt them. All I was only allowed to wear from then on was a smock. I know under drugs that I told them of all my hiding places back home. I could hear myself telling them whenever they gave me a certain drug. I always felt sick afterwards. My room was always kept spotless. Everything was sealed up. The window and doors were air tight. Air conditioning through filters had been fitted. They were leaving me with nowhere to go at all. I'd lost totally, my boltholes.

A man came in most days to continue my education. Time's been dragging on. I'm sixteen years old and I'm a prisoner. I know of two others held here with me. Boys, but no names are ever spoken. I've done no harm to anyone at all. Why me? Twice a week I have to lay down. They then attach wires to me. Give me an injection and then I have to soar up and hover. I'm only allowed thirty minutes. Any partials left in the room will be cleaned up while I'm away. They even inspect my nails to see that I have not split them off in any way. I don't want to die, so I do as they request.

At first they were shocked at how I disappeared. Even more so when I reappeared without any warning. Gone in an instant and back the same way. I had to demonstrate it to many people. Some I knew were important, but names were never given. Then the time came when I had to take up some sick people and try to cure them, something I was able to do in a fashion, but not like my friend whom I think of often.

I'd just been going up as normal one morning when I'm sure I saw it. Just out the side of my vision. Then it was gone. Had it been a trick of the light or just in my mind? I was so shocked that I missed the opportunity to find out for sure. Another mover, it had to be. That light had been big and so bright. I was so shocked, that I could not move at all. I only just made it back in the time span given.

They knew something had happened for sure. They could see it in my face.

'Someone's out there and he's big,' I said: 'His light is bright.'

I had to tell them every last detail. The only one with a light like that I'd ever seen before was my friend. I yelled with happiness. Now you'll find out and I screamed again with happiness. It was either tell them freely without drugs or they'd get it with them. What a flap it caused. The place totally closed down for a full week. I heard Edith speaking just after I arrived back.

'We're all in the shit if he's found us,' she was saying.

Only important people were given permission to come in. If only I had thought to go to him. I'd have been certain. One thing they don't know and have never asked me, is the fact that I read. I read a lot. Always newspapers. I watch the television when they let me. Always looking for something strange or unusual. France, Italy and Sicily. Switzerland was another. That had died down really quickly in Switzerland for some reason. All had one thing in common though: an unusual amount of ghostly apparitions appearing over a period of time. Always a few days afterwards there would be reports of people missing. What they didn't know was that those people had actually disappeared before the apparitions and not afterwards. I know of only one capable of doing that. I hope that he's outside.

BM

Four solid weeks of planning. I just took one weekend off to visit the family. Collected some more from a storage area. Then a slow ride back down by train. I could not risk my bike's number being taken. The spare one that was hidden had been bought under a different name.

I'd visited my old digs. The old couple were still happy with the arrangement. Then I found another place nearer the Mansion. I dressed smartly and they made me feel like one of the family. Maybe it was the daughter though. She was a right cracker I spent the evenings with her. Sue liked the fact that I had money to burn. I bought a nice car and she liked that. As for sex, she liked that too.

After a supposedly hard day working as a rep, I fell asleep travelling home by train. I hovered into the adjoining compartment and took the two sleeping passengers up for a sky ride. All that was left were two piles of clothes and two pairs of shoes in one compartment and an old set of clothes in another. A mystery to be solved. Maybe not though, because it would depend on the train cleaners and how honest they were.

Back down to one of my storage areas. Quickly dressing, then walked to the nearest station and headed into London on the next train. Headed up to Hatfield. My first set of lodging. Went to bed early after setting my alarm.

Woke up just before dawn. Relaxed, transferred to a small ball of light and headed into London. Inside to touch them and then take them up and out into the sky. Then it was just a matter of leaving them with their thoughts. An average of ten minutes apiece, for six men and two women. Let them scream, let them be torn apart by the ghosts of the night. It will be interesting to read the papers over the next few days. Travelled then on a general heading south west. Down to another of my storage areas. This one was my car. I'd just left a slight crack in the window so that I could enter. Again I put my clothes on and then went to a phone box.

She would just be getting ready to leave. Just be in time to make her jump. Not a little, but high up in the air. I'm parked just a few yards down from where she lives. No way will she escape. I wonder what it's like, to pick up your phone and a stranger tells you that some of your colleagues have resigned and gone on walkabouts forever. That your boss will not be coming into work today, nor tomorrow or ever again.

'Can you remember me Edith?' I said: 'I'm back. Would you like me to take some more, or would you like to go also? The Daily Mirror, put a message in. Remember only one minute long calls. Who have you got at the Mansion. Where is Rachel? Bye.'

I then put the phone down. It took her less than fifteen minutes to reach the mansion. Inside, she was shut off from me. I have all the time in the world. I had to wait, spend the evenings with Sue. Then early in the mornings I'd have a casual walk down the road for a paper. That first day there was nothing worth reading, but the second day it started. It had only taken two days and it was all there for me to read. The third day it was about people seeing ghosts at night. Not one, but dozens of reports were coming in. On the fourth day, I rang her number again.

Edith picked up.

'Do not speak, but listen to me,' I said: 'Remember the routine of a few years ago in Regents Park. Something similar, but a different delivery man. It will be the same place and the same time. Three days from now, don't have any second thoughts, this time. You must start to talk at 8.oo am prompt. I then put the phone down.

Chief Inspector Charles F Lewis

I've seen some strange things happen, whilst I've been in the police force. There is nothing to match what has happened over the last few days though. A sergeant and a detective constable made the first two investigations. A report of three piles of clothing left on a strain. The guard and ticket collector had both made statements. Both said that there had been two older men and a young one. They had been there one minute and then all three had disappeared within fifteen minutes.

What a load of crap I'd privately thought to myself whilst reading the report. It was only when I was called to a meeting around eleven o'clock the following day that it ceased to be a load of crap.

Six men and two women had disappeared in less than sixteen hours. Two were junior ministers and the six others were doctors of some form or other. All were prominent in their fields. All through the meeting we were told that it was of the highest confidence. I thought it very strange even at the beginning. Being told that we were after a ghost of some kind. It doesn't go down well, at first. Then to be told in the next breath that this ghost could become human was taking it a little too far. No way would I believe it and neither would the others. The long and the short of it ended up with having to travel to Winchester, for a demonstration.

All of it happened in total secrecy. This came all the way from the top. I mean the top. We were hit with reporters all day long. Never have I seen so many. It seems that somehow or other, word had got out about very strange happenings in London. Reports were coming in about ghosts and not just individuals seeing them.

At 8.20 last night an old man had walked into a packed bar. Give me a beer, he'd been heard to say. When he tried to pick it up. His hand had just passed straight through the glass. The barman had fainted at that point. Cracked his head and was in hospital suffering from shock. The bar had emptied in seconds.

Another incident was on a bus. The collector thought he'd got a drunk on board. When he tried to move him, he couldn't. His hands passed straight through him. At that one sighting alone, three people had been hospitalised. One man and a woman both with a broken ankles and one man with a broken leg, the ticket collector. They and a few more had jumped off the bus at over 30 mph. More reports were still flooding in. The disappearance of eight people was tied in somehow or other and people wanted answers quickly.

It took four cars to get every one down to Winchester. A police roadblock stopped any reporters from discovering our final destination. Army personnel were already digging in. No one was going to get in. How would you take it, being told that ghosts were real and that a demonstration was going to be shown to us?

We were all led into a room by a woman of forty plus. The room it contained nothing but a bed and around a dozen chairs. On it was a young man. He looked quite well and fit. Very pale though, as if he'd not seen much sun.

'My name at this moment does not concern you,' she said: 'What you are going to see is real. Believe me, it will shock some of you. We need you to all sit down. In the past, some have fainted.'

I for one, being a Chief Inspector, did not take her words to heart.

I thought that I'd seen every thing in this life. I should have paid more attention but didn't at that particular moment.

'Look closely at the boy,' she said. 'Now I'm going to ask him to go to sleep. 'Go to sleep Geoffrey and then rise up and hover.'

What a load of crap I was thinking but it happened before my eyes and I shot back in my chair. I was sweating by this time and feeling a bit giddy. Within just thirty seconds, he reappeared on the bed, naked as if nothing had happened.

'Boo,' he said quietly.

'That's enough Geoffrey,' the woman she said to him.

With that we were led out. Two people were being assisted from the room to the toilets. The rest of us were mystified.

Now you've seen it. You had better believe it. That is only a part of it. I have to go out and face the worst part myself from tomorrow onwards. I am staying hidden until it's over. I am safe for the next two days. After that, I'm out of it for life.

My resignation, it went in this morning. What you are about to face, is a cold-blooded killer. He's totally invisible to you in daylight. We made him what he is. We have three of them. A girl, very strong and two boys, slightly weaker but getting stronger. Research shows that if you sleep past dawn, he can have you in a moment. Your family is now at risk from the moment that you entered this place.

I have told you this to at least give you an idea of what you are facing and why you are facing it. I was not authorised to tell you anything but have just for your family's sakes. No one had been informed of the risk that we were taking by coming here to witness this display.

They now explained how the experiments had started down to the last detail. They had worked with the children two years before. There had been no progress and they had been released. They had then been recalled. This order had come from high up. Taking what I considered innocent children even if they are abnormal is a form of kidnap. If it had been done out in the open with full parental permission, none of us would have been put at risk. The children should have been allowed freedom of choice. Now we have someone loose outside. Someone, who would eliminate anyone in his way. After half an hour the woman was back in the room. She was the key to finding the man we were after, I thought. Otherwise why has she been allowed back in. She talked about many other things that had happened over the last few years. Listening to her words carefully, I heard her explaining that he can take people from their beds just by touching and it's into another dimension. Hell, we are in trouble. Deeply in trouble.

Being a high ranking police officer meant that the ball was put in my court, so to speak. Even then, I could not believe all that I'd heard. Written reports were to be sent to London by special carrier.

BM

I've sure stirred a nest up. I knew damn well that the place would be locked up tight. It was to be expected. Here's me hovering in the grounds, checking out the quaddies. None of them had a clue what was happening.

'Whitehall flap on,' remarked one soldier: 'Why one up the spout though, that's not normally?'

I watched closely for most of the morning, checking out the field of fire set out for them. A total waste of good men. Tomorrow morning, I'll clear the lot out.

Then out came the VIP's. Guy, in the police uniform with all the braid, I followed back to London right into the police HQ. Hovered right behind him, through the doors. Stopped to see what floor he was heading for and then shot through a window. In through another cracked window and I was waiting for him to come out of the lift. I was faster than the elevator.

He went straight into his office and sat down. He must have sat there for at least fifteen minutes without a word. He then made a phone call. Four minutes later his office was full of braid. I was hovering just above them all, listening to their plans. I glanced outside and it was time for me to leave. A quick trip and I'm down safely in the car again. Much better than the cold woods.

Soldiers are soldiers the world over, but nothing can prepare them for what I did to them. In no way were they at fault. Just guard this place, but against what, they hadn't been told. I hit them just as the sun came over the horizon. No tent could stop me. Four men to each tent. I took two at a time well up in the sky, for them to look around. It took just a minute at a time. All of the sleeping soldiers were taken up. Only those on guard remained safe. The last that I touched and took up was a Major. Sorry guys but you stood not a chance. Maybe if they'd told you to be awake before dawn, then nothing would have taken place.

You could see the upheaval below. I'd taken them up just before their normal time to wake up. Guards were chasing all over the place below me, looking for missing comrades. By that time I'd gotten you all safely out of the unusually high winds. You see, I have nothing against any of you. All a soldier does is follow orders, cannon fodder for politicians. That's why you're here now. Some of you, have already broken down, others are a little stronger. I even told the stronger one's to reach out and assist others, just to keep you together.

I am keeping you all here for only a short time. It's a demonstration for the politicians and for those who have hurt my innocent friends. I am a ghost, I told them. I have the power to keep you up here. For you to be ripped apart by night ghosts who crave your essence. You would be lost forever.

For those who are married and have children. Remember this, remember it well, that I am giving you back your life for your children's sake.

I then kept them milling around for a little while longer. I then took them one by one down to the bed from where I'd taken them. At the same time I had to calm them down to prevent insanity. One by one they reappeared. Each totally naked. Grown men wept with relief. They had been informed by me on the way down that any who crossed me were doomed. I watched for a while longer. Comrades, all coming together and all of them knowing that they'd survived. I watched them being led away. All would be questioned. It had been part of my plan. I noticed one thing and it made me little jealous. The way the men came together in a group, each knowing the others thoughts, their experiences. They had something in common. They were comrades. All I had was Rachel and the two lads.

Edith, it's nearly your time. Shall I just take you, or should I now make another friend.

I took off just before seven, on the third day. I knew she'd be there waiting. What I did not expect though was the people with her. A young girl was sat down beside her. On the other side was the policeman. Charles Lewis. What I could also see surrounding them were groups of men. All were within, thirty to forty feet. I had arranged the same routine, but with a twist. I never sent in the tramp. Time came around to the hour. No messenger, but she commenced to talk to herself on time. She definitely knew because my little girl sat back smiling just on the hour. It was Rachel, but with a difference. She was not just good to look at.

She was absolutely out of this world. I was just staring at her and listening to Edith, not believing what I was seeing. She was stunning in every possible, conceivable way.

Let's listen to Edith.

'This is Rachel. We have the two boys. We were ordered by the ministry to re-start the program. They thought that after two years not hearing of you that it was safe to proceed. I volunteered to work with the children. That was to ensure their well being. In the near future I would like to speak with you in private. At the moment I have to follow instructions. I am now going to ask Rachel to speak to you.'

'Hello,' she said: 'Edith is speaking the truth. Out of everyone at the mansion, she is our only protector. I have been sent to ask you not to carry on with what you are doing. You have made too many waves and too many people have been involved. They have promised not to harm you in any way. You will be allowed to come on go as you please. We, that's myself, plus the two boys, will be allowed our freedom at the same time. We are being classed as too valuable to be put away. At the side of me is a Chief Inspector. He is here to confirm this from the government. At the moment, nothing has been fully confirmed. They are trying to contain it has much as possible.'

Yes, I could see that she'd been primed to speak as she did. I never bothered to wait. Not even to hear the man speak. What I did do, was check out his extension number. At this point, I'd got all the information I required. What I did need to do was take Edith without any interference, for at least five to six hours. Her house was totally sealed off from me, or so I thought. She'd had one taste and I'm sure that she did not want another. Unless that is, that I could promise to return her safely.

How could I do it? You see I could read between the lines. She'd said a little bit too much. That part about wanting to speak to me privately. It did not ring true. I had a feeling that it should not have been part of the conversation.

I head up into the sky and hovered to get my correct bearings. When would they be allowed their freedom and out of their hands? When?

Edith

I have been involved in this project for nearly twenty years. I am now forty seven years old. I am in extremely good health. I am not married, except to my work. What can I really say about the last few years. We all knew that these children were abnormal. Care had to be taken at all times. That crazy old man had started it all up again. It was known that many people had some rare talent. Papers from the archives had established that fact. Special permission had been obtained just to get them in the first place.

Once read, they were unbelievable at first. Some form of mutation had taken place. We started to pin point the nearest children through directions given to us by the old man. We would get the first bearing and then move to another area to get the next. Doctors were then visited and all unusual reports were taken out.

It was established very quickly that there was a common factor. Flying. We asked many doctors if parents had discussed their children's dreams. This made it easy to find them. Some were able to only disappear for a short time. Whilst the three that we concentrated on could make themselves vanish at any time of the day.

We kept on losing the weaker ones. We do know of about thirty of them left. These we have estimated as weak. Some of them belonged to the same family. They have been left alone. They are the offspring of soldiers from a special unit from the war. That is the common factor. There is only one other clue. Two of them were seamen's children. They'd been conceived just prior to their fathers being killed. Their ship had been sunk shortly after.

It was known only that heavy material for the first H Bomb had been on that ship. It had been carried aboard by that special team. All the offspring had subsequently been born with special capabilities.

Who then, was this other one? Who then was this other one? The one that eludes our every effort to catch him.

The only thing for sure, he had to be a sailor's son. Records of the crew had gone down with the ship. David, had got the closest to him. He'd not kept any records though. All we got from him was the fact that this one was really special and that he lived in Scunthorpe.

Due to the town growing so fast with the steel works and the amount of children, he said it was hard. He had also mentioned that he felt sure that this one had spotted him right at the beginning. David had been lost in a shooting. We read the report, but none of us could foresee what it would mean to us down the line. The report should definitely have been taken more seriously. It was only when we had the girl for the very first time that we realised that we had made a serious error of judgement.

We had deluded ourselves into thinking that it was a one off incident with David. We had a boy in the beginning. He's now a man, with complete hatred of all we stand for. We have only ourselves to blame. He came for us the first time. He gave us just a small demonstration then. We have studied reports from four different countries. They had something in their midst all right and I believe sincerely that it was us to blame. He warned us back then, yet here we are again doing the same old thing.

We are facing someone who will show some mercy at times. He will then callously kill others that stand in his way. His method is total and final. He does not even leave a body. There's no actual proof anywhere at all. The episode with the soldiers was just a way of showing us that we are helpless. Totally helpless. I need to let him know my only wish is that he will give me the chance to explain. I've asked him for that chance whilst I sat in the park with Rachel and the policeman, Charles Lewis yesterday. My bosses have given me a hard time but it's my life that I want. I am unemployed now and no matter how they threaten me I will never work for them again. Maybe I will give some names out, just to save my life. Beware the world for what this one can do. He can take anyone. I have said, that I was going to lock myself away. Everyone believes that this is what I'm going to do but for how long could I do it? I have to eat and sleep. I cannot stay sealed up forever, hidden in my rooms. He will be there, of that I'm sure. Whoever you are. My windows are open.

Charles Lewis

Over the last forty eight hours this place, it as gone mad. From every day crime, to ghost hunting. Everyone, from doctors and soldiers have all been interviewed, not once, but many times. It has only led in one direction. That damn mansion. I sat in the park listening to a woman speaking into thin air. Then the young girl said a few words.

Yes, I did see what that boy did at the mansion. How can I conduct an investigation? There are no bodies, none at all. It all comes back to what the boy demonstrated. Where is the evidence? All we have at the moment is statements. What a bloody mess. If just this one person is able to do this at will, what would happen if there were more than one? The majority of my officers had looked at me astonished when I gave detailed information out. They will definitely learn quickly. Another demonstration was going to be shown. This was needed urgently, just to convince them all of the serious nature of the problem and the undertaking that would be required.

Chapter 19

BM

I'd just got my bearings correct and as I began to move I stopped. Two brilliant white lights had appeared. I hovered watching as the lights rose and headed towards me. I'd been looking for two lights since my first day in London. The girls from France. They stopped in front of me. A few thoughts came through to me. I opened up my thoughts and allowed them to speak to my mind.

A scream of delight came instantly from both of them. Over the next couple of hours I informed them all that had happened. They in turn told me that they'd been in the States together. The news had broken out on television. They had taken the first plane back. They knew of only one person who could create this havoc. Me.

Both wanted to take part in what I was doing. Neither of them had known that I'd just won the first round. Help was there for me if I needed it. I had other news from them. Both were now courting. From now on, the Daily Mirror could be put into use when we needed it. Fridays.

I had a couple of days lazing about and then took a ride to Hastings with Sue. I needed the heat off. Let them relax their guard a little. Give them time to get tired of looking for me and finding no clues. Who would have thought that I'd go for the top man? He's the one doing a job of work, so I must not harm him in any way at all. Just the same as all the soldiers: cannon fodder. With that in mind I got to work. I explained to Sue that I would be away for a few days. I then worked out the movements of the Charles Lewis. I was lucky really with it being summer, the days were long. This gave me the opportunity to find out his address. He very rarely stopped. Always on the go. I'd never realised how much work a policeman did. SW1. Got him.

Don't worry, Edith had not been forgotten. I found out that she was waiting for me. She knew that I could take her. I was staying in my first set of lodging. I gave the old man some cash. Car's outside and locked up. Just sat there with them for a change. Conversation came around to the strange happenings of recent days. I told them that I didn't believe in ghosts. No matter what the papers were saying. I went to the off licence for some beers. Took the old lady a bottle of sherry. She really appreciated it. It was time for bed. Caught the news first though. No further developments and no statements given out.

First light and I was on the road. Just a short drive in the car to the railway station. I'd told the old man I was taking a train and that my car would be at the station. I left a key with him and he'd pick it up from the station within two days.

I got in the back, made sure it was all clear and let myself go. Up I went fast and headed to SW1. Hunting time. Sure enough I got in and all it required was a light touch to bring the policeman with me. I let him see the members of his family. His wife was sleeping peacefully. His two teenaged sons were snoring away. I then took him through to his daughter's room. A pretty little girl, she was lying on the bed without a care in the world.

I then pulled him out and up into the sky. I let go and waited for the storm. He'd read enough reports in the last few days. He knew that he was at my mercy. I put my thoughts into him.

'Don't say one word. The answer is yes. I'm taking you home safe to your family. Those that are innocent have nothing to fear from me. It is only the guilty that will pay. You have some friends of mine. They have done nothing. They have committed no crimes and have broken no laws. You are supposed to uphold the law.'

I could feel him wanting to say something.

'Don't even think about it,' I said: 'Let me now take you home. We will pass your children on the way down. Think of the love that you and your wife have given them. My friends have had none at all, for years. They have been caged up like rats.'

With that I did as I had told him. I led him back to bed, ensuring that he could see his children, as promised. Let go of his circle of light and within an instant he was reformed, naked and unharmed on his bed. I gave him no power to do anything. Maybe he would think it just a dream.

I got out of there and went to see Edith. I've learnt to estimate the speed at which I can move. At a standard size, I have wind resistance. This cuts me down to around 174 mph. It does depend on which way the wind is blowing. If I make myself small though, then I estimate that I believe that I could break the sound barrier. Just a few minutes, that's all it takes and I'm at Edith's house. She wasn't in bed. She was damn well hovering just above it. Well what have we got here then. Just like a policeman.

At that she spun around to face me. Her ball was large and not very bright. I touched it and she became brighter.

'Would you mind if I don't say anything for a few minutes,' I projected into her mind.

No reply gave me the answer. So this is what she wanted to tell me. I'd changed her, she was now just like me, a weaker one sure, but still she was one of us now.

I remembered taking her up and prior to taking her back down. I had calmed her fears and had brightened her light before she reformed. What was it now, four or was it five years ago? She'd kept this quiet. I don't believe she ever told anyone.

'Rachel told me you protected them,' I projected to her: 'OK. What can you do, and who the hell have you told? Let actual go outside into the sky.'

I commence to move out of there.

'Wait, I cannot fly,' she put to me.

I had an answer to one of my questions. I touched her and pulled her slowly aloft. Slowly up. Two balls of what appeared to be bright light, but not as the light that we know. What spectrum of light is it, I thought, as I took her upwards into the heavens. I took her so high that we could see the difference between night and day. The temperature had no effect; we don't feel cold in this form.

'You can say your peace,' I said to her as we went up. Should I have said it differently to her? Like, you can make your peace? I didn't know at that moment because even though she was now one of us, I needed to hear her tell the truth of the last years.

Edith

I'm caught, just as I expected to be. There is nowhere to hide from him. Unless you stay buried underground for the rest of your life. I've called him a cold blooded killer. Yet, he has shown mercy as well. Look at what he did to the soldiers, and yet he returned them safely back down to the ground, totally against the grain of what we usually heard about him. I'd also had a telephone call a few days ago. That deepened the mystery. A slight acquaintance from the old place in London had called me in confidence: Dr Simon Evans.

I'd read the report about his daughter being cured. He'd knowledge that he should never have had. He'd asked for me to get in touch with the man I was now facing. The way he asked for me to do it was not outright but with an indirect approach. What will be the outcome of this meeting? I do not know and I'm scared. More than scared, because I could be going to my death.

I'd been hovering around my bed for four mornings.

'Why did you take so long, to come for me?' I asked him: 'It's as far as I can safely go normally. Sometimes I struggle to get back into my body.'

What would it mean to me now, on my second 'touching' with him? Can he just transfer his force from one person to another, just at will. If he can, then does he know that he has this power. If he already knows of it, then what are we facing in the future and if what I have been thinking is true, can he cure people when he wants to? On the other hand he has shown how quickly he can destroy.

I have always wished for him to return. In my own way, I have tried to safeguard the children. Living with the fact of what I can do made me realise that I was no different to them. My body is healthy, more than ever. Yearly medicals cannot lie. They show me as a woman of thirty and not forty-seven.

I have to tell him of all this, to tell him how I have fought for the children. Good god, I think to myself. They are not children any more. Would this one free them on an un-suspecting world without any knowledge of how to live and survive?

'Let me start from the beginning please?' I asked him.

And thus I told him what had transpired over the last few years. Right up to the present moment. It was while I was telling him that he gradually came closer and we touched. He totally transformed my power. I would from this day forth be able to fly with ease. He was altering the structure of my mind. The more he gave to me the more I wanted. I wanted it all. He pulled apart at that moment.

'The part I have not given you is the ability to read my mind,' he told me across the void between us: 'You see Edith, I can read your thoughts. What is the truth and what is not the truth. You tell a lie and I will know.'

That really set me back. I'd had no reason at all to explain it to him. No reason to speak to him. He could take it all from me and did not need to ask. He could just take it.

'I'll visit the doctor,' he said.

That was it.

'Beware of one thing Edith. What I give, I can take away.'

Charles.

I was given a demonstration today. The power that this person has is beyond belief. He could take anyone he wanted. He has maybe two or three weaknesses. They could be played upon but on the other hand, he will not let anything or anyone stand in his way to remain free. Do I resign and let someone else stand in the line of fire? For that's what it is. That's what he was asking me to do.

Checks and inquires would have to made on the legal side of what he has said. I must, under the circumstances, explain what happened this morning. I believe that he has a sense of fair play or I would be dead now. I shall call a meeting. I'd refused all phone calls for the last two hours, even from the ministry. I pick the phone up. Meeting in five minutes in the basement hall, everyone in the building involved on this case. Bring some masking tape I instructed.

That was it, my mind was made up. I had to stay with it, regardless of what might happen. I knew that if he came again for me, it would be the last time.

The basement was full when I got there.

'Where's the tape?' I asked: 'Seal that door.'

They may have thought that I was out of my mind In a few minutes they'd realise I wasn't. For those who had never seen it happen, it would be hard to believe it. Demonstrations could be arranged for any non-believers. I explained what we faced. The looks of disbelief were plain to see.

We have all seen many things serving in the police force. Nothing at all like this. This was totally alien. Science fiction. When I came to the part about this morning, a deadly hush was upon the room. It had sunk into the majority that what I was saying meant that anyone could be taken at any time.

No one was safe.

My first step was to make sure all the records from day one were double checked. We had to put a name to the person. This was going to go back twenty years. The next step was for me to find a sign writer to put up some signs, reading: 'I am doing my job.'

These were to be fastened in the bedrooms at home. One was to be hung on the wall in my office. Let's see what type of person we face. I found out later that the majority did the same. For maybe the first time in my life, I had to tell my wife why I was doing something very unusual. The signs had to stay. It was the only protection possible. The Ministry were stunned. Before I would speak to them, I insisted on a sealed room with no windows. I'd been called before them with my own boss. I explained it all again to them. Take me off the case if you wish. Put someone else's life at risk. To learn that he'd already taken me that morning shut them all up once and for all. No, I can't repeat this in public. We had to have a name. Playing him fairly and keeping malice out of it, may be our only chance. The children are still held and controlled. To my mind they should be free.

Chapter 20

BM

I was sure of one point. Edith's house was being watched. Cars were at either end of the street, a couple of people in each, pretending to read.

'Note the cars,' I said to her.

I then went on to tell her all the methods of moving from place to place. She knew finally that she was safe from me. At long last I'd extracted most of the truth from her and for me to give out this information meant that she now had my total trust.

Mind you, I have to say this; she carried herself very well indeed. Once I'd established the facts, I could not destroy her. Her life would never be the same again.

'Hi, is doc Simon in?' I asked into the mouthpiece of the telephone: 'Edith asked me to call.'

I was speaking to Simon's wife.

'Sorry, he's nothing to say to you,' I heard. With that the phone went dead. I gave it just one minute and I rang the same number. It was snatched up. The word Edith had done it.

'Sorry, but we've had that many calls from reporters. When my wife said Edith, I realised that the message had been passed on. We need your help June. You cured her, but there's something else wrong with her".

'What are her dreams?' I asked.

I heard the gasp at the other end of the telephone.

'How did you know what I was going to ask?' asked Simon.

'Have you been reading the papers lately?' I then asked him.

'Yes, but what is the truth, we need to know?'

'Would you trust me alone with your daughter, or would you prefer that her dreams get worse?

'No..'

'To cure her, I have to keep her out for longer than normal.'

'Can we think about it for a few days,' he asked me.

'I never know from one day to the next where I will be,' I said: 'Do not ring Edith, she is being watched. She also resigned, as of two days ago. In Friday's classified, in the Daily Mirror. Put it June, needs sweet dreams. This will be your permission for me to take her.

The cure would be total. June would be a Day Mover. Would they be able to live with it? To me, it was not their choice. The girl could choose whether or not, to use her power.

I could not get into the Police HQ. I could see the sign facing the widow. I flew to CI Lewis's house. They were on the walls there, too. I had to give this man credit for what he'd done. OK, fair play to those just doing a job. OK, if he keeps to his word, then it will be fair play. For those though, who don't play it that way. That's another deal altogether. I'll give him the answer tonight around ten thirty.

'Hello, Charles Lewis here.'

'You have asked for fair play, Charles. As long as it's that way, then you shall have it. You can take the signs down from the bedrooms. Your family is absolutely safe. All he said was; 'Thank You. You know…"

I then cut back into the conversation. 'Hold it. Your house is your castle, I will not enter it again unless I have your consent. I do understand how the game is played. You will get that and no more from me.'

With that I put the phone down. I felt sure, he'd now protect my three people. Sorry it's four, going on five.

Let's take a holiday to Bournemouth. It's a nice day for travelling by car. I quickly took a trip back to Edith's house. She was there practicing hovering, bless her.

As I got closer she spotted me coming and rose up to meet me.

'I never knew how wonderful it would be,' she said to me.

'Fancy a trip?' I asked.

'Where to,' was her reply.

I read her mind, but maintained a block on mine.

'Is he really going to meet me in the flesh,' were her thoughts.

'Look down and see if you can spot a way past the guards?' I put across to her: 'Take a train to "Bournemouth. You will be met whilst your walking along the beach, early in the morning.'

With that I left for my car. I had a drive in front of me. I'd clean clothes, in a case locked in the boot. I'd not be going back to my lodging again.

I was waiting as she stepped from the train. She walked straight by me, her eyes everywhere. When I didn't acknowledge her, her eyes swept elsewhere along the platform. I trailed behind her, checking to make sure that she'd got totally clear. I was close enough to hear her tell the taxi driver which hotel she wanted.

I waited to see if anyone asked for the same hotel, then watched for any cars following her. She'd done it. Clear for three days. One last check and then I would be sure. Back to my car, checked it was clear for me change. Up and over to the railway station, then along the main road.

I knew the location and was there before her. I watched her book in. Then I hovered above the desk. I estimated if she had been tailed they would only leave it fifteen minutes before checking out the room number.

I stayed there for a good hour. No one came to check. It was a definite go. She'd made it totally clear.

I travelled back to my car and checked around. Clear to get down and dress. I booked into the hotel and had dinner at the same time as Edith, though not at the same table. I was sat to the side a few tables along. Did I look my best though, you can bet. I'm just over 5ft 9" and built like a brick shit house; solid muscle all of it. Yes, the muscles of my arms are extremely big. I've compared myself to others and I know what I look like. You don't have to look twice; it is solid, hard, hard muscle. My teeth are white and straight. Hair is medium in length, and not what I call untidy. My eyes are dark brown. I must be OK because I find girls so easy without having to go out of my way. Look back at Sue, she was lovely and she came to me.

An old lady's dog had just pissed on the floor and didn't want to come into the dining room. I'll tell you why later. Poor thing. Not once did I let myself look at her fully. I had my meal and then went to the lounge. Ordered a beer and sat down to watch the television. Ten o'clock is the best time. Edith had disappeared upstairs about half an hour ago with a bottle of red wine. No news is good news.

I went to bed around ten thirty. I have the perfect alarm clock. It tells me when the day is arriving. At that precise moment, I leave my body. I waited above for her, maybe about half an hour and sure enough she came to join me. I'd positioned myself about fifty yards from the hotel. Fairly low down and about ten foot off the ground. I soared upwards briefly just to check we would be totally on our own.

'Where are you staying?' were her first words.

I laughed out aloud at that. It was the first ever time that she'd heard me laughing. Even though she could hear me, others could not.

'See you on the beach,' I projected into her mind: 'Go back down and no peeping.'

She did, laughingly. I gave her fifteen minutes start. I then returned to my bed and dressed in shorts and shirt and then I was outside looking for her. She was three hundred yards along the beach. Just staring out towards the ocean. Every so often I could see her head turn. I took a five foot jump from the wall onto the sand and walked to meet her.

'You,' she said: 'You were there last night, right in front of me. I was watching you and you never once looked at me. How cruel can you be, to do that to me? I was hoping that it would be someone like you. I shut her up by kissing her gently on the lips.

'You're not as tall as I'd thought you would be,' she said.

At that she paused for a few moments.

'Why now and why me, after all that I've done over the years?

I gave her an answer that she already knew.

'Read your own mind and look back over your own thoughts,' I said: 'Never once have you intended harm to any of those in your care. All you ever wished to do was study, to find out why. Let's not talk shop for the next two days. Live for a few days without cares.'

We went for a swim. Just like two ordinary people. I wined and dined her. We were nearly drunk and waiting for the right time. How would we break the little barrier that was holding us away from one another? It's maybe the easiest method, in an un-written book: Just say the words.

'Do you want a nightcap upstairs?'

On entering my room it broke the last bars holding us apart. Just two people, a man and a woman, wanting to love each other. Both of us realising that time would fly by quickly.

Not often do I let my guard down, but I did the next morning. I awoke to discover that she wasn't there and, after a moment's panic she reappeared beside me.

'Just been out for a check around,' she said.

Her body looked so beautiful when she appeared and I took full advantage.

'Let's have a picnic,' I shouted through to her whilst she was taking a shower.

'OK,' came the reply.

Imagine it, the two of us doing it. I smiled to myself. Edith was a happy woman, perhaps for the first time in her life.

A table cloth on the grass and little plates of sandwiches. Did we laugh that morning? Edith told me of her life, as a little girl growing up. Her always wanting to be a doctor. Everything came out.

She had money in the bank. Most of it had come from her father. It had been that money which kept her from marrying. She would never let anyone have part of her family's money. The sum gave me a shock. Well over two million. I told her how I had obtained my own little sums of money. I even told her how much I had banked and why I never went near it. How much I'd earned from one small job in Sicily. Only a small amount had been spent on personal pleasure. She told me of all the reports. How somehow she knew it was me and of the fear she'd sometimes felt, knowing that one day I would return.

It eventually came around to my own name. The one on the licence, "C. Windsor" and the address in Norfolk, she'd gather already that it was false. That is one big secret, that no one and I mean no one will ever find out from me. It's my last defence. Listening to me say this to her brought back sombre thoughts to both of us at the same time. Tonight would be possibly the last time. Neither of us was going to waste any more time. We packed up and went back to bed. First thing in the morning, I was out sharply for a paper. It was "Friday". Classified time. I left her to catch a train to London. We were both aware what we faced in the future.

Let's talk about Dogs, cats and birds. They just do not like me at all. That is, until I've touched them. Even as a child, many a dog has growled at me. When I got closer to them an attitude change came over them. A tail would go between a dog's legs. Once I'd let them sniff me or I'd gently stroked them, then it was all right. I was an unknown factor to them up until that moment. It was the same with cats. Birds though, with them it was different. I could always hear them singing first thing in the morning and yet even when I got closer. None stopped. I've had the wildest of birds unconcerned with my presence among them.

Remember the dog from the hotel dining room? It must have been terrified by the presence of not one, but two very strange human beings. I like dogs and birds and tolerate cats.

The children have not been released as promised.

Edith

My life has totally been turned upside down. In a matter of a few short days. I have no job. I'm being watched. I've been totally transformed, except for one little thing. Something that even he would not pass it on. It had to come from within yourself, the power to heal. It had been a secret between Rachel and myself. She had told me of that one difference. She can only do it on odd occasions.

I've been to bed with a stranger and yet he was not a stranger. He is twenty six years younger than myself and yet I felt like a young girl in his arms. He has managed to hide himself away from everyone for sixteen years. He has taken life. Even the lives of some of my friends, yet I do not hate him for it. He can read minds. What did he read in the minds of my friends to make him do what he did to them? I understand now about the ghosts of London and where they came from. The people transform from human form to a weak white sphere unable to defend themselves. They were taken up by him, left by him, for the ghosts to devour as the dark night comes in.

I am a Day Mover at last.

Down to earth though, I've people to see. Solicitors, in London will be my first call. I want them off my back. I did arrived in London by train. Took a black cab to my family solicitors. I had to be very careful what I said to him. My main priority was to be free of those watching me.

The fact that I'd resigned before most of the damage had occurred helped me a lot. It took a few telephone calls by my solicitor to make progress. First the denial, that I was being watched at all. Then finally a request came through asking if I would be prepared to make a statement.

No, was my immediate reply. Then came the request for an informal talk with CI: C. Lewis. I agreed to this as long as my solicitor could be present. One other item that I would not accept: a recording of the conversation. I also had another appointment set up for Saturday morning at ten o'clock with a girl named June.

BM

June's parents were sitting by her bed when I arrived on Saturday morning. The window was wide open. They never felt any sign of my presence. I touched against her and I let her disappear in front of their eyes. June was so much more alive from when I'd first seen her. I let go of her and let her roam slowly around the room. She hovered in front of her parents. Not a sign came from either of them. They just sat there looking at each other.

'June,' I said after just a few minutes: 'I was told about your dreams. Your father has asked me to help you. Does your mother agree?'

'Yes, they talked it through with me as well,' she said.

'It is your choice though and not theirs,' I explained to her.

'I want it,' came her response.

'OK, we are going to touch gently.'

With that I transformed her light until it was bright.

'Listen to me carefully,' I said to her: 'A woman named Edith will be calling today at ten o'clock sharp. She will be your teacher. You have a lot to learn and you must learn it fast. Just tell your parents her name and the time. I need you now to awaken and return to your body.'

With that she did so. Just to see the surprise on her parents faces.

Chapter 21

Edith and June

Precisely at ten o'clock, I rang the doorbell. It was opened sharply by Dr Simon and I was invited inside. We walked through to the lounge where I was invited to sit down. First I took my coat off where upon Simon took it from me quickly.

'Sorry,' he said: 'Even a doctor can get flustered. I know I'm one myself.'

How am I going to explain about June who was sitting there quietly smiling? It was Simon who broke the ice by telling me how he'd been taken by mistake. He did not know how he'd got away with it and had thought his last days on this earth had come when it happened.

'Who is he?' he asked me: 'I do not know his name. I only know what he is capable of doing. What I do know is that as of this morning, your daughter can do many strange things. She is also in great danger from the people that I've worked for during the last sixteen years. If they knew what she can do now, they would be knocking on this door. They would have been here before me.'

He has asked me to train her and this must be done immediately. She will be safe if she follows a few basic rules. The first rule and the most important is the daytime rule. Day moving only because she is now a Day Mover. I was looking at June while I explained this. Over the last sixteen years, we lost a few before we understood. It's only been, a few days since I found out exactly what happens at night.

Your sphere is pulled apart by any number of night ghosts. Small amounts at a time until you totally cease your existence. This happened a few days ago to a number of people. You must have read about the ghosts appearing over London. Now you know where they came from. At that Simon put his head down. He then lifted it and told me that he was perhaps responsible for one of them. You had no choice at all and no chance at all. You survive by telling him the truth. He can take it from your mind if you refuse to give it freely.

At this I told them all about a little boy. What he had to do, just to survive to manhood. If he says something, then you'd better believe it. How I have survived, I do not know. Maybe he'd been into my mind a few years ago. A few days ago I even called him a cold-blooded killer. He is all of that and maybe more. On the other hand and sometimes without any logical reason he will help someone, especially the very sick. June is a prime example. I believe that he lost someone close to him when he was younger, maybe before he knew what he could do.

I could not tell them of my last couple of days. That was mine and mine only. I did tell them about the bits of skin, clothes and anything that you have touched. That is the key to moving. Your daughter can transform both of you at any time, if you ever wish it. Another very important thing is never talk of what you know. You will not survive it. The people in charge would not believe that any of you could not do it. A catch twenty two. You are caught either way. After what has happened over the last few days, it would be wise to keep very quiet.

‘Have you any questions?’ I asked.

Simon’s wife said nothing but listened, still in shock from what she’d seen earlier in the morning. To see it happen does not mean that your mind believes it.

It took another hour of questions and answers until we finished. I left at noon.

I’ve decided to sell up and move north, live where it all began in his old stamping grounds. I didn’t want to be anywhere near London when the storm broke. It was bound to break soon; I knew him of old. I also knew the minds of those above me. The ones who were left that is. He had power that they wanted. He would not wait long, if they try again. The next time it would be from the top down and not the other way. I will be staying out of it.

Since the storm broke and just prior to leaving, I’d seen one report. Destroy or use as a weapon. It did not need a brilliant mind to understand that letter. They are fools. He just wanted to be left alone to live his life. Others would be searching for him, and all like him. Even the weak ones were not safe now. All the known ones would be taken.

The cold war would be concentrated here in England. Both sides would be searching for us. The West had the advantage at the moment. Hopefully I can hide with three of them, but I don’t know for how long.

BM

I’ve been away from home for a few weeks. Sent some money home with a letter to mum. I then started to compile a list. It was a long list of people directly involved with the kidnapping of

Rachel, Michael and Geoffrey. These were going to be my target. From Edith's mind I had taken a full list of names of all those able to transform. No matter how weak they were at doing it.

With it was a list of those involved throughout the project. Who they were and what they did to contribute to locking up children. Who would have thought to search in there? From it, my list was made up. I sorted it out to my advantage. Some had retired, but these older ones had ordered and set the standards of today. I started tracing these people. A library is the best place. Scanning through all the back papers and slowly moving up to the present day.

Every Friday, I search the classifieds. It has taken me nearly five solid weeks of research. The majority have been in the papers at sometime or other. I've been through all the electoral registers. There again I've hit a name or two. Find a few names and then find the people to match the names. An electoral register will give you an address. The children are still held captive. No lights have I seen.

Then it's confirmation time. Drive to the area and set up shop. Parked well clear of busy areas I can disappear into sphere form to investigate. The list it was whittled down slowly. Some had died, others had hidden but there was enough left for me to work on. A few minor details were the only things stopping me. Like a twenty-four hour guard for some of them. This time it was not all going to be one way. It's time though for a few days north before I start.

I arrived in the early hours. Total darkness met me at home. No sooner had I opened the door when my step-father came rushing down the stairs. My mother had been buried for three days. For a week they'd been trying to find me. I was really out of it, I can tell you. The only person in the world who I loved. The protector of my childhood and I'd not been there for her. Five weeks it had taken her to die and I'd not known. If I'd just come home two weeks earlier I could have used my skill to cure her.

Someone will pay for it, someone will pay dearly.

There was also something else missing from the sky. All the weak lights had disappeared. Except for one. One light. That I'd been looking out for. One that was now starting out on his young life. A genuine Day Mover. I had seen just a flash from him on the west side of Lincolnshire. I knew the exact location and Knew who it was going to be. My son.

CI: C Lewis.

The mansion is sealed off to everyone, unless they are accompanied by one of my officers. No one is left alone with the young adults. If they get out, then we will be in trouble. Deep trouble. It is a prison for the three of them and every door and window in the place is sealed. Three people at a time just to open a single door. One to open it, one to check that it's closed and then two to check that the door is sealed. It's the only method we know, other than the ultimate act. Who would give that order? Not me. I remember his promise. Every last little scrap of paper was taken from the mansion and it went back years. It's all been brought up to London. I have been reading it for the last few days. Twenty years worth of experiments, tracking suspects and endless failures. It was spread out in yearly sections to every officer we had available.

Long hours were ahead of us. The tracking section that was the most important on the agenda. We needed a name and a body that went by that name. Within a matter of days we had the general area. One of the searchers had been killed in Scunthorpe, Lincolnshire. His partner was seriously injured. We needed the full report for that one. Rachel the girl, came from Dunscroft, in Yorkshire. That was just twenty plus miles from Scunthorpe. Under the influence of drugs the second time she was taken. An escape route was in that direction. One report gave out that David had lost someone in Scunthorpe. Then he found another person in Hull.

Then reports that he'd written out later, were of both places one after the other. David had got close. He died when he got too close. What was the common link? Had he found the same person and was that person travelling from one place to another. Age? When did it all start? Just after the Second World War.

The report concerning the material transferred by boat was found early one morning. That was another link. Date it all together. Births, starting point to be nine months from the transfer of atomic material. We need to be in Lincolnshire. The transfer of officers will take time. Ministry is getting impatient despite the advances we've made. Some think it a waste of time. Time is a killer of interest and that's a problem. Others do not like the cost and yet some are chasing me for more progress, Why?

Further, the fact that for some reason or other, I feel that there are other parties involved now.

BM

I've spent the last few days with my brothers and sisters talking about mother. Remembering the good times that we had with her. There's nine of us. Eight of us were from my father. When mother was pregnant, he went back to sea. Then he came back and she was in the club again. That's what it seemed like. Mother had taught all of them well. None were as able as me as our ages differed, it made their power weaker. The youngest was my sister of six and a half years of age.

It was time to teach them. I took the three eldest out with me one night in the car. I had a lot of talking to do. They had to be given the facts, all the fact about what it would mean to them. How it would end if we were caught. I gave them information about many things. I'd avoided the issue of my brothers and sisters for along time. One thing I had never understood. Why was it only me who had the power to heal the sick.

I gave them one week to decide, with the younger ones, we would have to take a chance. How hard it was for me. I'm so bitter at the moment. One thing I could not leave to chance; that was the lodger. His suspicions had built up over the years. One thing about him, he was younger, than my mother and yet he married a woman with eight children. He became a father to them. I was proud of him for doing it. No, I will not harm him. He will be changed and in that way he is protected from me. That was what I thought to myself just before I took him away from his dream early the next morning.

I calmed him from his first fears.

'Hi,' I said to him: 'You're quite safe. Nothing can harm you.'

I then went on to explain why he was in this form. He called me every name under the sun, then said he would have rather been left to make his own decision. At that I commenced to read his mind, looking for information. I found it quickly for there was nothing to hide. I'd underestimated him in that respect. He already knew and had it confirmed by my mother a couple of years back. Yes, you could not have missed it, bringing up that many children.

'The rules where given to me by your mother,' he said.

With that I brightened his light a little. I needed him to have less power than my own kin.

Three items of information would save us all. At the time I didn't know how important it was. One place that I'd visited a few years back was the Registry Office. That's where I found the first information about my son. I'd then destroyed all the records for births, from one year before I was born until three years after. I then destroyed the records of my family surname at the rent office. That had been done once I'd arrived back in the UK, and found out mother had married the lodger. That place had gone up like a bomb. It was totally destroyed. I can make explosives so easy and it doesn't take much at all. Electoral Register. Forget it, my mother would never register to vote. They are all crooks and all as bad as each other, she used to say.

I met next day the woman who would become my future wife. My lover and my friend, my nurse and the mother of our two boys. Truth can be found on record. It is there for you to find. She was my ex-girlfriend. The girl from when I was seventeen and half, the mother of my adopted son. We met at the telephone box around the corner. We looked at each other and that was it. We held each other and cried. We headed for the woods and made love. I arranged to meet her over the next few days. It was my brother who found out about the strangers in town. The police were making door to door enquiries on different estates. The town was buzzing with talk.

CI: C Lewis

It's a shitty place when the wind blows towards the town. Appleby and Frodingham is only one of three steel works in this northern town. We found out immediately about the missing birth certificates. A copy of which was requested from Somerset House. Four years of births. He thinks he's clever does this one. Electoral Register next. Every single name on the list had to be found and traced somehow.

One consolation at least, it's boys only, now grown up and parents themselves now. Every single house we called at. We need this man. Found out about the main rent office being destroyed yesterday. Damn him, if he was responsible for that. He's covered his tracks. How many people move into a town for a few years and then leave? How many leave a town and never move back? With this one I'm sure his roots are still here. Everything points to that fact. We've pulled in a few already. All released. Still on with the house to house enquiries.

Where's that last report sent up? BM.

'This one is the average young man from this town,' I said to my men.

I did not realise at that time what I had in my hand. If I had only known then, maybe the outcome would have been totally different. He works all week and then he gets pissed on Saturday nights. He was still pissed Sunday morning when we interviewed him. All the time he was on about his mother. She died two weeks ago. We had confirmed that part as true. That's all what we got from this one. Do you damn well think, that our man will be pissed as a newt.

BM

Yes, I did have a few beers that Saturday night, with two of my brothers. I was sat in an armchair that Sunday morning when the two men passed the window. They knocked on the door a few seconds later.

'Just a second, Sis,' I said to my sister.

I grabbed a can of beer out of the cupboard and opened it. Had a quick swill.

'Let them in now and then go in the back,' I whispered to her.

What a sister. She opened the door and shouted back through to me.

'It's them coppers come round,' she shouted.

'Tell them to sod off,' I shouted back: 'We ain't pinced ow't.'

'Sorry sir, we have to speak to you,' came a voice from the door.

'Get your arses in then, I want to get back to my fucking beer,' I shouted.

A general enquiry about who you are and where you work? How long you have lived here? And so on. Whilst they were interviewing me, I took a few drinks from the can. Frod was one answer. It was short for where I worked. The full name must have been put in many times over the last few days. Appleby and Frodingham the main steel plant. First name I gave them but it wasn't mine. They were never going to find out. Three of us brothers have the same first initial for our Christian name. What I wasn't to know is what he put down at the side.

"Pissed".

It could have been why, they never found out about me. That interview finished quickly.

I'm going out with my girlfriend later on. We are re-establishing what we had nearly four years ago. Love for each other.

To make it legal for me to drive a car, I'd also applied to take my driving test. I'd been driving illegally for years. I brushed up on the Highway Code and duly took my test. Passed it first time. Sent the pink slip off with my provisional the same day. I wanted that full licence. Then I'm going to start back down south. I've a job in London to finish. Once I get back down there it should only take me a few days to wind it up. Do what I had to do to fully warn them away from me.

I parked my car outside the old man's house and knocked on the door. He and his wife had both been wondering where I'd got too. Soon settled it though. I explained that this would be my last time there and with that I gave him two hundred pounds in cash. They both loved the money more than me, but that's life.

I'm due out early in the morning and I went to bed around nine pm. My eyes opened with the dawn chorus. I closed my eyes and relaxed, feeling myself changing to a sphere of light, listening to all around me. Up and heading south. Under gaps on doors and through open windows, going quickly to each house on my list. Touching them gently, drawing them all out and into the sky. Leaving them alone one by one. Not a word did I say, not even one calming or healing thought. Retired politicians, ex MP's, a few doctors, policemen and ex policemen, retired military men. Women were included on the list.

What did they all have in common before I took them up? They'd used Rachel's healing power. Kept it totally to themselves. Her power to heal was there even though it wasn't very strong. This had been taken from Edith's mind. None of the children of those I took up that day had ever needed a doctor. A total abuse of power which could have been shared. I had to then start all over again taking them back down. All totally insane, for I'd given none of them comfort or healing at the point of taking them aloft. That is one of my secrets of what happens if I release them too soon.

The mind cannot take the impact unless I hold a person for longer than ten seconds. They all have tried to become Day Movers but have failed. The Day Mover choose who will be changed, not them. I'd taught Rachel very well. I'd had enough at this point. The ultimate choice would be given to them. They would give in at the next telephone call or else. Back to my car to have a check around before I head back north.

CI; C Lewis.

I answered the telephone and what I heard left me speechless. Twenty seven, very prominent people had been found, between the hours of 7.30 am and 10.00 am this morning. None could speak a word and were found cowering up on top of their beds. All were naked. Their minds had been taken from them. Damn it, he was in London. Had he been there all the time. Were we wasting our time here? At this point we were exhausted with the amount of ground we'd covered. It was arranged for most of the group to return while the rest carried on. A very fast car, for myself, it's a 168 miles to London, high speed down the A1.

BM

Well I'm not fancying the drive north. It's just passed 1.00 pm and I've hit the A1. Just driving along with the flow of traffic. A jack knifed lorry, two cars smashed up were ahead of me.

One was a police car. I could see all this as the traffic was waved by steadily. They were trying at that moment to cut metal away. Trying to release a man in the police car. I caught a glimpse and I decided to find out more about that accident.

I pulled up at the next Service Station, wound the window down a fraction. Had a good check around me first and then I was up and away.

I was being nosy this time. I was going to see how they were getting on. I'd done enough damage for one day and was hovering around seven feet in the air above the fireman's head. The car was a mess.

Of the two men in front, one was definitely gone from this world. The other was in a hell of a state. I could see where the dashboard had been hammered back with the impact. The seat was jammed underneath it. Let's move around the car for a better view.

I recognised his face, Charles Lewis. Bloody hell, I thought. The one man in this damn country who had the means to find me. What should I do? Should I leave him to his fate. What about his family at home, his wife and children? I'd promised not to harm them. What would he do for me if the roles were reversed? Without another thought, I went in and touched him. His body disappeared. I left behind such a commotion. Right before their very eyes, I took him from them.

They were staggering around each other asking questions. Others sat down, not believing. Others were rushing away, for telephones, no doubt. This was going to hit the news.

I took him upwards to around a hundred feet and then headed towards his house. On the way he was coming into his own. Not because I was feeding him with power, but the fact that I was commencing to heal his injuries. We are told about the need to wear seat belts and here we have a preacher, who hadn't one on at the time of the accident.

We talked on the way towards his house. He asked me what I was going to do with him. He hadn't a clue as to the direction we were heading in. The last thing he'd remembered was the car hitting the lorry. To wake up next to his quarry had him wondering alright.

I assured him that I would be taking him home. No harm would be coming his way. No powers would he inherit from me. Just the healing of his body. We paused above his house.

'How your investigation going on then?' I said: 'Have you found my lair.'

'Progressing well,' was his reply.

'Well I've a little for you,' I said: 'Your mind's an open book to me. They're not all drunks in Scunthorpe. I am also going to give you the ultimate choice. If my people are not released, then I will hit the very foundation of our country. All the family, beginning with the highest of the land.'

It was the biggest bluff that I was ever going to make.

‘By the way,’ I said: ‘I need permission to take you in. Remember my promise?’

His response came and down I took him home.

I’m now on my way north again. Stopping for a bite to eat and a drink. I listen to the news. There’s quite a commotion going on in London. Reporters will get the facts and then a little can be added to spice it up. Then the report came on about the disappearance of a police officer, how badly he’d been injured and who he was. No way could they hold that one back from the public. Too many people had seen it happen for a gag to be put on it.

Speculation was running high about how it had been done. It was the next day when it totally exploded out of all proportion. A reporter had come up with a photograph of Charles. Being hurried into the Police HQ, he had no visible injuries. Put two and two together and can you make five. Questions were now being asked. The questions were coming from the newspapers. People wanting to hear the truth. I am on my way to see my girl.

Chapter 22

CI; C Lewis

What is this person, that he can callously destroy one minute and save others the next. My life was over. I'd received terminal injuries in the car crash. My very existence is down to him. There was no justifiable reason for him to do what he did for me. I am trying to track him down and yet he came out of nowhere to save me. Just what would happen if we released the girl and the two boys? I have passed on his threat to take the highest in the land. Who did he class as the highest though? There is a nagging in my mind though, that it's a bluff.

What was that he said, about the drunks of Scunthorpe.

We caved in within three days. A truce really, just to give us the breathing space. Too much had happened in so short a time. We had to find out why he'd chosen the ones he did.

That Doctor Reynolds has been requested in to see a board. I was ordered to attend. I was beginning to really respect the man I'd been searching for.

Edith

A car from London will be arriving shortly. I have just time to reflect on what has happened over the last few days. My guards had been called off. Bit of a joke really, because they'd taken to watching from the house across the road. What havoc he's played over the last few days. When will it end and how will it end? Was he crazy to rescue that police officer. No, I don't think so. Underneath, there something that's good in him. I've seen what he's like in the flesh.

In two days, I will be house hunting. Here's the car. Not taken long really and we were there. Was asked to sit down and wait for a few minutes. Then requested in to sit around the table. That CI sat next to me. He caught me, looking at his face. I was wondering about his thoughts.

They got to the main point very quickly. A house to be chosen and the three children to be under my care. Did I give it to them all, there and then? I'd resigned. Did I let loose? They were trying to control what I did where I went. No way. I will not be dictated to by any man.

I stood up then and told them what I would do, under my own free will.

'First of all, what sum of money, have you in mind for a house?' I asked.

That sum I doubled immediately.

'Now you can forget,' I explained: 'Whatever else you have in mind. A capital sum now, for detention of minors without a justifiable reason. A means of changing, all surnames to those I choose. Only one other person to know the name I choose. That man is sitting next to me.'

With that I was asked to withdraw. An hour I was kept waiting and was finally requested to return. They still tried to sway me, to let them have a means of controlling the situation. I just stood up and said plainly for them to hear; 'Goodbye gentleman, it's be your turn next to feel his anger.'

With that I left. I could hear the commotion as I walked down the stairs. I also had someone walking down besides me. Charles Lewis. Chief Inspector.

'Good for you,' he said quietly to me.

Those words coming from him meant a lot to me, someone was now on my side. What I now firmly believed to be the right side. It took them just a matter of hours to cave into my demands. I was at home by that time and received the details by phone. I headed directly to the mansion by car. I told them to leave the doors open, for I was taking the children out with me. That certainly got them moving. Every door way was now open.

Rachel, she was first: 'Pack you bags, you are out of here in the next few minutes.'

The same with Michael and Geoffrey.

Astonishment was on all three faces and I'd no time at the moment to explain. All they had between them was a few bits and pieces. They were into my car in minutes and I drove them to my home first. I spent forty five minutes packing my cloths and we were out of there, heading north. Just the four of us heading north.

I sent Michael out in sphere form to check the rear. He appeared back in the car naked and was embarrassed with Rachel giggling. He dressed as fast as possible and then told me we were clear. No one was following us. Let's see if I can open their eyes to a little bit of pleasure. Blackpool, here we come. We all spent a mad four days shopping for clothes, on the ride and attractions at the fairground. Looking at all the lights strung up along the sea front, taking our minds from the past. On Monday morning, how we managed to put every thing in the car, I honestly don't know. It was time to head to Lincolnshire.

Rachel had already explained to the boys about the area. How flat it was, and how far you could see. That means a lot to a Day Mover. I'd already set out a schedule because they had to catch up on a lot of schooling. On a natural rise to the east of the River Trent, there is a little village close to Scunthorpe called Scawby. I'd seen a house advertised for sale and had arranged viewing for Monday afternoon.

Even on the outside it looked suitable. Inside it was found to be just what we wanted. It was vacant and ready for us to move into when formalities had been completed. I used my mother's maiden name to sign the legal documents. My solicitor had already been informed of my intentions so everything was soon cleared. I wanted to hide the fact of who we were. I hoped the village people would think that I was a widow with three children and left at that.

Michael first and then Geoffrey, asked if they can take driving lessons. They need to be mobile and I know the reason for that. Rachel has been teaching them both. Even though she is not yet seventeen, she is the leader of the three.

Michael four days later spotted the lights west and had come back down to his body quickly, opened his eyes and started screaming that they were coming. It woke the house up in seconds and we all ran to his room. Calming him down was a bit of a job until Rachel told him to grow up. We all listened carefully to what he had to say. Four lights were west of us and one of them had come very fast towards him. It was the fastest he'd ever seen a Day Mover move. It had been very close before he'd got back to his body. At that I just told them he's here and he's found us as I planned that he would.

All three then started to talk at once. Yes, I'd planned it all right, our protector, was within range. Rachel screamed for joy as soon as I managed to tell her who it was. The boys just smiled, knowing that at least someone was out there for them. I then sat down and told them what had happened over the last few weeks and what he'd done. I also asked them not to be surprised if he was listening in to the conversation. I only left out a couple of days. That was mine and mine alone.

In the mean time we have a lot to do. The garden needs clearing for winter. An old pond needs to be cleaned and repaired. I've just put an advert in the paper for a handy man. I'm not feeling well this morning and I'm going for a check up. I'm a doctor, damn it. I know what it is, but I have to have it confirmed.

BM

The week is up for the answer I need from my two brothers and sister. What a funny answer they give me. If we get married they began, will our children be affected? I answered that one with a yes. They would have the same power. That was the only honest answer that I could give them.

Now my sister wanted one week more and that then, it was to be taken from her. My two brothers wanted to retain the power but needed that little extra to move in and out safely.

You know something, we were all enjoying ourselves that morning. There was myself, two brothers and my step-father, just pratting about in the sky. Playing about, weaving up and down. It was there before my eyes and I had just time to call to them.

'Down, Quick,' I projected to them.

With that I was small and speeding up fast towards the light on the hill. I'd just time to catch it drop into that old house. I hovered there for just a few moments and then descended down to circle the house. I could hear the commotion going on in one bedroom. Listening in I heard the last part about a really fast light. Then I just hovered there, laughing to myself whilst the rest of it unfolded.

I had to go home in the end because I'd left three worried people descending in a hurry. Ended up telling them I'd met a friend. Yes, I'd succeeded, but had I? British Law is the greatest in the world in some respects. But the British Policeman has no equal. Armed with just a piece of wood, he patrols the streets. He commands respect from all sides. The arm of the British police force is long. Never will I forget that.

I've promised my girl friend to get a job. What do I know. Only how to be cannon fodder for the politicians. The army. Yes, I volunteered in the British Army. It's now 1967 and I'm twenty two years of age. Parachute Regiment here I come. Have just a couple of weeks left before I go and I have a few things to sort out.

First of all and I don't ever know how it started. A hard case from down town was rumoured to be looking for me. It was generally known by some of my old cronies. BM's back. Word gets passed about sometimes about fights and fighters, as everyone knows. It only takes a few beers and trouble's there before you, sometimes without you ever realising it's coming your way. Now very rarely did I ever get the chance to get into town. To me it's just a row of shops. Only if I wanted something special would it be a quick trip in and then back home. Now the girlfriend, she loves to shop. Even if she's no money, it's a need in her to go, just to look.

I'd never even thought anything about the rumour, couldn't give a damn really. Trouble was, it was the girlfriend who was threatened. She'd gone out with a friend shopping as usual. She was well known by everyone and that led to her being accosted by the town gang. Not kids but men of twenty or more and their girlfriends just outside a pub. The *Oswald* right on kicking out time. How unlucky can you get, to be just passing at that time? They knew she was my girl. She got punched in the mouth by a bastard and then they asked where I was. I'd recently had a telephone installed at the house. Our first ever phone. I answered the phone and was told by her friend. Go back to them and tell them I'll be there in fifteen minutes. It took me ten minutes to get there. Out of the car and straight over to the girlfriend. I took one look at her and asked which one.

She told me and I looked over to see him smirking away. Thinking he was safe in a gang. His mistake, because I just walked over. He saw me coming across the road and his smirk was coming off his face as if he couldn't believe what I was doing. I didn't pause, but nutted him straight across his nose.

At that I hit the one next to him before he'd time to react. Two were down and four to go. I took a lot of punishment in that fight, the second guy I'd hit even joined back in, but all of them I put down.

Then I finished it. The supposed hard-case was getting up when I grabbed him again. I just commenced to punch him. Head, body, head ,body. I stopped when I couldn't hold him up any longer. He was out cold. I just turned to their women.

'You tell these arseholes that I'll come back anytime, any day and any place.'

They were swearing all sorts at me. Hell, I'm bleeding but standing and my clothes are torn. Fuck them, their down. I was in a bit of a mess. My face was cut, I'd a black eye coming on. My knee was grazed. How was I going to get myself out of this. I couldn't disappear to hover form because I'd heal automatically. I'd just have to let nature take its course.

That fight made some doubt who I really was, and I was thankful for that.

By the way, in all the years since, I've never had another fight in that town. Mind you, I've only been back twice. Once, for just six years and the second time for two years.

Charles F Lewis

The case was squashed and shut down, orders from above. I'm off the case but I still have access to every report. For some reason, something important has been niggling at my subconscious.

I have been thinking about this one subject for a few days now. At every meeting, we were sealed in. How did he know about the report I'd thrown in a bin? OK, it had been recovered later in the day and I have it. This one particular person. Age eighteen. DOB but looked older. One of four brothers. He has four sisters. (one a step-sister) Frod. Mother and father deceased. Step-father. At the bottom was the word.

Pissed.

Something is not right. I'm going to do this one myself. Let's look at the father first and see what he used to do.

Dole Office, let's check out that surname. First thing National Insurance Number. With that I telephone that office in Scunthorpe. It came out. A certain man had come onto the registry there for only four years. Previous to that, he'd been a seaman. Can you check all the others with the same surname? Interesting this is. Let's check with Navy records next.

It was the following day before I had that answer. The ships were all there and there it was before me. This man could have been on that vessel. He'd been injured one night. The date coincided with the one ship that had carried radioactive material. The son of that seaman. Now where were the reports, on the others?

I was quietly satisfied in what I'd found out so far. Opening the other reports gave me a shock. There were three of the brothers with the same initial. One was far older than thought. He'd signed on once and had never gone back. Never ever collected any money. It was all there facing me. I had knowledge that could get some one killed. What was I to do with it? He'd said fair play. Would he keep to his word?

The case is finished but I need to know the answer. I put all the documents into my briefcase and left the building. I need to be home with my wife and as every woman knows, when her man is troubled. She came over and sat with me.

'Penny for your thoughts dear,' she said.

I now told her that I was sure I'd found him. I knew exactly where he was. The street, the house and his name.

'Go see him,' she said: 'It's not as if you're going to arrest him is it.'

I then received a beautiful kiss from my wife. She'd settled it for me. I'd done my job, but was stopped by the powers above from completing it. I stopped next morning hundred miles along the road and told the office I'd be away for a couple of days. I'd a few days due and I was taking them. I continued north along the A1, cut off at Newark and went through Lincoln. Twenty two miles to go and I'm feeling a little bit unsure by this time. I'm not in uniform. I'm now heading for a town called Brigg. On the map there's a short cut through Hibblestow. Next one is a little village. Nothing happens in villages.

That's it. No sooner in it than I'm out of it and I'm nearly in Scunthorpe. Ashby, a small village that now forms part of the town called Scunthorpe. I had to stop at that point. My heart was pumping fast and I was really sweating. What was going to be his reaction to my appearing before him. Having stopped and calmed down, I needed the directions to the street, which I got from a news shop. I bought a local paper, some cigarettes and matches.

Opened the packet and put one in my mouth. Lit it and for the first time in my life, I smoked a cigarette. I did so while reading the paper and sat in the car. I read about the normal, every day happenings in the town.

One story was about a gang fight the previous day. Drink was put down as the main reason. That struck a cord with me. Was it an omen. I folded the paper, put it on the seat beside me and thought.

Let's get it over and done with. I parking outside a very ordinary council house, not smartly painted, but clean and tidy. Kids were playing up and down the street. In and out the gates chasing each other. Was this where he lived? Could it be that with all the power he had, he preferred to live like this? That he just wanted to be normal, like everyone else? He could just take anything from anywhere.

I knocked on the door and it opened. Before me was a man of around twenty two by my estimate. It looked as if he'd tangled with a bull. His face was battered and bruised. I could see a massive black eye. He'd been fighting all right. Around 5 foot 9 inches. Built like a brick shit house. I've never even to this day seen a man of that size so broad in the shoulders. His arms were all muscle. Seeing the state of him at first glance threw me off immediately. My man could not be in this state, if he could heal people then surely he could heal himself? Did I really have the right man. I could only just get his name out at that point. What did he do? He just smiled at me and asked; 'Have you found that damn drunk yet.'

I'd got my man and yet I hadn't.

Next words were quiet simple really; 'Would you like to come in and have a coffee?'

With that I entered. Seeing the telephone I asked him; 'Can I call my wife, she's waiting for good news. She also wishes to speak to you.'

My wife must have been waiting at the side of the telephone. It was only one ringing tone and it was picked up.

'Everything OK?' she asked: 'Is he the right one and is he there with you.'

With that I passed him the telephone. Everything was fine. I was at the end of the trail. What should I do about It. At the end of his conversation with my wife, he replaced the phone and sat down in a chair facing me.

A young girl came in carrying a tray with two cups of coffee. A little smile on her face gave me the opportunity to smile back. At that BM smiled and then commenced to laugh. He told me everything and looking at him sat there, I knew that I was facing someone who, if he'd wished could kill me.

That story in the paper had been him taking on six grown men. All he'd done was to protect his own. Nothing more, nothing less. He could have done far worse but hadn't. He could make me disappear, without trace. The trouble was though, I was beginning to feel comfortable in his presence and he damn well knew that too. It was as if I'd known him all my life. Five solid hours of talking.

An evening meal was put before us and time continued to pass as we talked. What a life he'd had. Hunted from every corner. I could hear the rest of the family talking in the back room. They did not even know my name. Yet they had known immediately that I was someone important to their brother and we were left alone. I went to fetch my briefcase. In it was all the information I had collected, about him and his family.

He could see what it was. I put it in the fire page by page and let it burn to ashes. It was over for good, as far as I was concerned. I'd resign and take an early pension before looking for this person in the future. He could just disappear at will. How would anyone find him if he wanted to stay lost.

'Let's go find a hotel for you,' he said at long last: 'I'll stop and have a drink with you. You've got to keep up appearances in this town.'

Damn it, he knew all along that I'd trace him through that remark he'd made to me about drunks. He'd intentionally given me the means to find him. How did he know what I'd do? Something still was not quiet right.

That's exactly what we did though. I booked into a hotel and then sat and had a drink with him.

In the conversation he had come up with the possibility that others would try again and not necessary people from this country. My mind went back to my own thoughts on that subject. His words on that subject were:

'West and East.'

Chapter 23

BM

I'd spotted him just as he drew up in his car. He come alone and not in uniform. This was something for him alone and not to be discussed with others. For me the day ended as one of the best that I'd ever had. Never before had I ever talked with someone for so long. He was a gentleman in every respect. I had given him a clue to finding me and I cannot say even today whether it was intentional or not. Tomorrow I have to find a way to see some people in Scawby.

It was easy when you consider that a gardener was required. It was at the village shop that I spotted the notice in the window. The address given was where I needed to be. Even though I was well dressed and drove a car, I still got a few frowns from the person behind the counter.

My bruises and black eye was plain to see. It took just a minute to drive up the road. I stopped and walked down the drive to the house and knocked on the door.

A tall young man answered.

'About the advert for a gardener,' I said.

He just looked me up and down frowning away: 'She's in Brigg at the moment and shouldn't be long. You can sit on the porch if you like.'

Just like that, and he just shut the door. I could hear him talking to someone inside. I saw the curtain move a minute later. I was been watched and about thirty seconds later a young girl appeared from around the side. She was staring at me, trying to place me. I decided to put her out of her misery.

'Hello Rachel,' I said.

At that it was all arms and legs as she clung to me, laughing and crying both at the same time. The two boys appeared behind her

'It's him,' she screamed at them: 'It's him.'

She still hadn't a name for me. The young man from the door tried to mutter an apology for shutting me out but I just grinned at both of them and we all shook hands.

They asked me why I'd come and I explained that it had been my light they had seen the previous day.

Michael said that he'd never seen anything move so fast and he'd been petrified. I told him that I'd known that, as I had listened at the window. We had only got really talking, when we all heard the car arriving. It was Edith returning from Brigg. Her face lit up and we spent a couple of hours all talking at once. Then it settled down to talking about the future.

Michael wanted to be an airline pilot. Geoffrey a doctor. Now with Rachel it was a different matter. With her being so young, she had a hard time thinking about what she wanted to be. I put a thought into her head.

'Why not, Drama and Acting School,' I said,

After all she was very beautiful and I could just picture her as a leading lady.

It was time for me to leave. Edith asked if she could come to the car with me alone.

‘I have to tell you something,’ she said quietly to me: ‘I’m having a baby, yours.’

I just pulled her close and hugged her tightly. Then I whispered.

‘I know, I read it in your mind a few days ago and I also know what you wish to do. The answers yes.’

I kissed her knowing that I would not be returning to interfere in what she wanted. She had the means to do it. Only if she ever needed me would I return.

‘There’s one more thing to do,’ I said: ‘You know those little snuff boxes. I want you to buy six of them. Empty and clean them out. Each one to be filled with nail clippings and rubbed off flakes of skin. Do it for the baby when it’s born. Each name must be inscribed on a tin. Then wrap each one up with grease proof paper. Bury them together under the corner of that flag stone.’

I pointed the stone out to her. It was right up close to the hedge running around the property.

‘Tell no one under any circumstances,’ I said: ‘Here’s mine and I gave her a little bag.

I’d done some thinking about all of this. I could have had them out sooner if I’d done this earlier.

Little did I know what was in store for them and many others throughout the country? My own need for nail clippings was not necessary all the time now but I said nothing.

Let’s go back to myself at twenty two years of age. I needed to do something honest, a real job. That’s why I joined the Army. It was also a means to getting married and having a house. I have collected a fair amount of money from some of my hideouts. It's going to give me a clean start.

I had a warrant for Aldershot. I said my goodbye at the station.

I was on my way to Maida Barracks. I had nothing to fear, Foot slogging and training I could take in my stride. I have never ever stopped my own training but these days I always do it in secret. Can any of you remember platoon 303. You will know the year from that one. Can you also remember a recruit, very fit and strong? Can you remember when he bounced a corporal in the Naffi Club one night, to protect a young girl?

He didn't know at the time about the guy being a corporal. Can you remember the military police arriving at the barrack? Do you know how much the colonel fined him? One pound.

Only one pound you may say. The facts are these. I protected that girl from someone who would not leave her alone. It would have been an insult also for a Para not to have done what I did that night. The hardest part about any training is co-ordination. This comes to you by the drills and marching. Working together as a team. For the average recruit it is a shock to find out that although you classed yourself fit prior to joining. You soon found out how unfit you really were. Take a quarter of a mile run. That, at the start, was hell for most recruits. It's a build up of strength and stamina over a period of time.

Remember the milling sessions in the gym? How he just stood there for at least a minute and then put his opponent down with one blow. Some of you will remember me in *1 Para.* I could give you a couple of real names to set this straight.

Sgt Danny O'Mahney was in *1 Para*. So too was Joe Lee. He was well known to everyone. Abingdon at parachute training went like a breeze. Eight jumps to qualify. Yes, I did my training and ended up in *1 Para*. I never forgot about the little bright light I'd glimpsed though. I considered that it was now time for a close up visit.

It was one early Saturday morning when I decided on the spur of the moment to be there waiting. It was a free weekend rest at camp. What's a journey of less than one hundred and sixty miles to me, at the speed I can travel? I hovered above a mainline railway station waiting silently for it to appear. It came out and up without warning and stopped so quickly. He was watching me all right. Nervously watching and ready for immediate flight.

I could feel the fear coming from him. His young thoughts were fast. Fly away, stop or try to talk.

'I'm the brightest of the lights that you see,' I projected across and into his mind: 'I am not here to hurt you in any way. Sometimes you see me, many times it's others.'

'Who are you, what am I?' were his thoughts: 'My parents cry sometimes. They are worried that I will be taken away.'

It was his thoughts that I could feel and it moved me to feel them.

His childhood was going to be a mirror image of my own if I did not help him now. I gave him advice and instructions. I told him as much as possible. First thing was about the night. And why not to use the afternoon. How to come up into the sky properly. To keep low before rising. Then the thorough checks to be sure. I gave a message for his parents. This was to expect a letter very soon.

‘Try to be careful in everything that you do. I, or a friend of mine, will be back in the future to help you. Do not be afraid of any lights from the east because all of them are your friends.’

I moved away from him slowly and then turned and took off fast. I got married that year and my wife was pregnant again, for the second time.

No, I’m not flying these days. It’s a closely guarded secret. I’m just relying on long runs and fitness training in the gym. I still feel that people are wary of me for some reason. I always will be on my guard. I have three close friends and no more. My wife and I bought a caravan on Pegasus Village. This was where we had a small community of soldiers from all three battalions. Six months later, we got a married quarter.

Good job, because Aden came up.

A DC10 took us there. Radfan Camp, known to all. Lost three men in a few short weeks. One of which was my best friend at the time. 20th June, it happened. I received gunshot wounds. In total I ended up with thirteen scars from it.

I nearly went crazy at one point, but I’d promised myself never to go back to what I was. I ended up back in England. Medi-vac. I was not allowed to parachute. It was due to the metal in my spine, and they downgraded me. I was to go to another regiment, when something made me ask a question.

My signing on papers, I was sure that they had Para only on them. It was true. I became a civilian overnight.

It was SAFFA which got us the house back home. For three years I’d only disappeared into the air once. Once and for all, I’d had enough of what was wrong with my back. I became a sphere again, so bright, and way up in the sky. It took me over an hour to bring the bits and pieces out of me. Absolutely clean again and really healthy, in body and mind.

Charles Lewis

I have kept periodical checks on him now over the last couple of years. He's settled down to being a soldier. I had access to information so it wasn't hard. Gradually, I'd stopped thinking about him. That is until we started Terrorist and Hijack training. I had the perfect person, able to infiltrate anywhere. Trouble was he was in Aden.

It was a shock to see his name on a report that came in on 20th June with a full list of those killed and wounded that day. I wondered why he was not using his gift to cure himself. He could have run riot just on his own. What was stopping him? Two months later I found out that he was now a civilian. I had to travel up north again. I made a phone call to his old address. It was answered by his step-father. I gave my name and he recognised it from my previous visit, three years ago. I explained that it did not involve any trouble, but I wished to have his stepson's new address so that I could visit him. He asked for my number and told me that he'd pass on the message.

That's as close as I got and all I would get. I know that I could have obtained the address by other means but I didn't want other officers involved.

How lucky can you really get? I was later on introduced to not one Day Mover, but nine. It happened like this.

Two days had gone by and I picked the phone up as normal.

'You are invited to book in to the *Star Hotel* in Scunthorpe on Saturday if you want to meet me. No other way and no other place. Bring your wife if you wish.'

I arrived with my wife Saturday afternoon. A wedding party was taking place that afternoon and it would be going on through the evening. I spotted him with the party, but not before he'd spotted me. He waved and then walked over to shake my hand.

'Business or pleasure,' he asked outright.

'A bit of both,' I replied.

'Why don't you join us? My sister has just got married. Tomorrow morning we can talk about business.'

I was welcomed to the party. If I were a friend to this one, then I was a friend to the remainder. I had a jolly good time and so did my wife. I opened my eyes to feel myself floating out of the bedroom. There was nothing I could do about it. You bastard, I thought to myself. I should have known where we'd talk. Up in the sky.

He turned me slowly around. There were nine more orbs of light. In the distance to the west was another brighter one. Three of them were very close. Five were about five miles away, one of which was very small. On the horizon, flickering on and off were some weaker light spheres. 'There are nine strong ones and littered around the country a total of around thirty others. They have no real power at all,' he said: 'There are also three very strong ones in London. By now, there could be more. I have not kept a check.'

I explained why I'd want to see him, to ask him really, if he'd agree to join a team. His answer was immediate.

'No.'

He was in fact reading my mind, his answers arriving before I could think the words.

I was jealous of his powers, of what he could do. I'd never admitted it to myself, but it was all true.

He touched me then. Just a touch, to join our spheres. He gave me the power, to transform. Not the power to transform others, or the power to heal. He'd given it to me so that I could be the one to join the team and I would be get close in the event of an hijack or terrorist attack.

He then told me about his sister. She had lost her power the previous day. It had been a promise to take it away for her future children's sake. At that moment I felt proud of this man because he was not abusing what he had to give. He also went on to explain about the other lights, some of which would be losing power in the future.

He then asked me if I'd be informing my bosses.

'No way,' I said to him.

He left me floating there and away he went. For a second I was alarmed, until I realised that I didn't need him anymore. I thought myself down and awakened on my bed.

That was my introduction to the fact that ghosts do not have clothes. My wife was just turning over and I shot off the bed into the bathroom.

He called me within ten minutes, to inform me that a letter would be arriving on my desk next week.

'Follow the instructions to the letter or you will not survive,' he explained.

I have that letter locked up at home. My wife read the letter and knows that if anything ever goes wrong, she will burn it immediately.

BM

Over the last week, I have been bugged with something. Something was wrong with the sky. I just couldn't work out what was wrong. Then it came to me. The sky was getting empty. I broke the speed limit on my bike getting to Scawby. As I came level with the house, I slowed down to look. No lights were on, yet the car was in the driveway.

Then just a couple of hundred yards in front of me a car engine started. I whipped the bike around fast and nearly lost it. I took the junction at the end without checking for traffic and wound up the throttle. Around a couple of bends and then a sharp turn into the woods onto a narrow track.

Most people know of that track if they live in the area. That car was about two hundred yards behind me, following as fast as possible. I always check for escape routes. It paid dividends that night because the track narrows too much for vehicles with four wheels. It comes out on Holme Lane. From there, you have the road into Bottesford village.

I got away for sure and there was not a chance of them having my number plate. If they'd been just ten seconds earlier, then my family would have been found.

I never took the bike home again. I gave it away, the next day. That morning though I went back. Hovering silently above and then around the house. It was empty. It had started again. This time though, they had cleared the sky except for my family and a small light to the west. All done under the cover of darkness, and at the same time. It could have been only a few nights ago but they had a start on me.

Who, was the big question? Just who? Where do I start? They will have gone underground for sure this time. I cannot take revenge on innocent people and nor can I take anyone up without disclosing that I am hunting. This time I will really hunt them to the end. Sure it may take some time, but sooner or later they will want a demonstration from those taken. That will be their mistake.

They don't know where I'll be or in which direction to look. I have also found out an important fact. I can go up very high. It had been a mistake that I'd made one afternoon. I'd left it later than normal. Night ghosts had been on my tail. The only way out was upwards into the unknown, to find the light of the sun. They cannot follow me into sunlight. As I went up I angled north towards the pole. It was summer and night was just an hour away. It never gets dark there above the night shadow. I went higher, to find out how high I could go and it seemed as if I could have gone on endlessly to infinity and I had to come back down to earth again.

One more little secret that may come in handy and it may save me one day. The darkness I no longer fear. Millions fear the dark of the night and there will be more to join them before I'm finished.

Chapter 24

BM

Finding them will be hard, or so I thought. There will be no sign in this country.

Over the water west will be the place where I'll find them. I'm sure of that. Remember my talk with the CI. I remember my chat with the CI and we'd both agreed on that little point. How could I hit out at people at the top in this country, if they had no knowledge of it taking place? It would be just one man acting on his own. Someone, who would have been paid plenty of money, just to give out the information.

At some time in the future I would see a light, but it would be in a country to the west. I had to start somewhere. Where would they have flown from in England? Mildenhall, maybe. It's the closest and it would be a good start.

I had to break a rule then. I had a full passport in my real name from my army days. I went to the bank and drew out a large sum. There was a little bit of a commotion because this was the first time in years that I'd ever gone in there. Proof of who I was. I slammed my passport down before the manager and told him I needed his phone to ring head office. Who's damn money was it? His money or was it mine? I then told him it came every month from France, e the date when the account had been set up. I had signed my name four times in front of him.

He settled down after that. It's not every day someone walks in and asks for twenty thousand in cash. He's lucky, because how I was feeling then. I could have wrung his bloody neck.

From there I walked up the road and opened another account. Back to that bank within half an hour and transferred the lot to the new account.

My wife is no fool. She knew I had a secret and had asked many times about it. I always said to her that the past is best forgotten. We had a boy of three by then. I gave her the account number and told her that she was required to go up and sign for the joint account. She came back with surprise on her face.

The money had shocked her and now she was starting to fish for information. Where had it all come from and how had I got it? Most of it I told her, belongs to a man called Richard Martin. It was the truth because she was talking to him, one name that I'd used on the continent. I'd never disclosed anything about the years abroad. Our life together had started when I came back.

I also told her that she could use that money in an emergency. This settled her down. Told her I had to go away to do something private. No, I wasn't going to steal anything. Something I'd promised not to do. She'd always assumed that the money I had when we were younger had been stolen. Would I leave her with that money if I wasn't going to return? It took most of the night and a little bit of the other before it was finally settled. That must have been the night she fell pregnant again.

I was looking for at least four men. I'd watched the control tower from above for these men to leave. Air traffic control personnel who logged each flight out. I'd followed them home and to the barracks. Three were married and one single. He was my choice.

A week later, I watched him drive out of the gates and followed him. He drove to a little country pub about five miles from the base. I followed five minutes afterwards and sat next to him at the bar. Around the room were others from the base. There was also a few young lasses dreaming of marrying a yank. Nothing wrong with that if that's what they wanted to do.

I watched a couple playing cards and the controller next to me moved into a vacant seat.

Plenty of booze was drunk in the next two hours.

'Damn blasted cheat,' a raised voice shouted.

A free for all started. The table took off in a second. I stood watching. Four men were fighting, then six. Another two came in and I stepped forwards to stop a bottle hitting the man I wanted. He saw me, smiled and he continued fighting for another five minutes. Time to pay up for the damage. They had to, or be reported to the base and banned. I sat down facing out and my man walked up to thank me.

We got chatting and I told him I'd always want to see what happened at the control tower but had never had time to go. .up there but had never had time to go.

'No Problem, I can fix it,' he said: 'Light week for a change and only a couple of flights tomorrow afternoon.'

I slept well that night and prepared myself for a good day at the base. I checked the pouch containing my nail clipping and flakes of skin.

He walked down the road to meet me. Into the guardroom to sign in, and then a jeep ride to the tower. I was going in as a tourist. I always heard about air shows been held at this base but I never knew how big it was until then. I could sense after meeting the first people in there that he'd told them about me stopping the bottle. Maybe the fact that I'd not asked, the grand tour was given to me.

At each level I dropped skin particles, especially at the top level. I used the toilet to leave another few bits. The cleaners, if they cleaned away some would not get every little piece. I cracked the window in the toilet. Spotted another open on the floor below. The doors had wide open bottoms. Each door I passed through I checked for alarms. Nothing was visible. They relied on a locked door at the bottom and security on the base.

Night fell around eight. All work was normally finished and they shut up by seven. During the tour I was able to see log books open on desks. It ended and I arranged to see him the following night for a drink.

I was hovering just before seven, unseen and silent above a door. I thought to myself, why not. I passed under and moved upwards slowly. I went above people when they came down stairs and passed through behind them before the doors closed. I ended up on the top deck where I needed to be. I waited until I could just see the ghosts of the night before I came awake.

I was within three feet of where I'd seen the logbooks. I quickly scanned the flight details. Not local and European flights but flights west to the United States. Eight flights the previous week. Six flights last week. Kansas for two flights, Virginia four flights, Boston had five flights, New York had the remainder. I scanned it again to memorise it. A pencilled mark was notated next to one of the Virginia flights, faint, as if rubbed out. SPE… The rest I couldn't make out. I memorised the aircraft numbers for them all.

That SP was giving me hopes. Was this the mistake I'd hoped to find?

I cracked a window open just in case and then lay down planning again. I got a rude awakening just before dawn. The bottom door slammed open and I could hear feet pounding up the stairs. I was trapped. There was nowhere to go, except outside and up. Could I really chance it? How would night ghosts respond to me appearing before them?

I did it without another thought and moved fast. Outside and condensed myself as small as possible, building speed, moving upwards and eastwards like a bullet. Glancing behind, they were following hard on my trail. I could not even count how many. There was a shadow of whiteness behind me. Hard and fast they were travelling, closing the gap, matching my speed as I went faster and faster upwards. I felt an impact and realised what I'd finally done: I'd broken the sound barrier for the first time. It must have been heard loud and clear by those on the ground far below.

I hit sunlight at that very moment. The dawn had arrived to meet me and I stopped to hover basking in the rays of the sun.

Below, I could not have dreamed of how many ghosts there were, just watching, but staying in the shadow of night. Hundreds had taken up the chase. Where did they all hide during the daylight hours? I could see them moving downwards as the suns rays became more apparent below.

I descended with them, always in sunlight.

I was low enough by then to see what had caused the commotion. A prop engine aircraft was making an approach to land. Only two out of four blades were spinning. An emergency landing had nearly caught me out. I lazed about hovering until the sun finally hit the ground below and then headed for my digs.

Going to the United States would be my next step. At which airport would I enter the states and for what reason? Tourist? That would be on a limited time visa. Business would be another way, but still limited. I'd no addresses or contacts. I'd got one way of doing it and I'm sure it could give me an advantage. Wife's grandfather had been an American. When his father and mother split up and divorced. He'd brought his son to England. The search would be for my wife's relatives. An extended holiday. Three months was what I wanted on my passport.

I also took one other item down to London with me. Proof of financial status. I was waiting early for the Embassy Visa section to open. First one in and forms finished quickly. Money and documents on the counter. Only question asked me was when would I like to go.

'Next available flight,' I said. Not one more question was asked. When you have means, then it definitely helps. Four hours of sitting around and I was dully returned my passport and documents. Next stop a travel agent. Two days to wait and I'd be on my way. Traveller's checks for five thousand dollars. It was now time to go back home by train. The car I'd been using I dumped at Kings Cross station.

Home, to a surprised wife and family for a discussion. Next day it was straight to the bank to arrange a password for possible transfers. Then I made a phone call to France.

It took me five hours to get to the airport the following day. Three hours before my flight. Only thing I bought at the airport was a notebook and two pens. My first flight took me to New York, where I stopped for two days before going to Galveston.

A cab took me to a hotel. Driver was a young black guy. Throughout that ride he talked non stop about driving part time to cover his college fees. He got a tip but I also got his phone number. I had a feeling that I was going to need that cab again. I booked in and asked for a room right on top. Paid up front for the hotel and a little extra given as a prepaid tip, just for three days. Doing it that way ensures that you're left alone. Down to the bar to make a phone call.

Albert, the cab driver was there inside of ten minutes in his own car. I'd asked him over with something in mind. Just the fact of free beers and a meal thrown in brought him running.

'Bring a friend if you like,' was music to his ears.

The friend was his sister and she appeared to be around fifteen. He'd been looking after her for his parents. She was blind.

We sat down, chatted over a few beers and I ordered the meal. It was around one in the afternoon. I had to put him straight on one little fact. I did it before alcohol took effect. He excused himself to go to the toilet. That was the opportunity I'd been waiting for. Made a quick excuse to his sister and followed him.

In my hand I had an empty glass.

'Hi, Albert, before we continue, I need to show you something,' I said.

I held that glass out in front of him.

'Albert, you are studying to be an engineer. Is it possible to break this glass in one hand by squeezing it with your fingers?'

'No way man,' he replied.

'OK, look at it and check that it's not cracked.'

He gave me it back with a puzzled look on his face.

'Watch the glass,' I said.

I crushed it instantly to pieces.

'Don't ever take me for a fool,' I said and then turned and went back to join his sister.

He followed me back to the table and looked me up and down, looking at me in a different light. Noting now the size and not the tourist. Then asked him if he wanted a beer.

'How much do you earn on the cabs?' I asked.

'Just enough to get by,' he said.

'Here's hundred dollars for now,' I said: 'I need you here tomorrow in your car. Can you arrange time off from driving the cab?'

'Sure,' he replied.

I asked for his address. It was a small flat where he lived, mother and father, son and daughter. All worked hard to keep it going.

America. It was not a golden dream for many people. That was the fiction created by the movies. In every city you will find a ghetto. It's sad, but they are there for you to see. Albert showed me where he lived. Then he went on to show me another side of Galveston. No doubt he had something in mind and I let him continue.

We stopped at another bar and went inside. It was a sea of black faces all staring at me. I helped his sister to a chair by a table, while he went for drinks. Something was on and I waited for it to happen. This boy was a betting man and he was going to use me to gain some cash. I was going to let it unfold before me. I could see the arm actions. One young one even tried it. No joy and Albert got into his stride. Three guys then walked over with Albert.

'Still after money Albert?' I asked him: 'Have you told them that they will lose their money yet.'

I looked closely at the one next to him. Muscle rippled in his body.

'How about an arm wrestle afterwards to give you a chance to get your money back.'

I was going to set them back on there heels with this.

'Have you made a bet yet Albert?'

A nod confirmed it so I picked up not one but two glasses.

'Ready,' I asked a now silent bar full of people.

I just squeezed each one in turn to shatter them. Startled gasps broke out through out the room. Arm wrestling was going to follow.

'What's your rules?' I asked Albert.

'Best of three,' came his reply.

'Suits me,' I said and I sat waiting for number one to sit down. Elbow in the middle and I'm waiting. Muscles sat down with a smile. I whispered to him: 'Down in five seconds.'

That smile dropped off his face. He met my hand and tried to crush it. No bother, I just put the back of his hand down fast onto the table. That shook him to the core. Next one and it was a repeat of the first. Third and last one, so I squeezed hard first just to see the pain and then down again.

I'd pissed some people off and that was my intention. Outside it was still broad daylight. I disappeared right in front of them and watched the sudden panic. Immediately I reappeared and dressed in front of a silent crowd of coloured men.

I sat down to let them recover. Just sat there waiting for one of them to speak.

'Devil man,' came the words from an older man and he crossed himself fast.

'That's where you are wrong,' I said straight at that man: I am as human as you are, but I have a power. You want to listen to why I am here? If you do, then sit and I'll tell you. First though, lock the doors.'

I related to them nearly everything that had happened in the UK over the last few weeks. I ended my tale quickly. All had listened intently. Some cussed, others had their own views. The girl beside me would be proof of what I could really do.

'You now require proof and it will only be a few minutes to give you it,' I said: 'I need all of you to stay in here and to wait. Albert, forgive me for one thing.'

I tapped his sister, Thelma, unconscious. I went instantly into hover and took her up with me. I calmed her immediate reaction and took out the darkness from her.

'All will be explained back on the ground,' I projected into her mind: 'Never do this at night.'

It took me just another few minutes of holding and explaining before I took her back down. We appeared again naked before the crowd who were still silently waiting. Thelma silently dressed. I did just the same. She turned then and asked which one was Albert.

'I am,' her brother said.

She just said, 'I've always wanted to see you and now I can.'

With tears in her eyes, she ran to hold him.

'I can see you brother, I can see you,' she cried out to him. I had before me an army by then.

They'd listened to my tale. Proof had now been given to them. I sat down to talk seriously with them. No, I did not want to harm or kill anyone. I just wanted my friends back. If trouble did happen though, then others would have to start first. What I needed was a hide-out from officialdom, in this area. I gave them all a choice then: to be the next generation of Day Movers of America.

The silence of that room could be felt. I'd hit them hard, very hard. You have two days to think about it, no one else is to be brought in at all and no words to be spoken. Who would believe you anyway.

'Come on Albert, take me back.'

At that I left them to think about it. Before I commenced further with my search, I was going to leave America with a big present, regardless of the outcome. Albert drove me back to the hotel. New York would not be sleeping tonight. It would be buzzing with rumours and it would build up over the next two days.

I took Albert from his bed early next morning, the second person of America. All the information to safeguard him was passed over. One more warning was given: Do not abuse it. I asked him about his sister and the reaction of his parents. They'd gone to church last night and he'd missed them on their return. He'd been in a bar. I knew which one. Some of those men were maybe thieves. Some may have committed serious crimes. Pimps maybe. Others could be the honest

I will find my friends and I hope that it's not too late. If I do not find them then I'll create a monster. In every town, I will create a monster that they cannot control. It will just get larger and larger. They will be made to realise one thing. That they should have kept well clear of me, and my friends.

I moved to another hotel just to feel safer. It could have exploded in my face. One night had been a chance because Albert would have been asked where I was staying. He'd gotten far more than he could have wished for. He had the means to travel now if he planned ahead.

Once booked in again, I took myself high up and began a slow circle to monitor the ground below. I was searching for just one glimmering flash of light. For the rest of the day, I stayed aloft circling around slowly.

My mind was blank to anything else, but the search. They have only got to try it once and I'll be there fast. To the south and far away are the Blue Ridge Mountains.

Below me and slightly east was Yeager airport. Air traffic was up and down all day long. I'm higher than what a military plane can reach and safe from collision. I can see the night shadow slowly moving towards the land and down I go. Onto my bed and then up very quickly to make a phone call to Albert.

Albert must have been waiting.

'Where are you, I've been searching for you all day,' he said down the phone.

He was with me in minutes.

'The town's really buzzing with rumours,' I told me: 'Nothing outright, but they want to see you.'

'Sorry Albert, I told them two days and I will not change it.'

I spent half that morning picking up camping equipment. Three tents, four ground sheets and ten water bottles. Seven packets of hard-tack rations. Three spades of the folding stock type. Then I had to estimate some sizes from memory. Clothes and shoes for four people and some more clothes for a baby.

These we loaded into Albert's car and we set off south. Three hours later we were at a place called Bland. Here I headed up into some woods. It was going to be a storage area. Then we headed due west. Ended up at Clintwood, where I did the same thing. Next it was north west for the last stop of West Liberty. All the camping gear had been well hidden. I had water and food. Money was stashed at each place. Inside six socks at each site were clipping and skin flakes. I'd also torn up some clothes of mine to make sure.

I'd not forgotten about the small snuff tins. Somehow that single thought just a few weeks ago had paid off. I'd sneaked in and retrieved all the tins. I'd transferred the contents of each box into a separate envelope with a name written on each one.

It was early morning by the time we got back to Galveston. Albert went home for a couple of hours sleep. At ten o'clock I took a cab ride to within five minutes walk of the bar. With me I had some spare clothes in a parcel, which I placed in an open skip. I walked into the ghetto with an open mind. I could see men and women on each corner. Whispers began when they saw me. Piercing eyes were looking at me. The answer would be inside that door across the road.

I opened it and peered inside. They were waiting for me to enter. Albert sat to one side and was the only one smiling. I had my answer at that moment. I'd asked him to smile, if the answer was yes. Without that smile, I'd have been gone instantly. There were in that room two additions and I noticed it immediately. One was a priest and the other a little boy. There was also one person missing and it was the one who'd called me a Devil Man.

'You are all agreed then?' I asked and I was looking around the room at all of them: 'One is missing though. Can you tell me why he refused to join the rest of you?'

'He backed out last night, but his son is here,' said Rufas, the guy with the muscles.

I didn't have to ask the priest. He came forwards and stood before me. Not a smile on his lips, but a question.

'I have seen a blind child see again and I have heard confessions from most of these men. I need to see with my own eyes what you really are?'

'You'll have your answer and you can also tell anyone the truth if you really need to,' was my reply: 'Albert, tell them what you can do.'

'Tell them how you feel.'

Albert told them what he could do. I let him talk for nearly half an hour and then suggested that they all went home to try to sleep. I knew that most had been awake for nearly two days now. It wouldn't take long. Albert went with one group and I with another.

I flickered out of sight before Albert and began touring around the area. It took me some time before I caught the first one nodding off. Up he went with me and I began the process once again.

I gave all the necessary information to the first and he went back on his own to start a new life as a Day Mover.

I caught the priest half way through the group and let him see more than the others. I also explained more to him. My childhood and how I'd been hunted. The kidnappings and about my friends, the ill treatment given to them because of what we were. The facts of why we were born like we were. I let his light glow brightly.

He went back to the ground and a few minutes later I spotted him heading to the church. I could see the smile on his face. He'd had the truth given to him and nothing less.

During the next hour a little sphere kept dancing around me. I knew who it was and laughed to myself. A little boy was having fun and really enjoying himself. It all eventually came to an end. It had been completed.

This part of Charleston would be protecting it's own from this day forth.

I dressed in the bar. And men began to arrive. All of them wanted to help me find my friends.

'How many of you have relatives within a five hundred mile radius?' I asked.

Hands shot up.

Chapter 25

BM

I'll give you ten of the places mentioned and then you'll catch on to what I want to do. Ripley (north). Portsmouth, (north west). Lexington, (west). Burning Springs, (south west). Jonesville, (south, south west). Johnson City, (south). Norwood, (south). Buena Vista, (east). Luray, (east) and Morgan Town, (north east).

I was going to cover all this area. If necessary I would continue, until all the landing places of the lanes from England had been covered. The mention of money I made, it was shot down in flames by these hard men. That's what they were and had to be, to live in this area. I'd hit a common ideal with them. I wanted my friends back. Nothing else. They all protected their friends just as I did.

Over the next four days lights increased over a wide area. I'd asked them to condense down to small pinprick lights. To go high to make it hard to be seen, by anyone. They have my friends and one can change others. If she's began to change anyone. We will be seen. The signal would be for none to be up on the following day. Then I would have to make just one phone call.

It was on the seventeenth day when I went up early.

The sky around me was empty. For two hours, I waited for the sky to fill with lights. Then it was down to make a call. Not one, but two sightings had been seen and it was in the direction of Salem, south east of Charleston and just over the other side of the Blue Ridge mountain range.

I gave my thanks to the priest and asked him to call every one in.

Within an hour, I'd hired a car and was travelling in the direction of Salem. I drove towards Lexington first and then headed down to Timberlake. I took it easy all the way. Slept every so often and on the last leg stopped at Roanoke.

A motel room as a base would suit me. I would move in slowly by night and then move back to base. It would only be in the afternoons that I would go up. I needed the sun to be in the west. If a small flash of light was seen by those before me. I wanted them to think that it was the sun's rays reflecting off glass. Each hover would be up and down quickly just to look ahead. Then back down to dress and move forwards to another location.

On the third day I caught seven lights in front of me. I was well condensed and was hidden behind a building within seconds of seeing them. I moved quickly back under cover and into the car. I drove into a stream of traffic and continued away from their direction. My estimate was about ten miles to the lights. I could not believe that those lights belonged to anyone from the UK.

I moved by foot slowly to within five miles of the general area.

From where I stood in the woods, I could see a high wire fence. Government Property. That fence was new.

My heart leaped when I realised that this had to be the place. I had been fortunate to get onto that base in England and spot that faint writing on the logbook. I'd found them on the first try. How many, though were held here? Were all of them together, or just one at a time, held in different places?

I backed away slowly. Tomorrow I'd be ready and waiting for any that came up into the sky, no matter who, they would be mine in seconds.

No one but the priest knew what I'd discovered only a few weeks ago. Not even Rachel knew the full truth and she was the second strongest of our kind. If I succeeded to release my friends then I would I explain it all. Once and for all everyone needed to know the truth. Why and how we had come to be as we were and why throughout the ages it had continued time and time again.

Edith

The four of us were taken after dusk. Not a thing we could do about it. Just a single knock at the door. Rachel had opened it and men had burst in to take us. Not one of them was British. They were American soldiers in civilian clothing and carrying guns.

We were bundled into separate cars and driven off at high speed. Only consolation that I had was the baby in my arms. It seemed hours before we arrived at our destination.

Within minutes we were on a plane and heading westerly. That was the only direction these people were taking us. Into the long hours of the night and through part of the day we continued. We stopped only once to refuel before taking off again.

Looking around me during that flight I could see about fifteen soldiers and around thirty other worried young people. It came to me immediately who they all were. Every single light of England was being shipped abroad in one night. Except for those that they knew nothing about. Damn fools, I thought. You've missed the main one. Michael was next to me, Geoffrey was nearby and Rachel is laughing, no doubt at the same thoughts that had occurred to me. A man walked forwards and told her to be quiet.

'Fuck Off,' she said.

I spoke up then: 'Why don't you go back to your seat and carry on… playing with yourself.'

That did put him off his stride. We'd both got the measure of them all. We were taken off the aircraft one at a time in darkness and put into military vehicles. Within a few seconds they drove away. It was hours later when we finally stopped, inside a tunnel. My ears started popping with the difference in pressure as we went deeper. I could do nothing, when the baby was taken from me. I held back my tears. They separated us then and led us off with an escort of two people, and I was led through a door with my name written in chalk. A letter was below my name in red. 'A'. Passing some of the others I'd noticed the names of others in our group. Most had the letter 'B' under the name, all except one girls' name. It had an 'A'.

Who was this one, I thought to myself? I never got to see the rest of the names. The door was shut and locked behind me. That's when I cried.

I had a bed, table and a single chair. The toilet and bathroom were partitioned behind a curtain. On the table was a typewriter and paper. On the wall was a camera. At the side was a speaker.

'Sit down at the table,' a voice told me.

'Isolation for number two,' came the voice.

I knew the method because I'd done it myself in the past. Until I sat at that table I'd have no contact at all and no food or water. Lights, I thought, and sure enough, they went out in the next second. It was inky black. It would be for around four hours before they came back on. Standard procedure for a couple of seconds, it's just to see if you were at that table and sat down.

I lay on the bed to sleep. Thinking of every last little detail. Rachel said he would find us one day but how long would that be? I was brought awake by the sound of a baby crying. My baby and I knew that I was beaten. I crawled around until I felt the table leg and then found the chair. Sat down, I waited for the lights to come back on. They flickered on and then off and then came back on to stay. I began to type, sheet after sheet.

I stopped when I heard the door unlock. Two men entered with food and a plastic cup of water. Not a word was spoken. It was placed down and then they took what I'd typed. More paper had been left for me to continue. I typed away knowing that I was beaten. I slept for a while and then it was back to typing.

More food and water were brought to me. Sleep and then back again to typing. I finished at long last and by then, I'd lost track of night and day. A voice came over the speaker so sudden that I jumped.

'His name. We want his name.'

I had no name to give them. None of us had his name. Not even Rachel.

At the typewriter I leaned over and typed two words.

'Day Mover.'

I left it for them to take away. Around five minutes later, I had an afterthought and typed them a message.

'He will appear before you and take away those who confront him. He will show no mercy this time. If we are hurt in any way or form, your minds will be empty. Just a living body will remain. That body will cringe at every little sound and at anything passing before it's eyes. It will curl up into a ball. You will have to force feed it. You will have to clean it. It will be as I have said. It will be just a living shell of a human.'

Rachel

It was only the darkness and the sealed plane that had held me prisoner. Whatever they wanted would do them no good at all. He would guess in which direction we'd be taken. I'll give them whatever they want though.

Let's see them destroy themselves because without doubt that's what will happen. Only the chosen ones can survive. Somehow he can see into a person's mind. A chosen person can then control any others they change. He will find out one day why this is the way that it happens.

I've been put into a room on my own and many question have been answered by me. The request for his name repeatedly. What is it, one week or two now, that we've been held here. I've lost track. Now they want to see it happen. To see me, disappear in front of them. It's early the next day when I'm escorted to an upper chamber.

I can see the sky above me through the heavy windows over head. This room is sealed tight. There are cameras all around the room and facing towards a flat elevated couch.

I didn't waiting for the go from them but just relaxed down onto the couch and disappeared. I hovered brightly within the room for a few minutes to watch the reaction. It took less than thirty seconds for alarm bells to start ringing. Four bewildered men in white coats rushed into the room.

I reappeared before them naked and casually dressed. They just backed away from me, bewilderment turning into fear. They had seen the impossible happen before their eyes for the first time. An armed escort led me from that room. Another day passed slowly by my reckoning.

Then back to the same room again. This time a second bed was there besides the first. A man of about thirty was waiting.

'Take him with you,' said a voice over the speakers: 'Bring him back with his mind intact or gas will be applied on your return. The shutters will close after an hour.'

I really looked closely to see that there were in fact shutters to the sides of the windows. Fear entered me for the first time since my arrival. They knew about the ghosts of the night. They also knew that I could take people up into the sky with me. How did they know? Who had told them about us and why had they done so?

It was only days later that I found out that my fears were unfounded. I lay there beside him.

'You will have to sleep or I cannot take you,' I said to him.

'A drug will render me asleep within the next five minutes,' he replied.

'Are you an officer?' I asked him and he nodded his head.

Poor man, I thought, to volunteer for this. I lay there watching his eyes getting heavier and heavier and finally they closed in sleep. I took him in seconds and steadied his mind as I'd been taught. His thoughts were racing and I slowed them down.

'Remember this one fact,' I projected to him: 'You are now meat for night ghosts. You can rise up and go back down but you will never be in control. There is one of us coming. One, who will show you no mercy. We are but children to him.'

I left him to return on his own. I dressed and walked to the door to await my escort. He appeared behind me. I could hear him getting dressed.

'Tell me,' he quietly asked: 'Can just this one person do what you said.'

I just nodded my head without turn around.

'Your babies,' I repeated.

I wasn't to know but over three hundred men and women, all of them volunteers, were changed over the next two days.
SOMEONE DID NOT BELIEVE ME.

BM

I'm waiting and watching the lights in front of me, from in front of a glass building facing west and the sun his going down. More and more lights are appearing, then descending back down to disappear. I'm just a pinprick refection from a window to them.

Tomorrow morning I will surprise them.

I went to bed early and just laid there thinking of the past. What would the future be for me? How was I going to approach it and when would I be free to live a normal life?

Up with the sun and moving fast, I came upon the outer buildings before a large tunnel. I'm just a pinprick now and waiting just above a massive set of doors facing upwards. Just a small atom sized little light waiting for my first victims.

Those doors began to open slowly, then one, two and then four. Another six and then three more were ascending upwards into the sky.

'Keep going up,' I whisper into each mind: 'Just go up to where the sun shines forever above this earth. Stop and wait there until I call you.

Only one light quivered and tried to stop but it followed the others. From each of them I took their names and from those that were married, I took the names of their wives. I took telephone numbers and an address of a living relative. I'd ordered each one to ascend into the sky.

One solid hour passed. Not one inch did I move. Another light came upwards towards my hiding place and then six together. As they came close I burst outwards into a brilliant white light. So bright did I become that they were hardly visible to me.

'Stop,' I whispered into each of there minds.

All movement ceased before me.

'Who of you is in control?' I asked them.

It was from the second light to my left that gave me back a mind thought.

'I am. I was the first changed.'

'Look above you, high above you,' and I put this to them very loudly: 'All of you damn well look. Your friends are there and cannot come down. You in charge, stay where you are. The rest, join your friends above.'

In turn I took from each the same information as before. Up they went into the sky. My own mind controlled them all. The one before me, I would be sending back down to earth. I went down before him for my first visit.

Row upon row of men and women all asleep on beds. The empty beds of those I'd taken to one side. I brought the light down from above. I then altered his mind just before he became human again. As he appeared on one bed I was very busy indeed. Touching each of those sleeping people and I did not hesitate one little bit on my way around. Taking each of them into hover before they realised what had happened.

'Up and out,' I was whispering: 'Up and outside, wait above.'

Those doors were closing as I touched the last one. Pandemonium was before me. Total panic in just a couple of seconds.

From seeing that silent man appear, then to see him curling up in fear. It had hit them hard. To see all the sleepers go must have hit them harder.

I was out and up in the sky well before those doors finally rumbled closed. From each I took the same as before and then told them to join with those above. Only I knew where they were, but they were safe from harm. I headed back to my base fast. I had work to do and I needed to be in human form to complete it.

Rachel

I was just laid there on the bed when the bells rang. I did not even know what time it was. They rang loudly for over fifteen minutes. It must have been another three hours before my door opened. Outside between fifteen to twenty men.

'Come with me please,' said a man standing at the door.

That was the first time that I'd heard that word in weeks. 'Please'. Something had happened but what? I was going to find out soon enough. I was escorted into a massive cavern. Floodlights made it very bright. All around the floor were empty beds. At one side across the room, were a group of men and women, in white coats. But most were in uniform. It was an elderly man in uniform who asked me to come forwards. I could see the stars on his shoulders and realised that he was of a very high rank.

'I would like you to give me a few answers please?' he asked.

His voice was not demanding. I smiled then because I knew, even then, who was outside waiting.

'First I would like a seat and then a coffee,' I said.

He frowned back at me and just for an instance I thought I was wrong.

Seat, coffee,' he snapped out to another officer to the side of him. That seat appeared immediately and the coffee shortly afterwards.

'Behind me,' he began and those behind him moved for me to see a body curled up upon a bed.

I butted in then quickly: 'Would you like to see him cured?'

That did surprise them and the men in white coats gasped as if with disbelief. It had also shaken the man in front of me.

'You would do that for him?' he finally said to me: 'Even after what we have done to you.'

I just nodded my head and had my first sip of hot coffee. I was enjoying this immensely.

'What do you need in return though?' he asked.

'We can talk about that later,' I answer and I also looked around the room at all the others present: 'You also seem to have some others missing. The answer is no, I cannot fetch them back. He can.'

I'd now told them outright who was outside. It was fully intended.

'Open the doors above and I'll be only a short time in returning. I will be leaving here later, but not without my friends.'

Loud voices murmured but I was I was only looking at one person. The man in charge. He was stood there looking at me. Just staring into my face and I could feel the cogs of his mind turning around.

'Silence,' he suddenly shouted: 'Silence the damn lot of you. Get those fucking doors open now?'

He'd not taken his eyes off me for one second.

At the first glimmer of pure daylight above me I acted. I let my clothes fall crumpling to the ground, took a curled up body away from their sight and out we went together. I held that empty light and whispered gently.

'Come in to him, come into him,' I whispered. and the light stirred before me. I calmed him as he moved. His Soul had waited, as instructed. His mind, I kept it quiet. He was back into his own within just a few minutes and I returned to the cavern below.

I appeared naked and unashamed before them and dressed. A man was rising from his bed across from me and he put on a tracksuit. He then walked forwards slowly to stand in front of me. Three words he spoke to me.

'Thank You Lady.'

At that he turned and walked over to the man who had questioned me, and had also trusted me.

'Sir, they are all outside, but trapped high up. Outside somewhere is the one we were warned about.'

'I see,' said the senior officer.

'He could have destroyed all of us with a single word but for some reason he just sent all the rest upwards. His light is so bright that we were all blinded at once. He commands straight into your mind.'

I broke in: 'You have three days before he will carry out the same promise that he gave in England. He will commence at the top and work downwards. Over the next few days you will start to hear of strange things happening. That is just his way of warning you. He will start tomorrow morning. Any harm given to myself, or those held with me, and you will see the result. It would at my estimate take him about two hours to take into the sky thousand people. That will include children. He can force those taken up to start on others in turn. It's a pyramid effect with no end.'

I paused for a moment and then added: 'How long will it take before this country is swept clean?'

'Can this be true?' the senior officer asked and looked around for someone to say something. The blood drained from his face: 'Why wasn't we told this?'

I continued: 'He nearly did it in England, but they let me go free with my friends in time. All you will have left is the people who dare not sleep. Or those hidden underground, like your, never to have the sun on your face again or to feel the wind in your hair. None of this was written down. We never told anyone what he would do to gain our freedom.'

I paused again for it to sink in to the people before me.

'What if he uses those already held up in the sky. You are lucky that he found us quickly. Think on one simple little item. At this moment no one is dead by his hand. You are now fully warned of what to expect.'

I then asked a woman if she would escort me to see a friend and also to pick up a baby. I'd sometimes heard that baby crying in the room next to mine and he was crying for his mother. I left the room erupting with loud voices.

Chapter 26

BM

I made the phone calls. As each one answered, I told them the name of one of those held high in the sky. It was mothers of the unmarried men, husbands to worried wives. Then a few odd men of the women trapped with them. A call to a newspaper and a word left to call a certain address.

I'd started a panic of calls to military bases. Then a call to a radio station, those there to call other numbers. Men were missing, in a secret project was the topic that I mentioned over the phone. I then left that area and drove south to a place called Martinsville and booked into a motel. I signed the first name that came into my head: Richard Martin. Paid for the night and headed for a bar across the street for a long cool beer. I would now wait for one day to see what developed.

It started first on a local radio station next day around 11.00 am. Just a little report about missing soldiers. By 1.00 pm it had started to grow. It hit the television stations. By nightfall the news had grown massive, just as I'd hoped.

A priest had called in. He'd given them information and then he was thrust before the media. He told them about an injustice and then he explained what had happened.

In the end, he told them to prepare for a practical demonstration. Albert walked towards the camera.

‘Watch closely because this is what we face,’ the priest stated loud and clear. Albert then vanished before their eyes. It took just five seconds for the television screen to go blank before me. They’d cut it fast. People next to me in the bar were now muttering and talking about what they’d just witnessed. I just carried on drinking my beer.

It’s the beginning of another bright day. Eyes closed listening and as I felt the sun’s rays brighten the room, I left it quickly. Up and small really quickly to gain speed and heading towards that camp. I could see twinkling lights high above me. Not the stars of the night sky, but the stars of the men and women I’d sent there. I was soon above the doors that are closed below. I’m just waiting for my answer. It was not long before I heard the rumble of them opening. Not six, but eight lights appeared below me and this surprise me.

I’d expected only six at the most. They came up fast and then stopped right in front of me. Edith and the boy. Rachel. Michael and Geoffrey. Then the answer to who had betrayed us. Sue and Sam were hovering before me. That did change my plans.

‘At the main entrance gate and just to the left are some trees. On one is a parcel. I want this parcel to be put on a bed below. Only the four senior personnel are to stay in that room.’

This I put to the last light in front of me. That officer, he’d dared to come up again. He’d gone as soon as I’d said the last word.

From each of them, I listened to what had happened since their capture. We then waited and watched below. It took fifteen minutes before a light flashed below us and I descended down to meet him coming upwards once again.

‘Stay until I return,’ I told them.

On the bed below I transformed, dressed in a track suit taken from the parcel and appeared, but not as a young man. I’d altered myself to look fat and old. A camera would be on somewhere down here. Not saying one word until I was ready. I turned around and then stood up facing four men before me. Then a fifth appeared and dressed.

‘Do you gentlemen realise what you have done to that man getting dressed?’ and I pointed across to the fifth man: ‘Do you also realise what you have done to all those who will start to appear in just a few moments. They no longer fit in with life as you know it. That man there.’

I turned and pointed across to him: ‘He is dead and yet he does not know it.’

That got the reaction I’d been waiting for. I heard a deep gasp.

The four men staggered backwards in shock at my words. They were all grey faced and one looked as if he was going to fall at any second.

‘Dead, explain it too us. We need to know?’ This came from a man with stars on his shoulder pads. It was at that moment that others started to appear on the beds around me.

‘All of them are dead,’ I repeated: ‘I have returned half of them to you. You have committed murder without knowing but it does not change the facts. Each one dies at the change for just a few seconds. They were dead to this world.’

I stood there looking as the first one collapse with the realisation of what they had done.

I heard another say; 'God, what have we done.'

'No use calling God now. It's to late for that,' I said: 'England could have warned you, so why did you not ask them first?'

I paused to let it all sink in before speaking again: 'I can change it for you.

It was the fifth man who slowly approached me and stood looking into my eyes.

'You can change me back?' he asked quietly.

I just nodded the answer and he believed me. I heard a door open at the side and told the man.

'Tell them all to stay outside. Any that enter I'll take up and leave them up.'

Not only did he shout at them to stay outside, he moved fast towards the doors to stand before them.

'Keep the hell out of here,' he was bellowing.

The view seen from the camera had shown the arrival of the missing people. Assuming it was over, they'd jumped the gun.

'What now?' he asked.

'A plane, for two girls and for all of the other weak ones that you have hidden.'

I'd not forgotten the weaker ones from England. Sue and Sam will be safe with the weaker ones.

'The plane will take them to England. It's Wednesday now, on Saturday I will return. You will have *The Daily Mirror*, from Friday, here in this room and I will read it.

'Can you not start now?' one asked from the side.

I turned towards him and smiled. He couldn't see me then because I'd gone. In my place within a few minutes were Sue and Sam. Remaining now here in America would be just six of the originals.

We headed for Bland. There we appeared one by one in the trees and well hidden. From this hiding place, I sorted out all the clothes that I'd stashed. Not long afterwards, we headed into town, individually or in pairs. I bought a truck and drove the group to a motel where we spent the next two days keeping out of sight.

Always we were on guard, especially at night. I never took a chance and had made up a bed in the back of the truck. It was never parked in the same place twice. Early Saturday morning we were ready. I drove the truck in an easterly direction until we found an ideal spot in the woods. It was then up to me. Plans had already been made, just in case. I was away fast and high within a moment. Heading back to read a newspaper.

I entered that big open cavern of a room slowly and invisible to all of them assembled. There were a few new faces there. Men of importance. The braid was thick to see. I gently cruised above and all around them. Listening in to low muttered words between different men and women. I then appeared right there before them.

Tell the gentlemen to disarm and I pointed at different men in that room. I disappeared again to watch the proceedings. It shook them rigid to see me and then not to see me all in less than five seconds. What an uproar I caused. It was clear that no one had informed the senior officer that weapons were hidden. He was pissed off and cussing at one of the newcomers, who complained bitterly that they'd been told; 'Have a go.' If the chance appeared.

I came down fast and hit the speaker hard. He went down and disappeared in another second to join me as a sphere. That informed them there and then what I could really do.

Every person in that room was immediately ordered to strip or leave. Three left and seven stripped off down to their underpants. I re-appeared down again.

'Where's the Senator?' I was asked.

'Just above your head,' I replied: 'He can watch from there.'

There was not one person present, who did not look above. I took *The Daily Mirror* from the senior officer's hand. On one of the pages was a message for me. I read to them.

"Mover wanted".

They were home and safe. I wondered how much it had cost to get that message in so quickly.

'First fifty when you're ready,' I said looking up.

It took a few seconds to realise what I said to them. Within minutes there were people laid out on the beds and white coats were giving them injections to make them sleep again. Each in turn, I took up and then brought them back down, without the power to ever be able to do it again.

They became living breathing men and women of this earth. The only way they'd ever fly again would be by aircraft or by jumping off a cliff edge. That last flight would be straight down though and not upwards.

I did the same with another hundred before I brought back the Senator. I brought him back insane.

'That's a present for those above you,' I said. If he had got his way, they would have remained up there for ever.'

I'd taken his mind away because of what I'd read from it.

'Another two aircraft, tomorrow please, at Yeager airport.

Again I disappeared and hovered above listening until I heard the rumble of the doors closing.

I went back to my friends and gave them an account of the day. We now had a long drive in front of us. As I relaxed for the remainder of the day. I thought how easy it would be to go home the easy way. It would have taken a trip straight upwards and then a wait of a few hours, then straight down. We had to make them think otherwise.

I arrived in the back of that truck the next morning as they were approaching the Yeager airport. Not knowing how many and also not knowing my face gave us an advantage. Edith passed something to me as we got closer. They'd been spotted some time on the drive to the airport. From the sky at night it's very easy to pick up a lone vehicle travelling in the direction of that airport. Other cars and trucks pulled out in front and led the way in. Others tagged on behind but stayed well back.

We finally pulled up before two aircraft. We waited then until an officer approached the truck.

'I would like a quick look on those aircraft,' I told him. His pause before speaking confirmed my doubts to all of us. We were out in the open and well away from the buildings.

'Sure go ahead,' he finally said.

I was up them steps in seconds. Forwards and inside quickly. I took from my inside pocket a miniature hand drill with a 1/8" drill bit already attached. Low down and to the left of the pilot's cabin door. I drilled three holes. It had taken less that a minute and I headed back outside to the next plane. Glancing back I saw the officer going on to the first plane. Would he spot those three holes? They would take a good man to find them, I thought. I did the same on the next plane. It was then back to the truck to wait for him. He came out and back down and I couldn't see anything in his expression. This had to succeed to get us clear once and for all.

He asked if everything was all right onboard. I nodded my head and faded away in front of his eyes. That really made him move back from the truck. He'd been warned to expect the abnormal but not this. Edith told him that in two hours time they would board and not before. She then drove across to the terminal.

They all got out as if they hadn't a care in the world and walked into the terminal. Behind them armed soldiers appeared.. Close but not too close.

I was watching all of this from above. Listening also to an officer's conversation on the phone. His instructions were clear for me to hear. First part was over, now to finish it. I climbed upwards and headed fast towards the hillside cavern to complete my part of the bargain with America.

I appeared and set about curing all of them and not even bothering to stop to see the out come.

I headed back to Yeager. I landed, dressed before anyone saw me and got out of what they thought was an empty truck.

They were very nervous and fidgety. I just calmly walked off to find the others. It was easy to spot where they'd holed up. I couldn't miss the guard. I was just a little old fat man to them. An arm tried to block my way as I approached. It was removed quickly when a voice to the side advised him to let me through. It was the officer who'd been there when we had arrived.

I entered a private VIP lounge.

'Ready folks,' I said and they all spun round at hearing my voice. Up and out quickly. Five went to one plane and I went alone to the other. I saw the pilot and co-pilot just before the cabin door shut. I heard the click as it was locked tight.

No one but myself was in that cabin. Not another soul. I went into hover and began to get smaller and smaller and smaller. I moved forwards and lowered in front of a drilled hole. I passed through to enter the cockpit behind two men. I watched first the taxi and then the long take off.

We turned eastwards back to England. To the side of us was the second plane, matching this one for height and speed. Just as I knew they would. A normal flight would climb to cruising height fast. It is more than twenty thousand feet but these two planes stayed low and the estimate of speed was only around two hundred miles an hour. The game would be played out until the end.

In an hour and a half, we were over the coast of America. That's when it started to happen. The pilot stood up, moved to a cupboard and dressed in heavier clothing. He removed a parachute and slipped it on. Then back to his seat to take control from the co pilot. He did exactly the same. They knew how we Day Movers were able to enter a place and how to contain us. They thought that once I was cocooned in a sealed area, that I would be helpless. It was in all the reports written about us. It indicated this one fact. We could not enter or leave a sealed area.

I watched closely. The box right in between the seats, was opened with two keys. Both put in a code and each pressed a little button at the same time. Engine revs were increased slowly and a climb commenced. The co-pilot stood up quickly and a lever was pulled down. Under the floor a panel dropped clear. The pilot pulled another lever and three green lights appeared. Then he flicked into auto pilot. I didn't wait any longer but followed the first man as he removed another panel. I beat him too it. I was outside and clear in a second. I paced that plane until it was confirmed that both men had dropped clear.

Looking downwards I could see the helicopter so clearly. Plus the ship in the distance. I swung around and headed for the second plane.

One light appeared and then two came out together, then the remaining two. We were all clear and heading upwards into the air. I continued watching below as the two aircraft rose upwards, slowly flying east. They were soon too small to follow.

We are in the sunlight basking in it's glow, watching and waiting. Later two bright lights appeared in the sky. They destroyed millions of other dim lights. The balance had been drastically altered forever. It has just taken one split second of madness, the same as had happened in nineteen forty-five.

The earth was lucky that time because the dark side had been destroyed in a war lasting six years. They kept the balance even while testing a weapon of war. It was mainly underground and in isolated areas. The light side and the dark side never hide in those areas of isolation. They are where the people are, or in the path of where the circling earth will bring the people too them.

The dark side has the upper hand once again. Who is it and where will he be born? It may be a woman. What country will be ruled first and which one will be taken first? There may even be more than one. We are six strong one's and we hope that we can always be on the light side. America had never been beaten in a war. They did what they thought was right. They think that we are gone and they have only one to find.

Albert is on the run, for sure. He knows where his friends can be found and if he needs to, he will find us. The remaining men and the priest have only a limited means of transformation. They can harm no one but themselves.

We all have an unknown amount of time on this earth.

Some of you will think of spirit and others our soul. They are the same really. Many different words can have the same meaning. Joy, it has an opposite word. It is sadness. You can even say happiness, is opposite to sadness. Catch = Drop. Good = Bad. Light = Dark.

Need I go on with it. For each of us living we can have a good side or a bad side. Spirits of the day = Spirits of the night. It's an equal balance that sometimes moves one way, sometimes the other.

We are all born at sometime and our souls are either good or bad. If both parents are bad, then the child would be bad. One good parent and a bad parent would be the half way equation. The dominant side will sometimes win, but not always. Two good parents will normally have a good child.

At night you have the spirits or souls of the dead who die during darkness. Where are the spirits of the dead who die at night?

During the daylight hours, they hide away in all the dark corners the earth but most are following the night shadow hidden from the sun.

It's easier for the day spirits. They rise upwards when the dark shadow comes close. Right high up and out of the shadow of the earth to bathe in full sunlight. They descend to the earth during the day.

Both the night and day spirits or souls if you want to call them that are seeking to return to this earth. A child is born and it means one spirit or soul succeeded. What if a baby is born during the night? That is where the balance is upset. Good parent and bad parent. It is just the same with a child born in the daytime. It's the swaying of balance.

"I am a ghost".

I died as a baby. It was in those first few seconds of my death that my spirit left an empty shell of a human and then for some reason the same one returned. I was alive again. It was the chemicals of this earth that allowed my spirit to return, giving back to me my life.

It happened to all my brothers and sisters each in turn. It was more than likely passed to me through my father. As he got older it must have grown weaker. Edith had given me information. It confirmed most of what I believed happened. I'd seen a foot long scar on my father's body. It was wide at the top and narrowing towards the bottom. Just the sort of scar a falling object would make.

I can now leave and come back at any time during the day. My touch in spirit form is death and then life at will.

I have the ability to keep the original spirit in place and then urn it, forming again a human body as if nothing had happened. It ave me the means to take from a sick person the dark side that was eating into them.

It allows me to live as a normal person on this earth, to have children. I am at present on the light side of the world and this I did not understand until I went high up above this earth and what I saw up there told me what I was. There were millions of bright little lights spinning and twirling. All of them waiting for an opportunity.

To become human beings, alive and living on the earth. So it will go on and on throughout time.

I am called a Day Mover.

You may think of me as a ghost. When you see me though, I'm as solid as anyone. I shudder to think what will happen when the Night Movers appear. Who will fight them on this earth?

YOU AND YOUR KIND?

OR WILL IT BE ME AND MY KIND.

Epilogue

I'll give you what happened to them now. The two boys did it. The day "Michael" qualified as a pilot. Dual engine rated, night time and instrument rated. He asked for all his powers to be removed for safety reasons. He is still a pilot. "Geoffrey". He is a "Surgeon". He also had his powers removed. "Rachel", well everyone sees her. She is married to the silver screen and is very famous. She still has her powers. Every single one of them. "Edith", she had a little boy. He fly's by day and his power to do so, as never been told to anyone. Occasionally I still meet him. I always ask him about his mother. Somehow or other, I'm sure that he knows that I'm his father. He's a policeman. "Edith" she is eighty-four years of age now. She still does not look her age. No one has ever bothered them. It was me that they wanted. They still do. I have seen the searchers occasionally but they never get too close. Whichever hotel they stay at, is always easy to find. I have friends. Hard fighting friends. The searchers all leave. They take back with them the evidence. Bruises, black eyes and an occasional broken bone.